Charles Lamb, Alfred Ainger

The Letters of Charles Lamb

Charles Lamb, Alfred Ainger

The Letters of Charles Lamb

ISBN/EAN: 9783337017132

Printed in Europe, USA, Canada, Australia, Japan

Cover: Foto ©Raphael Reischuk / pixelio.de

More available books at **www.hansebooks.com**

OF

CHARLES LAMB

Newly Arranged, with Additions

EDITED, WITH INTRODUCTION AND NOTES, BY

ALFRED AINGER

London

MACMILLAN AND CO., Limited

NEW YORK: THE MACMILLAN COMPANY

1897

First Edition, March 1888
Reprinted September 1888, 1891, 1897

TO MY OLD FRIEND

ADOLPHUS WILLIAM WARD

M.A. LITT.D.

OF OWENS COLLEGE, MANCHESTER

THIS EDITION OF

THE WORKS AND CORRESPONDENCE OF CHARLES LAMB

IS

AFFECTIONATELY INSCRIBED

CONTENTS OF VOL. I.

		PAGE
SONNET TO ELIA	.	xiv
INTRODUCTION	. .	xv

CHAPTER I.
1796–1800.

LETTERS TO COLERIDGE, SOUTHEY, AND MANNING.

LETTER			DATE	PAGE
I. To SAMUEL TAYLOR COLERIDGE			May 27, 1796	1
II.	,,	,,	. [No Month] 1796	3
III.	,,	,,	. June 10, 1796	10
IV.	,,	,,	. June 13, 1796	21
V.	,,	,,	. June 14, 1796	23
VI.	,,	,,	. July 1, 1796	26
VII.	,,	,,	. July 5, 1796	28
VIII.	,,	,,	Sept. 27, 1796	32
IX.	,,	,,	. Oct. 3, 1796	33
X.	,,	,,	. Oct. 17, 1796	38
XI.	,,	,,	. Oct. 24, 1796	39
XII.	,,	,,	. Oct. 28, 1796	41
XIII.	,,	,,	. Nov. 8, 1796	43
XIV.	,,	,,	Nov. 14, 1796	46

LETTER			DATE	PAGE
XV. To Samuel Taylor Cole-ridge	.	.	Dec. 2, 1796	49
XVI.	,,	,,	Dec. 5, 1796	52
XVII.	,,	,,	Dec. 10, 1796	52
XVIII.	,,	,,	Dec. 1796	55
XIX.	,,	,,	Jan. 2, 1797	56
XX.	,,	,,	Jan. 5, 1797	57
XXI.	,,	,,	Jan. 10, 1797	63
XXII.	,,	,,	Jan. 16, 1797	67
XXIII.	,,	,,	Feb. 13, 1797	69
XXIV.	,,	,,	April 7, 1797	73
XXV.	,,	,,	April 15, 1797	75
XXVI.	,,	,,	1797	76
XXVII.	,,	,,	June 13, 1797	76
XXVIII.	,,	,,	June 24, 1797	78
XXIX.	,,	,,	July 1797	79
XXX.	,,	,,	Sept. 1797	81
XXXI.	,,	,,	Dec. 10, 1797	83
XXXII.	,,	,,	Jan. 28, 1798	85
XXXIII. To Robert Southey	.	.	July 28, 1798	87
XXXIV.	,,	,,	Oct. 18, 1798	90
XXXV.	,,	,,	...	90
XXXVI.	,,	,,	Nov. 3, 1798	93
XXXVII.	,,	,,	Nov. 8, 1798	95
XXXVIII.	,,	,,	Nov. 28, 1798	96
XXXIX.	,,	,,	Dec. 27, 1798	99
XL.	,,	,,	Jan. 21, 1799	100
XLI.	,,	,,	Mar. 15, 1799	102
XLII.	,,	,,	Mar. 20, 1799	104
XLIII.	,,	,,	April 20, 1799	107

LETTER		DATE	PAGE
XLIV.	To Robert Southey .	May 20, 1799	107
XLV.	,, ,,	Oct. 31, 1799	109
XLVI.	To Thomas Manning .	Dec. 28, 1799	110
XLVII.	,, ,,	Dec. 1799	111

CHAPTER II.

1800–1809.

LETTERS TO COLERIDGE, MANNING, AND OTHERS.

LETTER		DATE	PAGE
XLVIII.	To Samuel Taylor Coleridge	Jan. 2, 1800	113
XLIX.	To Thomas Manning . .	Mar. 1, 1800	114
L.	,, ,, .	Mar. 17, 1800	115
LI.	To Samuel Taylor Coleridge	May 12, 1800	116
LII.	To Thomas Manning .	(Before June) 1800	117
LIII.	,, ,, . .	1800	118
LIV.	To Samuel Taylor Coleridge	June 22, 1800	119
LV.	,, ,,	Aug. 6, 1800	120
LVI.	To Thomas Manning . .	Aug. 1800	123
LVII.	,, ,, . .	1800	125
LVIII.	,, ,, . .	[Aug. 9, 1800]	127
LIX.	,, ,, . .	Aug. 11, 1800	128
LX.	To Samuel Taylor Coleridge	Aug. 14, 1800	129
LXI.	To Thomas Manning . .	Aug. 22, 1800	132
LXII.	To Samuel Taylor Coleridge	[Aug. or Sep.] 1800	134
LXIII.	,, ,,	Aug. 26, 1800	135
LXIV.	To Thomas Manning . .	Oct. 5, 1800	139
LXV.	To Samuel Taylor Coleridge	Oct. 9, 1800	140
LXVI.	To Wordsworth . .	Oct. 13, 1800	142
LXVII.	To Thomas Manning .	Oct. 16, 1800	143

LETTER		DATE	PAGE
LXVIII.	To Thomas Manning	Nov. 3, 1800	145
LXIX.	,, ,,	Nov. 28, 1800	148
LXX.	To William Godwin	Dec. 4, 1800	149
LXXI.	,, ,, .	Dec. 11, 1800	150
LXXII.	To Thomas Manning .	Dec. 13, 1800	151
LXXIII.	To William Godwin .	Dec. 14, 1800	153
LXXIV.	To Thomas Manning .	Dec. 16, 1800	154
LXXV.	,, ,, .	Dec. 27, 1800	157
LXXVI.	To Samuel Taylor Cole-		
	ridge . . [No date—end of 1800]		159
LXXVII.	To William Wordsworth	Jan. 1801	162
LXXVIII.	,, ,,	Jan. 30, 1801	164
LXXIX.	To Thomas Manning	[Feb. or Mar.] 1801	166
LXXX.	,, ,,	April 1801	169
LXXXI.	To William Godwin .	June 29, 1801	170
LXXXII.	To Mr. Walter Wilson .	Aug. 14, 1801	170
LXXXIII.	To Thomas Manning	[Aug.] 1801	171
LXXXIV.	,, ,, .	Aug. 31, 1801	172
LXXXV.	To William Godwin	Sept. 9, 1801	175
LXXXVI.	,, ,, .	Sept. 17, 1801	177
LXXXVII.	To Thomas Manning .	Feb. 15, 1802	179
LXXXVIII.	To Mr. Rickman . .	April 10, 1802	180
LXXXIX.	To Samuel Taylor Cole-		
	ridge	Sept. 8, 1802	180
XC.	To Mrs. Godwin .	[Early in Sept. 1802?]	181
XCI.	To Thomas Manning .	Sept. 24, 1802	181
XCII.	To Samuel Taylor Cole-		
	ridge .	Oct. 9, 1802	185
XCIII.	,, ..	Oct. 11, 1802	187
XCIV.		Oct. 23, 1802	189

LETTER		DATE	PAGE
XCV.	To Samuel Taylor Coleridge . . .	Nov. 4, 1802	191
XCVI.	To Thomas Manning .	Nov. 1802	193
XCVII.	„ „ .	Feb. 19, 1803	194
XCVIII.	„ „	Feb. 1803	196
XCIX.	„ „ .	Mar. 1803	198
C.	To Samuel Taylor Coleridge . . .	Mar. 20, 1803	199
CI.	„ „	April 13, 1803	201
CII.	To Thomas Manning . .	April 23, 1803	202
CIII.	To Samuel Taylor Coleridge	May 27, 1803	204
CIV.	To Mr. Rickman .	July 16, 1803	206
CV.	To William Godwin .	Nov. 8, 1803	207
CVI.	„ „ . .	Nov. 10, 1803	207
CVII.	To Robert Southey . .	Nov. 7, 1804	209
CVIII.	To Thomas Manning . .	Feb. 24, 1805	210
CIX.	To Miss Wordsworth .	June 14, 1805	212
CX.	To William Wordsworth	June 26, 1805	215
CXI.	To Thomas Manning . .	[July 27, 1805]	216
CXII.	To William Wordsworth	Sept. 28, 1805	216
CXIII.	To William Hazlitt .	Nov. 10, 1805	219
CXIV.	To Thomas Manning . .	[Nov. 15, 1805]	221
CXV.	To William Hazlitt .	Jan. 15, 1806	222
CXVI.	To Mr. Rickman .	Jan. 25, 1806	223
CXVII.	To William Hazlitt .	Feb. 19, 1806	224
CXVIII.	To Mr. Rickman . .	Mar. 1806	226
CXIX.	To William Hazlitt	Mar. 15, 1806	227
CXX.	To Thomas Manning . .	May 10, 1806	228
CXXI.	To William Wordsworth	June 1806	230

LETTER		DATE	PAGE
CXXII.	To Thomas Manning	Dec. 5, 1806	234
CXXIII.	To Miss Stoddart . .	Dec. 11 [1806]	239
CXXIV.	To William Wordsworth	Dec. 11, 1806	239
CXXV.	To William Godwin .	1806	240
CXXVI.	To William Wordsworth	Jan. 29, 1807	241
CXXVII.	To Rev. W. Hazlitt .	Feb. 18, 1808	242
CXXVIII.	To Thomas Manning .	Feb. 26, 1808	243
CXXIX.	To William Godwin	Mar. 11, 1808	247
CXXX.	To Mrs. Hazlitt	Dec. 10, 1808	248

CHAPTER III.

1809–1816.

LETTERS TO MANNING, COLERIDGE, WORDSWORTH, AND OTHERS.

LETTER		DATE	PAGE
CXXXI.	To Thomas Manning	Mar. 28, 1809	249
CXXXII.	To Samuel Taylor Coleridge .	June 7, 1809	251
CXXXIII.	,, ,,	Oct. 30, 1809	254
CXXXIV.	To Thomas Manning	Jan. 2, 1810	255
CXXXV.	To John Mathew Gutch	[April 9, 1810]	259
CXXXVI.	To Basil Montagu . .	July 12, 1810	260
CXXXVII.	To William Hazlitt	[Aug. 9, 1810]	261
CXXXVIII.	To Miss Wordsworth .	[Aug. 1810]	262
CXXXIX.	To William Wordsworth	Oct. 19, 1810	262
CXL.	To Miss Wordsworth .	Nov. 23, 1810	264
CXLI.	To William Hazlitt .	Nov. 28, 1810	265
CXLII.	To Henry Crabb Robinson	[1810]	266
CXLIII.	To William Hazlitt	Oct. 2, 1811	267

LETTER		DATE	PAGE
CXLIV. To WILLIAM GODWIN . .		[1811]	268
CXLV. To SAMUEL TAYLOR COLE-			
RIDGE		Aug. 13, 1814	269
CXLVI. To WILLIAM WORDSWORTH		Aug. 14, 1814	271
CXLVII. To SAMUEL TAYLOR COLE-			
RIDGE		Aug. 26, 1814	274
CXLVIII. To WILLIAM WORDSWORTH		Aug. 29, 1814	276
CXLIX.	,, ,,	1814	278
CL.	,, ,,	1814	280
CLI.	,, ,,	[1815]	283
CLII.	,, ,,	1815	286
CLIII. To ROBERT SOUTHEY . .		May 6, 1815	290
CLIV.	,, ,, . .	Aug. 9, 1815	292
CLV. To WILLIAM WORDSWORTH		Aug. 9, 1815	294
CLVI. To MISS HUTCHINSON . .		Oct. 19, 1815	297
CLVII. To THOMAS MANNING . .		Dec. 25, 1815	298
CLVIII.	,, ,, . .	Dec. 26, 1815	300
CLIX. To WILLIAM WORDSWORTH		April 9, 1816	302
CLX.	,, ,,	April 26, 1816	304
CLXI. To MISS MATILDA BETHAM .		June 1, 1816	306
CLXII. To H. DODWELL . . .		July 1816	308
NOTES			311

SONNET TO ELIA.

Thou gentle Spirit, sweet and pure and kind,
Though strangely witted—"high fantastical"—
Who clothest thy deep feelings in a pall
Of motley hues, that twinkle to the mind,
Half hiding, and yet heightening, what's enshrined
Within ;—who by a power unknown to all
Save thee alone, canst bring up at a call
A thousand seeming opposites, entwined
In wondrous brotherhood—fancy, wild wit,
Quips, cranks, and wanton wiles, with deep sweet thought,
And stinging jests, with honey for the wound ;
All blent in intermixture full and fit,—
A banquet for the choicest souls :—can aught
Repay the solace which from thee I've found?

J. H. (JOHN HUNTER OF CRAIGCROOK)
From *Friendship's Offering*, 1832.

INTRODUCTION.

As I have elsewhere told the story of Charles Lamb's life to the best of my ability, I have not thought it necessary, in editing his Letters, to tell it over again in my own words. The letters themselves contain his story—at least from the year when he came of age and began in earnest the battle of his difficult and lonely life. From the year 1796 to a date preceding his death by only a few days, there are few incidents of that life that are not related or referred to in those letters. When read consecutively, and with the help of such supplementary information as can be provided in notes, they form an almost complete biography.

Material for a final collection of Lamb's Letters has been gradually accumulating since the appearance of Talfourd's well-known volumes—the *Letters of Charles Lamb, with a Sketch of his Life*, in 1837, and the *Final Memorials* published after the death of Mary Lamb in 1848. It would take long to unfold the complicated history of the various editions of Lamb's correspondence that have since appeared. No change in the form of Talfourd's work would seem to have been made until the year 1868, when an edition of the writings of Lamb was published by Mr. Moxon, preceded by a collection of the Letters, freshly arranged according to the persons to whom they were addressed. This edition was in the first instance prefaced by an " Essay on the Genius of Lamb " from the hand of Mr. G. A. Sala. Two years later the first volume was withdrawn, and re-issued with a substituted Preface by Mr. Thomas Purnell. This edition was in its turn replaced in 1875 by another in six volumes, bearing the name of the same publishers, and under the editorship of Mr. Percy Fitzgerald. In this last-named edition the narrative portion of Talfourd's two works was retained, digested into one continuous narrative, with additions both in the text and notes. The Letters were separated from Talfourd's original matter, arranged (as in the two preceding editions) in groups—the Letters to Coleridge being followed by those addressed to Southey, and so forth. Mr. Fitzgerald was able to announce that he had added forty new letters to the collection.

More than ten years after Mr. Fitzgerald's edition, Mr. W. C. Hazlitt edited for Mr. George Bell a fresh *Life and Letters*, announced as Talfourd's, "carefully revised and greatly enlarged." The edition consists of Talfourd's text, freely interspersed with original matter, and the Letters rearranged, with certain additions to their number. The edition has this advantage over Mr. Fitzgerald's in that it aims at giving the Letters in chronological order, and not broken up into groups on any other plan. But I certainly cannot think that Talfourd's work, which, whatever be its defects, has long taken its place as an English Classic, should be re-issued under its author's name after additions and alterations so extensive have been introduced into it. I have preferred, therefore, to omit Talfourd's own narrative altogether, and to print the Letters only, with such additions to their number as I have been fortunate in obtaining, and in chronological order, so far as their dates are discoverable, reserving all elucidatory matter for the notes at the end of the respective volumes.

The editors of Lamb's Letters who have succeeded Talfourd have been, I think, unduly severe upon his methods of procedure. Mr. Fitzgerald, for instance, complains that in Talfourd's hands the Letters were edited "in accordance with his peculiar views—being cut up, altered, and dealt with in very summary fashion." This may be correct, but it should not be forgotten that the former of Talfourd's two works—the Life and Letters published in 1837—was produced under exceptionally difficult circumstances. Charles Lamb's history was bound up with that of his sister, and with the consequences of one most terrible event in her life. As long as Mary Lamb survived her brother, no letters, however interesting, which bore upon that calamity or the sacrifices it entailed, or upon the frequent recurrence of the malady in the life of the sister, could be printed without large omissions. Hence the Letters in the volumes of 1837 were in many cases fragments only, and made no claim to be anything else.

After the death of Mary Lamb in 1847 the fuller narrative of the sad fortunes of the brother and sister, vaguely hinted in the Preface to the former volumes, became possible. It is easy to pronounce upon the course Talfourd ought to have pursued. He should have prepared a new edition of his former book, adding new letters and restoring the omitted passages with such additional explanatory matter of his own as would have made the whole intelligible. Talfourd was evidently aware that this would have been the simplest and most satisfactory course, and apologises for not adopting it on the ground that it would be unfair to purchasers of the former work. He therefore chose the alternative plan of a second collection of letters with fresh connecting matter. But unfortunately he too often supplied the missing portions of letters with no indication of those in his former book to which they belonged. This was, beyond all question, a grave error of judgment, and the consequence was that if Talfourd's former work had of necessity a "scrappy" character, for reasons that were entitled to all respect, the second work was more fragmentary still. The charge against Talfourd of "cutting and carving" must at least, therefore, be made with due allowance for the difficulties of his position. For Mr. Fitzgerald's further complaint that Talfourd "altered" the Letters, a different defence must be found. It is certainly true that here and there, though very rarely, Lamb makes use in writing of certain freedoms of expression—principally of the expletive kind—which were common enough in letters and in conversation eighty years since, but are now happily out of fashion. If Talfourd, on a principle long ago accepted as sound, that such expletives have "had their day," ventured to soften them down into more harmless equivalents, I yet cannot agree with Mr. Fitzgerald that any serious treason against Lamb was committed in so doing. As to the omissions or changes of other kinds—of passages bearing upon persons then still living, or of intimate confidences as to the writer's own self, the publication of which must always be matter for editorial discretion — Talfourd showed himself neither timid nor capricious. I am not speaking without good reason. The autographs of two of the most important series of letters—those to Manning and those to Bernard Barton—have been in my hands, and except for the mutilations already referred to, made necessary by the Mary Lamb difficulty, I can testify that omissions or changes due to Talfourd are not only insignificant in amount, but were at the time amply justifiable. Many of such omissions have been since Talfourd's day supplied, and I have been able to restore some passages and correct others in the present edition.

A more important defect in Talfourd's method as editor must, however, be admitted. It certainly could never have been an easy task to determine the dates of Lamb's various letters. He rarely dated a letter, especially in early life, and postmarks are too often torn or illegible. To arrange the Letters, therefore, in anything like chronological order must have been, as it is still, matter of great difficulty. But Talfourd, we must agree, might have come something nearer to success. Even where the postmarks existed, he does not seem to have noticed them, or to have cared for any more precise reference to a letter than that it was written "about this time." Sometimes, even in the absence of both date and postmark, references in the Letters to incidents in the lives of Lamb or his correspondent might have saved the editor from many errors. A single illustration of this may suffice. In the summer of 1797 Coleridge was living at Nether Stowey, whither he had betaken himself, with his young friend Charles Lloyd, to be near Thomas Poole, who had his tannery hard by. Cruikshank and his wife were there, and Citizen Thelwall was not far off. Wordsworth and his sister, from Racedown, were on a visit, and Charles and Mary Lamb—the former little more than a youth of twenty-two—joined the party to spend their brief holiday. It was during this visit that Coleridge, having injured his leg, and being thus prevented from joining his friends in an excursion, stayed at home and wrote the lines, familiar to all lovers of Coleridge and Lamb—"This Lime-tree Bower my prison," containing touching reference to both Lamb and his sister. The poem was printed soon after in the *Annual Anthology* at Bristol, with a prefatory note relating the circumstances. After Lamb's return to London he writes Coleridge a letter (see vol. i. p. 79 of this edition) referring to this visit, to Coleridge's accident, to Poole, Wordsworth, and the rest, and to the incident of little Hartley Coleridge cutting his teeth. This letter Talfourd placed three years later, in 1800, and no subsequent editor has corrected the mistake. It must be admitted, however, that errors are not always so easy to amend as in this instance. Internal evidence is not always present to supplement the external, and after careful examination and balancing of probabilities, I have had to leave many letters, notably of the period between 1800 and 1802, with many misgivings as to the place finally assigned to them. The originals of the Letters to Coleridge, I should add, are dispersed, and no longer accessible for purposes of collation.

The autographs of the Manning Letters have been in my hands, through the kindness of their owner, the Rev. C. R. Manning, Rector of Diss, the nephew of the famous orientalist and traveller. Among these I have been so fortunate as to find several not before printed,—one of singular interest, containing Lamb's criticism on the second volume of the *Lyrical Ballads,* and an account of the passage at arms between himself and the author of the volume. Talfourd suppressed the letter, there can be no doubt, because Wordsworth was then still living. It came under my notice too late for insertion in its place in the text of the correspondence, but I have found room for it in my notes. Some new letters to Manning of later date will be found in their proper places. The Barton Letters I have also carefully examined with the valuable assistance of Bernard Barton's daughter, Mrs. Edward Fitzgerald, who has also favoured me with much interesting information throwing light upon allusions occurring in the letters. To Mrs. Procter I have to express my warm acknowledgments for entrusting me with the originals of the letters to her husband ("Barry Cornwall"), from which I have been able to make both corrections and additions. To Mrs. Cowden Clarke (the Mary Victoria Novello of the Letters) I am also deeply indebted for her "cordial permission" to include in this edition the Letters of Lamb to her husband, and to her father, Vincent Novello, first printed in Mr. and Mrs. Cowden Clarke's interesting *Recollections of Writers.*

Other letters, as yet unpublished, will be found in the present edition. A series addressed to Mr. J. B. Dibdin I am able to include, by the kindness of his nephew, Mr. R. W. Dibdin. Readers of Lamb's correspondence may remember a reference to this gentleman, "the grandson of the songster," as having died early of consumption, after seeking in vain the restorative climate of Madeira. I have told in my notes the story of Lamb's chance introduction to the young man, to whom he was thenceforth drawn by kindred literary tastes, and even more by that which always deeply moved Charles Lamb,—the sight of patient suffering or struggle. Mr. Dibdin, a clerk in a city merchant's house, was often obliged to visit some southern watering-place for his health, and most of the present letters were evidently composed by Lamb with the single object of amusing his friend, and relieving for a moment the tedium of his enforced idleness. It is as such that these letters must be judged. If their fun is at times of the most extravagant, the true kindness of heart that prompted them will not be overlooked.

It will be seen that I have not attempted to make this edition of Lamb's Letters "complete," in the sense of having retained all the notes (or "notelets," as they have been called) included in former collections. It happens to any man of mark and genius, such as Charles Lamb, that his most trivial notes are naturally preserved by correspondents as autographs, but it assuredly does not follow that they are therefore worth printing. Dozens of hasty notes written by Lamb are extant, but it seems to me little short of an insult to his memory and to his readers to fill page after page with communications, of which the following is a sample :—

"DEAR A.—I am better. Mary quite well. We expected to see you before. I can't write long letters. So a friendly love to you all."

At the same time I have not lightly omitted any scrap of a note containing a characteristic flash of humour or felicity of expression, or supplying any link in the chain of incidents that made up his own life or Mary's. Even now, when finally parting from a task that has employed my leisure for some years, I feel reluctant altogether to omit certain fragments—illustrations of that rare union of tenderness, humour, and invention—that for various reasons have not found a place in the text of these volumes. In an early note to Manning (January 1800) occurs one more of the many touching tributes to his early friend, his "guardian angel": "I have given up my house and must look out for lodgings. I expect Mary will get better before many weeks are gone; but at present I feel my daily and hourly prop has fallen from me. I totter and stagger with weakness, for nobody can supply her place to me. White has *all kindness*, but not *sympathy*. C. Lloyd, my only correspondent, you except, is a good being, but a weak one. I know not where to look but to you. If you will suffer me to weary your shoulders with part of my burden, I shall write again to let you know how I go on."

He is in a more cheerful mood in another letter of the same year to the same correspondent, in which occurs this passage (not without interest just now in its prophecies and speculations): "By the way, I am anxious to get specimens of all English turkeys. Pray send me at your leisure separate specimens from every county in Great Britain, including Wales, for I hate nationalities. The Irish turkeys I will let alone till the union is determined." And, finally, I cannot keep back the droll and wonderful imagination of the following—an extract from a letter to Mr. Procter. Lamb, who was himself always writing verses for his young friends' albums, wanted Procter to do the same kind office for a young lady in whose veins was a tinge of blood darker than European. Assuming that Procter might make his verses a vehicle for some compliments, Lamb writes: "And now, Procter, I will tell you a story. Hierocles, the Sicilian Tyrant, who lived in the thirtieth Olympiad, just seven hundred and sixty years *ante* A.D., by the Gregorian Computation, having won the Prize in a Race of Mules, besought the Poet Simonides, with the incentive moreover of a donative of 1200 Sesterces, which might be about £12 : 7 : 3¼ of our money, to write him an Olympic Hymn in praise of the mules. But Simonides, declining to vulgarise his Muse with the mention of any such mongrels, the Tyrant (which signifies in the Greek of that age only *king*) rounds him in the ear that he shall have 8000 sesterces if he will touch up his beasts handsomely. Whereupon Simonides—the 'tender Simonides,' as antiquity delights to phrase him—began to relent, and

stringing his golden lyre begins a lofty ode to the cattle
with—

   ' Hail ! daughters of the swift-winged steed.'

Sinking, you see, one part of their genealogy. Now for
the application. What I told you, dear Procter, about
my young friend was nothing but the exact truth. But
I sunk the circumstance that her mother was a negro, or
half-caste—which convinces me, what I always thought,
that something of the tender genius of Simonides lives
again in my strains. Mary corrects me, and will have it
that the lady's mother was a Hindostanee half-caste, and
no negress, but was I to send you wool-gathering over the
vast plains watered by the Ganges, or the more bewilder-
ing wilds of Timbuctoo, to search for images ?" There
is *genius* in nonsense such as this. I have willingly
suppressed no "fooling" of this kind; but notes of
invitation to a supper party, or acceptance of one, have no
justification for appearing merely because they were once
in Charles Lamb's handwriting.

I have elsewhere spoken of the peculiar value and
interest of the literary and other criticism scattered
through these Letters, and I may be permitted to repeat
here a few sentences. It is remarkable that the intel-
lectual accomplishment in Lamb which asserts itself
earliest is just that which ordinarily it takes years, with
their increased reading and experience, to mature—the
critical faculty. Lamb's earliest letters that have sur-
vived begin when he was just of age, and his two chief
correspondents for the next three years were young men
like himself—one his schoolfellow, Samuel Taylor Cole-
ridge, three years his senior; and the other, whom he had
come to know through Coleridge, and who was associated
with Coleridge by so many ties, Robert Southey. All
three were starting on a literary career, full of ambition;
two of them with the intention of making it their pro-
fession, the other, happily for himself, settling down to
that desk in Leadenhall Street which was to prove,
though he knew it not, his best blessing and safeguard

for thirty years to come. Apart from the family matters —sad and terrible they were—discussed in these Letters, the chief topics dealt with are literary and critical. Coleridge and Southey forward to their friend their verses, their lyrics and eclogues, for his judgment and suggestions ; and he in turn submits to them his sonnets and elegies, plaintive and tender after his model, William Lisle Bowles. Coleridge and Southey, endowed with a poetic gift far stronger and richer than Lamb's, yet at once recognise in their companion—no University man like themselves, lowly in his home and traditions, humble in his life's occupation—this rare and precious gift of critical insight. These earliest letters of Lamb show how amply justified was their confidence in his powers. If the art or science of poetical criticism could be made matter of instruction, I know no better introduction to the study than these scattered criticisms of his, first upon Coleridge's and Southey's verse, then upon Wordsworth's, and generally upon all poetry ancient or modern quoted or referred to in the Letters. Lamb was one of the very first to detect the great powers and the real importance of Coleridge and Wordsworth before the wit of the Anti-Jacobin and "English Bards" had opened its batteries upon these poets, and while the *Edinburgh* and *Quarterly Reviews* were yet unborn. This boy of twenty-one was already showing that, together with the keenest eye for the weaker side of these poetical reformers, and with a true humorist's enjoyment of what was absurd or puerile in their methods, that enjoyment in no way disturbed his appreciation of their genius. With all his prejudices and petulances (and Lamb had plenty of these), the distinguishing feature of his critical power is its width and its versatility. The deepest of all his literary affections, that for Milton, no more interfered with his intense enjoyment of Pope, than did his delight in Pope delay for an instant his recognition of the worth of Cowper, Burns, and their successors. Lamb is our best and wholesomest example of that rare capacity for valuing and enjoying

one literary school without at the same time disparaging its
opposites. And he could recognise that the same writer
often rises above, and often sinks below, himself. He
laughs as frankly at what was namby-pamby in Coleridge
and Wordsworth as he descants with enthusiasm on the
Ancient Mariner and the "Lines written above Tintern
Abbey."

Nor is it only on the great men—the Coleridges and
Wordsworths—that Lamb's criticism is so instructive.
Scarcely anything was too poor or insignificant, if written
by a friend or by one who needed his friendship, for him
to exercise his critical faculty upon; and if in the dead
waste of Joseph Cottle's blank-verse a redeeming line
appears, Lamb detects it on the spot, and by his words
of approval almost imprints the stamp of classicality
upon the poem. If he says almost the best thing possible
about Cervantes, he does not disdain to do the same
thing for the author of the *Farmer's Boy*. But it is not
only about books that Lamb's judgments are so acute.
As we pass from letter to letter in this collection, nothing
will strike us more than the transition from wildest
burlesque to the nicest and most delicate estimates of
human conduct. Even in the same letter, as in one
to Mr. Basil Montagu on the proposal to erect a monu-
ment to Clarkson in his lifetime, the two sides of the
writer appear in a contrast almost startling. It is the
letter in which he says that he should not like his name
to be absent from the list of subscribers, if the project
were carried out, but adds, "Otherwise I frankly own
that to pillarise a man's good feelings in his life-time is
not to my taste. Monuments to goodness, even after death,
are equivocal. Goodness blows no trumpet, nor desires
to have it blown. *We should be modest for a modest
man*, as he is for himself. The vanities of life—art,
poetry, skill military—are subjects for trophies; not
the silent thoughts arising in a good man's mind in lonely
places." This ethical good taste that appears whenever
Lamb's opinion is seriously called for, is one of the many

pleasures and surprises, if I am not mistaken, to be enjoyed by those who think of Lamb mainly as a jester, who did not always observe a corresponding moderation in his jests.

In certain respects I have tried to improve upon Talfourd's method as an editor of these Letters. But I have little sympathy with those who have spoken slightingly of the obligations he has laid upon all lovers of Charles Lamb. Least of all can I understand the covert charges against him of having, in the interest of his friend, over-coloured his virtues or concealed any of his frailties or foibles. When Talfourd put together the *Final Memorials* after the death of Mary Lamb in 1847, he attempted a fresh estimate of Lamb's character, as affected by the evidence of facts then for the first time published to the world. He headed these last pages, "Lamb fully known." I believe that those who know Lamb best must acknowledge both the generosity and the discriminating justice of this estimate. It may be true that a certain daintiness, a certain hothouse flavour, in Talfourd's style is a little out of keeping with his subject, but it certainly is not for the critical fashions of this age to look back scornfully on the "preciosity" of forty years since. But if Talfourd wraps up his judgments with something of an over-elegant elaboration, these judgments appear to me for the most part admirable. And although the number of Lamb's collected letters has largely grown in the last forty years, and his scattered writings have been collected and published, no record has "leaped to light" which need in any degree modify the estimate then formed.

It was remarked by Mr. Sala, that among the reasons for Lamb's memory enduring among us, is the circumstance that "he was passionately loved by his friends. He had, not one, but half-a-dozen Boswells." This is certainly true. We know Lamb as he was known to troops of friends the most various in character and genius. Either in prose or verse, or both, we possess descriptions, estimates, anecdotes of Lamb from Wordsworth, Coleridge, Hood,

Procter, Landor, Hazlitt, Leigh Hunt, Talfourd, Patmore, and many others; and through all these eyes, we see one and the same man. The same rare and sterling qualities impress all these alike. There are some forgotten verses by that friend of Lamb's earlier days, Charles Lloyd, written in 1820,—verses often obscure and sounding curious depths of bathos, but not without gleams of poetry and genuine insight. They are called "Desultory thoughts in London," and include, among other such thoughts, an elaborate tribute to Coleridge, and a description of Lloyd's other dearest friend, Charles Lamb. No names are mentioned, but the allusions are unmistakable. Lloyd could only then hint at the sorrows of his friend's early life :—

> " He walked along his path in steadiness,
> In solitude, and in sublimity ;
> None ever knew his desolate distress,
> And none shall ever know it now from me."

And when, after many stanzas of strange digression, he comes back to his theme :

> " And now, my friend, I turn again to thee,
> Thou pure receptacle of all that's good ! "

he admits that Lamb has "contrived an art" he had never conceived as possible :

> " The child of impulse ever to appear,
> And yet through duty's path strictly to steer.
>
> Nay more, thou hast contrived *to be* that child,
> And not alone hast held, through duty's path,
> In lofty unimpeachableness, and mild,
> Thy way—but through strange suffering and scathe
> Of worldly comfort, hast been unbeguiled
> Of life's first innocence :—God's blessing hath—
> Like Shadrach, Meshach, and Abednego—
> Through fiery furnace made thee safely go."

There is no mistaking tributes such as these for the mere language of literary compliment. There was no conspiracy among Landor and Lloyd, Wordsworth and Thomas Hood, Coleridge and Procter, to uphold the reputation of a favourite member of their clique. When we read such words, we know that they mean what they say, and that they are true. And it is because I believe that Talfourd justly interpreted the character of his hero, and was in full harmony with the judgments of those other friends of Lamb, that I have ventured to add these few words in his vindication.

To the names already mentioned of those to whom I am indebted for many kind services, I must add that of Mr. George Bentley of New Burlington Street, for the use of an unpublished letter; of Mr. C. Kegan Paul, for permission to include the Letters of Lamb to Godwin, originally printed in Mr. Paul's *Life of William Godwin*; of Messrs. Longmans, and the editor of the *Century Magazine* and Mr. R. S. Chilton, for a like permission to use letters addressed respectively to Miss Matilda Betham and to Mr. John Howard Payne. Mr. B. M'George of Glasgow kindly collated two of the letters here given with originals in his possession; and my old friend Dr. Edward Calvert of Shrewsbury has taken a lively interest in extracting meanings and allusions from some of Lamb's rather frolicsome Latin. And I owe a final word of special gratitude to Mr. James Dykes Campbell, who has allowed me to consult him throughout, and whose minute and exact knowledge of all matters touching Coleridge, Wordsworth, and Lamb, has materially enriched my notes.

ALFRED AINGER.

Hampstead, *November* 1887.

LETTERS OF CHARLES LAMB.

CHAPTER I.

1796–1800.

To SAMUEL TAYLOR COLERIDGE.

LETTER I.]   *May* 27, 1796.

Dear Coleridge—Make yourself perfectly easy about May. I paid his bill when I sent your clothes. I was flush of money, and am so still to all the purposes of a single life; so give yourself no further concern about it. The money would be superfluous to me if I had it.

When Southey becomes as modest as his predecessor, Milton, and publishes his Epics in duodecimo, I will read 'em; a guinea a book is somewhat exorbitant, nor have I the opportunity of borrowing the work. The extracts from it in the *Monthly Review*, and the short passages in your *Watchman*, seem to me much superior to any thing in his partnership account with Lovell. Your poems I shall procure forthwith. There were noble lines in what you inserted in one of your Numbers from *Religious Musings*; but I thought them elaborate. I am somewhat glad you have given up that paper: it must have

VOL. I.   S   B

been dry, unprofitable, and of "dissonant mood" to your disposition. I wish you success in all your undertakings, and am glad to hear you are employed about the *Evidences of Religion.* There is need of multiplying such books a hundredfold in this philosophical age, to *prevent* converts to atheism, for they seem too tough disputants to meddle with afterwards.

Le Grice is gone to make puns in Cornwall. He has got a tutorship to a young boy living with his mother, a widow lady. He will, of course, initiate him quickly in "whatsoever things are honest, lovely, and of good report." He has cut Miss Hunt completely: the poor girl is very ill on the occasion; but he laughs at it, and justifies himself by saying, "she does not see me laugh." Coleridge, I know not what suffering scenes you have gone through at Bristol. My life has been somewhat diversified of late. The six weeks that finished last year and began this, your very humble servant spent very agreeably in a madhouse, at Hoxton. I am got somewhat rational now, and don't bite any one. But mad I was; and many a vagary my imagination played with me, enough to make a volume, if all were told. My Sonnets I have extended to the number of nine since I saw you, and will some day communicate to you. I am beginning a poem in blank verse, which, if I finish, I publish. White is on the eve of publishing (he took the hint from *Vortigern*) "Original letters of Falstaff, Shallow," etc.; a copy you shall have when it comes out. They are without exception the best imitations I ever saw. Coleridge, it may convince you of my regards for you when I tell you my head ran on you in my madness, as much almost as on another person, who I am inclined to think was the more immediate cause of my temporary frenzy.

The Sonnet I send you has small merit as poetry; but you will be curious to read it when I tell you it was written in my prison-house in one of my lucid intervals.

TO MY SISTER.

If from my lips some angry accents fell,
  Peevish complaint, or harsh reproof unkind,
  'Twas but the error of a sickly mind
And troubled thoughts, clouding the purer well
  And waters clear of Reason ; and for me,
  Let this my verse the poor atonement be—
  My verse, which thou to praise wert e'er inclined
Too highly, and with a partial eye to see
No blemish.   Thou to me didst ever show
  Kindest affection ; and would'st oft-times lend
  An ear to the desponding love-sick lay,
  Weeping my sorrows with me, who repay
But ill the mighty debt of love I owe,
  Mary, to thee, my sister and my friend.

With these lines, and with that sister's kindest remembrances to C——, I conclude.

Yours sincerely,   LAMB.

Your *Conciones ad Populum* are the most eloquent politics that ever came in my way.

Write when convenient—not as a task, for there is nothing in this letter to answer.

We cannot send our remembrances to Mrs. C., not having seen her, but believe me our best good wishes attend you both.

My civic and poetic compliments to Southey if at Bristol. Why, he is a very Leviathan of Bards !—the small minnow, I !

LETTER II.]   [No Month] 1796.

I am in such violent pain with the headache, that I am fit for nothing but transcribing, scarce for that. When I get your poems, and the *Joan of Arc*, I will exercise my presumption in giving you my opinion of 'em. The mail does not come in before to-morrow (Wednesday) morning. The following Sonnet was composed during a walk down into Hertfordshire early in last Summer :—

The Lord of Light shakes off his drowsyhed.
  Fresh from his couch up springs the lusty sun,
  And girds himself his mighty race to run ;
Meantime, by truant love of rambling led,
I turn my back on thy detested walls,
  Proud City, and thy sons I leave behind,
  A selfish, sordid, money-getting kind,
Who shut their ears when holy Freedom calls.
I pass not thee so lightly, humble spire,
  That mindest me of many a pleasure gone,
  Of merriest days, of Love and Islington,
Kindling anew the flames of past desire ;
  And I shall muse on thee, slow journeying on,
To the green plains of pleasant Hertfordshire.

The last line is a copy of Bowles's, "To the green Hamlet in the peaceful Plain." Your ears are not so very fastidious ; many people would not like words so prosaic and familiar in a Sonnet as Islington and Hertfordshire. The next was written within a day or two of the last, on revisiting a spot where the scene was laid of my first Sonnet that "mock'd my step with many a lonely glade."

When last I roved these winding wood-walks green,
  Green winding walks, and shady pathways sweet,
Oft-times would Anna seek the silent scene,
  Shrouding her beauties in the lone retreat.
No more I hear her footsteps in the shade ;
  Her image only in these pleasant ways
  Meets me self-wandering, where in happier days
I held free converse with my fair-hair'd maid.
I pass'd the little cottage which she loved,
The cottage which did once my all contain :
It spake of days that ne'er must come again ;
  Spake to my heart, and much my heart was moved.
Now "Fair befall thee, gentle maid," said I ;
And from the cottage turn'd me with a sigh.

The next retains a few lines from a Sonnet of mine which you once remarked had no "body of thought" in it. I agree with you, but have preserved a part of it, and it runs thus. I flatter myself you will like it :—

A timid grace sits trembling in her eye,
  As loth to meet the rudeness of men's sight

> Yet shedding a delicious lunar light,
> That steeps in kind oblivious ecstacy
> The care-crazed mind, like some still melody :
>   Speaking most plain the thoughts which do possess
>   Her gentle sprite, peace and meek quietness,
> And innocent loves, and maiden purity :
>   A look whereof might heal the cruel smart
> Of changed friends, or Fortune's wrongs unkind ;
>   Might to sweet deeds of mercy move the heart
> Of him who hates his brethren of mankind.
>   Turn'd are those beams from me, who fondly yet
>   Past joys, vain loves, and buried hopes regret.

The next and last I value most of all. 'Twas composed close upon the heels of the last, in that very wood I had in mind when I wrote "Methinks how dainty sweet."

> We were two pretty babes, the youngest she,
>   The youngest, and the loveliest far, I ween,
>   And Innocence her name. The time has been
> We two did love each other's company ;
>   Time was, we two had wept to have been apart :
>   But when, with show of seeming good beguiled,
>   I left the garb and manners of a child,
> And my first love for man's society,
>   Defiling with the world my virgin heart,
> My loved companion dropp'd a tear and fled,
> And hid in deepest shades her awful head.
>   Beloved ! who can tell me where thou art—
>   In what delicious Eden to be found—
>   That I may seek thee the wide world around?

Since writing it, I have found in a poem by Hamilton of Bangor, these two lines to "Happiness :"—

> " Nun, sober and devout, where art thou fled
>   To hide in shades thy meek, contented head?"

Lines eminently beautiful ; but I do not remember having read them previously, for the credit of my tenth and eleventh lines. Parnell has two lines (which probably suggested the above) to "Contentment :"

> " Whither, ah ! whither art thou fled,
>   To hide thy meek, contented head?"

Cowley's exquisite "Elegy on the death of his friend Harvey," suggested the phrase of "we two."

> "Was there a tree that did not know
> The love betwixt us two?"

So much for acknowledged plagiarisms, the confession of which I know not whether it has more of vanity or modesty in it. As to my blank verse, I am so dismally slow and sterile of ideas (I speak from my heart) that I much question if it will ever come to any issue. I have hitherto only hammered out a few independent, unconnected snatches, not in a capacity to be sent. I am very ill, and will rest till I have read your poems, for which I am very thankful. I have one more favour to beg of you, that you never mention Mr. May's affair in any sort, much less *think* of repaying. Are we not flocci-nauci-what-d'ye-call-'em-ists? We have just learned that my poor brother has had a sad accident: a large stone, blown down by yesterday's high wind, has bruised his leg in a most shocking manner; he is under the care of Cruikshanks. Coleridge! there are 10,000 objections against my paying you a visit at Bristol; it cannot be else; but in this world 'tis better not to think too much of pleasant possibles, that we may not be out of humour with present insipids. Should anything bring you to London, you will recollect No. 7, Little Queen Street, Holborn.

I shall be too ill to call on Wordsworth myself, but will take care to transmit him his poem, when I have read it. I saw Le Grice the day before his departure, and mentioned incidentally his "teaching the young idea how to shoot." Knowing him and the probability there is of people having a propensity to pun in his company, you will not wonder that we both stumbled on the same pun at once, he eagerly anticipating me,—"he would teach him to shoot!" Poor Le Grice! if wit alone could entitle a man to respect, etc., he has written a very witty little pamphlet lately, satirical, upon college declamations. When I send White's book, I will add that. I am sorry there should be any difference between you and Southey.

"Between you two there should be peace," tho' I must say I have borne him no good will since he spirited you away from among us. What is become of Moschus? You sported some of his sublimities, I see, in your *Watchman*. Very decent things. So much for to-night from your afflicted, headachey, sorethroaty, humble servant, C. LAMB.

Tuesday Night.—Of your *Watchman*, the Review of Burke was the best prose. I augured great things from the first Number. There is some exquisite poetry interspersed. I have re-read the extract from the *Religious Musings*, and retract whatever invidious there was in my censure of it as elaborate. There are times when one is not in a disposition thoroughly to relish good writing. I have re-read it in a more favourable moment, and hesitate not to pronounce it sublime. If there be any thing in it approaching to tumidity (which I meant not to infer; by *elaborate* I meant simply laboured), it is the gigantic hyperbole by which you describe the evils of existing society : "snakes, lions, hyenas, and behemoths," is carrying your resentment beyond bounds. The pictures of "The Simoom," of "Frenzy and Ruin," of "The Whore of Babylon," and "The Cry of the Foul Spirits disherited of Earth," and "the strange beatitude" which the good man shall recognise in heaven, as well as the particularising of the children of wretchedness (I have unconsciously included every part of it), form a variety of uniform excellence. I hunger and thirst to read the poem complete. That is a capital line in your sixth Number :

"This dark, frieze-coated, hoarse, teeth-chattering month."

They are exactly such epithets as Burns would have stumbled on, whose poem on the ploughed-up daisy you seem to have had in mind. Your complaint that some of your readers thought there was too much, some too little original matter in your Numbers, reminds me of poor dead Parsons in the *Critic.* "Too little incident! Give me leave to tell you, sir, there is too much incident." I had like to have forgot thanking you for that exquisite little morsel, the first Sclavonian Song. The expression in the second,—"more happy to be unhappy in hell :" is it not very quaint? Accept my thanks, in common with those of all who love good poetry, for "The Braes of Yarrow." I congratulate you on the enemies you must have made by your splendid invective against the barterers in human flesh and sinews. Coleridge! you will rejoice to hear that Cowper is recovered from his lunacy, and is employed on his translation of the Italian, etc., poems of Milton for an edition where Fuseli presides as designer. Coleridge! to an idler like myself, to write and receive letters are both very pleasant; but I wish not to break in upon your valuable time by expecting to hear very frequently from you. Reserve that obligation for your moments of lassitude, when you have nothing else to do; for your loco-restive and all your idle propensities, of course, have given way to the duties of providing for a family. The mail is come in, but no parcel; yet this is Tuesday. Farewell, then, till to-morrow; for a niche and a nook I must leave for criticisms. By the way, I hope you do not send your only copy of *Joan of Arc:* I will in that case return it immediately.

Your parcel *is* come: you have been *lavish* of your presents.

Wordsworth's poem I have hurried through, not without delight. Poor Lovell! my heart almost accuses me for the light manner I lately spoke of him, not dreaming of his death. My heart bleeds for your accumulated troubles: God send you through 'em with patience. I conjure you, dream not that I will ever think of being repaid; the very word is galling to the ears. I have read all your *Religious Musings* with uninterrupted feelings of profound admiration. You may safely rest your fame on it. The best remaining things are what I have before read, and they lose nothing by my recollec tion of your manner of reciting 'em, for I too bear in mind "the voice, the look" of absent friends, and can occasionally mimic their manner for the amusement of those who have seen 'em. Your impassioned manner of recitation I can recall at any time to mine own heart and to the ears of the bystanders. I rather wish you had left the monody on Chatterton concluding, as it did, abruptly. It had more of unity. The conclusion of your *Religious Musings*, I fear, will entitle you to the reproof of your beloved woman, who wisely will not suffer your fancy to run riot, but bids you walk humbly with your God. The last words,

> "I discipline my young and novice thought
> In ministeries of heart-stirring song,"

though not now new to me, cannot be enough admired. To speak politely, they are a well-turned compliment to Poetry. I hasten to read *Joan of Arc*, etc. I have read your lines at the beginning of the second book: they are worthy of Milton; but in my mind yield to your *Religious Musings*. I shall read the whole carefully, and in some future letter take the liberty to particularise my opinions of it. Of what is new to me among your poems next to the "Musings," that beginning "My Pensive Sara" gave me most pleasure: the lines in it I just alluded to are most exquisite; they made my sister and self smile, as conveying a pleasing picture of Mrs. C. checking your wild wanderings, which we were so fond of hearing you indulge when among us. It has endeared us more than any thing to your good lady; and your own self-reproof that follows, delighted us. 'Tis a charming poem throughout. (You have well remarked that *charming, admirable, exquisite* are the words expressive of feelings more than conveying of ideas; else I might plead very well want of room in my paper as excuse for generalising.) I want room to tell you how we are charmed with your verses in the manner of Spenser, etc., etc., etc., etc., etc. I am glad you resume the *Watchman*. Change the name: leave out all articles of news, and whatever things are peculiar to newspapers, and confine yourself to ethics, verse, criticism; or, rather do not confine yourself. Let your plan be as diffuse as the *Spectator*, and I'll answer for it the work prospers. If I am vain enough to think I can be a contributor; rely on my inclinations. Coleridge! in reading your *Religious Musings* I felt a transient superiority over you. I *have* seen Priestley. I love to see his name repeated in your writings. I love and honour him, almost profanely. You would be charmed with his *Sermons*, if you never read 'em. You have doubtless read his books illustrative of the doctrine of Necessity. Prefixed to a late work of his, in answer to Paine, there is a Preface, giving an account of the man, and his services to men, written by Lindsey, his dearest friend, well worth your reading.

Tuesday Eve.—Forgive my prolixity, which is yet too brief for all I could wish to say. God give you comfort, and all that are of your household! Our loves and best good wishes to Mrs. C.　　　　　　　　　　C. LAMB.

LETTER III.]　　　　　　　　　　　　*June* 10, 1796.

With *Joan of Arc* I have been delighted, amazed. I had not presumed to expect any thing of such excellence from Southey. Why, the poem is alone sufficient to redeem the character of the age we live in from the imputation of degenerating in Poetry, were there no such beings extant as Burns, and Bowles, Cowper, and ———: fill up the blank how you please; I say nothing. The subject is well chosen. It opens well. To become more particular, I will notice in their order a few passages that chiefly struck me on perusal. Page 26, " Fierce and terrible Benevolence !" is a phrase full of grandeur and originality. The whole context made me feel *possessed*, even like Joan herself. Page 28, " It is most horrible with the keen sword to gore the finely-fibred human frame," and what follows, pleased me mightily. In the 2nd Book, the first forty lines in particular are majestic and high-sounding. Indeed the whole vision of the Palace of Ambition and what follows are supremely excellent. Your simile of the Laplander,.

> . . . . . "by Niemi lake
> Or Balda Zhiok, or the mossy stone
> Of Solfar-kapper,"

will bear comparison with any in Milton for fulness of circumstance and lofty pacedness of versification. Southey's similes, though many of 'em are capital, are all inferior. In one of his books, the simile of the oak in the storm occurs, I think, four times. To return : the light in which you view the heathen deities is accurate and beautiful. Southey's personifications in this book are so many fine and faultless pictures. I was much pleased with your manner of accounting for the reason why monarchs take delight in war. At the 447th line you have placed Prophets and Enthusiasts check by jowl, on too intimate a footing for the dignity of the former. Necessarian-like-speaking, it is correct. Page 98, "Dead is the Douglas! cold thy warrior frame, illustrious Buchan," etc., are of kindred excellence with Gray's "Cold is Cadwallo's tongue," etc. How famously the Maid baffles the Doctors, Seraphic and Irrefragable, "with all their trumpery!" Page 126, the procession, the appearances of the Maid, of the Bastard Son of Orleans and of Tremouille, are full of fire and fancy, and exquisite melody of versification. The personifications from line 303 to 309, in the heat of the battle, had better been omitted ; they are not very striking, and only encumber. The converse which Joan and Conrade hold on the banks of the Loire is altogether beautiful. Page 313, the conjecture that in dreams "all things are that seem," is one of those conceits which the Poet delights to admit into his creed ; a creed, by the way, more marvellous and mystic than ever Athanasius dreamed of. Page 315, I need only *mention* those lines ending with "She saw a serpent gnawing at her heart !" They are good imitative lines, "he toiled and toiled, of toil to reap no end, but endless toil and never-ending woe." Page 347, Cruelty is such as Hogarth might have painted her. Page 361, all the passage about Love (where he seems to confound conjugal love with creating and preserving love) is very confused, and sickens me with a load of useless personifications ; else that ninth Book is the finest in the volume —an exquisite combination of the ludicrous and the terrible : I have never read either, even in translation, but such I conceive to be the manner of Dante or Ariosto. The tenth Book is the most languid. On the whole, considering the celerity wherewith the poem was finished, I was astonished at the infrequency of weak lines. I had expected to find it verbose. Joan, I think, does too little in battle ; Dunois perhaps the same ; Conrade too much. The anecdotes interspersed among the battles refresh the mind very agreeably, and I am delighted with the very many passages of simple pathos abounding throughout the poem ; passages which the author of "Crazy Kate" might have written. Has not Master Southey spoke very slightingly, in his Preface, and disparagingly of Cowper's Homer? What makes him reluctant to give Cowper his fame? And does not Southey use too often the expletives "did," and "does?" They have a good effect at times, but are too inconsiderable, or rather become blemishes, when they mark a style. On the whole, I expect Southey one day to rival Milton : I already deem him equal to Cowper, and superior to all living poets besides. What says Coleridge? The "Monody on Henderson" is *immensely good :* the rest of that little volume is *readable, and above mediocrity.* I proceed to a more pleasant task ; pleasant because the poems are yours ; pleasant because you impose the task on me ; and pleasant, let me add, because it will confer a whimsical importance on me to sit in judgment upon your rhymes. First, though, let me thank you again and again, in my own and my sister's name, for your invitations. Nothing could give us more pleasure than to come, but (were there no other reasons) while my brother's leg is so bad it is out of the question. Poor fellow! he is very feverish and light-headed; but Cruikshanks has pronounced the symptoms favourable, and gives us every hope that there will be no need of amputation: God send not! We are necessarily confined with him all the afternoon and evening till very late, so that I am stealing a few minutes to write to you.

Thank you for your frequent letters: you are the only correspondent, and I might add, the only friend I have in the world. I go nowhere, and have no acquaintance. Slow of speech, and reserved of manners, no one seeks or cares for my society; and I am left alone. Allen calls only occasionally, as though it were a duty rather, and seldom stays ten minutes. Then judge how thankful I am for your letters! Do not, however, burthen yourself with the correspondence. I trouble you again so soon, only in obedience to your injunctions. Complaints apart, proceed we to our task. I am called away to tea; thence must wait upon my brother; so must delay till to-morrow. Farewell!—*Wednesday.*

Thursday.—I will first notice what is new to me. Thirteenth page: "The thrilling tones that concentrate the soul" is a nervous line; and the first six lines of page 14 are very pretty; the twenty-first effusion is a perfect thing. That in the manner of Spenser is very sweet, particularly at the close: the thirty-fifth effusion is most exquisite; that line in particular, "And, tranquil, muse upon tranquillity." It is the very reflex pleasure that distinguishes the tranquillity of a thinking being from that of a shepherd, a modern one I would be understood to mean, a Damætas, one that keeps other people's sheep. Certainly, Coleridge, your letter from Shurton Bars has less merit than most things in your volume; personally, it may chime in best with your own feelings, and therefore you love it best. It has, however, great merit. In your fourth epistle, *that* is an exquisite paragraph, and fancy-full, of "A stream there is which rolls in lazy flow," etc., etc. "Murmurs sweet under-song 'mid jasmine bowers" is a sweet line; and so are the three next. The concluding simile is far-fetched—"tempest-honoured" is a quaintish phrase. Of the Monody on Henderson I will here only notice these lines, as superlatively excellent. That energetic one, "Shall I not praise thee, scholar, Christian, friend," like to that beautiful climax of Shakspeare's "King, Hamlet, Royal Dane, Father;" "yet memory turns from little men to thee," "And sported careless round their fellow child." The whole, I repeat it, is immensely good.

Yours is a poetical family. I was much surprised and pleased to see the signature of Sara to that elegant composition, the fifth epistle. I dare not *criticise* the *Religious Musings:* I like not to select any part, where all is excellent. I can only admire, and thank you for it in the name of a Christian, as well as a lover of good poetry : only let me ask, Is not that thought and those words in Young, "stands in the sun,"—or is it only such as Young, in one of his *better moments*, might have writ ?—

> "Believe thou, O my soul,
> Life is a vision, shadowy of Truth ;
> And vice, and anguish, and the wormy grave,
> Shapes of a dream !"

I thank you for these lines in the name of a necessarian, and for what follows in the next paragraph, in the name of a child of fancy. After all, you cannot, nor ever will, write any thing with which I shall be so delighted as what I have heard yourself repeat. You came to town, and I saw you at a time when your heart was yet bleeding with recent wounds. Like yourself, I was sore galled with disappointed hope. You had

> . . . "many an holy lay
> That, mourning, soothed the mourner on his way."

I had ears of sympathy to drink them in, and they yet vibrate pleasant on the sense. When I read in your little volume, your nineteenth effusion, or the twenty-eighth or twenty-ninth, or what you call the "Sigh," I think I hear *you* again. I image to myself the little smoky room at the *Salutation and Cat*, where we have sat together through the winter nights, beguiling the cares of life with Poesy. When you left London I felt a dismal void in my heart. I found myself cut off, at one and the same time, from two most dear to me. "How blest with ye the path could I have trod of quiet life!" In your conversation you had blended so many pleasant fancies that they cheated me of my grief. But in your absence the tide of melancholy rushed in again, and did its worst mischief by overwhelming my reason. I have recovered, but feel a stupor that makes me in-different to the hopes and fears of this life. I sometimes wish to introduce a religious turn of mind; but habits are strong things, and my religious fervours are confined, alas! to some fleeting moments of occasional solitary devotion. A correspondence, opening with you, has roused me a little from my lethargy, and made me con-scious of existence. Indulge me in it: I will not be very troublesome. At some future time I will amuse you with an account, as full as my memory will permit, of the strange turn my frenzy took. I look back upon it at times with a gloomy kind of envy; for, while it lasted, I had many, many hours of pure happiness. Dream not, Coleridge, of having tasted all the grandeur and wildness of fancy till you have gone mad! All now seems to me vapid, comparatively so. Excuse this selfish digression. Your "Monody" is so superlatively excellent, that I can only wish it perfect, which I can't help feeling it is not quite. Indulge me in a few conjectures. What I am going to propose would make it more compressed, and, I think, more energetic, though I am sensible at the expense of many beautiful lines. Let it begin "Is this the land of song-ennobled line?" and proceed to "Otway's famish'd form;" then, "Thee, Chatterton," to "harps of Seraphim;" then, "clad in Nature's rich array," to "orient day;" then, "but soon the scathing lightning," to "blighted land;" then, "sublime of thought," to "his bosom glows;" then

> " But soon upon his poor unshelter'd head
> Did Penury her sickly mildew shed :
> Ah ! where are fled the charms of vernal Grace,
> And Joy's wild gleams that lighten'd o'er his face ?"

Then "youth of tumultuous soul" to "sigh," as before. The rest may all stand down to "gaze upon the waves below." What follows now may come next as detached verses, suggested by the Monody, rather than a part of it. They are indeed, in themselves, very sweet :

> " And we, at sober eve, would round thee throng
> Hanging, enraptured, on thy stately song,"

in particular, perhaps. If I am obscure, you may understand me by counting lines. I have proposed omitting twenty-four lines. I feel that thus compressed it would gain energy, but think it most likely you will not agree with me ; for who shall go about to bring opinions to the bed of Procrustes, and introduce among the sons of men a monotony of identical feelings? I only propose with diffidence. Reject, if you please, with as little remorse as you would the colour of a coat or the pattern of a buckle, where our fancies differed. The lines " Friend to the Friendless," etc., which you may think rudely disbranched from the Chatterton, will patch in with the Man of Ross, where they were at once at home, with two more which I recollect,

> " And o'er the dowried virgin's snowy cheek
> Bade bridal Love suffuse his blushes meek,"

very beautiful.

The "Pixies" is a perfect thing; and so are the "Lines on the Spring," page 28. The "Epitaph on an Infant," like a Jack-o'-lantern, has danced about (or like Dr. Forster's scholars) out of the *Morning Chronicle* into the *Watchman*, and thence back into your Collection. It is very pretty, and you seem to think so ; but, may be, o'erlooked its chief merit, that of filling up a whole page.   I had once deemed Sonnets of unrivalled use that way ; but your Epitaphs, I find, are the more diffuse. "Edmund" still holds its place among your best verses. "Ah ! fair delights" to "roses round," in your Poem called "Absence," recall (none more forcibly) to my mind the tones in which *you recited it.*   I will not notice, in this tedious (to you) manner, verses which have been so long delightful to me, and which you already know my opinion of.   Of this kind are Bowles, Priestley, and that most exquisite and most Bowles-like of all, the nineteenth effusion.   It would have better ended with "agony of care :" the last two lines are obvious and unnecessary, and you need not now make fourteen lines of it : now it is rechristened from a Sonnet to an Effusion.   Schiller might have written the twentieth Effusion : 'tis worthy of him in any sense.   I was glad to meet with those lines you sent me, when my sister was so ill : I had lost the copy, and I felt not a little proud at seeing my name in your verse.   The "Complaint of Ninathoma" (first stanza in particular) is the best, or only good imitation, of Ossian I ever saw, your "Restless Gale" excepted. "To an Infant" is most sweet.   Is not "foodful," though, very harsh ?   Would not "dulcet" fruit be less harsh, or some other friendly bi-syllable ?   In "Edmund," "Frenzy, fierce-eyed child," is not so well as "frantic," though that is an epithet adding nothing to the meaning.   Slander *couching* was better than "squatting."   In the "Man of Ross" it *was* a better line thus :

"If 'neath this roof thy wine-cheer'd moments pass,"

than as it stands now.   Time nor nothing can reconcile me to the concluding five lines of "Kosciusko :" call it any thing you will but sublime.   In my twelfth effusion I had rather have seen what I wrote myself, though they bear no comparison with your exquisite lines—

"On rose-leaf'd beds, amid your faery bowers," etc.

I love my Sonnets because they are the reflected images

of my own feelings at different times. To instance, in
the thirteenth—

"How reason reel'd," etc.,

are good lines, but must spoil the whole with me, who
know it is only a fiction of yours, and that the "rude
dashings" did in fact not "rock me to repose." I grant
the same objection applies not to the former Sonnet; but
still I love my own feelings: they are dear to memory,
though they now and then wake a sigh or a tear.
"Thinking on divers things foredone," I charge you,
Coleridge, spare my ewe lambs; and though a gentleman
may borrow six lines in an epic poem (I should have no
objection to borrow five hundred, and without acknow-
ledging), still, in a sonnet, a personal poem, I do not
"ask my friend the aiding verse." I would not wrong
your feelings by proposing any improvements (did I think
myself capable of suggesting 'em) in such personal poems
as "Thou bleedest, my poor heart!"—'od so,—I am
caught—I have already done it; but that simile I pro-
pose abridging, would not change the feeling or introduce
any alien ones. Do you understand me? In the twenty-
eighth, however, and in the "Sigh," and that composed
at Clevedon, things that come from the heart direct, not
by the medium of the fancy, I would not suggest an
alteration. When my blank verse is finished, or any
long fancy poems, *propino tibi alterandum, cut-up-andum,
abridgandum*, just what you will with it; but spare my
ewe lambs! That to "Mrs. Siddons," now, you were
welcome to improve, if it had been worth it; but I say
unto you again, Coleridge, spare my ewe lambs! I must
confess were they mine, I should omit, *in editione secundâ*,
Effusions two and three, because satiric, and below the
dignity of the poet of *Religious Musings*, fifth, seventh,
half of the eighth, that "Written in early youth," as far
as "thousand eyes,"—though I part not unreluctantly
with that lively line—

"Chaste joyance dancing in her bright blue eyes,"

and one or two more just thereabouts. But I would substitute for it that sweet poem called "Recollection," in the fifth Number of the *Watchman;* better, I think, than the remainder of this poem, though not differing materially: as the poem now stands it looks altogether confused. And do not omit those lines upon the "Early Blossom," in your sixth Number of the *Watchman:* and I would omit the tenth Effusion or, what would do better, alter and improve the last four lines. In fact, I suppose, if they were mine, I should *not* omit 'em; but your verse is, for the most part, so exquisite, that I like not to see aught of meaner matter mixed with it. Forgive my petulance, and often, I fear, ill-founded criticisms; and forgive me that I have, by this time, made your eyes and head ache with my long letter; but I cannot forego hastily the pleasure and pride of thus conversing with you. You did not tell me whether I was to include the *Conciones ad Populum* in my remarks on your poems. They are not unfrequently sublime; and I think you could not do better than to turn 'em into verse, if you have nothing else to do. Allen, I am sorry to say, is a *confirmed* Atheist. Stoddart, a cold-hearted, well-bred, conceited disciple of Godwin, does him no good. His wife has several daughters (one of 'em as old as himself). Surely there is something unnatural in such a marriage.

How I sympathise with you on the dull duty of a reviewer, and heartily damn with you Ned Evans and the Prosodist. I shall, however, wait impatiently for the articles in the *Critical Review,* next month, because they are *yours.* Young Evans (W. Evans, a branch of a family you were once so intimate with) is come into our office, and sends his love to you! Coleridge, I devoutly wish that Fortune, who has made sport with you so long, may play one freak more,—throw you into London, or some spot near it, and there snug-ify you for life. 'Tis a selfish, but natural wish for me, cast as I am "on life's wide plain, friendless." Are you acquainted with Bowles ?   I see, by his last Elegy (written at Bath), you are near neighbours.—*Thursday.*

"And I can think I can see the groves again—was it the voice of thee—turns not the voice of thee, my buried friend—who dries with her dark locks the tender tear," are touches as true to Nature as any in his other Elegy, written at the Hot Wells, about poor Kassell, etc.   You are doubtless acquainted with it.

I do not know that I entirely agree with you in your stricture upon my Sonnet "To Innocence."   To men whose hearts are not quite deadened by their commerce with the world, innocence (no longer familiar) becomes an awful idea.   So I felt when I wrote it.   Your other censures (qualified and sweetened, though, with praises somewhat extravagant) I perfectly coincide with ; yet I choose to retain the word "lunar."   Indulge a "lunatic" in his loyalty to his mistress the Moon !   I have just been reading a most pathetic copy of verses on Sophia Pringle, who was hanged and burnt for coining.   One of the strokes of pathos (which are very many, all somewhat obscure), is "She lifted up her guilty forger to heaven." A note explains, by "forger," her right hand, with which she forged or coined the base metal.   For "pathos" read *bathos.*   You have put me out of conceit with my blank verse by your *Religious Musings.*   I think it will come to nothing.   I do not like 'em enough to send 'em.   I have just been reading a book which I may be too partial to, as it was the delight of my childhood ; but I will recommend it to you : it is Izaak Walton's *Complete Angler.*   All the scientific part you may omit in reading. The dialogue is very simple, full of pastoral beauties, and will charm you.   Many pretty old verses are interspersed. This letter, which would be a week's work reading only, I do not wish you to answer it in less than a month.   I shall be richly content with a letter from you some day early in July ; though, if you get any how *settled* before then, pray let me know it immediately ; 'twould give me so much satisfaction.   Concerning the Unitarian chapel,

the salary is the only scruple that the most rigid moralist
would admit as valid. Concerning the tutorage, is not
the salary low, and absence from your family unavoidable?
London is the only fostering soil for genius. Nothing
more occurs just now; so I will leave you, in mercy, one
small white spot empty below, to repose your eyes upon,
fatigued as they must be with the wilderness of words
they have by this time painfully travelled through. God
love you, Coleridge, and prosper you through life; though
mine will be loss if your lot is to be cast at Bristol, or
at Nottingham, or anywhere but London. Our loves to
Mrs. C——. C. L.

Friday, 10*th June* 1796.

Letter IV.] *Monday Night, June* 13, 1796.

Unfurnished at present with any sheet-filling subject,
I shall continue my letter gradually and journal-wise.
My second thoughts entirely coincide with your comments
on *Joan of Arc,* and I can only wonder at my childish
judgment which overlooked the 1st book, and could pre-
fer the 9th : not that I was insensible to the soberer
beauties of the former; but the latter caught me with its
glare of magic : the former, however, left a more pleasing
general recollection in my mind. Let me add, the 1st
book was the favourite of my sister; and *I* now, with
Joan, often "think on Domremi and the fields of Arc."
I must not pass over without acknowledging my obliga-
tions to your full and satisfactory account of personifica-
tions. I have read it again and again, and it will be a
guide to my future taste. Perhaps I had estimated
Southey's merits too much by number, weight, and
measure. I now agree completely and entirely in your
opinion of the genius of Southey. Your own image of
Melancholy is illustrative of what you teach, and in itself
masterly. I conjecture it is "disbranched" from one of
your embryo "hymns." When they are mature of birth
(were I you) I should print 'em, in one separate volume,

with *Religious Musings* and your part of the *Joan of Arc*. Birds of the same soaring wing should hold on their flight in company. Once for all (and by renewing the subject you will only renew in me the condemnation of Tantalus), I hope to be able to pay you a visit (if you are then at Bristol) some time in the latter end of August or beginning of September, for a week or fortnight : before that time office business puts an absolute veto on my coming.

" And if a sigh that speaks regret of happier times appear,
  A glimpse of joy that we have met shall shine and dry the tear."

Of the blank verses I spoke of, the following lines are the only tolerably complete ones I have writ out of not more than one hundred and fifty. That I get on so slowly you may fairly impute to want of practice in composition, when I declare to you that (the few verses which you have seen excepted) I have not writ fifty lines since I left school. It may not be amiss to remark that my grandmother (on whom the verses are written) lived housekeeper in a family the fifty or sixty last years of her life—that she was a woman of exemplary piety and goodness—and for many years before her death was terribly afflicted with a cancer in her breast, which she bore with true Christian patience. You may think that I have not kept enough apart the ideas of her heavenly and her earthly master; but recollect I have designedly given in to her own way of feeling; and if she had a failing 'twas that she respected her master's family too much, not reverenced her Maker too little. The lines begin imperfectly, as I may probably connect 'em if I finish at all: and if I do, Biggs shall print 'em (in a more economical way than you yours), for, Sonnets and all, they won't make a thousand lines as I propose completing 'em, and the substance must be wire-drawn.

Letter V.]   *Tuesday Evening, June* 14, 1796.

I am not quite satisfied now with the Chatterton, and, with your leave, will try my hand at it again. A master joiner, you know, may leave a cabinet to be finished by his journeyman, when his own hands are full.

. To your list of illustrative personifications, into which a fine imagination enters, I will take leave to add the following from Beaumont and Fletcher's *Wife for a Month;* 'tis the conclusion of a description of a sea fight: —" The game of *death* was never played so nobly : the meagre thief grew wanton in his mischiefs ; and his shrunk, hollow eyes smiled on his ruins." There is fancy in these of a lower order, from *Bonduca ;*—" Then did I see these valiant men of Britain, like boding owls creep into tods of ivy, and hoot their fears to one another nightly." Not that it is a personification ; only it just caught my eye in a little extract book I keep, which is full of quotations from Beaumont and Fletcher in particular, in which authors I can't help thinking there is a greater richness of poetical fancy than in any one, Shakspeare excepted. Are you acquainted with Massinger ? At a hazard I will trouble you with a passage from a play of his called *A Very Woman.* The lines are spoken by a lover (disguised) to his faithless mistress. You will remark the fine effect of the double endings. You will by your ear distinguish the lines, for I write 'em as prose. " Not far from where my father lives, *a lady*, a neighbour by, blest with as great a *beauty* as Nature durst bestow without *undoing*, dwelt, and most happily, as I thought then, and blest the house a thousand times she *dwelt* in. This beauty, in the blossom of my youth, when my first fire knew no adulterate *incense*, nor I no way to flatter but my *fondness ;* in all the bravery my friends could *show me*, in all the faith my innocence could *give me*, in the best language my true tongue could *tell me*, and all the broken sighs my sick heart *lend me*, I sued and served. Long did I serve this *lady*, long was my travail, long my trade to *win her :* with all the duty of my soul I SERVED HER." "Then she must love." "She did, but never me : she could not *love me ;* she would not love, she hated,—more, she *scorn'd me ;* and in so poor and base a way *abused me* for all my services, for all my *bounties,* so bold neglects flung on me." "What out of love, and worthy love, I *gave her* (shame to her most unworthy mind!), to fools, to girls, to fiddlers, and her boys she flung, all in disdain of me." One more passage strikes my eye from Beaumont and Fletcher's *Palamon and Arcite.* One of 'em complains in prison :

" This is all our world :
We shall know nothing here but one another ;
Hear nothing but the clock that tells our woes.
The vine shall grow, but we shall never see it."

Is not the last circumstance exquisite ? I mean not to lay myself open by saying they exceed Milton, and perhaps Collins, in sublimity. But don't you conceive all poets, after Shakspeare, yield to 'em in variety of genius ? Massinger treads close on their heels ; but you are most probably as well acquainted with his writings as your humble servant. My quotation, in that case, will only serve to show my barrenness of matter. Southey, in simplicity and tenderness, is excelled decidedly only, I think, by Beaumont and Fletcher—in his " Maid's Tragedy " and some parts of " Philaster " in particular, and elsewhere occasionally ; and perhaps by Cowper in his " Crazy Kate," and in parts of his translation : such as the speeches of Hecuba and Andromache. I long to know your opinion of that translation. The Odyssey especially is surely very Homeric. What nobler than the appearance of Phœbus at the beginning of the Iliad—the lines ending with " Dread sounding, bounding on the silver bow !"

I beg you will give me your opinion of the translation ; it afforded me high pleasure. As curious a specimen of translation as ever fell into my hands is a young man's in our office, of a French novel. What in the original was literally "amiable delusions of the fancy," he proposed to render "the fair frauds of the imagination!" I had much trouble in licking the book into any meaning at all. Yet did the knave clear fifty or sixty pounds by subscription and selling the copyright: the book itself not a week's work! To-day's portion of my journalising epistle has been very dull and poverty-stricken. I will here end.

Tuesday Night.—I have been drinking egg-hot and smoking Oronooko (associated circumstances, which ever forcibly recall to my mind our evenings and nights at the *Salutation*). My eyes and brain are heavy and asleep, but my heart is awake; and if words came as ready as ideas, and ideas as feelings, I could say ten hundred kind things. Coleridge, you know not my supreme happiness at having one on earth (though counties separate us) whom I can call a friend. Remember you those tender lines of Logan's?—

> " Our broken friendships we deplore,
> And loves of youth that are no more;
> No after-friendships e'er can raise
> Th' endearments of our early days,
> And ne'er the heart such fondness prove
> As when we first began to love."

I am writing at random, and half-tipsy, what you may not *equally* understand, as you will be sober when you read it; but *my* sober and *my* half-tipsy hours you are alike a sharer in. Good-night.

> " Then up rose our bard, like a prophet in drink,
> Craigdoroch, thou'lt soar when creation shall sink."
>
> BURNS.

Thursday.—I am now in high hopes to be able to visit you, if perfectly convenient on your part, by the end of next month—perhaps the last week or fortnight in July. A change of scene and a change of faces would do me good, even if that scene were not to be Bristol, and those faces Coleridge's and his friends. In the words of Terence, a little altered, *Tædet me hujus quotidiani mundi,*

I am heartily sick of the every-day scenes of life.   I shall
half wish you unmarried (don't show this to Mrs. C.) for
one evening only, to have the pleasure of smoking with
you and drinking egg-hot in some little smoky room in a
pot-house, for I know not yet how I shall like you in a
decent room and looking quite happy.   My best love and
respects to Sara notwithstanding.

Yours sincerely,
CHARLES LAMB.

LETTER VI.]   *July* 1, 1796.

The first moment I can come I will; but my hopes of
coming yet a while yet hang on a ticklish thread.   The
coach I come by is immaterial, as I shall so easily, by
your direction, find ye out.   My mother is grown so
entirely helpless (not having any use of her limbs) that
Mary is necessarily confined from ever sleeping out, she
being her bed-fellow.   She thanks you though, and will
accompany me in spirit.   Most exquisite are the lines
from Withers.   Your own lines, introductory to your poem
on " Self," run smoothly and pleasurably, and I exhort
you to continue 'em.   What shall I say to your " Dactyls "?
They are what you would call good *per se ;* but a parody
on some of 'em is just now suggesting itself, and you shall
have it rough and unlicked.   I mark with figures the
lines parodied :—

> 4.—Sorely your Dactyls do drag along limp-footed.
> 5.—Sad is the measure that hangs a clod round 'em so.
> 6.—Meagre and languid, proclaiming its wretchedness.
> 1.—Weary, unsatisfied, not a little sick of 'em.
> 11.—Cold is my tired heart, I have no charity.
> 2.—Painfully travelling thus over the rugged road.
> 7.—O begone, measure, half Latin, half English, then.
> 12.—Dismal your Dactyls are, God help ye, rhyming ones !

I possibly may not come this fortnight; therefore all
thou hast to do is not to look for me any particular day,
only to write word immediately, if at any time you quit

Bristol, lest I come and Taffy be not at home. I *hope* I can come in a day or two; but young Savory, of my office, is suddenly taken ill in this very nick of time, and I must officiate for him till he can come to work again. Had the knave gone sick, and died, and putrefied, at any other time, philosophy might have afforded one comfort; but just now I have no patience with him. Quarles I am as great a stranger to as I was to Withers. I wish you would try and do something to bring our elder bards into more general fame. I writhe with indignation when, in books of criticism, where commonplace quotation is heaped upon quotation, I find no mention of such men as Massinger, or Beaumont and Fletcher,—men with whom succeeding dramatic writers (Otway alone excepted) can bear no manner of comparison. Stupid Knox hath noticed none of 'em among his extracts.

Thursday.—Mrs. C—— can scarce guess how she has gratified me by her very kind letter and sweet little poem. I feel that I *should* thank her in rhyme; but she must take my acknowledgment, at present, in plain honest prose. The uncertainty in which I yet stand, whether I can come or no, damps my spirits, reduces me a degree below prosaical, and keeps me in a suspense that fluctuates between hope and fear. Hope is a charming, lively, blue-eyed wench, and I am always glad of her company, but could dispense with the visitor she brings with her—her younger sister, Fear,—a white-livered, lily-cheeked, bashful, palpitating, awkward hussy, that hangs, like a green girl, at her sister's apron-strings, and will go with her whithersoever *she* goes. For the life and soul of me I could not improve those lines in your poem on the Prince and Princess; so I changed them to what you bid me, and left 'em at Perry's. I think 'em altogether good, and do not see why you were solicitous about *any* alteration. I have not yet seen, but will make it my business to see, to-day's *Chronicle*, for your verses on Horne Tooke. Dyer stanza'd him in one of the papers t'other day; but, I think, unsuccessfully. Tooke's friends' meeting was, I suppose, a dinner of condolence. I am not sorry to find you (for all Sara) immersed in clouds of smoke and metaphysics. You know I had a sneaking kindness for this last noble science, and you taught me some smattering of it. I look to become no mean proficient under your tuition. Coleridge, what do you mean by saying you wrote to me about Plutarch and Porphyry? I received no such letter, nor remember a syllable of the matter, yet am not apt to forget any part of your epistles, least of all, an injunction like that. I will cast about for 'em, tho' I am a sad hand to know what books are worth, and both worthy gentlemen are alike out of my line. To-morrow I shall be less suspensive, and in better cue to write; so good-bye at present.

Friday Evening.—That execrable aristocrat and knave, Richardson, has given me an absolute refusal of leave. The *poor man* cannot guess at my disappointment. Is it not hard, "this dread dependence on the low-bred mind?" Continue to write to me tho', and I must be content. Our loves and best good wishes attend upon you both.   LAMB.

Savory did return, but there are two or three more ill and absent, which was the plea for refusing me. I will never commit my peace of mind by depending on such a wretch for a favour in future, so I shall never have heart to ask for holidays again. The man next him in office, Cartwright, furnished him with the objections.

C. LAMB.

LETTER VII.]   *July 5, 1796.*

Let us prose.

What can I do till you scud word what priced and placed house you should like? Islington, possibly, you would not like; to me 'tis classical ground. Knights-bridge is a desirable situation for the air of the parks. St. George's Fields is convenient for its contiguity to the Bench. Choose! But are you really coming to town? The hope of it has entirely disarmed my petty disappoint-ment of its nettles; yet I rejoice so much on my own account, that I fear I do not feel enough pure satisfaction on yours. Why, surely, the joint editorship of the [*Morning*] *Chronicle* must be a very comfortable and secure living for a man. But should not you read French, or do you? and can you write with sufficient moderation, as 'tis called, when one suppresses the one half of what one feels or could say on a subject, to chime in the better with popular lukewarmness? White's "Letters" are near publication. Could you review 'em, or get 'em reviewed? Are you not connected with the *Critical Review?* His frontispiece is a good conceit: Sir John learning to dance to please Madame Page, in dress of doublet, etc., forms the upper half; and modern panta-loons, with shoes, etc., of the eighteenth century, form the lower half; and the whole work is full of goodly quips and rare fancies, "all deftly masqued like hoar antiquity" —much superior to Dr. Kenrick's *Falstaff's Wedding,* which you have seen. Allen sometimes laughs at super-stition, and religion, and the like. A living fell vacant lately in the gift of the Hospital: White informed him that he stood a fair chance for it. He scrupled and scrupled about it, and at last, to use his own words, "tampered" with Godwin to know whether the thing was honest or not. Godwin said nay to it, and Allen rejected the living! Could the blindest poor papist have bowed more servilely to his priest or casuist? Why sleep the *Watchman's* answers to that Godwin? I beg you will not delay to alter, if you mean to keep, those last lines I sent you. Do that, and read these for your pains :—

TO THE POET COWPER.

Cowper, I thank my God that thou art heal'd !
Thine was the sorest malady of all ;
And I am sad to think that it should light
Upon thy worthy head !   But thou art heal'd,
And thou art yet, we trust, the destined man,
Born to reanimate the lyre, whose chords
Have slumber'd, and have idle lain so long ;
To the immortal sounding of whose strings
Did Milton frame the stately-pacèd verse ;
Among whose wires with light finger playing,
Our elder bard, Spenser, a gentle name,
The lady Muses' dearest darling child,
Elicited the deftest tunes yet heard
In hall or bower, taking the delicate ear
Of Sidney and his peerless Maiden Queen.

Thou, then, take up the mighty epic strain,
Cowper, of England's Bards, the wisest and the best.

1796.

I have read your climax of praises in those three
Reviews.   These mighty spouters out of panegyric waters
have, two of 'em, scattered their spray even upon me, and
the waters are cooling and refreshing.   Prosaically, the
Monthly reviewers have made indeed a large article of it,
and done you justice.   The *Critical* have, in their wisdom,
selected not the very best specimens, and notice not,
except as one name on the muster-roll, the *Religious
Musings.*   I suspect Master Dyer to have been the writer
of that article, as the substance of it was the very remarks
and the very language he used to me one day.   I fear
you will not accord entirely with my sentiments of Cowper,
as *expressed* above (perhaps scarcely just), but the poor
gentleman has just recovered from his lunacies, and that
begets pity, and pity love, and love admiration ; and then
it goes hard with people, but they lie !   Have you read
the Ballad called "Leonora," in the second Number of
the *Monthly Magazine?*   If you have ! ! ! !   There is
another fine song, from the same author (Burger), in the
third Number, of scarce inferior merit ; and (vastly below

these) there are some happy specimens of English hexameters, in an imitation of Ossian, in the fifth Number. For your Dactyls—I am sorry you are so sore about 'em —a very Sir Fretful! In good troth, the Dactyls are good Dactyls, but their measure is naught. Be not yourself "half anger, half agony," if I pronounce your darling lines not to be the best you ever wrote—you have written much.

Have a care, good Master Poet, of the Statute *de Contumeliâ*. What do you mean by calling Madame Mara "harlot" and other naughty things? The goodness of the verse would not save you in a Court of Justice. But are you really coming to town? Coleridge, a gentleman called in London lately from Bristol, and inquired whether there were any of the family of a Mr. Chambers living: this Mr. Chambers, he said, had been the making of a friend's fortune, who wished to make some return for it. He went away without seeing her. Now, a Mrs. Reynolds, a very intimate friend of ours, whom you have seen at our house, is the only daughter, and all that survives, of Mr. Chambers; and a very little supply would be of service to her, for she married very unfortunately, and has parted with her husband. Pray find out this Mr. Pember (for that was the gentleman's friend's name); he is an attorney, and lives at Bristol. Find him out, and acquaint him with the circumstances of the case, and offer to be the medium of supply to Mrs. Reynolds, if he chooses to make her a present. She is in very distressed circumstances. Mr. Pember, attorney, Bristol. Mr. Chambers lived in the Temple; Mrs. Reynolds, his daughter, was my schoolmistress, and is in the room at this present writing. This last circumstance induced me to write so soon again. I have not further to add. Our loves to Sara. C. LAMB.

Thursday.

LETTER VIII.]   *September* 27, 1796.

My dearest Friend—White, or some of my friends, or the public papers, by this time may have informed you of the terrible calamities that have fallen on our family. I will only give you the outlines :—My poor dear, dearest sister, in a fit of insanity, has been the death of her own mother. I was at hand only time enough to snatch the knife out of her grasp. She is at present in a madhouse, from whence I fear she must be moved to an hospital. God has preserved to me my senses : I eat, and drink, and sleep, and have my judgment, I believe, very sound. My poor father was slightly wounded, and I am left to take care of him and my aunt. Mr. Norris, of the Blue-coat School, has been very very kind to us, and we have no other friend ; but, thank God, I am very calm and com posed, and able to do the best that remains to do. Write as religious a letter as possible, but no mention of what is gone and done with. With me " the former things are passed away," and I have something more to do than to feel.

God Almighty have us all in His keeping !

C. LAMB.

Mention nothing of poetry. I have destroyed every vestige of past vanities of that kind. Do as you please, but if you publish, publish mine (I give free leave) without name or initial, and never send me a book, I charge you.

Your own judgment will convince you not to take any notice of this yet to your dear wife. You look after your family ; I have my reason and strength left to take care of mine. I charge you, don't think of coming to see me. Write. I will not see you if you come. God Almighty love you and all of us !

C. LAMB.

LETTER IX.]   *October* 3, 1796.

My dearest Friend—Your letter was an inestimable treasure to me. It will be a comfort to you, I know, to know that our prospects are somewhat brighter. My poor dear, dearest sister, the unhappy and unconscious instrument of the Almighty's judgments on our house, is restored to her senses,—to a dreadful sense and recollection of what has past, awful to her mind, and impressive (as it must be to the end of life), but tempered with religious resignation and the reasonings of a sound judgment, which, in this early stage, knows how to distinguish between a deed committed in a transient fit of frenzy and the terrible guilt of a mother's murder. I have seen her. I found her, this morning, calm and serene; far, very very far from an indecent forgetful serenity : she has a most affectionate and tender concern for what has happened. Indeed, from the beginning—frightful and hopeless as her disorder seemed—I had confidence enough in her strength of mind and religious principle, to look forward to a time when *even she* might recover tranquillity. God be praised, Coleridge ! wonderful as it is to tell, I have never once been otherwise than collected and calm ; even on the dreadful day, and in the midst of the terrible scene, I preserved a tranquillity which bystanders may have construed into indifference—a tranquillity not of despair. Is it folly or sin in me to say that it was a religious principle that *most* supported me ? I allow much to other favourable circumstances. I felt that I had something else to do than to regret. On that first evening my aunt was lying insensible—to all appearance like one dying ; my father, with his poor forehead plaistered over from a wound he had received from a daughter, dearly loved by him, and who loved him no less dearly ; my mother a dead and murdered corpse in the next room ; yet was I wonderfully supported. I closed not my eyes in sleep that night, but lay without terrors and without despair. I have lost no sleep since. I had been long used not to rest in things of sense,—had endeavoured after a comprehension of mind, unsatisfied with the " ignorant present time ;" and *this* kept me up.   I had the whole weight of the family thrown on me ; for my brother, little disposed (I speak not without tenderness for him) at any time to take care of old age and infirmities, had now, with his bad leg, an exemption from such duties, and I was now left alone.   One little incident may serve to make you understand my way of managing my mind : Within a day or two after the fatal one, we dressed for dinner a tongue, which we had had salted for some weeks in the house. As I sat down, a feeling like remorse struck me : this tongue poor Mary got for me ; and can I partake of it now, when she is far away ?   A thought occurred and relieved me :—if I give into this way of feeling, there is not a chair, a room, an object in our rooms, that will not awaken the keenest griefs.   I must rise above such weaknesses.   I hope this was not want of true feeling. I did not let this carry me, though, too far.   On the very second day (I date from the day of horrors), as is usual in such cases, there were a matter of twenty people, I do think, supping in our room : they prevailed on me to eat *with them* (for to eat I never refused).   They were all making merry in the room !   Some had come from friendship, some from busy curiosity, and some from interest. I was going to partake with them, when my recollection came that my poor dead mother was lying in the next room—the very next room ;—a mother who, through life, wished nothing but her children's welfare.   Indignation, the rage of grief, something like remorse, rushed upon my mind.   In an agony of emotion I found my way mechanically to the adjoining room, and fell on my knees by the side of her coffin, asking forgiveness of Heaven, and sometimes of her, for forgetting her so soon.   Tranquillity returned, and it was the only violent emotion that mastered me.   I think it did me good.

I mention these things because I hate concealment, and love to give a faithful journal of what passes within me. Our friends have been very good. Sam Le Grice, who was then in town, was with me the first three or four days, and was as a brother to me; gave up every hour of his time, to the very hurting of his health and spirits, in constant attendance and humouring my poor father; talked with him, read to him, played at cribbage with him (for so short is the old man's recollection, that he was playing at cards, as though nothing had happened, while the coroner's inquest was sitting over the way!) Samuel wept tenderly when he went away, for his mother wrote him a very severe letter on his loitering so long in town, and he was forced to go. Mr. Norris, of Christ's Hospital, has been as a father to me—Mrs. Norris as a mother; though we had few claims on them. A gentleman, brother to my godmother, from whom we never had right or reason to expect any such assistance, sent my father twenty pounds; and to crown all these God's blessings to our family at such a time, an old lady, a cousin of my father and aunt's, a gentlewoman of fortune, is to take my aunt and make her comfortable for the short remainder of her days. My aunt is recovered, and as well as ever, and highly pleased at thoughts of going—and has generously given up the interest of her little money (which was formerly paid my father for her board) wholely and solely to my sister's use. Reckoning this, we have, Daddy and I, for our two selves and an old maid-servant to look after him, when I am out, which will be necessary, £170 (or £180 rather) a-year, out of which we can spare £50 or £60 at least for Mary while she stays at Islington, where she must and shall stay during her father's life, for his and her comfort. I know John will make speeches about it, but she shall not go into an hospital. The good lady of the madhouse, and her daughter, an elegant, sweet-behaved young lady, love her, and are taken with her amazingly; and I know from her own mouth she loves them, and longs to be with them as much. Poor thing, they say she was but the other morning saying she knew she must go to Bethlem for life; that one of her brothers would have it so, but the other would wish it not, but be obliged to go with the stream; that she had often as she passed Bethlem thought it likely, "here it may be my fate to end my days," conscious of a certain flightiness in her poor head oftentimes, and mindful of more than one severe illness of that nature before. A legacy of £100, which my father will have at Christmas, and this £20 I mentioned before, with what is in the house, will much more than set us clear. If my father, an old servant-maid, and I, can't live, and live comfortably, on £130 or £120 a-year, we ought to burn by slow fires; and I almost would, that Mary might not go into an hospital. Let me not leave one unfavourable impression on your mind respecting my brother. Since this has happened, he has been very kind and brotherly; but I fear for his mind: he has taken his case in the world, and is not fit himself to struggle with difficulties, nor has much accustomed himself to throw himself into their way; and I know his language is already, "Charles, you must take care of yourself; you must not abridge yourself of a single pleasure you have been used to," etc. etc., and in that style of talking. But you, a Necessarian, can respect a difference of mind, and love what *is amiable* in a character not perfect. He has been very good; but I fear for his mind. Thank God, I can unconnect myself with him, and shall manage all my father's moneys in future myself, if I take charge of Daddy, which poor John has not even hinted a wish, at any future time even, to share with me. The lady at this madhouse assures me that I may dismiss immediately both doctor and apothecary, retaining occasionally a composing draught or so for a while; and there is a less expensive establishment in her house, where she will only not have a room and nurse to herself, for £50 or guineas a-year—the outside would be £60. You know, by economy, how much more even I shall be able to spare for her comforts. She will I fancy, if she stays, make one of the family, rather than of the patients; and the old and young ladies I like exceedingly, and she loves dearly; and they, as the saying is, take to her very extraordinarily, if it is extraordinary that people who see my sister should love her. Of all the people I ever saw in the world, my poor sister was most and thoroughly devoid of the least tincture of selfishness. I will enlarge upon her qualities, poor dear, dearest soul, in a future letter, for my own comfort, for I understand her thoroughly; and, if I mistake not, in the most trying situation that a human being can be found in, she will be found—(I speak not with sufficient humility, I fear), but humanly and foolishly speaking, she will be found, I trust, uniformly great and amiable. God keep her in her present mind!—to whom be thanks and praise for all His dispensations to mankind.

C. Lamb.

These mentioned good fortunes and change of prospects had almost brought my mind over to the extreme, the very opposite to despair. I was in danger of making myself too happy. Your letter brought me back to a view of things which I had entertained from the beginning. I hope (for Mary I can answer)—but I hope that *I* shall through life never have less recollection nor a fainter impression of what has happened than I have now. 'Tis not a light thing, nor meant by the Almighty to be received lightly. I must be serious, circumspect, and deeply religious through life; and by such means may *both* of us escape madness in future, if it so please the Almighty.

Send me word how it fares with Sara. I repeat it, your letter was, and will be, an inestimable treasure to me. You have a view of what my situation demands of me, like my own view, and I trust a just one.

Coleridge, continue to write; but do not for ever offend me by talking of sending me cash. Sincerely, and on my soul, we do not want it. God love you both!

I will write again very soon. Do you write directly.

Letter X.]   *October* 17, 1796.

My dearest Friend—I grieve from my very soul to observe you, in your plans of life, veering about from this hope to the other, and settling nowhere. Is it an untoward fatality (speaking humanly) that does this for you —a stubborn, irresistible concurrence of events? or lies the fault, as I fear it does, in your own mind? You seem to be taking up splendid schemes of fortune only to lay them down again; and your fortunes are an *ignis fatuus* that has been conducting you, in thought, from Lancaster Court, Strand, to somewhere near Matlock; then jumping across to Dr. Somebody's, whose son's tutor you were likely to be; and would to God the dancing demon *may* conduct you at last, in peace and comfort, to the "life and labours of a cottager." You see, from the above awkward playfulness of fancy, that my spirits are not quite depressed. I should ill deserve God's blessings, which, since the late terrible event, have come down in mercy upon us, if I indulged regret or querulousness. Mary continues serene and cheerful. I have not by me a little letter she wrote to me; for, though I see her almost every day, yet we delight to write to one another, for we can scarce see each other but in company with some of the people of the house.

I have not the letter by me, but will quote from memory what she wrote in it: "I have no bad terrifying dreams. At midnight, when I happen to awake, the nurse sleeping by the side of me, with the noise of the poor mad people around me, I have no fear. The spirit of my mother seems to descend and smile upon me, and bid me live to enjoy the life and reason which the Almighty has given me. I shall see her again in heaven: she will then understand me better. My grandmother, too, will understand me better, and will then say no more, as she used to do, 'Polly, what are those poor crazy moythered brains of yours thinking of always?'" Poor Mary! my mother indeed *never understood* her right.

She loved her, as she loved us all, with a mother's love ; but in opinion, in feeling, and sentiment, and disposition, bore so distant a resemblance to her daughter, that she never understood her right; never could believe how much *she* loved her; but met her caresses, her protestations of filial affection, too frequently with coldness and repulse. Still she was a good mother. God forbid I should think of her but *most* respectfully, *most* affectionately. Yet she would always love my brother above Mary, who was not worthy of one-tenth of that affection which Mary had a right to claim. But it is my sister's gratifying recollection that every act of duty and of love she could pay, every kindness (and I speak true, when I say to the hurting of her health, and, most probably, in great part to the derangement of her senses), through a long course of infirmities and sickness, she could show her, she ever did. I will, some day, as I promised, enlarge to you upon my sister's excellences : 'twill seem like exaggeration ; but I will do it. At present, short letters suit my state of mind best. So take my kindest wishes for your comfort and establishment in life, and for Sara's welfare and comforts with you ! God love you ! God love us all !   C. LAMB.

LETTER XI.]   *October* 24, 1796.

Coleridge, I feel myself much your debtor for that spirit of confidence and friendship which dictated your last letter. May your soul find peace at last in your cottage life ! I only wish you were but settled. Do continue to write to me. I read your letters with my sister, and they give us both abundance of delight. Especially they please us when you talk in a religious strain : not but we are offended occasionally with a certain freedom of expression, a certain air of mysticism, more consonant to the conceits of pagan philosophy than consistent with the humility of genuine piety. To instance now, in your last letter you say, " It is by the press that

God hath given finite spirits, both evil and good (I suppose you mean *simply* bad men and good men), a portion as it were of His Omnipresence!" Now, high as the human intellect comparatively will soar, and wide as its influence, malign or salutary, can extend, is there not, Coleridge, a distance between the Divine Mind and it, which makes such language blasphemy? Again, in your first fine consolatory epistle, you say, "you are a temporary sharer in human misery, that you may be an eternal partaker of the Divine Nature." What more than this do those men say who are for exalting the man Christ Jesus into the second person of an unknown Trinity?—men whom you or I scruple not to call idolaters. Man, full of imperfections at best, and subject to wants which momentarily remind him of dependence; man, a weak and ignorant being, "servile" from his birth "to all the skiey influences," with eyes sometimes open to discern the right path, but a head generally too dizzy to pursue it; man, in the pride of speculation, forgetting his nature, and hailing in himself the future God, must make the angels laugh. Be not angry with me Coleridge: I wish not to cavil; I know I cannot instruct you; I only wish to remind you of that humility which best becometh the Christian character. God, in the New Testament (*our best guide*), is represented to us in the kind, condescending, amiable, familiar light of a *parent;* and in my poor mind 'tis best for us so to consider of him, as our *heavenly* father, and our *best friend*, without indulging too bold conceptions of his nature. Let us learn to think humbly of ourselves, and rejoice in the appellation of "dear children," "brethren," and "co-heirs with Christ of the promises," seeking to know no further.

I am not insensible, indeed I am not, of the value of that first letter of yours, and I shall find reason to thank you for it again and again, long after that blemish in it is forgotten. It will be a fine lesson of comfort to us, whenever we read it; and read it we often shall, Mary and I.

Accept our loves and best kind wishes for the welfare of yourself and wife and little one. Nor let me forget to wish you joy on your birthday, so lately past ; I thought you had been older. My kind thanks and remembrances to Lloyd.

God love us all !—and may He continue to be the father and the friend of the whole human race !

Sunday Evening. C. LAMB.

LETTER XII.] *October* 28, 1796.

My dear Friend—I am not ignorant that to be "a partaker of the Divine Nature" is a phrase to be met with in Scripture : I am only apprehensive, lest we in these latter days, tinctured (some of us perhaps pretty deeply) with mystical notions and the pride of meta-physics, might be apt to affix to such phrases a meaning, which the primitive users of them, the simple fishermen of Galilee for instance, never intended to convey. With that other part of your apology I am not quite so well satisfied. You seem to me to have been straining your comparing faculties to bring together things infinitely distant and unlike,—the feeble narrow-sphered operations of the human intellect and the everywhere diffused mind of Deity, the peerless wisdom of Jehovah. Even the expression appears to me inaccurate—"portion of Omni-presence." Omnipresence is an attribute the very essence of which is unlimitedness. How can Omnipresence be affirmed of anything in part ? But enough of this spirit of disputatiousness. Let us attend to the proper business of human life, and talk a little together respecting our domestic concerns. Do you continue to make me ac-quainted with what you are doing, and how soon you are likely to be settled, once for all.

I have satisfaction in being able to bid you rejoice with me in my sister's continued reason, and composed-ness of mind. Let us both be thankful for it. I continue to visit her very frequently, and the people of the house are vastly indulgent to her. She is likely to be as comfortably situated in all respects as those who pay twice or thrice the sum. They love her, and she loves them, and makes herself very useful to them. Benevolence sets out on her journey with a good heart, and puts a good face on it, but is apt to limp and grow feeble, unless she calls in the aid of self-interest, by way of crutch. In Mary's case, as far as respects those she is with, 'tis well that these principles are so likely to co-operate. I am rather at a loss sometimes for books for her : our reading is somewhat confined, and we have nearly exhausted our London library. She has her hands too full of work to read much ; but a little she must read, for reading was her daily bread.

Have you seen Bowles's new poem on " Hope ?" What character does it bear ? Has he exhausted his stores of tender plaintiveness ? or is he the same in this last as in all his former pieces ? The duties of the day call me off from this pleasant intercourse with my friend : so for the present adieu.

Now for the truant borrowing of a few minutes from business. Have you met with a new poem called the *Pursuits of Literature?* From the extracts in the *British Review* I judge it to be a very humorous thing. In particular, I remember what I thought a very happy character of Dr. Darwin's poetry. Among all your quaint readings did your ever light upon Walton's *Complete Angler ?* I asked you the question once before: it breathes the very spirit of innocence, purity, and simplicity of heart. There are many choice old verses interspersed in it. It would sweeten a man's temper at any time to read it ; it would Christianise every discordant angry passion. Pray make yourself acquainted with it. Have you made it up with Southey yet ? Surely one of you two must have been a very silly fellow, and the other not much better, to fall out like boarding-school misses. Kiss, shake hands, and make it up.

When will he be delivered of his new epic ? *Madoc*

I think, is to be the name of it; though that is a name
not familiar to my ears. What progress do you make
in your hymns? What Review are you connected with?
If with any, why do you delay to notice White's book?
You are justly offended at its profaneness; but surely
you have undervalued its *wit*, or you would have been
more loud in its praises. Do not you think that in
Slender's death and madness there is most exquisite
humour, mingled with tenderness, that is irresistible,
truly Shakspearian? Be more full in your mention of it.
Poor fellow, he has (very undeservedly) lost by it; nor
do I see that it is likely ever to reimburse him the charge
of printing, etc. Give it a lift, if you can. I suppose
you know that Allen's wife is dead, and he, just situated
as he was, never the better, as the worldly people say,
for her death, her money with her children being taken
off his hands. I am just now wondering whether you
will ever come to town again, Coleridge; 'tis among the
things I dare not hope, but can't help wishing. For
myself, I can live in the midst of town luxury and super-
fluity, and not long for them, and I can't see why your
children might not hereafter do the same. Remember,
you are not in Arcadia when you are in the west of
England, and they may catch infection from the world
without visiting the metropolis. But you seem to have
set your heart upon this same cottage plan; and God
prosper you in the experiment! I am at a loss for more
to write about; so 'tis as well that I am arrived at the
bottom of my paper.

God love you, Coleridge!—Our best loves and tenderest
wishes await on you, your Sara, and your little one.

C. L.

Letter XIII.]*November* 8, 1796.

My brother, my friend,—I am distress'd for you,
believe me I am; not so much for your painful, trouble-
some complaint, which, I trust, is only for a time, as for

those anxieties which brought it on, and perhaps even now may be nursing its malignity. Tell me, dearest of my friends, is your mind at peace? or has anything, yet unknown to me, happened to give you fresh disquiet, and steal from you all the pleasant dreams of future rest? Are you still (I fear you are) far from being comfortably settled? Would to God it were in my power to contribute towards the bringing of you into the haven where you would be! But you are too well skilled in the philosophy of consolation to need my humble tribute of advice. In pain, and in sickness, and in all manner of disappointments, I trust you have that within you which shall speak peace to your mind. Make it, I entreat you, one of your puny comforts, that I feel for you, and share all your griefs with you. I feel as if I were troubling you about *little* things, now I am going to resume the subject of our last two letters; but it may divert us both from unpleasanter feelings to make such matters, in a manner, of importance. Without further apology, then, it was not that I did not relish, that I did not in my heart thank you for those little pictures of your feelings which you lately sent me, if I neglected to mention them. You may remember you had said much the same things before to me on the same subject in a former letter, and I considered those last verses as only the identical thoughts better clothed; either way (in prose or verse) such poetry must be welcome to me. I love them as I love the Confessions of Rousseau, and for the same reason: the same frankness, the same openness of heart, the same disclosure of all the most hidden and delicate affections of the mind. They make me proud to be thus esteemed worthy of the place of friend-confessor, brother-confessor, to a man like Coleridge. This last is, I acknowledge, language too high for friendship; but it is also, I declare, too sincere for flattery. Now, to put on stilts, and talk magnificently about trifles,—I condescend, then, to your counsel, Coleridge, and allow my first Sonnet (sick to death am I to make mention of my Sonnets, and I blush

to be so taken up with them, indeed I do) ; I allow it to
run thus : *Fairy Land*, etc. etc., as I last wrote it.

The Fragments I now send you, I want printed to
get rid of 'em ; for, while they stick burr-like to my
memory, they tempt me to go on with the idle trade of
versifying, which I long (most sincerely I speak it) I long
to leave off, for it is unprofitable to my soul ; I feel it
is ; and these questions about words, and debates about
alterations, take me off, I am conscious, from the properer
business of my life. Take my Sonnets, once for all ; and
do not propose any reamendments, or mention them
again in any shape to me, I charge you. I blush that
my mind can consider them as things of any worth.
And, pray, admit or reject these fragments as you like or
dislike them, without ceremony. Call 'em Sketches,
Fragments, or what you will ; but do not entitle any of
my *things* Love Sonnets, as I told you to call 'em ; 'twill
only make me look little in my own eyes ; for it is a
passion of which I retain nothing. 'Twas a weakness,
concerning which I may say, in the words of Petrarch
(whose Life is now open before me), "if it drew me out
of some vices, it also prevented the growth of many
virtues, filling me with the love of the creature rather
than the Creator, which is the death of the soul." Thank
God, the folly has left me for ever. Not even a review
of my love verses renews one wayward wish in me ; and
if I am at all solicitous to trim 'em out in their best
apparel, it is because they are to make their appearance
in good company. Now to my fragments. Lest you
have lost my "Grandame," she shall be one. 'Tis among
the few verses I ever wrote : that to Mary is another,
which profit me in the recollection. God love her !—and
may we two never love each other less !

These, Coleridge, are the few sketches I have thought
worth preserving. How will they relish thus detached ?
Will you reject all or any of them ? They are thine : do
whatsoever thou listest with them. My eyes ache with

writing long and late, and I wax wondrous sleepy. God bless you and yours, me and mine ! Good-night.

C. LAMB.

I will keep my eyes open reluctantly a minute longer to tell you that I love you for those simple, tender, heart-flowing lines with which you conclude your last, and in my eyes best, " Sonnet " (so you call 'em)—

> " So, for the mother's sake, the child was dear ;
>   And dearer was the mother for the child."

Cultivate simplicity, Coleridge ; or rather, I should say, banish elaborateness ; for simplicity springs spontaneous from the heart, and carries into daylight its own modest buds, and genuine, sweet, and clear flowers of expression. I allow no hot-beds in the gardens of Parnassus. I am unwilling to go to bed and leave my sheet unfilled (a good piece of night-work for an idle body like me), so will finish with begging you to send me the earliest account of your complaint, its progress, or (as I hope to God you will be able to send me) the tale of your recovery, or at least amendment. My tenderest remembrances to your Sara——

Once more, Good-night.

November 14, 1796.

LETTER XIV.]

Coleridge, I love you for dedicating your poetry to Bowles. Genius of the sacred fountain of tears, it was he who led you gently by the hand through all this valley of weeping ; showed you the dark green yew trees, and the willow shades, where, by the fall of waters, you might indulge an uncomplaining melancholy, a delicious regret for the past, or weave fine visions of that awful future,

> " When all the vanities of life's brief day
>   Oblivion's hurrying hand hath swept away,
>   And all its sorrows, at the awful blast
>   Of the archangel's trump, are but as shadows past."

I have another sort of dedication in my head for my

few things, which I want to know if you approve of, and can insert. I mean to inscribe them to my sister. It will be unexpected, and it will give her pleasure; or do you think it will look whimsical at all? As I have not spoke to her about it I can easily reject the idea. But there is a monotony in the affections, which people living together, or, as we do now, very frequently seeing each other, are apt to give in to; a sort of indifference in the expression of kindness for each other, which demands that we should sometimes call to our aid the trickery of surprise. Do you publish with Lloyd, or without him? In either case my little portion may come last; and after the fashion of orders to a country correspondent, I will give directions how I should like to have 'em done. The title-page to stand thus:—

POEMS,

BY

CHARLES LAMB, OF THE INDIA HOUSE.

Under this title the following motto, which, for want of room, I put over leaf, and desire you to insert, whether you like it or no. May not a gentleman choose what arms, mottoes, or armorial bearings the Herald will give him leave, without consulting his republican friend, who might advise none? May not a publican put up the sign of the *Saracen's Head*, even though his undiscerning neighbour should prefer, as more genteel, the *Cat and Gridiron?*

[Motto.]

" This beauty, in the blossom of my youth,
　When my first fire knew no adulterate incense,
　Nor I no way to flatter but my fondness,
　In the best language my true tongue could tell me,
　And all the broken sighs my sick heart lend me,
　I sued and served. Long did I love this lady."

MASSINGER.

THE DEDICATION.

THE FEW FOLLOWING POEMS,
CREATURES OF THE FANCY AND THE FEELING
IN LIFE'S MORE VACANT HOURS,
PRODUCED, FOR THE MOST PART, BY
LOVE IN IDLENESS,
ARE,
WITH ALL A BROTHER'S FONDNESS,
INSCRIBED TO
MARY ANNE LAMB,
THE AUTHOR'S BEST FRIEND AND SISTER.

This is the pomp and paraphernalia of parting, with which I take my leave of a passion which has reigned so royally (so long) within me; thus, with its trappings of laureatship, I fling it off, pleased and satisfied with myself that the weakness troubles me no longer. I am wedded, Coleridge, to the fortunes of my sister and my poor old father. Oh, my friend! I think sometimes, could I recall the days that are past, which among them should I choose? not those "merrier days," not the "pleasant days of hope," not "those wanderings with a fair-hair'd maid," which I have so often and so feelingly regretted, but the days, Coleridge, of a *mother's* fondness for her *school-boy*. What would I give to call her back to earth for *one* day!—on my knees to ask her pardon for all those little asperities of temper which, from time to time, have given her gentle spirit pain!—and the day, my friend, I trust, will come. There will be "time enough" for kind offices of love, if "Heaven's eternal year" be ours. Hereafter, her meek spirit shall not reproach me. Oh, my friend, cultivate the filial feelings! and let no man think himself released from the kind "charities" of relationship: these shall give him peace at the last; these are the best foundation for every species of benevolence. I rejoice to hear, by certain channels, that you, my friend, are reconciled with all your relations. 'Tis the most kindly and natural species of love, and we have all the associated train of early feelings to secure its strength and perpetuity. Send me an account of your health : *indeed* I am solicitous about you. God love you and yours. C. LAMB.

LETTER XV.] *December* 2, 1796.

I have delayed writing thus long, not having by me my copy of your poems, which I had lent. I am not satisfied with all your intended omissions. Why omit 40, 63, 84? Above all, let me protest strongly against your rejecting the "Complaint of Ninathoma," 86. The words, I acknowledge, are Ossian's, but you have added to them the "music of Caril." If a vicarious substitute be wanting, sacrifice (and 'twill be a piece of self-denial too), the "Epitaph on an Infant," of which its author seems so proud, so tenacious. Or, if your heart be set on *perpetuating* the four-line wonder, I'll tell you what do ; sell the copyright of it at once to a country statuary. Commence in this manner Death's prime poet-laureate ; and let your verses be adopted in every village round, instead of those hitherto famous ones :—

> " Afflictions sore long time I bore ;
> Physicians were in vain."

I have seen your last very beautiful poem in the *Monthly Magazine :* write thus, and you most generally have written thus, and I shall never quarrel with you about simplicity. With regard to my lines—

> "Laugh all that weep," etc.,

I would willingly sacrifice them ; but my portion of the volume is so ridiculously little, that, in honest truth, I can't spare 'em. As things are, I have very slight pretensions to participate in the title-page. White's book is at length reviewed in the *Monthly ;* was it your doing, or Dyer's, to whom I sent him?—or, rather, do you not write in the *Critical ?*—for I observed, in an article of

this month's, a line quoted out of that Sonnet on Mrs.
Siddons,

"With eager wondering, and perturb'd delight."

And a line from *that* Sonnet would not readily have
occurred to a stranger. That sonnet, Coleridge, brings
afresh to my mind the time when you wrote those on
Bowles, Priestley, Burke ;—'twas two Christmases ago,
and in that nice little smoky room at the *Salutation*, which
is even now continually presenting itself to my recollection,
with all its associated train of pipes, tobacco, egg-hot,
welsh-rabbit, metaphysics, and poetry.—Are we *never* to
meet again? How differently I am circumstanced now!
I have never met with anyone—never shall meet with
anyone—who could or can compensate me for the loss
of your society. I have no one to talk all these matters
about to; I lack friends. I lack books to supply their
absence; but these complaints ill become me. Let me
compare my present situation, prospects, and state of
mind, with what they were but two months back—but
two months! O my friend, I am in danger of forgetting
the awful lessons then presented to me! Remind me of
them; remind me of my duty! Talk seriously with me
when you do write! I thank you, from my heart I
thank you, for your solicitude about my sister. She is
quite well, but must not, I fear, come to live with us yet
a good while. In the first place, because, at present, it
would hurt her, and hurt my father, for them to be
together; secondly, from a regard to the world's good
report; for, I fear, tongues will be busy whenever that
event takes place. Some have hinted, one man has
pressed it on me, that she should be in perpetual confine-
ment: what she hath done to deserve, or the necessity
of such an hardship, I see not; do you? I am starving
at the India House,—near seven o'clock without my
dinner; and so it has been, and will be, almost all the
week. I get home at night o'erwearied, quite faint, and
then to cards with my father, who will not let me enjoy

a meal in peace; but I must conform to my situation; and I hope I am, for the most part, not unthankful.

I am got home at last, and, after repeated games at cribbage, have got my father's leave to write awhile; with difficulty got it, for when I expostulated about playing any more, he very aptly replied, "If you won't play with me, you might as well not come home at all." The argument was unanswerable, and I set to afresh. I told you I do not approve of your omissions; neither do I quite coincide with you in your arrangements. I have not time to point out a better, and I suppose some self-associations of your own have determined their place as they now stand. Your beginning, indeed, with the *Joan of Arc* lines, I coincide entirely with. I love a splendid outset—a magnificent portico; and the diapason is grand. When I read the *Religious Musings*, I think how poor, how unelevated, unoriginal, my blank verse is—"Laugh all that weep," especially, where the subject demanded a grandeur of conception; and I ask what business they have among yours? but friendship covereth a multitude of defects. I want some loppings made in the "Chatterton:" it wants but a little to make it rank among the finest irregular lyrics I ever read. Have you time and inclination to go to work upon it?—or is it too late?—or do you think it needs none? Don't reject those verses in your *Watchman*, "Dear native brook," etc.; nor I think those last lines you sent me, in which "all effortless" is without doubt to be preferred to "inactive." If I am writing more than ordinarily dully, 'tis that I am stupified with a tooth-ache. Hang it! do not omit 48, 52, and 53: what you do retain, though, call Sonnets, for heaven's sake, and not Effusions. Spite of your ingenious anticipation of ridicule in your Preface, the last five lines of 50 are too good to be lost; the rest are not much worth. My tooth becomes importunate: I must finish. Pray, pray, write to me: if you knew with what an anxiety of joy I open such a long packet as you last sent me, you would not grudge giving a few minutes now and then to this intercourse (the only intercourse I fear we two shall ever have)—this conversation with your friend: such I boast to be called. God love you and yours! Write to me when you move, lest I should direct wrong. Has Sara no poems to publish? Those lines, 129, are probably too light for the volume where the *Religious Musings* are; but I remember some very beautiful lines, addressed by somebody at Bristol to somebody in London. God bless you once more. *Thursday Night.*   C. LAMB.

LETTER XVI.]   [Fragment.]   *December* 5, 1796.

At length I have done with verse-making; not that I relish other people's poetry less: theirs comes from 'em without effort; mine is the difficult operation of a brain scanty of·ideas, made more difficult by disuse. I have been reading "The Task" with fresh delight. I am glad you love Cowper. I could forgive a man for not enjoying Milton; but I would not call that man my friend who should be offended with the "divine chit-chat of Cowper." Write to me, God love you and yours!   C. L.

LETTER XVII.]   *December* 10, 1796.

I had put my letter into the post rather hastily, not expecting to have to acknowledge another from you so soon. This morning's present has made me alive again. My last night's epistle was childishly querulous: but you have put a little life into me, and I will thank you for your remembrance of me, while my sense of it is yet warm; for if I linger a day or two I may use the same phrase of acknowledgment, or similar, but the feeling that dictates it now will be gone. I shall send you a *caput mortuum*, not a *cor vivens*. Thy *Watchman's*, thy bellman's verses, I do retort upon thee, thou libellous varlet! Why you cried the hours yourself, and who made you so proud! But I submit, to show my humility most implicitly to your dogmas. I reject entirely the copy of verses you reject. With regard to my leaving off versifying, you have said so many pretty things, so many fine compliments, ingeniously decked out in the garb of sincerity, and undoubtedly springing from a present feeling somewhat like sincerity, that you might melt the most un-muse-ical soul—did you not (now for a Rowland compliment for your profusion of Olivers!) did you not in your very epistle, by the many pretty fancies and profusion of heart displayed in it, dissuade and discourage me from attempting anything after you. At present I have not leisure to make verses, nor anything approaching to a fondness for the exercise. In the ignorant present time, who can answer for the future man? "At lovers' perjuries Jove laughs;" and poets have sometimes a disingenuous way of forswearing their occupation. This though is not my case. The tender cast of soul, sombred with melancholy and subsiding recollections, is favourable to the Sonnet or the Elegy; but from

> " The sainted growing woof
> The teasing troubles keep aloof."

The music of poesy may charm for a while the importunate teasing cares of life; but the teased and troubled man is not in a disposition to make that music.

You sent me some very sweet lines relative to Burns, but it was at a time when in my highly agitated and perhaps somewhat distorted state of mind I thought it a duty to read 'em hastily and burn 'em. I burned all my own verses; all my book of extracts from Beaumont and Fletcher and a thousand sources; I burned a little journal of my foolish passion which I had a long time kept—

> " Noting ere they past away
> The little lines of yesterday."

I almost burned all your letters,—I did as bad, I lent 'em to a friend to keep out of my brother's sight, should he come and make inquisition into our papers; for, much as he dwelt upon your conversation while you were among us, and delighted to be with you, it has been his fashion ever since to depreciate and cry you down : you were the cause of my madness—you and your "damned foolish sensibility and melancholy ;" and he lamented, with a true brotherly feeling, that we ever met ; even as the sober citizen, when his son went astray upon the mountains of Parnassus, is said to have "cursed Wit and Poetry and Pope." I quote wrong, but no matter. These letters I lent to a friend to be out of the way for a season ; but I have claimed 'em in vain, and shall not cease to regret their loss. Your packets, posterior to the date of my misfortunes, commencing with that valuable consolatory epistle, are every day accumulating : they are sacred things with me.

Publish your Burns when and how you like, it will be new to me : my memory of it is very confused, and tainted with unpleasant associations. Burns was the god of my idolatry, as Bowles is of yours. I am jealous of your fraternising with Bowles, when I think you relish him more than Burns, or my old favourite, Cowper. But you conciliate matters when you talk of the "divine chit-chat" of the latter : by that expression I see you thoroughly relish him. I love Mrs. Coleridge for her excuses an hundredfold more dearly than if she heaped "line upon line," out-Hannah-ing Hannah More ; and would rather hear you sing "Did a very little baby," by your family fire-side, than listen to you when you were repeating one of Bowles's sweetest sonnets, in your sweet manner, while we two were indulging sympathy, a solitary luxury, by the fire-side at the *Salutation*. Yet have I no higher ideas of heaven. Your company was one "cordial in this melancholy vale :" the remembrance of it is a blessing partly, and partly a curse. When I can abstract myself from things present, I can enjoy it with a freshness of relish ; but it more constantly operates to an unfavourable comparison with the uninteresting converse I always and *only* can partake in. Not a soul loves Bowles here ; scarce one has heard of Burns ; few but laugh at me for reading my Testament. They talk a language I understand not. I conceal sentiments that would be a puzzle to them. I can only converse with you by letter, and with the dead in their books. My sister, indeed, is all I can wish in a companion; but our spirits are alike poorly, our reading and knowledge from the self-same sources; our communication with the scenes of the world alike narrow. Never having kept separate company, or any "company" "*together*"—never having read separate books, and few books *together*—what knowledge have we to convey to each other? In our little range of duties and connections, how few sentiments can take place, without friends, with few books, with a taste for religion, rather than a strong religious habit! We need some support, some leading-strings to cheer and direct us. You talk very wisely; and be not sparing of *your advice.* Continue to remember us, and to show us you do remember us: we will take as lively an interest in what concerns you and yours. All I can add to your happiness will be sympathy: you can add to mine *more;* you can teach me wisdom. I am indeed an unreasonable correspondent; but I was unwilling to let my last night's letter go off without this qualifier: you will perceive by this my mind is easier, and you will rejoice. I do not expect or wish you to write till you are moved; and, of course, shall not, till you announce to me that event, think of writing myself. Love to Mrs. Coleridge and David Hartley, and my kind remembrance to Lloyd, if he is with you.　　　　　　　　　　　　　C. LAMB.

I will get *Nature and Art:* have not seen it yet, nor any of Jeremy Taylor's works.

LETTER XVIII.]　　　　　　　　　　*December,* 1796.

In truth, Coleridge, I am perplexed, and at times almost cast down. I am beset with perplexities. The old hag of a wealthy relation who took my aunt off our hands in the beginning of trouble, has found out that she is "indolent and mulish "—I quote her own words, and that her attachment to us is so strong that she can never be happy apart. The lady, with delicate irony, remarks, that if I am not an hypocrite I shall rejoice to receive her again ; and that it will be a means of making me more fond of home to have so dear a friend to come home to ! The fact is, she is jealous of my aunt's bestowing any kind recollections on us while she enjoys the patronage of her roof. She says she finds it inconsistent with her own "ease and tranquillity," to keep her any longer ; and, in fine, summons me to fetch her home. Now, much as I should rejoice to transplant the poor old crea- ture from the chilling air of such patronage, yet I know how straitened we are already, how unable already to answer any demand which sickness or any extraordinary expense may make. I know this ; and all unused as I am to struggle with perplexities, I am somewhat non- plussed, to say no worse. This prevents me from a thorough relish of what Lloyd's kindness and yours have furnished me with. I thank you though from my heart, and feel myself not quite alone in the earth.

C. LAMB.

LETTER XIX.] January 2, 1797.

If the fraternal sentiment conveyed in the following lines will atone for the total want of anything like merit or genius in it, I desire you will print it next after my other Sonnet to my Sister.

> Friend of my earliest years and childish days,
> My joys, my sorrows, thou with me hast shared,
> Companion dear ; etc.

This has been a sad long letter of business, with no room in it for what honest Bunyan terms heart-work. I have just room left to congratulate you on your removal to Stowey ; to wish success to all your projects ; to " bid fair peace " be to that house ; to send my love and best wishes, breathed warmly, after your dear Sara, and her little David Hartley. If Lloyd be with you, bid him write to me: I feel to whom I am obliged primarily for two very friendly letters I have received already from him. A dainty sweet book that *Nature and Art* is. I am at present re-re-reading Priestley's Examination of the Scotch Doctors: how the rogue strings 'em up! three together! You have no doubt read that clear, strong, humorous, most entertaining piece of reasoning. If not, procure it, and be exquisitely amused. I wish I could get more of Priestley's works. Can you recommend me to any more books, easy of access, such as circulating shops afford? God bless you and yours.

Monday Morning, at Office.

Poor Mary is very unwell with a sore throat and a slight species of scarlet fever. God bless her too.

LETTER XX.]   *January 5, 1797.*

Sunday Morning.—You cannot surely mean to degrade the Joan of Arc into a pot-girl. You are not going, I hope, to annex to that most splendid ornament of Southey's poem all this cock-and-a-bull story of Joan, the publican's daughter of Neufchatel, with the lamentable episode of a waggoner, his wife, and six children. The texture will be most lamentably disproportionate. The first forty or fifty lines of these addenda are, no doubt, in their way, admirable, too; but many would prefer the Joan of Southey.

> " On mightiest deeds to brood
>   Of shadowy vastness, such as made my heart
>   Throb fast; anon I paused, and in a state
>   Of half expectance listen'd to the wind ;"

> " They wonder'd at me, who had known me once
>   A cheerful careless damsel ;"

> " The eye,
>   That of the circling throng and of the visible world
>   Unseeing, saw the shapes of holy phantasy ;"

I see nothing in your description of the Maid equal to

these.   There is a fine originality certainly in those lines—

> "For she had lived in this bad world
> As in a place of tombs,
> And touch'd not the pollutions of the dead ;"

but your "fierce vivacity" is a faint copy of the "fierce and terrible benevolence" of Southey; added to this, that it will look like rivalship in you, and extort a comparison with Southey,—I think to your disadvantage. And the lines, considered in themselves as an addition to what you had before written (strains of a far higher mood), are but such as Madame Fancy loves in some of her more familiar moods, at such times as she has met Noll Goldsmith, and walked and talked with him, calling him "old acquaintance." Southey certainly has no pretensions to vie with you in the sublime of poetry; but he tells a plain tale better than you. I will enumerate some woful blemishes, some of 'em sad deviations from that simplicity which was your aim. "Hail'd who might be near" (the "canvas-coverture moving," by the by, is laughable); "a woman and six children" (by the way,— why not nine children? It would have been just half as pathetic again): "statues of sleep they seem'd :" "frost-mangled wretch :" "green putridity:" "hail'd him immortal" (rather ludicrous again): "voic'd a sad and simple tale" (abominable !): "unprovender'd :" "such his tale :" "Ah ! suffering to the height of what was suffer'd" (a most *insufferable line*). "amazements of affright :" "the hot sore brain attributes its own hues of ghastliness and torture" (what shocking confusion of ideas) !

In these delineations of common and natural feelings, in the familiar walks of poetry, you seem to resemble Montauban dancing with Roubigné's tenants, "*much of his native loftiness remained in the execution.*"

I was reading your *Religious Musings* the other day, and sincerely I think it the noblest poem in the language, next after the *Paradise Lost ;* and even that was not made the vehicle of such grand truths. "There is one mind," etc., down to "Almighty's throne," are without a rival in the whole compass of my poetical reading.

> "Stands in the sun, and with no partial gaze
> Views all creation."

I wish I could have written those lines. I rejoice that I am able to relish them. The loftier walks of Pindus are your proper region. There you have no compeer in modern times. Leave the lowlands, unenvied, in possession of such men as Cowper and Southey. Thus am I pouring balsam into the wounds I may have been inflicting on my poor friend's vanity.

In your notice of Southey's new volume you omit to mention the most pleasing of all, the "Miniature"—

> "There were
> Who form'd high hopes and flattering ones of thee
> Young Robert,
> Spirit of Spenser!—was the wanderer wrong?"

Fairfax I have been in quest of a long time. Johnson, in his "Life of Waller," gives a most delicious specimen of him, and adds, in the true manner of that delicate critic, as well as amiable man, "It may be presumed that this old version will not be much read after the elegant translation of my friend, Mr. Hoole." I endeavoured— I wished to gain some idea of Tasso from this Mr. Hoole, the great boast and ornament of the India House, but soon desisted. I found him more vapid than smallest small beer "sun-vinegared." Your "Dream," down to that exquisite line—

> "I can't tell half his adventures,"

is a most happy resemblance of Chaucer. The remainder is so so. The best line, I think, is, "He belong'd, I believe, to the witch Melancholy." By the way, when will our volume come out? Don't delay it till you have written a new Joan of Arc. Send what letters you please by me, and in any way you choose, single or double. The India Company is better adapted to answer the cost than the generality of my friend's correspondents,—such poor and honest dogs as John Thelwall, particularly. I cannot say I know Colson, at least intimately. I once supped with him and Allen: I think his manners very pleasing. I will not tell you what I think of Lloyd, for he may by chance come to see this letter, and that thought puts a restraint on me. I cannot think what subject would suit your epic genius; some philosophical subject, I conjecture, in which shall be blended the sublime of poetry and of science. Your proposed "Hymns" will be a fit preparatory study wherewith "to discipline your young noviciate soul." I grow dull; I'll go walk myself out of my dulness.

Sunday Night.—You and Sara are very good to think so kindly and so favourably of poor Mary; I would to God all did so too. But I very much fear she must not think of coming home in my father's lifetime. It is very hard upon her; but our circumstances are peculiar, and we must submit to them. God be praised she is so well as she is. She bears her situation as one who has no right to complain. My poor old aunt, whom you have seen, the kindest, goodest creature to me when I was at school; who used to toddle there to bring me good things, when I, school-boy like, only despised her for it, and used to be ashamed to see her come and sit herself down on the old coal-hole steps as you went into the old grammar-school, and open her apron, and bring out her bason, with some nice thing she had caused to be saved for me; the good old creature is now lying on her death-bed. I cannot bear to think on her deplorable state. To the shock she received on that our evil day, from which she never completely recovered, I impute her illness. She says, poor thing, she is glad she is come home to die with me. I was always her favourite:

> " No after friendship e'er can raise
>   The endearments of our early days,
> Nor e'er the heart such fondness prove,
>   As when it first began to love."

Lloyd has kindly left me, for a keep-sake, *John Woolman.* You have read it, he says, and like it. Will you excuse one short extract? I think it could not have escaped you:—"Small treasure to a resigned mind is sufficient. How happy is it to be content with a little, to live in humility, and feel *that* in us, which breathes out this language—Abba! Father!"——I am almost ashamed to patch up a letter in this miscellaneous sort; but I please myself in the thought, that anything from me will be acceptable to you. I am rather impatient, childishly so, to see our names affixed to the same common volume. Send me two, when it does come out; two will be enough—or indeed one—but two better. I have a dim recollection that, when in town, you were talking of the Origin of Evil as a most prolific subject for a long poem. Why not adopt it, Coleridge?—there would be room for imagination. Or the description (from a Vision or Dream, suppose) of an Utopia in one of the planets (the Moon, for instance). Or a Five Days' Dream, which shall illustrate, in sensible imagery, Hartley's five Motives to Conduct:—1. Sensation; 2. Imagination; 3. Ambition; 4. Sympathy; 5. Theopathy:—*First.* Banquets, music, etc., effeminacy,—and their insufficiency. *Second.* "Beds of hyacinth and roses, where young Adonis oft reposes;" "Fortunate Isles;" "The pagan Elysium," etc.; poetical pictures; antiquity as pleasing to the fancy;—their emptiness, madness, etc. *Third.* Warriors, Poets; some famous yet more forgotten; their fame or oblivion now alike indifferent; pride, vanity, etc. *Fourth.* All manner of pitiable stories, in Spenser-like verse; love; friendship, relationship, etc. *Fifth.* Hermits; Christ and his apostles; martyrs; heaven, etc. An imagination like yours, from these scanty hints, may expand into a thousand great ideas, if indeed you at all comprehend my scheme, which I scarce do myself.

Monday Morn.—"A London letter—Ninepence halfpenny!" Look you, master poet, I have remorse as well as another man, and my bowels can sound upon occasion.

But I must put you to this charge, for I cannot keep back my protest, however ineffectual, against the annexing your latter lines to those former—this putting of new wine into old bottles. This my duty done, I will cease from writing till you invent some more reasonable mode of conveyance. Well may the "ragged followers of the Nine" set up for flocci-nauci-what-do-you-call-'em-ists! and I do not wonder that in their splendid visions of Utopias in America they protest against the admission of those *yellow*-complexioned, *copper*-coloured, *white*-livered gentlemen, who never proved themselves their friends. Don't you think your verses on a "Young Ass" too trivial a companion for the "Religious Musings?"— "Scoundrel monarch," alter that; and the "Man of Ross" is scarce admissible, as it now stands, curtailed of its fairer half: reclaim its property from the "Chatterton," which it does but encumber, and it will be a rich little poem. I hope you expunge great part of the old notes in the new edition: that, in particular, most barefaced, unfounded, impudent assertion, that Mr. Rogers is indebted for his story to *Loch Lomond*, a poem by Bruce! I have read the latter. I scarce think you have. Scarce anything is common to them both. The poor author of the *Pleasures of Memory* was sorely hurt, Dyer says, by the accusation of unoriginality. He never saw the poem. I long to read your poem on Burns; I retain so indistinct a memory of it. In what shape and how does it come into public? As you leave off writing poetry till you finish your Hymns, I suppose you print, now, all you have got by you. You have scarce enough unprinted to make a second volume with Lloyd. Tell me all about it. What is become of Cowper? Lloyd told me of some verses on his mother. If you have them by you, pray send 'em me. I do so love him! Never mind their merit. May be *I* may like 'em, as your taste and mine do not always exactly *identify*. Yours,

C. LAMB.

 January 10, 1797.

I need not repeat my wishes to have my little sonnets printed *verbatim* my last way. In particular, I fear lest you should prefer printing my first sonnet, as you have done more than once, " Did the wand of Merlin wave?" It looks so like *Mr.* Merlin, the ingenious successor of the immortal Merlin, now living in good health and spirits, and flourishing in magical reputation in Oxford Street; and, on my life, one half who read it would understand it so. Do put 'em forth, finally, as I have in various letters settled it; for first a man's self is to be pleased, and then his friends; and, of course, the greater number of his friends, if they differ *inter se.* Thus taste may safely be put to the vote. I do long to see our names together; not for vanity's sake, and naughty pride of heart altogether, for not a living soul I know, or am intimate with, will scarce read the book: so I shall gain nothing, *quoad famam;* and yet there is a little vanity mixes in it, I cannot help denying. I am aware of the unpoetical cast of the six last lines of my last sonnet, and think myself unwarranted in smuggling so tame a thing into the book; only the sentiments of those six lines are thoroughly congenial to me in my state of mind, and I wish to accumulate perpetuating tokens of my affection to poor Mary. That it has no originality in its cast, nor anything in the feelings but what is common and natural to thousands, nor ought properly to be called poetry, I see; still it will tend to keep present to my mind a view of things which I ought to indulge. These six lines, too, have not, to a reader, a connectedness with the foregoing.—Omit it, if you like.— What a treasure it is to my poor, indolent, and unemployed mind, thus to lay hold on a subject to talk about, though 'tis but a sonnet, and that of the lowest order! How mournfully inactive I am!—'Tis night: Good-night.

My sister, I thank God, is nigh recovered: she was seriously ill. Do, in your next letter, and that right soon, give me some satisfaction respecting your present situation at Stowey. Is it a farm you have got? And what does your worship know about farming?

Coleridge, I want you to write an epic poem. Nothing short of it can satisfy the vast capacity of true poetic genius. Having one great end to direct all your poetical faculties to, and on which to lay out your hopes, your ambition will show you to what you are equal. By the sacred energies of Milton! by the dainty, sweet, and soothing phantasies of honey-tongued Spenser! I adjure you to attempt the epic, or do something more ample than writing an occasional brief ode or sonnet; something, " to make yourself for ever known,—to make the age to come your own." But I prate; doubtless you meditate something. When you are exalted among the lords of epic fame, I shall recall with pleasure, and exultingly, the days of your humility, when you disdained not to put forth, in the same volume with mine, your *Religious Musings* and that other poem from the *Joan of Arc*, those promising first-fruits of high renown to come. You have learning, you have fancy, you have enthusiasm, you have strength, and amplitude of wing enow for flights like those I recommend. In the vast and unexplored regions of fairy-land there is ground enough unfound and uncultivated : search there, and realise your favourite Susquehannah scheme. In all our comparisons of taste, I do not know whether I have ever heard your opinion of a poet, very dear to me,—the now-out-of-fashion Cowley. Favour me with your judgment of him, and tell me if his prose essays, in particular, as well as no inconsiderable part of his verse, be not delicious. I prefer the graceful rambling of his essays, even to the courtly elegance and ease of Addison; abstracting from this the latter's exquisite humour.

When the little volume is printed, send me three or four, at all events not more than six copies, and tell me if I put you to any additional expense, by printing with you. I have no thought of the kind, and in that case must reimburse you.

Priestley, whom I sin in almost adoring, speaks of "such a choice of company as tends to keep up that right bent and firmness of mind which a necessary intercourse with the world would otherwise warp and relax." "Such fellowship is the true balsam of life ; its cement is infinitely more durable than that of the friendships of the world ; and it looks for its proper fruit and complete gratification to the life beyond the grave." Is there a possible chance for such an one as I to realise in this world such friendships? Where am I to look for 'em? What testimonials shall I bring of my being worthy of such friendship? Alas! the great and good go together in separate herds, and leave such as I to lag far, far behind in all intellectual, and, far more grievous to say, in all moral accomplishments. Coleridge, I have not one truly elevated character among my acquaintance : not one Christian : not one but undervalues Christianity. Singly, what am I to do? Wesley (have you read his life ?) was *he* not an elevated character? Wesley has said, "Religion is not a solitary thing." Alas! it necessarily is so with me, or next to solitary. 'Tis true you write to me ; but correspondence by letter, and personal intimacy, are very widely different. Do, do write to me, and do some good to my mind, already how much "warped and relaxed" by the world! 'Tis the conclusion of another evening. Good night. God have us all in his keeping !

If you are sufficiently at leisure, oblige me with an account of your plan of life at Stowey—your literary occupations and prospects ; in short, make me acquainted with every circumstance which, as relating to you, can be interesting to me. Are you yet a Berkleyan? Make me one. I rejoice in being, speculatively, a Necessarian. Would to God, I were habitually a practical one! Confirm me in the faith of that great and glorious doctrine, and keep me steady in the contemplation of it. You some time since expressed an intention you had of finishing some extensive work on the Evidences of Natural and Revealed Religion. Have you let that intention go?

Or are you doing anything towards it? Make to yourself other ten talents. My letter is full of nothingness. I talk of nothing. But I must talk. I love to write to you. I take a pride in it. It makes me think less meanly of myself. It makes me think myself not totally disconnected from the better part of mankind. I know I am too dissatisfied with the beings around me; but I cannot help occasionally exclaiming, "Woe is me, that I am constrained to dwell with Meshech, and to have my habitation among the tents of Kedar!" I know I am noways better in practice than my neighbours, but I have a taste for religion, an occasional earnest aspiration after perfection, which they have not. I gain nothing by being with such as myself: we encourage one another in mediocrity. I am always longing to be with men more excellent than myself. All this must sound odd to you; but these are my predominant feelings when I sit down to write to you, and I should put force upon my mind were I to reject them. Yet I rejoice, and feel my privilege with gratitude, when I have been reading some wise book, such as I have just been reading, *Priestley on Philosophical Necessity*, in the thought that I enjoy a kind of communion, a kind of friendship even, with the great and good. Books are to me instead of friends. I wish they did not resemble the latter in their scarceness.

And how does little David Hartley? "*Ecquid in antiquam virtutem?*" Does his mighty name work wonders yet upon his little frame and opening mind? I did not distinctly understand you: you don't mean to make an actual ploughman of him! Is Lloyd with you yet? Are you intimate with Southey? What poems is he about to publish? He hath a most prolific brain, and is indeed a most sweet poet. But how can you answer all the various mass of interrogation I have put to you in the course of this sheet? Write back just what you like, only write something, however brief. I have now nigh finished my page, and got to the end of another evening (Monday evening), and my eyes are heavy and sleepy.

and my brain unsuggestive. I have just heart enough awake to say good-night once more, and God love you, my dear friend; God love us all! Mary bears an affectionate remembrance of you. CHARLES LAMB.

LETTER XXII.] *January* 16, 1797.

Dear C——,—You have learned by this time, with surprise, no doubt, that Lloyd is with me in town. The emotions I felt on his coming so unlooked for, are not ill expressed in what follows, and what (if you do not object to them as too personal, and to the world obscure, or otherwise wanting in worth) I should wish to make a part of our little volume. I shall be sorry if that volume comes out, as it necessarily must do, unless you print those very schoolboy-ish verses I sent you on not getting leave to come down to Bristol last Summer. I say I shall be sorry that I have addressed you in nothing which can appear in our joint volume; so frequently, so habitually, as you dwell in my thoughts, 'tis some wonder those thoughts came never yet in contact with a poetical mood. But you dwell in my heart of hearts, and I love you in all the naked honesty of prose. God bless you, and all your little domestic circle! My tenderest remembrances to your beloved Sara, and a smile and a kiss from me to your dear dear little David Hartley. The verses I refer to above, slightly amended, I have sent (forgetting to ask your leave, tho' indeed I gave them only your initials) to the *Monthly Magazine*, where they may possibly appear next month, and where I hope to recognise your poem on Burns.

TO CHARLES LLOYD, AN UNEXPECTED VISITOR.

Alone, obscure, without a friend,
A cheerless, solitary thing,
Why seeks my Lloyd the stranger out?
What offering can the stranger bring

Of social scenes, home-bred delights,
  That him in aught compensate may
For Stowey's pleasant winter nights,
  For loves and friendships far away,

In brief oblivion to forego
  Friends, such as thine, so justly dear,
And be awhile with me content
  To stay, a kindly loiterer, here?

For this a gleam of random joy
  Hath flush'd my unaccustomed cheek ;
And, with an o'er-charged bursting heart,
  I feel the thanks I cannot speak.

O ! sweet are all the Muse's lays,
  And sweet the charm of matin bird—
'Twas long, since these estranged ears
  The sweeter voice of friend had heard.

The voice hath spoke : the pleasant sounds,
  In memory's ear, in after time
Shall live, to sometimes rouse a tear,
  And sometimes prompt an honest rhyme.

For when the transient charm is fled,
  And when the little week is o'er,
To cheerless, friendless solitude
  When I return, as heretofore—

Long, long, within my aching heart
  The grateful sense shall cherished be ;
I 'll think less meanly of myself,
  That Lloyd will sometimes think on me.

O Coleridge, would to God you were in London with us, or we two at Stowey with you all ! Lloyd takes up his abode at the *Bull and Mouth ;* the *Cat and Salutation* would have had a charm more forcible for me. *O noctes cœnæque Deûm !* Anglice—Welsh rabbit, punch, and poesy. Should you be induced to publish those very schoolboy-ish verses, print 'em as they will occur, if at all, in the *Monthly Magazine ;* yet I should feel ashamed that to you I wrote nothing better : but they are too personal, and almost trifling and obscure withal. Some

lines of mine to Cowper were in the last *Monthly Maga-
zine :* they have not body of thought enough to plead for
the retaining of 'em.   My sister's kind love to you all.

C. LAMB.

LETTER XXIII.] *February* 13, 1797.

Your poem is altogether admirable : parts of it are
even exquisite ; in particular, your personal account of
the Maid far surpasses anything of the sort in Southey.
I perceived all its excellences, on a first reading, as readily
as now you have been removing a supposed film from my
eyes.   I was only struck with a certain faulty dispropor-
tion in the matter and the *style*, which I still think I
perceive, between these lines and the former ones.   I had
an end in view : I wished to make you reject the poem
only as being discordant with the other ; and, in subser-
vience to that end, it was politically done in me to over-
pass and make no mention of merit, which, could you
think me capable of *overlooking*, might reasonably damn
for ever in your judgment all pretensions, in me, to be
critical.   There—I will be judged by Lloyd, whether I
have not made a very handsome recantation.   I was in
the case of a man whose friend has asked him his opinion
of a certain young lady.   The deluded wight gives judg-
ment against her *in toto*—doesn't like her face, her walk,
her manners ; finds fault with her eyebrows ; can see no
wit in her.   His friend looks blank ; he begins to smell
a rat ; wind veers about ; he acknowledges her good sense,
her judgment in dress, a certain simplicity of manners
and honesty of heart, something too in her manners
which gains upon you after a short acquaintance ; and
then her accurate pronunciation of the French language,
and a pretty uncultivated taste in drawing.   The recon-
ciled gentleman smiles applause, squeezes him by the
hand, and hopes he will do him the honour of taking a
bit of dinner with Mrs. —— and him,—a plain family
dinner,   some day next week ; "for, I suppose, you

never heard we were married. I'm glad to see you like my wife, however; you'll come and see her, ha?" Now am I too proud to retract entirely? Yet I do perceive I am in some sort straitened. You are manifestly wedded to this poem; and what fancy has joined let no man separate. I turn me to the *Joan of Arc*, second book.

The solemn openings of it are with sounds which, Lloyd would say, "are silence to the mind." The deep preluding strains are fitted to initiate the mind, with a pleasing awe, into the sublimest mysteries of theory concerning man's nature, and his noblest destination—the philosophy of a first cause — of subordinate agents in creation superior to man—the subserviency of pagan worship and pagan faith to the introduction of a purer and more perfect religion, which you so elegantly describe as winning, with gradual steps, her difficult way northward from Bethabara. After all this cometh Joan, a *publican's* daughter, sitting on an ale-house *bench*, and marking the *swingings* of the *signboard*, finding a poor man, his wife, and six children, starved to death with cold, and thence roused into a state of mind proper to receive visions, emblematical of equality ; which, what the devil Joan had to do with, I don't know, or indeed with the French and American revolutions ; though that needs no pardon, it is executed so nobly. After all, if you perceive no disproportion, all argument is vain : I do not so much object to parts. Again, when you talk of building your fame on these lines in preference to the *Religious Musings*, I cannot help conceiving of you, and of the author of that, as two different persons, and I think you a very vain man.

I have been re-reading your letter. Much of it I *could* dispute ; but with the latter part of it, in which you compare the two Joans with respect to their predispositions for fanaticism, I, *toto corde*, coincide ; only I think that Southey's strength rather lies in the description of the emotions of the Maid under the weight of inspiration. These (I see no mighty difference between *her* describing them or *your* describing them), these if you only equal, the previous admirers of his poem, as is natural, will prefer his. If you surpass, prejudice will scarcely allow it, and I scarce think you will surpass, though your specimen at the conclusion (I am in earnest) I think very nigh equals them. And in an account of a fanatic or of a prophet, the description of her *emotions* is expected to be most highly finished. By the way, I spoke far too disparagingly of your lines, and I am ashamed to say, purposely. I should like you to specify or particularise. The story of the "Tottering Eld," of "his eventful years all come and gone," is too general. Why not make him a soldier, or some character, however, in which he has been witness to frequency of "cruel wrong and strange distress!" I think I should. When I laughed at the "miserable man crawling from beneath the coverture," I wonder I did not perceive that it was a laugh of horror—such as I have laughed at Dante's picture of the famished Ugolino. Without falsehood, I perceive an hundred beauties in your narrative. Yet I wonder you do not perceive something out-of-the-way, something unsimple and artificial in the expression, "voiced a sad tale." I hate made-dishes at the muses' banquet. I believe I was wrong in most of my other objections. But surely "hailed him immortal," adds nothing to the terror of the man's death, which it was your business to heighten, not diminish by a phrase which takes away all terror from it. I like that line, "They closed their eyes in sleep, nor knew 'twas death." Indeed there is scarce a line I do not like. "*Turbid* ecstacy," is surely not so good as what you *had* written, "troublous." Turbid rather suits the muddy kind of inspiration which London porter confers. The versification is, throughout, to my ears unexceptionable, with no disparagement to the measure of the *Religious Musings*, which is exactly fitted to the thoughts.

You were building your house on a rock when you rested your fame on that poem. I can scarce bring my-

self to believe that I am admitted to a familiar corres-
pondence, and all the licence of friendship, with a man
who writes blank verse like Milton.   Now, this is delicate
flattery, *indirect* flattery.   Go on with your *Maid of
Orleans*, and be content to be second to yourself.   I shall
become a convert to it when 'tis finished.

This afternoon I attend the funeral of my poor old
aunt, who died on Thursday.   I own I am thankful that
the good creature has ended all her days of suffering and
infirmity.   She was to me the "cherisher of infancy,"
and one must fall on those occasions into reflections,
which it would be commonplace to enumerate, concerning
death, "of chance and change, and fate in human life."
Good God, who could have foreseen all this but four
months back!   I had reckoned, in particular, on my
aunt's living many years; she was a very hearty old
woman.   But she was a mere skeleton before she died,
looked more like a corpse that had lain weeks in the
grave, than one fresh dead.   "Truly the light is sweet,
and a pleasant thing it is for the eyes to behold the sun;
but if a man live many years and rejoice in them all, yet
let him remember the days of darkness, for they shall be
many."   Coleridge, why are we to live on after all the
strength and beauty of existence is gone, when all the
life of life is fled, as poor Burns expresses it?   Tell Lloyd
I have had thoughts of turning Quaker, and have been
reading, or am rather just beginning to read, a most
capital book, good thoughts in good language, William
Penn's *No Cross, no Crown*.   I like it immensely.   Un-
luckily I went to one of his meetings, tell him, in St.
John Street, yesterday, and saw a man under all the
agitations and workings of a fanatic, who believed him-
self under the influence of some "inevitable presence."
This cured me of Quakerism.   I love it in the books of
Penn and Woolman; but I detest the vanity of a man
thinking he speaks by the Spirit, when what he says an
ordinary man might say without all that quaking and
trembling.   In the midst of his inspiration (and the

effects of it were most noisy) was handed into the midst
of the meeting a most terrible blackguard Wapping sailor.
The poor man, I believe, had rather have been in the
hottest part of an engagement, for the congregation of
broad-brims, together with the ravings of the prophet,
were too much for his gravity, though I saw even he had
delicacy enough not to laugh out. And the inspired gentle-
man, though his manner was so supernatural, yet neither
talked nor professed to talk anything more than good
sober sense, common morality, with now and then a
declaration of not speaking from himself. Among other
things, looking back to his childhood and early youth, he
told the meeting what a graceless young dog he had been;
that in his youth he had a good share of wit. Reader,
if thou hadst seen the gentleman, thou wouldst have
sworn that it must indeed have been many years ago, for
his rueful physiognomy would have scared away the play-
ful goddess from the meeting, where he presided, for ever.
A wit! a wit! what could he mean? Lloyd, it minded
me of *Falkland* in the *Rivals*, "Am I full of wit and
humour? No, indeed you are not. Am I the life and
soul of every company I come into? No, it cannot be
said you are." That hard-faced gentleman, a wit! Why,
Nature wrote on his fanatic forehead fifty years ago, " Wit
never comes, that comes to all." I should be as scandalised
at a *bon mot* issuing from his oracle-looking mouth, as to
see Cato go down a country dance. God love you all!
You are very good to submit to be pleased with reading
my nothings. 'Tis the privilege of friendship to talk non-
sense, and to have her nonsense respected.—Yours ever,

C. LAMB.

LETTER XXIV.]   *April* 7, 1797.

Your last letter was dated the 10th of February; in it
you promised to write again the next day. At least, I
did not expect so long, so unfriend-like a silence. There
was a time, Col., when a remissness of this sort in a
dear friend would have lain very heavy on my mind; but

latterly I have been too familiar with neglect to feel much from the semblance of it. Yet, to suspect one's self overlooked, and in the way to oblivion, is a feeling rather humbling ; perhaps, as tending to self-mortification, not unfavourable to the spiritual state. Still, as you meant to confer no benefit on the soul of your friend, you do not stand quite clear from the imputation of unkindliness (a word, by which I mean the diminutive of unkindness).

Lloyd tells me he has been very ill, and was on the point of leaving you. I addressed a letter to him at Birmingham : perhaps he got it not, and is still with you. I hope his ill-health has not prevented his attending to a request I made in it, that he would write again very soon to let me know how he was. I hope to God poor Lloyd is not very bad, or in a very bad way. Pray satisfy me about these things.

And then David Hartley was unwell ; and how is the small philosopher, the minute philosopher ? and David's mother ? Coleridge, I am not trifling ; nor are these matter-of-fact questions only. You are all very dear and precious to me. Do what you will, Coleridge, you may hurt me and vex me by your silence, but you cannot estrange my heart from you all. I cannot scatter friendships like chuck-farthings, nor let them drop from mine hand like hour-glass sand. I have but two or three people in the world to whom I am more than indifferent, and I can't afford to whistle them off to the winds.

By the way, Lloyd may have told you about my sister. I told him. If not, I have taken her out of her confinement, and taken a room for her at Hackney, and spend my Sundays, holidays, etc., with her. She boards herself. In a little half-year's illness, and in such an illness, of such a nature, and of such consequences, to get her out into the world again, with a prospect of her never being so ill again,—this is to be ranked not among the common blessings of Providence. May that merciful God make tender my heart, and make me as thankful, as in my distress I was earnest, in my prayers. Congratulate me on an ever-present and never-alienable friend like her. And do, do insert, if you have not *lost*, my Dedication. It will have lost half its value by coming so late. If you really are going on with that volume, I shall be enabled in a day or two to send you a short poem to insert. Now, do answer this. Friendship, and acts of friendship, should be reciprocal, and free as the air. A friend should never be reduced to beg an alms of his fellow ; yet I will beg an alms : I entreat you to write, and tell me all about poor Lloyd, and all of you. God love and preserve you all !   C. LAMB.

LETTER XXV.]   *April* 15, 1797.

The above you will please to print immediately before the blank verse fragments. Tell me if you like it. I fear the latter half is unequal to the former, in parts of which I think you will discover a delicacy of pencilling not quite un-Spenser-like. The latter half aims at the *measure*, but has failed to attain the *poetry* of Milton in his *Comus*, and Fletcher in that exquisite thing ycleped the *Faithful Shepherdess*, where they both use eight-syllable lines. But this latter half was finished in great haste, and as a task, not from that impulse which affects the name of inspiration.

By the way, I have lit upon Fairfax's *Godfrey of Bullen*, for half-a-crown. Rejoice with me.

Poor dear Lloyd ! I had a letter from him yesterday ; his state of mind is truly alarming. He has, by his own confession, kept a letter of mine unopened three weeks ; afraid, he says, to open it, lest I should speak upbraidingly to him ; and yet this very letter of mine was in answer to one, wherein he informed me that an alarming illness had alone prevented him from writing. You will pray with me, I know, for his recovery ; for surely, Coleridge, an exquisiteness of feeling like this must border on derangement. But I love him more and more, and will not give up the hope of his speedy recovery, as he tells me he is under Dr. Darwin's regimen.

God bless us all, and shield us from insanity, which is "the sorest malady of all."

My kind love to your wife and child.

C. LAMB.

Pray write now.

LETTER XXVI.]   1797.

I discern a possibility of my paying you a visit next week. May I, can I, shall I, come so soon? Have you *room* for me, *leisure* for me? and are you pretty well? Tell me all this honestly—immediately. And by what *day* coach could I come soonest and nearest to Stowey? A few months hence may suit you better; certainly me, as well. If so, say so. I long, I yearn, with all the longings of a child do I desire to see you, to come among you—to see the young philosopher, to thank Sara for her last year's invitation in person—to read your tragedy— to read over together our little book—to breathe fresh air—to revive in me vivid images of " *Salutation* scenery." There is a sort of sacrilege in my letting such ideas slip out of my mind and memory. Still that Richardson remaineth—a thorn in the side of Hope, when she would lean towards Stowey. Here I will leave off, for I dislike to fill up this paper (which involves a question so con- nected with my heart and soul) with meaner matter, or subjects to me less interesting. I can talk, as I can think, nothing else.

Thursday.   C. LAMB.

LETTER XXVII.]   *June* 13, 1797.

I stared with wild wonderment to see thy well-known hand again. It revived many a pleasing recollection of an epistolary intercourse, of late strangely suspended, once the pride of my life. Before I even opened thy letter I figured to myself a sort of complacency which my little hoard at home would feel at receiving the new.

comer into the little drawer where I keep my treasures of this kind.   You have done well in writing to me. The little room (was it not a little one?) at the *Salutation* was already in the way of becoming a fading idea! It had begun to be classed in my memory with those "wanderings with a fair hair'd maid," in the recollection of which I feel I have no property.   You press me, very kindly do you press me, to come to Stowey.   Obstacles, strong as death, prevent me at present; maybe I may be able to come before the year is out.   Believe me, I will come as soon as I can; but I dread naming a probable time.   It depends on fifty things, besides the expense, which is not nothing.   Lloyd wants me to come to see him; but, besides that you have a prior claim on me, I should not feel myself so much at home with him, till he gets a house of his own.   As to Richardson, caprice may grant what caprice only refused; and it is no more hardship, rightly considered, to be dependent on him for pleasure, than to lie at the mercy of the rain and sunshine for the enjoyment of a holiday: in either case we are not to look for a suspension of the laws of Nature. " Gryll will be Gryll."   Vide Spenser.

I could not but smile at the compromise you make with me for printing Lloyd's poems first; but there is in nature, I fear, too many tendencies to envy and jealousy not to justify you in your apology.   Yet, if any one is welcome to pre-eminence from me, it is Lloyd, for he would be the last to desire it.   So pray, let his name *uniformly* precede mine, for it would be treating me like a child to suppose it could give me pain.   Yet, alas! I am not insusceptible of the bad passions.   Thank God, I have the ingenuousness to be ashamed of them.   I am dearly fond of Charles Lloyd; he is all goodness; and I have too much of the world in my composition to feel myself thoroughly deserving of his friendship.

Lloyd tells me that Sheridan put you upon writing your tragedy.   I hope you are only Coleridgeising when you talk of finishing it in a few days.   Shakspeare was a more modest man; but you best know your own power.

Of my last poem you speak slightingly. Surely the longer stanzas were pretty tolerable: at least there was one good line in it,

> " Thick-shaded trees, with dark green leaf rich clad."

To adopt your own expression, I call this a "rich" line, a fine full line. And some others I thought even beautiful. Believe me, my little gentleman will feel some repugnance at riding behind in the basket; though, I confess, in pretty good company. Your picture of idiocy, with the sugar-loaf head, is exquisite; but are you not too severe upon our more favoured brethren in fatuity? Lloyd tells me how ill your wife and child have been. I rejoice that they are better. My kindest remembrances, and those of my sister. I send you a trifling letter; but you have only to think that I have been skimming the superficies of my mind, and found it only froth. Now, do write again! You cannot believe how I long and love always to hear about you. Yours most affectionately,   CHARLES LAMB.

Monday Night.

LETTER XXVIII.]   *June* 24, 1797.

Did you seize the grand opportunity of seeing Kos-ciusko while he was at Bristol? I never saw a hero; I wonder how they look. I have been reading a most curious romance-like work, called the *Life of John Buncle, Esq.* 'Tis very interesting, and an extraordinary compound of all manner of subjects, from the depth of the ludicrous to the heights of sublime religious truth. There is much abstruse science in it above my cut, and an infinite fund of pleasantry. John Buncle is a famous fine man, formed in Nature's most eccentric hour. I am ashamed of what I write; but I have no topic to talk of. I see nobody. I sit and read, or walk alone, and hear nothing. I am quite lost to conversation from disuse; and out of the sphere of my little family (who, I am thankful, are dearer and dearer to me every day) I see no face that brightens up at my approach. My friends are at a distance. Worldly hopes are at a low ebb with me, and unworldly thoughts are familiarised to me, though I occasionally indulge in them. Still I feel a calm not unlike content. I fear it is sometimes more akin to physical stupidity than to a heaven-flowing serenity and peace. What right have I to obtrude all this upon you? and what is such a letter to you? and if I come to Stowey, what conversation can I furnish to compensate my friend for those stores of knowledge and of fancy; those delightful treasures of wisdom which I know he will open to me? But it is better to give than to receive; and I was a very patient hearer and docile scholar, in our winter evening meetings at Mr. May's; was I not, Col.? What I have owed to thee, my heart can ne'er forget.

God love you and yours!   C. L.
Saturday.

LETTER XXIX.]   *July* 1797.

I am scarcely yet so reconciled to the loss of you, or so subsided into my wonted uniformity of feeling, as to sit calmly down to think of you and write to you. But I reason myself into the belief that those few and pleasant holidays shall not have been spent in vain. I feel improvement in the recollection of many a casual conversation. The names of Tom Poole, of Wordsworth and his good sister, with thine and Sara's, are become "familiar in my mouth as household words." You would make me very happy if you think W. has no objection, by transcribing for me that inscription of his. I have some scattered sentences ever floating on my memory, teasing me that I cannot remember more of it. You may believe I will make no improper use of it. Believe me I can think now of many subjects on which I had planned gaining information from you; but I forgot my "treasure's worth" while I possessed it. Your leg is now become to me a matter of much more importance; and many a little thing, which when I was present with you seemed scarce to *indent* my notice, now presses painfully on my remembrance. Is the Patriot come? Are Wordsworth and his sister gone yet? I was looking out for John Thelwall all the way from Bridgewater; and had I met him, I think it would have moved almost me to tears. You will oblige me, too, by sending me my great-coat, which I left behind in the oblivious state the mind is thrown into at parting. Is it not ridiculous that I sometimes envy that great-coat lingering so cunningly behind! At present I have none: so send it to me by a Stowey waggon, if there be such a thing, directing for C. L., No. 45, Chapel Street, Pentonville, near London. But above all, *that Inscription!* It will recall to me the tones of all your voices, and with them many a remembered kindness to one who could and can repay you all only by the silence of a grateful heart. I could not talk much while I was with you; but my silence was not sullenness, nor I hope from any bad motive; but, in truth, disuse has made me awkward at it. I know I behaved myself, particularly at Tom Poole's, and at Cruikshank's, most like a sulky child; but company and converse are strange to me. It was kind in you all to endure me as you did.

Are you and your dear Sara—to me also very dear, because very kind—agreed yet about the management of little Hartley? And how go on the little rogue's teeth! I will see White to-morrow and he shall send you information on that matter; but as perhaps I can do it as well, after talking with him, I will keep this letter open.

My love and thanks to you and all of you.

C. L.

Wednesday Evening.

LETTER XXX.]   *September* 1797.

WRITTEN A TWELVEMONTH AFTER THE EVENTS.

[*Friday next, Coleridge, is the day on which my Mother died.*]

Alas ! how I am changed !   Where be the tears
The sobs, and forced suspensions of the breath
And all the dull desertions of the heart
With which I hung o'er my dear mother's corse?
Where be the blest subsidings of the storm
Within ; the sweet resignedness of hope
Drawn heavenward, and strength of filial love,
In which I bow'd me to my Father's will?
My God and my Redeemer, keep not thou
My heart in brute and sensual thanklessness
Seal'd up, oblivious ever of that dear grace,
And health restor'd to my long-loved friend,
Long-lov'd, and worthy known ! Thou didst not leave
Her soul in death.   O leave not now, my Lord,
Thy servants in far worse—in spiritual death
And darkness—blacker than those feared shadows
O' the valley all must tread.   Lend us thy balms,
Thou dear Physician of the sin-sick soul,
And heal our cleansed bosoms of the wounds
With which the world hath pierc'd us thro' and thro' !
Give us new flesh, new birth ; Elect of heaven
May we become, in thine election sure
Contain'd, and to one purpose steadfast drawn—
Our souls' salvation.
                          Thou and I, dear friend,
With filial recognition sweet, shall know
One day the face of our dear mother in heaven,
And her remember'd looks of love shall greet
With answering looks of love, her placid smiles
Meet with a smile as placid, and her hand
With drops of fondness wet, nor fear repulse.

Be witness for me, Lord, I do not ask
Those days of vanity to return again
(Nor fitting me to ask, nor thee to give),
Vain loves, and " wanderings with a fair-hair'd maid ;"
(Child of the dust as I am), who so long
My foolish heart steep'd in idolatry,
And creature-loves.   Forgive it, O my Maker !
If in a mood of grief, I sin almost
In sometimes brooding on the days long past,

(And from the grave of time wishing them back),
Days of a mother's fondness to her child—
Her little one! Oh, where be now those sports
And infant play-games? Where the joyous troops
Of children, and the haunts I did so love?
O my companions! O ye loved names
Of friend, or playmate dear, gone are ye now.
Gone divers ways ; to honour and credit some ;
And some, I fear, to ignominy and shame !
I only am left, with unavailing grief
One parent dead to mourn, and see one live
Of all life's joys bereft, and desolate :
Am left, with a few friends, and one above
The rest, found faithful in a length of years,
Contented as I may, to bear me on,
'T' the not unpeaceful evening of a day
Made black by morning storms.

The following I wrote when I had returned from
Charles Lloyd, leaving him behind at Burton, with
Southey. To understand some of it you must remember
that at that time he was very much perplexed in mind.

A stranger, and alone, I pass'd those scenes
We pass'd so late together ; and my heart
Felt something like desertion, as I look'd
Around me, and the pleasant voice of friend
Was absent, and the cordial look was there
No more, to smile on me. I thought on Lloyd—
All he had been to me ! And now I go
Again to mingle with a world impure ;
With men who make a mock of holy things,
Mistaken, and of man's best hope think scorn.
The world does much to warp the heart of man ;
And I may sometimes join its idiot laugh :
Of this I now complain not. Deal with me,
Omniscient Father, as thou judgest best,
And in *thy* season soften thou my heart.
I pray not for myself : I pray for him
Whose soul is sore perplexed. Shine thou on him,
Father of lights ! and in the difficult paths
Make plain his way before him : his own thoughts
May he not think—his own ends not pursue—
So shall he best perform thy will on earth.
Greatest and Best, Thy will be ever ours !

The former of these poems I wrote with unusual

celerity t'other morning at office.   I expect you to like it
better than anything of mine; Lloyd does, and I do myself.

You use Lloyd very ill, never writing to him.   I tell
you again that his is not a mind with which you should
play tricks.   He deserves more tenderness from you.

For myself, I must spoil a little passage of Beaumont
and Fletcher's to adapt it to my feelings :—

> "I am prouder
> That I was once your friend, tho' now forgot,
> Than to have had another true to me."

If you don't write to me now, as I told Lloyd, I shall
get angry, and call you hard names—Manchineel, and I
don't know what else.   I wish you would send me my
great-coat.   The snow and the rain season is at hand,
and I have but a wretched old coat, once my father's, to
keep 'em off, and that is transitory.

> "When time drives flocks from field to fold,
> When ways grow foul and blood gets cold,"

I shall remember where I left my coat.   Meet emblem
wilt thou be, old Winter, of a friend's neglect—cold, cold,
cold !   C. LAMB.

LETTER XXXI.]   *December* 10, 1797.

I am sorry I cannot now relish your poetical present so
thoroughly as I feel it deserves ; but I do not the less
thank Lloyd and you for it.

Before I offer, what alone I have to offer, a few obvious
remarks on the poems you sent me, I can but notice the
odd coincidence of two young men, in one age, carolling
their grandmothers.   Love, what L. calls the "feverish
and romantic tie," hath too long domineered over all the
charities of home : the dear domestic ties of father, brother,
husband.   The amiable and benevolent Cowper has a
beautiful passage in his "Task,"—some natural and pain-
ful reflections on his deceased parents : and Hayley's sweet
lines to his mother are notoriously the best things he ever
wrote.   Cowper's lines, some of them are—

> " How gladly would the man recall to life
> The boy's neglected sire ! a Mother, too,
> That softer friend, perhaps more gladly still,
> Might he demand them at the gates of death."

I cannot but smile to see my granny so gaily decked forth : though, I think, whoever altered " thy " praises to " her " praises—" thy " honoured memory to " her " honoured memory, did wrong ; they best expressed my feelings.   There is a pensive state of recollection in which the mind is disposed to apostrophise the departed objects of its attachment ; and, breaking loose from grammatical precision, changes from the first to the third, and from the third to the first person, just as the random fancy or the feeling directs.   Among Lloyd's sonnets, the 6th, 7th, 8th, 9th, and 11th, are eminently beautiful.   I think him too lavish of his expletives : the *do's* and *did's*, when they occur too often, bring a quaintness with them along with their simplicity, or rather air of antiquity, which the patrons of them seem desirous of conveying.

Another time, I may notice more particularly Lloyd's, Southey's, Dermody's Sonnets.   I shrink from them now : my teasing lot makes me too confused for a clear judgment of things, too selfish for sympathy ; and these ill-digested, meaningless remarks, I have imposed on myself as a task, to lull reflection, as well as to show you I did not neglect reading your valuable present.   Return my acknowledgments to Lloyd ; you two seem to be about realising an Elysium upon earth, and, no doubt, I shall be happier. Take my best wishes.   Remember me most affectionately to Mrs. C——, and give little David Hartley (God bless its little heart !) a kiss for me.   Bring him up to know the meaning of his Christian name, and what that name (imposed upon him) will demand of him.

God love you !   C. LAMB.

I write, for one thing, to say that I shall write no more till you send me word where you are, for you are so soon to move.

My sister is pretty well, thank God. We think of you very often. God bless you : continue to be my correspondent, and I will strive to fancy that this world is *not* " all barrenness."

Letter XXXII.]   *January* 28, 1798.

You have writ me many kind letters, and I have answered none of them. I don't deserve your attentions. An unnatural indifference has been creeping on me since my last misfortunes, or I should have seized the first opening of a correspondence with *you.* To you I owe much, under God. In my brief acquaintance with you in London, your conversations won me to the better cause, and rescued me from the polluting spirit of the world. I might have been a worthless character without you ; as it is, I do possess a certain improvable portion of devotional feelings, tho' when I view myself in the light of divine truth, and not according to the common measures of human judgment, I am altogether corrupt and sinful. This is no cant. I am very sincere.

These last afflictions, Coleridge, have failed to soften and bend my will. They found me unprepared. My former calamities produced in me a spirit of humility and a spirit of prayer. I thought they had sufficiently disciplined me ; but the event ought to humble me. If God's judgment now fail to take away from me the heart of stone, what more grievous trials ought I not to expect ? I have been very querulous, impatient under the rod— full of little jealousies and heart burnings. I had wellnigh quarrelled with Charles Lloyd ; and for no other reason, I believe, than that the good creature did all he could to make me happy. The truth is, I thought he tried to force my mind from its natural and proper bent. He continually wished me to be from home ; he was drawing me *from* the consideration of my poor dear Mary's situation, rather than assisting me to gain a proper view of it with religious consolations. I wanted to be left to the tendency of my own mind, in a solitary state, which, in times past, I knew had led to quietness and a patient bearing of the yoke. He was hurt that I was not more constantly with him; but he was living with White, a man to whom I had never been accustomed to impart my *dearest feelings*, tho' from long habits of friendliness, and many a social and good quality, I loved him very much. I met company there sometimes—indiscriminate company. Any society almost, when I am in affliction, is sorely painful to me. I seem to breathe more freely, to think more collectedly, to feel more properly and calmly, when alone. All these things the good creature did with the kindest intentions in the world, but they produced in me nothing but soreness and discontent. I became, as he complained, "jaundiced" towards him . . . but he has forgiven me; and his smile, I hope, will draw all such humours from me.) I am recovering, God be praised for it, a healthiness of mind, something like calmness; but I want more religion. I am jealous of human helps and leaning-places. I rejoice in your good fortunes. May God at the last settle you!—You have had many and painful trials; humanly speaking they are going to end; but we should rather pray that discipline may attend us thro' the whole of our lives. . . . A careless and a dissolute spirit has advanced upon *me* with large strides. Pray God that my present afflictions may be sanctified to me! Mary is recovering; but I see no opening yet of a situation for her. Your invitation went to my very heart; but you have a power of exciting interest, of leading all hearts captive, too forcible to admit of Mary's being with you. I consider her as perpetually on the brink of madness. I think you would almost make her dance within an inch of the precipice: she must be with duller fancies, and cooler intellects. I know a young man of this description, who has suited her these twenty years, and may live to do so still, if we are one day restored to each other. In answer to your suggestions of occupation for me, I must say that I do not think my capacity altogether suited for disquisitions of that kind. . . . I have read little, I have a very weak memory, and retain little of what I read; am unused to compositions in which any methodising is required; but I thank you sincerely for the hint, and shall receive it as far as I am able; that is, endeavour to engage my mind in some constant and innocent pursuit. I know my capacities better than you do.

Accept my kindest love, and believe me yours, as ever. C. L.

S. T. Coleridge,
at the Reverend A. Rowe's,
Shrewsbury.

To ROBERT SOUTHEY.

LETTER XXXIII.] *July* 28, 1798.

Dear Southey—I am ashamed that I have not thanked you before this for the *Joan of Arc*, but I did not know your address, and it did not occur to me to write through Cottle. The poem delighted me, and the notes amused me; but methinks she of Neufchatel, in the print, holds her sword too "like a dancer." I sent your *notice* to Phillips, particularly requesting an immediate insertion, but I suppose it came too late. I am sometimes curious to know what progress you make in that same "Calendar:" whether you insert the nine worthies and Whittington? what you do or how you can manage when two Saints meet and quarrel for precedency? Martlemas, and Candlemas, and Christmas, are glorious themes for a writer like you, antiquity-bitten, smit with the love of boars' heads and rosemary; but how you can ennoble the 1st of April I know not. By the way, I had a thing to say, but a certain false modesty has hitherto prevented me : perhaps I can best communicate my wish by a hint. My birthday is on the 10th of February, New Style; but if it interferes with any remarkable event, why rather than my country should lose her fame, I care not if I put my nativity back eleven days.   Fine family patronage for your "Calendar," if that old lady of prolific memory were living, who lies (or lyes) in some church in London (saints forgive me, but I have forgot *what* church), attesting that enormous legend of as many children as days in the year.   I marvel her impudence did not grasp at a leap-year.   Three hundred and sixty-five dedications, and all in a family !   You might spit, in spirit, on the oneness of Mæcenas's patronage !

Samuel Taylor Coleridge, to the eternal regret of his native Devonshire, emigrates to Westphalia : "Poor Lamb" (these were his last words), "if he wants any *knowledge*, he may apply to me."   In ordinary cases I thanked him.   I have an "Encyclopædia" at hand ; but on such an occasion as going over to a German university, I could not refrain from sending him the following propositions, to be by him defended or oppugned (or both) at Leipsic or Gottingen.

THESES QUÆDAM THEOLOGICÆ.

I.

"Whether God loves a lying angel better than a true man ?"

II.

"Whether the archangel Uriel *could* knowingly affirm an untruth, and whether, if he *could*, he *would* ?"

III.

"Whether honesty be an angelic virtue, or not rather belonging to that class of qualities which the schoolmen term ' virtutes minus splendidæ et hominis et terræ nimis participes ?'"

IV.

"Whether the seraphim ardentes do not manifest their goodness by the way of vision and theory? and whether practice be not a sub-celestial, and merely human virtue?"

V.

"Whether the higher order of seraphim illuminati ever *sneer?*"

VI.

"Whether pure intelligences can *love*, or whether they can love anything besides pure intellect?"

VII.

"Whether the beatific vision be anything more or less than a perpetual representment to each individual angel of his own present attainments, and future capabilities, something in the manner of mortal looking-glasses?"

VIII.

"Whether an 'immortal and amenable soul' may not come *to be damned at last, and the man never suspect it beforehand?*"

Samuel Taylor Coleridge hath not deigned an answer. Was it impertinent of me to avail myself of that offered source of knowledge?

Wishing *Madoc* may be born into the world with as splendid promise as the second birth, or purification, of the Maid of Neufchatel,—I remain yours sincerely,

C. LAMB.

I hope Edith is better; my kindest remembrances to her. You have a good deal of trifling to forgive in this letter.

"Love and remembrances to Cottle."

LETTER XXXIV.]   *October* 18, 1798.

Dear Southey—I have at last been so fortunate as to pick up Wither's Emblems for you, that "old book and quaint," as the brief author of *Rosamund Gray* hath it; it is in a most detestable state of preservation, and the cuts are of a fainter impression than I have seen. Some child, the curse of antiquaries and bane of bibliopical rarities, hath been dabbling in some of them with its paint and dirty fingers; and, in particular, hath a little sullied the author's own portraiture, which I think valuable, as the poem that accompanies it is no common one; this last excepted, the Emblems are far inferior to old Quarles. I once told you otherwise, but I had not then read old Quarles with attention. I have picked up, too, another copy of Quarles for ninepence!!! O tempora! O lectores! so that if you have lost or parted with your own copy, say so, and I can furnish you, for you prize these things more than I do. You will be amused, I think, with honest Wither's "Supersedeas to all them whose custom it is, without any deserving, to importune authors to give unto them their books." I am sorry 'tis imperfect, as the lottery board annexed to it also is. Methinks you might modernise and elegantise this Supersedeas, and place it in front of your *Joan of Arc*, as a gentle hint to Messrs. Parke, etc. One of the happiest emblems, and comicalest cuts, is the owl and little chirpers, page 63.

Wishing you all amusement, which your true emblem-fancier can scarce fail to find in even bad emblems, I remain your caterer to command,   C. LAMB.

Love and respects to Edith. I hope she is well. How does your Calendar prosper?

LETTER XXXV.]

Dear Southey—I thank you heartily for the Eclogue; it pleases me mightily, being so full of picture work and circumstances. I find no fault in it, unless perhaps that Joanna's ruin is a catastrophe too trite; and this is not the first or second time you have clothed your indignation, in verse, in a tale of ruined innocence. The old lady, spinning in the sun, I hope would not disdain to claim some kindred with old Margaret. I could almost wish you to vary some circumstances in the conclusion. A gentleman seducer has so often been described in prose and verse. What if you had accomplished Joanna's ruin by the clumsy arts and rustic gifts of some country-fellow? I am thinking, I believe, of the song—

> " An old woman clothed in gray,
> Whose daughter was charming and young,
> And she was deluded away
> By Roger's false flattering tongue."

A Roger-Lothario would be a novel character; I think you might paint him very well. You may think this a very silly suggestion, and so indeed it is; but, in good truth, nothing else but the first words of that foolish ballad put me upon scribbling my *Rosamund*. But I thank you heartily for the poem. Not having anything of my own to send you in return (though, to tell truth, I am at work upon something, which, if I were to cut away and garble, perhaps I might send you an extract or two that might not displease you; but I will not do that; and whether it will come to anything I know not, for I am as slow as a Fleming painter, when I compose anything) I will crave leave to put down a few lines of old Christopher Marlow's; I take them from his tragedy, *Jew of Malta*. The Jew is a famous character, quite out of nature; but, when we consider the terrible idea our simple ancestors had of a Jew, not more to be discommended for a certain discolouring (I think Addison calls it) than the witches and fairies of Marlow's mighty successor. The scene is betwixt *Barabbas*, the Jew, and *Ithamore*, a Turkish captive, exposed to sale for a slave.

BARABBAS.

(*A precious rascal.*)

" As for myself, I walk abroad a-nights,
And kill sick people groaning under walls;
Sometimes I go about, and poison wells;
And now and then, to cherish Christian thieves,
I am content to lose some of my crowns,
That I may, walking in my gallery,
See 'm go pinion'd along by my door.
Being young, I studied physic, and began
To practise first upon the Italian:
There I enrich'd the priests with burials,
And always kept the sexton's arms in use
With digging graves, and ringing dead men's knells:
Aud after that was I an engineer,
And in the wars 'twixt France and Germany,
Under pretence of serving Charles the Fifth,
Slew friends and enemy with my stratagems.
Then after that was I an usurer,
And with extorting, cozening, forfeiting,
And tricks belonging unto brokery,
I fill'd the jails with bankrupts in a year,
And with young orphans planted hospitals,
And every moon made some or other mad,
And now and then one hang himself for grief,
Pinning upon his breast a long great scroll,
How I with interest had tormented him."

(Now hear Ithamore, the other gentle nature.)

ITHAMORE.

(*A comical dog.*)

" Faith, master, and I have spent my time
In setting Christian villages on fire,
Chaining of eunuchs, binding galley slaves.
One time I was an hostler at an inn,
And in the night time secretly would I steal
To travellers' chambers, and there cut their throats
Once at Jerusalem, where the pilgrims kneel'd,
I strew'd powder on the marble stones,
And therewithal their knees would rankle so,
That I have laugh'd a good to see the cripples
Go limping home to Christendom on stilts."

BARABBAS.

" Why, this is something."

There is a mixture of the ludicrous and the terrible in these lines, brimful of genius and antique invention, that at first reminded me of your old description of cruelty in hell, which was in the true Hogarthian style. I need not tell *you* that Marlow was author of that pretty madrigal, " Come live with me and be my Love," and of the tragedy of Edward II., in which are certain *lines* unequalled in our English tongue. Honest Walton mentions the said madrigal under the denomination of " certain smooth verses made long since by Kit Marlow."

I am glad you have put me on the scent after old Quarles. If I do not put up those eclogues, and that shortly, say I am no true-nosed hound. I have had a letter from Lloyd; the young metaphysician of Caius is well, and is busy recanting the new heresy, metaphysics, for the old dogma, Greek. My sister, I thank you, is quite well. She had a slight attack the other day, which frightened me a good deal, but it went off unaccountably. Love and respects to Edith.

Yours sincerely,   C. LAMB.

LETTER XXXVI.]   *November* 3, 1798.

I have read your Eclogue repeatedly, and cannot call it bald, or without interest; the cast of it and the design are completely original, and may set people upon thinking. It is as poetical as the subject requires, which asks no poetry; but it is defective in pathos. The woman's own story is the tamest part of it; I should like you to remould that : it too much resembles the young maid's history; both had been in service. Even the omission would not injure the poem : after the words " growing wants," you might, not unconnectedly, introduce " look at that little chub" down to " welcome

one."   And, decidedly, I would have you end it somehow
thus,—

> " Give them at least this evening a good meal.
>   [*Gives her money.*
>   Now, fare thee well ; hereafter you have taught me
>   To give sad meaning to the village bells," etc.,

which would leave a stronger impression (as well as
more pleasingly recall the beginning of the Eclogue) than
the present commonplace reference to a better world, which
the woman " must have heard at church."   I should like
you too a good deal to enlarge the most striking part, as
it might have been, of the poem—" Is it idleness?" etc. :
that affords a good field for dwelling on sickness, and
inabilities, and old age.   And you might also a good
deal enrich the piece with a picture of a country wedding.
The woman might very well, in a transient fit of oblivion,
dwell upon the ceremony and circumstances of her own
nuptials six years ago, the snugness of the bridegroom,
the feastings, the cheap merriment, the welcomings, and
the secret envyings of the maidens ; then dropping all
this, recur to her present lot.   I do not know that I can
suggest anything else, or that I have suggested anything
new or material.   I do not much prefer this Eclogue to
the last.   Both are inferior to the former.

> " And when he came to shake me by the hand,
>   And spake as kindly to me as he used,
>   I hardly knew his voice—"

is the only passage that affected me.   When servants
speak, their language ought to be plain, and not much
raised above the common else I should find fault with
the pathos of this passage,—

> " And when I heard the bell strike out,
>   I thought (what?) that I had never heard it toll
>   So dismally before."

I like the destruction of the martens' old nests hugely,
having just such a circumstance in my memory.   I shall
be very glad to see your remaining Eclogue, if not too

much trouble, as you give me reason to expect it will be the second best. I shall be very glad to see some more poetry ; though, I fear, your trouble in transcribing will be greater than the service my remarks may do them.

Yours affectionately,   C. LAMB.

I cut my letter short because I am called off to business.

LETTER XXXVII.]   *November* 8, 1798.

I perfectly accord with your opinion of old Wither ; Quarles is a wittier writer, but Wither lays more hold of the heart. Quarles thinks of his audience when he lectures ; Wither soliloquizes in company from a full heart. What wretched stuff are the " Divine Fancies " of Quarles ! Religion appears to him no longer valuable than it furnishes matter for quibbles and riddles ; he turns God's grace into wantonness. Wither is like an old friend, whose warm-heartedness and estimable qualities make us wish he possessed more genius, but at the same time make us willing to dispense with that want. I always love Wither, and sometimes admire Quarles. Still that portrait poem is a fine one ; and the extract from " Shepherds' Hunting " places him in a starry height far above Quarles. If you wrote that review in the *Critical Review*, I am sorry you are so sparing of praise to the *Ancient Marinere*. So far from calling it as you do, with some wit, but more severity, a " Dutch Attempt," etc., I call it a right English attempt, and a successful one, to dethrone German sublimity. You have selected a passage fertile in unmeaning miracles, but have passed by fifty passages as miraculous as the miracles they celebrate. I never so deeply felt the pathetic as in that part,

> " A spring of love gush'd from my heart,
> And I bless'd them unaware."

It stung me into high pleasure through sufferings. Lloyd

does not like it; his head is too metaphysical, and your taste too correct; at least I must allege something against you both, to excuse my own dotage—

> " So lonely 'twas, that God himself
> Scarce seem'd there to be !"—etc. etc.

But you allow some elaborate beauties: you should have extracted 'em. The *Ancient Marinere* plays more tricks with the mind than that last poem, which is yet one of the finest written. But I am getting too dogmatical; and before I degenerate into abuse, I will conclude with assuring you that I am

Sincerely yours,

C. Lamb.

I am going to meet Lloyd at Ware on Saturday, to return on Sunday. Have you any commands or commendations to the metaphysician? I shall be very happy if you will dine or spend any time with me in your way through the great ugly city; but I know you have other ties upon you in these parts.

Love and respects to Edith, and friendly remembrances to Cottle.

LETTER XXXVIII.]   *November* 28, 1798.

I can have no objection to your printing " Mystery of God " with my name, and all due acknowledgments for the honour and favour of the communication ; indeed, 'tis a poem that can dishonour no name. Now, that is in the true strain of modern modestovanitas. . . . But for the sonnet, I heartily wish it, as I thought it was, dead and forgotten. If the exact circumstances under which I wrote could be known or told, it would be an interesting sonnet; but to an indifferent and stranger reader it must appear a very bald thing, certainly inadmissible in a compilation. I wish you could affix a different name to the volume. There is a contemptible book, a wretched assortment of vapid feelings, entitled *Pratt's Gleanings*, which hath damned and impropriated the title for ever. Pray think of some other. The gentleman is better known (better had he remained unknown) by an Ode to Benevolence, written and spoken for and at the annual dinner of the Humane Society, who walk in procession once a year, with all the objects of their charity before them, to return God thanks for giving them such benevolent hearts.

I like "Bishop Bruno," but not so abundantly as your "Witch Ballad," which is an exquisite thing of its kind.

I showed my "Witch" and "Dying Lover" to Dyer last night; but George could not comprehend how *that* could be poetry which did not go upon ten feet, as George and his predecessor had taught it to do; so George read me some lectures on the distinguishing qualities of the Ode, the Epigram, and the Epic, and went home to illustrate his doctrine, by correcting a proof sheet of his own Lyrics. George writes odes where the rhymes, like fashionable man and wife, keep a comfortable distance of six or eight lines apart, and calls that "observing the laws of verse!" George tells you, before he recites, that you must listen with great attention, or you'll miss the rhymes. I did so, and found them pretty exact. George, speaking of the dead Ossian, exclaimeth, "Dark are the poet's eyes!" I humbly represented to him that his own eyes were dark, and many a living bard's besides, and recommended "Closed are the poet's eyes." But that would not do. I found there was an antithesis between the darkness of his eyes and the splendour of his genius; and I acquiesced.

Your recipe for a Turk's poison is invaluable, and truly Marlowish. . . . Lloyd objects to "shutting up the womb of his purse" in my curse (which, for a Christian witch in a Christian country, is not too mild, I hope). Do you object? I think there is a strangeness in the idea, as well as "shaking the poor like snakes from his door," which suits the speaker. Witches illustrate, as

fine ladies do, from their own familiar objects, and snakes
and the shutting up of wombs are in their way. I don't
know that this last charge has been before brought
against 'em nor either the sour milk or the mandrake
babe ; but I affirm these be things a witch would do if
she could.

My Tragedy will be a medley (as I intend it to be a
medley) of laughter and tears, prose and verse, and in
some places rhyme, songs, wit, pathos, humour, and, if
possible, sublimity ; at least it is not a fault in my inten-
tion if it does not comprehend most of these discordant
atoms. Heaven send they dance not the "Dance of
Death !" I hear that the Two Noble Englishmen have
parted no sooner than they set foot on German earth ; but
I have not heard the reason. Possibly to give moralists
an handle to exclaim, " Ah me ! what things are perfect?"
I think I shall adopt your emendation in the "Dying
Lover," though I do not myself feel the objection against
"Silent Prayer."

My tailor has brought me home a new coat lapelled,
with a velvet collar. He assures me everybody wears
velvet collars now. Some are born fashionable, some
achieve fashion, and others, like your humble servant,
have fashion thrust upon them. The rogue has been
making inroads hitherto by modest degrees, foisting upon
me an additional button, recommending gaiters ; but to
come upon me thus, in a full tide of luxury, neither
becomes him as a tailor nor the ninth of a man. My
meek gentleman was robbed the other day, coming with
his wife and family in a one-horse shay from Hampstead.
The villains rifled him of four guineas, some shillings and
half-pence, and a bundle of customers' measures, which
they swore were bank notes. They did not shoot him,
and when they rode off he addrest them with profound
gratitude, making a congee : " Gentlemen, I wish you
good-night, and we are very much obliged to you that
you have not used us ill !" And this is the cuckoo that
has had the audacity to foist upon me ten buttons on a

side, and a black velvet collar!   A cursed ninth of a
scoundrel!

When you write to Lloyd, he wishes his Jacobin cor-
respondents to address him as *Mr*. C. L.   Love and
respects to Edith.   I hope she is well.

Yours sincerely,   C. LAMB.

LETTER XXXIX.   *December* 27, 1798.

Dear Southey—Your friend John May has formerly
made kind offers to Lloyd of serving me in the India
House, by the interest of his friend Sir Francis Baring.
It is not likely that I shall ever put his goodness to the
test on my own account, for my prospects are very com-
fortable; but I know a man, a young man, whom he
could serve through the same channel, and, I think,
would be disposed to serve if he were acquainted with
his case.   This poor fellow (whom I know just enough
of to vouch for his strict integrity and worth) has lost
two or three employments from illness, which he cannot
regain; he was once insane, and, from the distressful
uncertainty of his livelihood, has reason to apprehend a
return of that malady.   He has been for some time
dependent on a woman whose lodger he formerly was,
but who can ill afford to maintain him; and I know that
on Christmas night last he actually walked about the
streets all night, rather than accept of her bed, which
she offered him, and offered herself to sleep in the kitchen;
and that, in consequence of that severe cold, he is labour-
ing under a bilious disorder, besides a depression of spirits,
which incapacitates him from exertion when he most needs
it.   For God's sake, Southey, if it does not go against
you to ask favours, do it now; ask it as for me: but do
not do a violence to your feelings, because he does not
know of this application, and will suffer no disappoint-
ment.   What I meant to say was this,—there are in the
India House, what are called *extra clerks*, not on the
establishment, like me, but employed in extra business,

by-jobs; these get about £50 a year, or rather more, but never rise.   A director can put in at any time a young man in this office, and it is by no means considered so great a favour as making an established clerk.   He would think himself as rich as an emperor if he could get such a certain situation, and be relieved from those disquietudes which, I do fear, may one day bring back his distemper.

You know John May better than I do, but I know enough to believe that he is a good man.   He did make me that offer I have mentioned, but you will perceive that such an offer cannot authorise me in applying for another person.

But I cannot help writing to you on the subject, for the young man is perpetually before my eyes, and I shall feel it a crime not to strain all my petty interest to do him service, though I put my own delicacy to the question by so doing.   I have made one other unsuccessful attempt already.   At all events I will thank you to write, for I am tormented with anxiety.   C. LAMB.

LETTER XL.   *January* 21, 1799.

I am requested by Lloyd to excuse his not replying to a kind letter received from you.   He is at present situated in most distressful family perplexities, which I am not at liberty to explain, but they are such as to demand all the strength of his mind, and quite exclude any attention to foreign objects.   His brother Robert (the flower of his family) hath eloped from the persecutions of his father, and has taken shelter with me.   What the issue of his adventure will be, I know not.   He hath the sweetness of an angel in his heart, combined with admirable firmness of purpose; an uncultivated, but very original, and I think superior, genius.   But this step of his is but a small part of their family troubles.

I am to blame for not writing to you before on *my own account;* but I know you can dispense with the expressions of gratitude, or I should have thanked you before for all May's kindness. He has liberally supplied the person I spoke to you of with money, and had procured him a situation just after himself had lighted upon a similar one, and engaged too far to recede. But May's kindness was the same, and my thanks to you and him are the same. May went about on this business as if it had been his own. But you knew John May before this, so I will be silent.

I shall be very glad to hear from you when convenient. I do not know how your Calender and other affairs thrive; but above all, I have not heard a great while of your "Madoc"—the *opus magnum*. I would willingly send you something to give a value to this letter; but I have only one slight passage to send you, scarce worth the sending, which I want to edge in somewhere into my play, which, by the way, hath not received the addition of ten lines, besides, since I saw you. A father, old Walter Woodvil (the witch's *protégé*), relates this of his son John, who "fought in adverse armies," being a royalist, and his father a parliamentary man :—

" I saw him in the day of Worcester fight,
Whither he came at twice seven years,
Under the discipline of the Lord Falkland
(His uncle by the mother's side,
Who gave his youthful politics a bent
Quite *from* the principles of his father's house);
There did I see this valiant Lamb of Mars,
This sprig of honour, this unbearded John,
This veteran in green years, this sprout, this Woodvil
(With dreadless ease guiding a fire-hot steed,
Which seem'd to scorn the manage of a boy),
Prick forth with such a *mirth* into the field,
To mingle rivalship and acts of war
Even with the sinewy masters of the art.
You would have thought the work of blood had been
A play-game merely, and the rabid Mars
Had put his harmful hostile nature off
To instruct raw youth in images of war,
And practice of the unedged players' foils.
The rough fanatic and blood-practised soldiery
Seeing such hope and virtue in the boy,

> Disclosed their ranks to let him pass unhurt,
> Checking their swords' uncivil injuries,
> As loth to mar that curious workmanship
> Of Valour's beauty portray'd in his face."

Lloyd objects to "portray'd in his face," do you? I like the line.

I shall clap this in somewhere. I think there is a spirit through the lines; perhaps the 7th, 8th, and 9th owe their origin to Shakspere, though no image is borrowed.

He says in *Henry the Fourth*—

> "This infant Hotspur,
> Mars in swathing clothes."

But pray did Lord Falkland die before Worcester fight? In that case I must make bold to unclify some other nobleman.

Kind love and respects to Edith. C. LAMB.

LETTER XLI.   *March* 15, 1799.

Dear Southey—I have received your little volume, for which I thank you, though I do not entirely approve of this sort of intercourse, where the presents are all one side. I have read the last Eclogue again with great pleasure. It hath gained considerably by abridgment, and now I think it wants nothing but enlargement. You will call this one of tyrant Procrustes's criticisms, to cut and pull so to his own standard; but the old lady is so great a favourite with me, I want to hear more of her; and of "Joanna" you have given us still less. But the picture of the rustics leaning over the bridge, and the old lady travelling abroad on summer evening to see her garden watered, are images so new and true, that I decidedly prefer this "Ruin'd Cottage" to any poem in the book. Indeed I think it the only one that will bear comparison with your "Hymn to the Penates," in a former volume.

I compare dissimilar things, as one would a rose and a

star, for the pleasure they give us, or as a child soon learns to choose between a cake and a rattle; for dissimilars have mostly some points of comparison.

The next best poem, I think, is the first Eclogue; 'tis very complete, and abounding in little pictures and realities. The remainder Eclogues, excepting only the "Funeral," I do not greatly admire. I miss *one*, which had at least as good a title to publication as the "Witch," or the "Sailor's Mother." You call'd it the "Last of the Family." The "Old Woman of Berkeley" comes next; in some humours I would give it the preference above any. But who the devil is Matthew of Westminster? You are as familiar with these antiquated monastics, as Swedenborg, or, as his followers affect to call him, the Baron, with his invisibles. But you have raised a very comic effect out of the true narrative of Matthew of Westminster. 'Tis surprising with how little addition you have been able to convert, with so little alteration, his incidents, meant for terror, into circumstances and food for the spleen. The Parody is *not* so successful; it has one famous line, indeed, which conveys the finest death-bed image I ever met with :—

" The doctor whisper'd the nurse, and the surgeon knew what he said."

But the offering the bride three times bears not the slightest analogy or proportion to the fiendish noises three times heard! In "Jaspar," the circumstance of the great light is very affecting. But I had heard you mention it before. The "Rose" is the only insipid piece in the volume; it hath neither thorns nor sweetness; and, besides, sets all chronology and probability at defiance.

"Cousin Margaret," you know, I like. The allusions to the *Pilgrim's Progress* are particularly happy, and harmonise tacitly and delicately with old cousins and aunts. To familiar faces we do associate familiar scenes and accustomed objects : but what hath Apollidon and

his sea-nymphs to do in these affairs? Apollyon I could
have borne, though he stands for the devil; but who is
Apollidon? I think you are too apt to conclude faintly,
with some cold moral, as in the end of the poem called
" The Victory "—

> " Be thou her comforter, who art the widow's friend :"

a single commonplace line of comfort, which bears no
proportion in weight or number to the many lines which
describe suffering. This is to convert religion into
mediocre feelings, which should burn, and glow, and
tremble. A moral should be wrought into the body and
soul, the matter and tendency of a poem, not tagged to
the end, like a "God send the good ship into harbour,"
at the conclusion of our bills of lading. The finishing of
the "Sailor" is also imperfect. Any dissenting minister
may say and do as much.

These remarks, I know, are crude and unwrought,
but I do not lay much claim to accurate thinking. I
never judge system-wise of things, but fasten upon par-
ticulars. After all, there is a great deal in the book
that I must, for time, leave *unmentioned*, to deserve my
thanks for its own sake, as well as for the friendly
remembrances implied in the gift. I again return you
my thanks.

Pray present my love to Edith.   C. L.

LETTER XLII.]   *March* 20, 1799.

I am hugely pleased with your "Spider," "your old
freemason," as you call him. The first three stanzas are
delicious; they seem to me a compound of Burns and
Old Quarles, the kind of home-strokes, where more is felt
than strikes the ear; a terseness, a jocular pathos, which
makes one feel in laughter. The measure, too, is novel
and pleasing. I could almost wonder Robert Burns in
his lifetime never stumbled upon it. The fourth stanza
is less striking, as being less original. The fifth falls

off. It has no felicity of phrase, no old-fashioned phrase or feeling.

"Young hopes, and love's delightful dreams,"

savour neither of Burns nor Quarles; they seem more like shreds of many a modern sentimental sonnet. The last stanza hath nothing striking in it, if I except the two concluding lines, which are Burns all over. I wish, if you concur with me, these things could be looked to. I am sure this is a kind of writing, which comes tenfold better recommended to the heart, comes there more like a neighbour or familiar, than thousands of Hammels, and Zillahs, and Madelons. I beg you will send me the "Holly Tree," if it at all resemble this, for it must please me. I have never seen it. I love this sort of poems, that open a new intercourse with the most despised of the animal and insect race. I think this vein may be further opened. Peter Pindar hath very prettily apostrophised a fly; Burns hath his mouse and his louse; Coleridge less successfully hath made overtures of intimacy to a jackass, therein only following, at unresembling distance, Sterne, and greater Cervantes. Besides these, I know of no other examples of breaking down the partition between us and our "poor earth-born companions." It is sometimes revolting to be put in a track of feeling by other people, not one's own immediate thoughts, else I would persuade you, if I could (I am in earnest), to commence a series of these animals' poems, which might have a tendency to rescue some poor creatures from the antipathy of mankind. Some thoughts came across me: for instance—to a rat, to a toad, to a cockchafer, to a mole. People bake moles alive by a slow oven fire to cure consumption. Rats are, indeed, the most despised and contemptible parts of God's earth. I killed a rat the other day by punching him to pieces, and feel a weight of blood upon me to this hour. Toads you know are made to fly, and tumble down and crush all to pieces. Cockchafers are old sport. Then again to a worm, with an apostrophe to anglers, those patient tyrants, meek inflictors of pangs intolerable, cool devils; to an owl; to all snakes, with an apology for their poison; to a cat in boots or bladders. Your own fancy, if it takes a fancy to these hints, will suggest many more. A series of such poems, suppose them accompanied with plates descriptive of animal torments, cooks roasting lobsters, fishmongers crimping skates, etc. etc., would take excessively. I will willingly enter into a partnership in the plan with you: I think my heart and soul would go with it too—at least, give it a thought. My plan is but this minute come into my head; but it strikes me instantaneously as something new, good, and useful, full of pleasure, and full of moral. If old Quarles and Wither could live again, we would invite them into our firm. Burns hath done his part.

Poor Sam. Le Grice! I am afraid the world, and the camp, and the university, have spoilt him among them. 'Tis certain he had at one time a strong capacity of turning out something better. I knew him, and that not long since, when he had a most warm heart. I am ashamed of the indifference I have sometimes felt towards him. I think the devil is in one's heart. I am under obligations to that man for the warmest friendship, and heartiest sympathy exprest both by word and deed and tears for me, when I was in my greatest distress. But I have forgot that! as, I fear, he has nigh forgot the awful scenes which were before his eyes when he served the office of a comforter to me. No service was too mean or troublesome for him to perform. I can't think what but the devil, "that old spider," could have suck'd my heart so dry of its sense of all gratitude. If he does come in your way, Southey, fail not to tell him that I retain a most affectionate remembrance of his old friendliness, and an earnest wish to resume our intercourse. In this I am serious. I cannot recommend him to your society, because I am afraid whether he be quite worthy of it; but I have no right to dismiss him from *my* regard. He was at one time, and in the worst of times, my own familiar friend, and great comfort to me then. I have known him to play at cards with my father, meal-times excepted, literally all day long, in long days too, to save me from being teased by the old man, when I was not able to bear it.

God bless him for it, and God bless you, Southey.

C. L.

LETTER XLIII.]   *April* 20, 1799.

The following is a second extract from my tragedy—*that is to be*. 'Tis narrated by an old Steward to Margaret, orphan ward of Sir Walter Woodvil. . . . This and the Dying Lord I gave you are the only extracts I can give without mutilation. . . . I expect you to like the old woman's curse :—

> *Old Steward.*—One summer night, Sir Walter, as it chanced,
> Was pacing to and fro in the avenue
> That westward fronts our house,
> Among those aged oaks, said to have been planted
> Three hundred years ago
> By a neighbouring Prior of the Woodvil name, etc.

This is the extract I bragged of as superior to that I sent you from Marlow : perhaps you will smile. But I should like your remarks on the above, as you are deeper witch-read than I.

Yours ever,   C. LAMB.

Rob. Southey, Esq.,
  Mr. Cottle's, Bookseller,
    High Street, Bristol.

LETTER XLIV.]   *May* 20, 1799.

Dear Southey—I thank you heartily for your intended presents, but do by no means see the necessity you are under of burthening yourself thereby. You have read old Wither's Supersedeas to small purpose. You object to my pauses being at the end of my lines ; I do not know any great difficulty I should find in diversifying or changing my blank verse; but I go upon the model of Shakspeare in my Play, and endeavour after a colloquial ease and spirit, something like him. I could as easily imitate Milton's versification, but my ear and feeling would reject it, or any approaches to it, in the *drama*. I do not know whether to be glad or sorry that witches have been detected aforetimes in the shutting up of wombs. I certainly invented that conceit, and its coincidence with fact is accidental, for I never heard it. I have not seen those verses on Colonel Despard: I do not read any newspapers. Are they short to copy without much trouble? I should like to see them.

I just send you a few rhymes from my play, the only rhymes in it. A forest liver gives an account of his amusements :—

> What sports have you in the forest?
> Not many,—some few,—as thus,
> To see the sun to bed, to see him rise,
> Like some hot amourist with glowing eyes,
> Bursting the lazy bands of sleep that bound him;
> With all his fires and travelling glories round him; etc.

I love to anticipate charges of unoriginality : the first line is almost Shakspeare's :—

> "To have my love to bed and to arise."
>
> *A Midsummer Night's Dream.*

I think there is a sweetness in the versification not unlike some rhymes in that exquisite play, and the last line but three is yours :

> " An eye
> That met the gaze, or turn'd it knew not why."
>
> *Rosamund's Epistle.*

I shall anticipate all my play, and have nothing to show you. An idea for Leviathan: Commentators on Job have been puzzled to find out a meaning for Leviathan. 'Tis a whale, say some; a crocodile, say others. In my simple conjecture, Leviathan is neither more nor less than the Lord Mayor of London for the time being.

Rosamund sells well in London, malgré the non-revival of it. I sincerely wish you better health, and better health to Edith. Kind remembrances to her.

C. LAMB.

My sister Mary was never in better health or spirits than now.

LETTER XLV.] *October* 31, 1799.

Dear Southey—I have but just got your letter, being returned from Herts, where I have passed a few red-letter days with much pleasure. I would describe the county to you, as you have done by Devonshire; but alas! I am a poor pen at that same. I could tell you of an old house with a tapestry bedroom, the " Judgment of Solomon " composing one pannel, and " Actæon spying Diana naked " the other. I could tell of an old marble hall, with Hogarth's prints, and the Roman Cæsars in marble hung round. I could tell of a *wilderness*, and of a village church, and where the bones of my honoured grandam lie; but there are feelings which refuse to be translated, sulky aborigines, which will not be naturalised in another soil. Of this nature are old family faces, and scenes of infancy.

I have given your address, and the books you want, to the Arches; they will send them as soon as they can get them, but they do not seem quite familiar to their names. I have seen Gebor! Gebor aptly so denominated from Geborish, *quasi* Gibberish. But Gebor hath some lucid intervals. I remember darkly one beautiful simile veiled in uncouth phrases about the youngest daughter of the Ark. I shall have nothing to communicate, I fear, to the Anthology. You shall have some fragments of my play, if you desire them; but I think I would rather print it whole. Have you seen it, or shall I lend you a copy? I want your opinion of it.

I must get to business; so farewell. My kind remembrances to Edith.

C. LAMB.

To THOMAS MANNING.

LETTER XLVI.]   *December* 28, 1799.

Dear Manning—Having suspended my correspondence a decent interval, as knowing that even good things may be taken to satiety, a wish cannot but recur to learn whether you be still well and happy.   Do all things continue in the state I left them in Cambridge?

Do your night parties still flourish? and do you continue to bewilder your company with your thousand faces, running down through all the keys of idiotism (like Lloyd over his perpetual harpsichord), from the smile and the glimmer of half-sense and quarter-sense, to the grin and hanging lip of Betty Foy's own Johnny?   And does the face-dissolving curfew sound at twelve?   How unlike the great originals were your petty terrors in the postscript! not fearful enough to make a fairy shudder, or a Lilliputian fine lady, eight months full of child, miscarry. Yet one of them, which had more beast than the rest, I thought faintly resembled *one* of your brutifications.   But, seriously, I long to see your own honest Manning-face again.   I did not mean a pun,—your *man's* face, you will be apt to say, I know your wicked will to pun.   I cannot now write to Lloyd and you too; so you must convey as much interesting intelligence as this may contain, or be thought to contain, to him and Sophia, with my dearest love and remembrances.

By the by, I think you and Sophia both incorrect with regard to the *title* of the *play*.   Allowing your objection (which is not necessary, as pride may be, and is in real life often, cured by misfortunes not directly originating from its own acts, as Jeremy Taylor will tell you a naughty desire is sometimes sent to cure it; I know you read these *practical divines*)—but allowing your objection, does not the betraying of his father's secret directly spring from pride?—from the pride of wine, and a full heart, and a proud over-stepping of the ordinary rules of morality, and contempt of the prejudices of mankind, which are not to bind superior souls—"as *trust* in *the matter* of *secrets* all *ties* of *blood*, etc. etc., keeping of *promises*, the feeble mind's religion, binding our *morning knowledge* to the performance of what *last night's ignorance* spake"—does he not prate, that "*Great Spirits*" must do more than die for their friend? Does not the pride of wine incite him to display some evidence of friendship, which its own irregularity shall make great? This I know, that I meant his punishment not alone to be a cure for his daily and habitual *pride*, but the direct consequence and appropriate punishment of a particular act of pride.

If you do not understand it so, it is my fault in not explaining my meaning.

I have not seen Coleridge since, and scarcely expect to see him,—perhaps he has been at Cambridge.

Need I turn over to blot a fresh clean half-sheet, merely to say, what I hope you are sure of without my repeating it, that I would have you consider me, dear Manning, Your sincere friend,

C. LAMB.

LETTER XLVII.] *December* 1799.

Dear Manning—The particular kindness, even up to a degree of attachment, which I have experienced from you, seems to claim some distinct acknowledgment on my part. I could not content myself with a bare remembrance to you, conveyed in some letter to Lloyd.

Will it be agreeable to you, if I occasionally recruit your memory of me, which must else soon fade, if you consider the brief intercourse we have had. I am not likely to prove a troublesome correspondent. My scribbling days are past. I shall have no sentiments to communicate, but as they spring up from some living and worthy occasion.

I look forward with great pleasure to the performance of your promise, that we should meet in London early in the ensuing year. The century must needs commence auspiciously for me, that brings with it Manning's friendship, as an earnest of its after gifts.

I should have written before, but for a troublesome inflammation in one of my eyes, brought on by night travelling with the coach windows sometimes up.

What more I have to say shall be reserved for a letter to Lloyd. I must not prove tedious to you in my first outset, lest I should affright you by my ill-judged loquacity.

I am, yours most sincerely,   C. Lamb.

CHAPTER II.

1800–1809.

To SAMUEL TAYLOR COLERIDGE.

LETTER XLVIII.]   *January* 2, 1800.

DEAR COLERIDGE—Now I write, I cannot miss this opportunity of acknowledging the obligations myself, and the readers in general of that luminous paper, the *Morning Post*, are under to you for the very novel and exquisite manner in which you combined political with grammatical science in your yesterday's dissertation on Mr. Wyndham's unhappy composition. It must have been the death-blow to that ministry. I expect Pitt and Grenville to resign. More especially the delicate and Cottrellian grace with which you officiated, with a ferula for a white wand, as gentleman usher to the word "also," which it seems did not know its place.

I expect Manning of Cambridge in town to-night. Will you fulfil your promise of meeting him at my house? He is a man of a thousand. Give me a line to say what day, whether Saturday, Sunday, Monday, etc., and if Sara and the Philosopher can come. I am afraid if I did not at intervals call upon you, I should *never see you.* But I forget, the affairs of the nation engross your time and your mind.

Farewell.   C. L.

To THOMAS MANNING.

LETTER XLIX.]   *March* 1, 1800.

I hope by this time you are prepared to say, the
" Falstaff's letters " are a bundle of the sharpest, queerest,
profoundest humours, of any these juice-drained latter
times have spawned.   I should have advertised you, that
the meaning is frequently hard to be got at; and so are
the future guineas, that now lie ripening and aurifying in
the womb of some undiscovered Potosi; but dig, dig, dig,
dig, Manning!   I set to, with an unconquerable propul-
sion to write, with a lamentable want of what to write.
My private goings on are orderly as the movements of
the spheres, and stale as their music to angels' ears.
Public affairs—except as they touch upon me, and so
turn into private,—I cannot whip up my mind to feel
any interest in.   I grieve, indeed, that War, and Nature,
and Mr. Pitt, that hangs up in Lloyd's best parlour,
should have conspired to call up three necessaries, simple
commoners as our fathers knew them, into the upper
house of luxuries; bread, and beer, and coals, Manning.
But as to France and Frenchmen, and the Abbé Sièyes
and his constitutions, I cannot make these present times
present to me.   I read histories of the past, and I live in
them; although, to abstract senses, they are far less
momentous than the noises which keep Europe awake.
I am reading *Burnet's History of his own Times*.   Did
you ever read that garrulous, pleasant history?   He tells
his story like an old man past political service, bragging
to his sons on winter evenings of the part he took in
public transactions, when his "old cap was new."   Full
of scandal, which all true history is.   No palliatives;
but all the stark wickedness, that actually gives the
momentum to national actors.   Quite the prattle of age,
and out-lived importance.   Truth and sincerity staring
out upon you perpetually in *alto relievo*.   Himself a party

man—he makes you a party man. None of the cursed philosophical Humeian indifference, so cold, and unnatural, and inhuman! None of the cursed Gibbonian fine writing, so fine and composite! None of Dr. Robertson's periods with three members. None of Mr. Roscoe's sage remarks, all so apposite, and coming in so clever, lest the reader should have had the trouble of drawing an inference. Burnet's good old prattle I can bring present to my mind: I can make the revolution present to me: the French revolution, by a converse perversity in my nature, I fling as far *from* me. To quit this tiresome subject, and to relieve you from two or three dismal yawns, which I hear in spirit, I here conclude my more than commonly obtuse letter; dull, up to the dulness of a Dutch commentator on Shakspeare.

My love to Lloyd and to Sophia. C. L.

LETTER L.] *March* 17, 1800.

Dear Manning—I am living in a continuous feast. Coleridge has been with me now for nigh three weeks, and the more I see of him in the quotidian undress and relaxation of his mind, the more cause I see to love him, and believe him a *very good man*, and all those foolish impressions to the contrary fly off like morning slumbers. He is engaged in translations, which I hope will keep him this month to come. He is uncommonly kind and friendly to me. He ferrets me day and night to *do something*. He tends me, amidst all his own worrying and heart-oppressing occupations, as a gardener tends his young *tulip*. Marry come up; what a pretty similitude, and how like your humble servant! He has lugged me to the brink of engaging to a newspaper, and has suggested to me, for a first plan, the forgery of a supposed manuscript of Burton, the anatomist of melancholy. I have even written the introductory letter; and if I can pick up a few guineas this way, I feel they will be most *refreshing*, bread being so dear. If I go on with it, I will apprise you of it, as you may like to see my things! and the *tulip*, of all flowers, loves to be admired most.

Pray pardon me, if my letters do not come very thick. I am so taken up with one thing or other, that I cannot pick out (I will not say time, but) fitting times to write to you. My dear love to Lloyd and Sophia, and pray split this thin letter into three parts, and present them with the *two biggest* in my name.

They are my oldest friends; but, ever the new friend driveth out the old, as the ballad sings! God bless you all three! I would hear from Lloyd if I could.

Flour has just fallen nine shillings a sack: we shall be all too rich.

Tell Charles I have seen his mamma, and have almost fallen in love with *her*, since I mayn't with Olivia. She is so fine and graceful, a complete matron-lady-quaker. She has given me two little books. Olivia grows a charming girl—full of feeling, and thinner than she was; but I have not time to fall in love.

Mary presents her *general compliments*. She keeps in fine health.

Huzza boys! and down with the Atheists!

To SAMUEL TAYLOR COLERIDGE.

Letter LI.]   *May* 12, 1800.

My dear Coleridge—I don't know why I write, except from the propensity which misery has to tell her griefs. Hetty died on Friday night, about eleven o'clock, after eight days' illness. Mary, in consequence of fatigue and anxiety, is fallen ill again, and I was obliged to remove her yesterday. I am left alone in a house with nothing but Hetty's dead body to keep me company. To-morrow I bury her, and then I shall be quite alone, with nothing but a cat, to remind me that the house has been full of living beings like myself. My heart is quite sunk, and I don't know where to look for relief. Mary will get better again, but her constantly being liable to such relapses is dreadful; nor is it the least of our evils that her case and all our story is so well known around us. We are in a manner *marked*. Excuse my troubling you, but I have nobody by me to speak to me. I slept out last night, not being able to endure the change and the stillness; but I did not sleep well, and I must come back to my own bed. I am going to try and get a friend to come and be with me to-morrow. I am completely shipwrecked. My head is quite bad. I almost wish that Mary were dead. God bless you! Love to Sara and Hartley. C. LAMB.

Monday.

To THOMAS MANNING.

LETTER LII.]   (Before June) 1800.

Dear Manning—I feel myself unable to thank you sufficiently for your kind letter. It was doubly acceptable to me, both for the choice poetry and the kind honest prose which it contained. It was just such a letter as I should have expected from Manning.

I am in much better spirits than when I wrote last. I have had a very eligible offer to lodge with a friend in town. He will have rooms to let at Midsummer; by which time I hope my sister will be well enough to join me. It is a great object to me to live in town, where we shall be much more *private*, and to quit a house and a neighbourhood where poor Mary's disorder, so frequently recurring, has made us a sort of marked people. We can be nowhere private except in the midst of London. We shall be in a family where we visit very frequently; only my landlord and I have not yet come to a conclusion. He has a partner to consult. I am still on the tremble, for I do not know where we could go into lodgings that would not be, in many respects, highly exceptionable. Only God send Mary well again, and I hope all will be well! The prospect, such as it is, has made me quite happy. I have just time to tell you of it, as I know it will give you pleasure.—Farewell.   C. LAMB.

LETTER LIII.]   1800.

Dear Manning—Olivia is a good girl, and if you turn to my letter you will find that this very plea you set up to vindicate Lloyd, I had made use of as a reason why he should never have employed Olivia to make a copy of such a letter!—a letter I could not have sent to my Enemy's B——, if she had thought proper to seek me in the way of marriage. But you see it in one view, I in another. Rest you merry in your opinion! Opinion is a species of property; and though I am always desirous to share with my friend to a certain extent, I shall ever like to keep some tenets, and some property, properly my own. Some day, Manning, when we meet, substituting Corydon and fair Amaryllis, for Charles Lloyd and Mary Hayes, we will discuss together this question of moral feeling, "In what cases, and how far, sincerity is a virtue?" I do not mean Truth, a good Olivia-like creature, God bless her, who, meaning no offence, is always ready to give an answer when she is asked why she did so and so ; but a certain forward-talking half-brother of hers, Sincerity, that amphibious gentleman, who is so ready to perk up his obnoxious sentiments unasked into your notice, as Midas would his ears into your face, uncalled for. But I despair of doing anything by a letter in the way of explaining or coming to explanations. A good wish, or a pun, or a piece of secret history, may be well enough that way conveyed ; nay, it has been known, that intelligence of a turkey hath been conveyed by that medium, without much ambiguity. Godwin I am a good deal pleased with. He is a very well-behaved, decent man ; nothing very brilliant about him or imposing, as you may suppose; quite another guess sort of gentleman from what your anti-jacobin Christians imagine him.   I was well pleased to find he has neither horns nor claws; quite a tame creature, I assure you: a middle-sized man, both in stature and in understanding; whereas, from his noisy fame, you would expect to find a Briareus Centimanus, or a Tityus tall enough to pull Jupiter from his heavens.

I begin to think you atheists not quite so tall a species!   Coleridge inquires after you pretty often.   I wish to be the Pandar to bring you together again once before I die.   When we die, you and I must part; the sheep, you know, take the right-hand sign-post, and the goats the left.   Stript of its allegory, you must know the sheep are—I, the Apostles, and the martyrs, and the Popes, and Bishop Taylor, and Bishop Horsley, and Coleridge, etc. etc.   The goats are the atheists, and adulterers, and fornicators, and dumb dogs, and Godwin, and M——g, and that Thyestæan crew!   Egad, how my saintship sickens at the idea!   You shall have my play and the Falstaff's Letters in a day or two.   I will write to Ll[oyd] by this day's Post.

Pray, is it a part of your sincerity to show my letters to Lloyd? for, really, gentlemen ought to explain their virtues upon a first acquaintance, to prevent mistakes.

God bless you, Manning.   Take my trifling *as trifling;* and believe me, seriously and deeply,

Your well-wisher and friend,

C. L.

To SAMUEL TAYLOR COLERIDGE.

LETTER LIV.]   *June* 22, 1800.

By some fatality, unusual with me, I have mislaid the list of books which you want.   Can you, from memory, easily supply me with another?

I confess to Statius and I detained him wilfully, out

of a reverent regard to your style. Statius, they tell me, is turgid. As to that other Latin book, since you know neither its name nor subject, your wants (I crave leave to apprehend) cannot be very urgent. Meanwhile, dream that it is one of the lost Decades of Livy.

Your partiality to me has led you to form an erroneous opinion as to the measure of delight you suppose me to take in obliging. Pray be careful that it spread no further. 'Tis one of those heresies that is very pregnant. Pray rest more satisfied with the portion of learning which you have got, and disturb my peaceful ignorance as little as possible with such sort of commissions.

Did you never observe an appearance well known by the name of the man in the moon? Some scandalous old maids have set on foot a report that it is Endymion.

Your theory about the first awkward step a man makes being the consequence of learning to dance, is not universal. We have known many youths bred up at Christ's, who never learned to dance, yet the world imputes to them no very graceful motions. I remember there was little Hudson, the immortal preceptor of St. Paul's, to teach us our quavers; but, to the best of my recollection, there was no master of motions when we were at Christ's.

Farewell, in haste.   C. L.

Dear Coleridge—I have taken to-day, and delivered to L. and Co., *Imprimis :* your books, viz., three ponderous German dictionaries, one volume (I can find no more) of German and French ditto, sundry other German books unbound, as you left them, *Percy's Ancient Poetry*, and one volume of *Anderson's Poets.* I specify them, that you may not lose any. *Secundo :* a dressing gown (value, fivepence) in which you used to sit and look like a conjuror, when you were translating *Wallenstein.* A case of two razors, and a shaving-box and strap. This it has cost me a severe struggle to part with. They are in a brown-paper parcel, which also contains sundry papers and poems, sermons, *some few Epic* Poems,—one about Cain and Abel, which came from Poole, etc. etc., and also your tragedy; with one or two small German books, and that drama in which Got-fader performs. *Tertio:* a small oblong box containing *all your letters*, collected from all your waste papers, and which fill the said little box. All other waste papers, which I judged worth sending, are in the paper parcel aforesaid. But you will find *all* your letters in the box by themselves. Thus have I discharged my conscience and my lumber-room of all your property, save and except a folio entitled *Tyrrell's Bibliotheca Politica*, which you used to learn your politics out of when you wrote for the *Post, mutatis mutandis, i.e.,* applying past inferences to modern *data.* I retain that, because I am sensible I am very deficient in the politics myself; and I have torn up (don't be angry, waste paper has risen forty per cent., and I can't afford to buy it) all *Buonaparte's Letters, Arthur Young's Treatise on Corn,* and one or two more light-armed infantry, which I thought better suited the flippancy of London discussion than the dignity of Keswick thinking. Mary says you will be in a passion about them, when you come to miss them; but you must study philosophy. Read *Albertus Magnus de Chartis Amissis* five times over after phlebotomising,—'tis Burton's recipe,—and then be angry with an absent friend if you can.

Sara is obscure. Am I to understand by her letter, that she sends a *kiss* to Eliza Buckingham? Pray tell your wife that a note of interrogation on the superscription of a letter is highly ungrammatical: she proposes writing my name *Lambe?* Lamb is quite enough. I have had the Anthology, and like only one thing in it, *Lewti;* but of that the last stanza is detestable, the rest most exquisite: the epithet *enviable* would dash the finest poem. For God's sake (I never was more serious) don't make me ridiculous any more by terming me gentle-hearted in

print, or do it in better verses. It did well enough five
years ago when I came to see you, and was moral coxcomb
enough at the time you wrote the lines, to feed upon such
epithets; but, besides that, the meaning of "gentle" is
equivocal at best, and almost always means poor-spirited;
the very quality of gentleness is abhorrent to such vile
trumpetings. My *sentiment* is long since vanished. I
hope my *virtues* have done *sucking*. I can scarce think
but you meant it in joke. I hope you did, for I should
be ashamed to believe that you could think to gratify me
by such praise, fit only to be a cordial to some green-sick
sonneteer.

I have hit off the following in imitation of old English
poetry, which, I imagine, I am a dab at. The measure
is unmeasurable; but it most resembles that beautiful
ballad, the "Old and Young Courtier;" and in its feature
of taking the extremes of two situations for just parallel,
it resembles the old poetry certainly. If I could but
stretch out the circumstances to twelve more verses, *i.e.*,
if I had as much genius as the writer of that old song, I
think it would be excellent. It was to follow an imita-
tion of Burton in prose, which you have not seen. But
fate "and wisest Stewart" say No.

I can send you 200 pens and six quires of paper
immediately, if they will answer the carriage by coach.
It would be foolish to pack 'em up *cum multis libris et
cæteris;* they would all spoil. I only wait your commands
to coach them. I would pay five-and-forty thousand
carriages to read W.'s tragedy, of which I have heard so
much and seen so little—only what I saw at Stowey.
Pray give me an order in writing on Longman for
Lyrical Ballads. I have the first volume, and, truth to
tell, six shillings is a broad shot. I cram all I can in, to
save a multiplying of letters,—those pretty comets with
swinging tails.

I'll just crowd in, God bless you!   C. LAMB.

Wednesday night.

To THOMAS MANNING.

Dear Manning—I am going to ask a favour of you, and am at a loss how to do it in the most delicate manner. For this purpose I have been looking into Pliny's Letters, who is noted to have had the best grace in begging of all the ancients (I read him in the elegant translation of Mr. Melmoth), but not finding any case there exactly similar with mine, I am constrained to beg in my own barbarian way. To come to the point then, and hasten into the middle of things : have you a copy of your Algebra to give away? I do not ask it for myself; I have too much reverence for the Black Arts ever to approach thy circle, illustrious Trismegist! But that worthy man, and excellent Poet, George Dyer, made me a visit yesternight, on purpose to borrow one ; supposing, rationally enough, I must say, that you had made me a present of one before this ; the omission of which I take to have proceeded only from negligence ; but it is a fault. I could lend him no assistance. You must know he is just now diverted from the pursuit of the BELL LETTERS by a paradox, which he has heard his friend Frend (that learned mathematician) maintain, that the negative quantities of mathematicians were *meræ nugæ*, things scarcely *in rerum naturâ*, and smacking too much of mystery for gentlemen of Mr. Frend's clear Unitarian capacity. However, the dispute once set a-going, has seized violently on George's pericranick ; and it is necessary for his health that he should speedily come to a resolution of his doubts. He goes about teasing his friends with his new mathematics : he even frantically talks of purchasing Manning's Algebra, which shows him far gone ; for, to my knowledge, he has not been master of seven shillings a good time. George's pockets and ——'s brain are two things in nature which do not abhor a vacuum. . . . Now, if you could step in, in this trembling suspense of his reason, and he should find on Saturday morning, lying for him at the Porter's Lodge, Clifford's Inn (his safest address), Manning's Algebra, with a neat manuscription in the blank leaf, running thus "From the Author," it might save his wits, and restore the unhappy author to those studies of poetry and criticism which are at present suspended, to the infinite regret of the whole literary world. *N.B.*—Dirty backs, smeared leaves, and dogs' ears, will be rather a recommendation than otherwise. *N.B.*—He must have the book as soon as possible, or nothing can withhold him from madly purchasing the book on tick. . . . Then shall we see him sweetly restored to the chair of Longinus—to dictate in smooth and modest phrase the laws of verse; to prove that Theocritus first introduced the Pastoral, and Virgil and Pope brought it to its perfection; that Gray and Mason (who always hunt in couples in George's brain) have shown a great deal of poetical fire in their lyric poetry; that Aristotle's rules are not to be servilely followed, which George has shown to have imposed great shackles upon modern genius. His poems, I find, are to consist of two vols.—reasonable octavo; and a third book will exclusively contain criticisms, in which he asserts he has gone *pretty deeply* into the laws of blank verse and rhyme—epic poetry, dramatic and pastoral ditto—all which is to come out before Christmas. But, above all, he has *touched* most *deeply* upon the Drama, comparing the English with the modern German stage, their merits and defects. Apprehending that his *studies* (not to mention his *turn*, which I take to be chiefly towards the lyrical poetry) hardly qualified him for these disquisitions, I modestly inquired what plays he had read? I found by George's reply that he *had* read Shakspeare, but that was a good while since: he calls him a great but irregular genius, which I think to be an original and just remark.

Beaumont and Fletcher, Massinger, Ben Jonson, Shirley
Marlowe, Ford, and the worthies of Dodsley's Collection
—he confessed he had read none of them, but professed
his *intention* of looking through them all, so as to be
able to *touch* upon them in his book. So Shakspeare,
Otway, and I believe Rowe, to whom he was naturally
directed by Johnson's Lives, and these not read lately,
are to stand him in stead of a general knowledge of the
subject. God bless his dear absurd head!

By the by, did I not write you a letter with some-
thing about an invitation in it? But let that pass; I
suppose it is not agreeable.

N.B.—It would not be amiss if you were to accom-
pany your *present* with a dissertation on negative
quantities. C. L.

Letter LVII.] 1800.

George Dyer is an Archimedes, and an Archimagus,
and a Tycho Brahe, and a Copernicus; and thou art the
darling of the Nine, and midwife to their wandering babe
also! We take tea with that learned poet and critic on
Tuesday night, at half-past five, in his neat library. The
repast will be light and Attic, with criticism. If thou
couldst contrive to wheel up thy dear carcass on the
Monday, and after dining with us on tripe, calves' kid-
neys, or whatever else the Cornucopia of St. Clare may
be willing to pour out on the occasion, might we not
adjourn together to the Heathen's—thou with thy Black
Back, and I with some innocent volume of the Bell
Letters, Shenstone, or the like : it would make him wash
his old flannel gown (that has not been washed to my
knowledge since it has been *his*—Oh the long time!)
with tears of joy. Thou shouldst settle his scruples and
unravel his cobwebs, and sponge off the sad stuff that
weighs upon his dear wounded pia mater. Thou shouldst
restore light to his eyes, and him to his friends and the
public. Parnassus should shower her civic crowns upon

thee for saving the wits of a citizen !   I thought I saw a lucid interval in George the other night ; he broke in upon my studies just at tea-time, and brought with him Dr. Anderson, an old gentleman who ties his breeches' knees with packthread, and boasts that he has been disappointed by ministers.   The Doctor wanted to see *me ;* for I being a Poet, he thought I might furnish him with a copy of verses to suit his *Agricultural Magazine.*   The Doctor, in the course of the conversation, mentioned a poem called the " Epigoniad," by one Wilkie, an epic poem, in which there is not one tolerable good line all through, but every incident and speech borrowed from Homer.   George had been sitting inattentive, seemingly, to what was going on—hatching of negative quantities—when, suddenly, the name of his old friend Homer stung his pericranicks, and, jumping up, he begged to know where he could meet with Wilkie's works.   It was a curious fact, he said, that there should be such an epic poem and he not know of it ; and he *must* get a copy of it, as he was going to touch pretty deeply upon the subject of the Epic—and he was sure there must be some things good in a poem of 8000 lines !   I was pleased with this transient return of his reason and recurrence to his old ways of thinking : it gave me great hopes of a recovery, which nothing but your book can completely insure.   Pray come on Monday, if you *can*, and stay your own time.   I have a good large room with two beds in it, in the handsomest of which thou shalt repose a-nights, and dream of Spheroides.   I hope you will understand by the nonsense of this letter that I am *not* melancholy at the thoughts of thy coming : I thought it necessary to add this, because you love *precision.*   Take notice that our stay at Dyer's will not exceed eight o'clock ; after which our pursuits will be our own.   But indeed I think a little recreation among the Bell Letters and poetry will do you some service in the interval of severer studies.   I hope we shall fully discuss with George Dyer what I have never yet heard done to my satisfaction, the reason of Dr. Johnson's malevolent strictures on the higher species of the Ode.

LETTER LVIII.]   [*August* 9, 1800.]

Dear Manning—I suppose you have heard of Sophia Lloyd's good fortune, and paid the customary compliments to the parents. Heaven keep the new-born infant from star blasting and moon blasting, from epilepsy, marasmus, and the devil! May he live to see many days, and they good ones; some friends, and they *pretty regular correspondents!* with as much wit and wisdom as will eat their bread and cheese together under a poor roof without quarrelling! as much goodness as will earn heaven. Here I must leave off, my benedictory powers failing me.

And now, when shall I catch a glimpse of your honest face-to-face countenance again?—your fine *dogmatical sceptical* face by punch-light? Oh! one glimpse of the human face, and shake of the human hand, is better than whole reams of this cold, thin correspondence; yea, of more worth than all the letters that have sweated the fingers of sensibility, from Madame Sévigné and Balzac to Sterne and Shenstone.

Coleridge is settled with his wife and the young philosopher at Keswick, with the Wordsworths. They have contrived to spawn a new volume of lyrical ballads, which is to see the light in about a month, and causes no little excitement in the *literary world.* George Dyer too, that good-natured heathen, is more than nine months gone with his twin volumes of ode, pastoral, sonnet, elegy, Spenserian, Horatian, Akensidish, and Masonic verse. Clio prosper the birth! it will be twelve shillings out of somebody's pocket. I find he means to exclude "personal satire," so it appears by his truly original advertisement. Well, God put it into the hearts of the English gentry to come in shoals and subscribe to his poems, for

He never put a kinder heart into flesh of man than George Dyer's!

Now farewell, for dinner is at hand.   C. L.

                    August 11, 1800.

My dear fellow (*N.B.* mighty familiar of late!) for me to come to Cambridge now is one of heaven's impossibilities. Metaphysicians tell us, even it can work nothing which implies a contradiction. I can explain this by telling you that I am engaged to do double duty (this hot weather!) for a man who has taken advantage of this very weather to go and cool himself in "green retreats" all the month of August.

But for you to come to London instead!—muse upon it, revolve it, cast it about in your mind. I have a bed at your command. You shall drink rum, brandy, gin, aqua-vitæ, usquebaugh, or whiskey a' nights; and for the after-dinner trick, I have eight bottles of genuine port, which, mathematically divided, gives $1\frac{1}{7}$ for every day you stay, provided you stay a week. Hear John Milton sing,

> "Let Euclid rest and Archimedes pause."
> *Twenty-first Sonnet.*

And elsewhere,—

> "What neat repast shall feast us, light[1] and choice,
> Of Attic taste, with wine,[2] whence we may rise
> To hear the lute well touch'd, or artful voice
> Warble immortal notes and Tuscan air?"

Indeed the poets are full of this pleasing morality,—

> "Veni cito, Domine Manning!"

Think upon it. Excuse the paper; it is all I have.

C. Lamb.

[1] We poets generally give *light* dinners.

[2] No doubt the poet here alludes to port wine at 38s. the dozen.

To SAMUEL TAYLOR COLERIDGE.

LETTER LX.] *August* 14, 1800.

My head is playing all the tunes in the world, ringing such peals! It has just finished the "Merry Christ Church Bells," and absolutely is beginning "Turn again, Whittington," Buz, buz, buz, bum, bum, bum, wheeze, wheeze, wheeze, fen, fen, fen, tinky, tinky, tinky, *cr'annch*. I shall certainly come to be condemned at last. I have been drinking too much for two days running. I find my moral sense in the last stage of a consumption, and my religion getting faint. This is disheartening; but I trust the devil will not overpower me. In the midst of this infernal larum, Conscience is barking and yelping as loud as any of them. I have sat down to read over again your satire upon me in the *Anthology*, and I think I do begin to spy out something like beauty and design in it. I perfectly accede to all your alterations, and only desire that you had cut deeper, when your hand was in.

In sober truth, I cannot see any great truth in the little dialogue called "Blenheim." It is rather novel and pretty, but the thought is very obvious and is but poor prattle, a thing of easy imitation. *Pauper vult videri et est.*

In the next edition of the *Anthology* (which Phœbus avert, and those nine other wandering maids also!) please to blot out "gentle-hearted," and substitute drunken dog, ragged head, seld-shaven, odd-eyed, stuttering, or any other epithet which truly and properly belongs to the gentleman in question. And for Charles read Tom, or Bob, or Richard for mere delicacy. Hang you, I was beginning to forgive you, and believe in earnest that the lugging in of my proper name was purely unintentional on your part, when looking back for further conviction, stares me in the face, "Charles Lamb of the *India House*." Now I am convinced it was all done in malice, heaped sack-upon-sack, congregated, studied malice. You dog! your 141st page shall not save you. I own I was just ready to acknowledge that there is a something not unlike good poetry in that page, if you had not run into the unintelligible abstraction-fit about the manner of the Deity's making spirits perceive his presence. No created thing alive can receive any honour from such thin show-box attributes. By the by, where did you pick up that scandalous piece of private history about the angel and the Duchess of Devonshire? If it is a fiction of your own, why truly it was a very modest one *for you*. Now I do affirm, that "Lewti" is a very beautiful poem. I *was* in earnest when I praised it. It describes a silly species of one not the wisest of passions. *Therefore* it cannot deeply affect a disenthralled mind. But such imagery, such novelty, such delicacy, and such versification never got into an *Anthology* before. I am only sorry that the cause of all the passionate complaint is not greater than the trifling circumstance of Lewti being out of temper one day. "Ganlberto" certainly has considerable originality, but sadly wants finishing. It is, as it is, one of the very best in the book. Next to "Lewti" I like the "Raven," which has a good deal of humour. I was pleased to see it again, for you once sent it me, and I have lost the letter which contained it. Now I am on the subject of Anthologies, I must say I am sorry the old pastoral way has fallen into disrepute. The gentry which now indite sonnets are certainly the legitimate descendants of the ancient shepherds. The same simpering face of description, the old family face, is visibly continued in the line. Some of their ancestors' labours are yet to be found in Allan Ramsay's and Jacob Tonson's Miscellanies. But miscellanies decaying, and the old pastoral way dying of mere want, their successors (driven from their paternal acres) now-a-days settle and lie upon Magazines and Anthologies. This race of men are uncommonly addicted to superstition. Some of them are idolators, and worship the moon. Others deify qualities, as Love, Friendship, Sensibility; or bare accidents, as Solitude. Grief and Melancholy have their respective altars and temples among them, as the heathens builded theirs to Mors, Febris, Pallor, etc. They all agree in ascribing a peculiar sanctity to the number 14. One of their own legislators affirmeth, that whatever exceeds that number "encroacheth upon the province of the elegy"—*vice versa*, whatever "cometh short of that number abutteth upon the premises of the epigram." I have been able to discover but few *images* in their temples, which, like the caves of Delphos of old, are famous for giving *echoes*. They impute a religious importance to the letter O, whether because by its round-ness it is thought to typify the moon, their principal goddess, or for its analogies to their own labours, all ending where they began, or for whatever other high and mystical reference, I have never been able to discover, but I observe they never begin their invocations to their gods without it, except indeed one insignificant sect among them, who use the Doric A, pronounced like Ah! broad, instead. These boast to have restored the old Dorian mood.

Now I am on the subject of poetry, I must announce to you, who doubtless in your remote part of the island have not heard tidings of so great a blessing, that George Dyer hath prepared two ponderous volumes full of poetry and criticism. They impend over the town, and are threatened to fall in the Winter. The first volume con-tains every sort of poetry, except personal satire, which George, in his truly original prospectus, renounceth for ever, whimsically foisting the intention in between the price of his book and the proposed number of subscribers. (If I can, I will get you a copy of his *handbill*.) He has tried his *vein* in every species besides—the Spenserian, Thomsonian, Masonic, and Akensidish more especially. The second volume is all criticism; wherein he demon-strates to the entire satisfaction of the literary world, in a way that must silence all reply for ever, that the

Pastoral was introduced by Theocritus, and polished by Virgil and Pope; that Gray and Mason (who always hunt in couples in George's brain) have a good deal of poetical fire and true lyric genius; that Cowley was ruined by excess of wit (a warning to all moderns); that Charles Lloyd, Charles Lamb, and William Wordsworth, in later days, have struck the true chords of poesy. O George, George! with a head uniformly wrong, and a heart uniformly right, that I had power and might equal to my wishes : then I would call the gentry of thy native island, and they should come in troops, flocking at the sound of thy prospectus trumpet, and crowding who shall be first to stand in thy list of subscribers ! I can only put twelve shillings into thy pocket (which, I will answer for them, will not stick there long), out of a pocket almost as bare as thine. Is it not a pity so much fine writing should be erased? But, to tell the truth, I began to scent that I was getting into that sort of style which Longinus and Dionysius Halicarnassus aptly call "the affected."   C. L.

To THOMAS MANNING.

Letter LXI.]   *August* 22, 1800.

Dear Manning—You needed not imagine any apology necessary. Your fine hare and fine birds (which are just now dangling by our kitchen blaze) discourse most eloquent music in your justification. You just nicked my palate. For with all due decorum and leave may it be spoken, my worship hath taken physic to-day, and being low and puling, requireth to be pampered. Foh ! how beautiful and strong those buttered onions come to my nose ! For you know we extract a divine spirit of gravy from those materials, which, duly compounded with a consistence of bread and cream (y'clept bread-sauce), each to each giving double grace, do mutually illustrate and set off (as skilful gold foils to rare jewels) your partridge, pheasant, woodcock, snipe, teal, widgeon. and the other lesser daughters of the ark. My friendship, struggling with my carnal and fleshly prudence (which suggests that a bird a man is the proper allotment in such cases), yearneth sometimes to have thee here to pick a wing or so. I question if your Norfolk sauces match our London culinarie.

George Dyer has introduced me to the table of an agreeable old gentleman, Dr. Anderson, who gives hot legs of mutton and grape pies at his sylvan lodge at Isleworth ; where, in the middle of a street, he has shot up a wall most preposterously before his small dwelling, which, with the circumstance of his taking several panes of glass out of bed-room windows (for air), causeth his neighbours to speculate strangely on the state of the good man's pericranicks. Plainly, he lives under the reputation of being deranged. George does not mind this circumstance ; he rather likes him the better for it. The Doctor, in his pursuits, joins agricultural to poetical science, and has set George's brains mad about the old Scotch writers, Barbour, Douglas's Æneid, Blind Harry, etc. We returned home in a return postchaise (having dined with the Doctor), and George kept wondering and wondering, for eight or nine turnpike miles, what was the name, and striving to recollect the name, of a poet anterior to Barbour. I begged to know what was remaining of his works. "There is nothing *extant* of his works, Sir ; but by all accounts he seems to have been a fine genius !" This fine genius, without anything to show for it, or any title beyond George's courtesy, without even a name ; and Barbour, and Douglas, and Blind Harry, now are the predominant sounds in George's pia mater, and their buzzings exclude politics, criticism, and algebra—the late lords of that illustrious lumber-room. Mark, he has never read any of these books, but is impatient till he reads them *all* at the Doctor's suggestion. Poor Dyer ! his friends should be careful what sparks they let fall into such inflammable matter.

Could I have my will of the heathen, I would lock him up from all access of new ideas; I would exclude all critics that would not swear me first (upon their Virgil) that they would feed him with nothing but the old, safe, familiar notions and sounds (the rightful aborigines of his brain)—Gray, Akenside, and Mason. In these sounds, reiterated as often as possible, there could be nothing painful, nothing distracting.

God bless me, here are the birds, smoking hot! All that is gross and unspiritual in me rises at the sight!

Avaunt friendship, and all memory of absent friends!

C. LAMB.

To SAMUEL TAYLOR COLERIDGE.

LETTER LXII.   [*August or September*] 1800.

Dear Coleridge—Soon after I wrote to you last, an offer was made me by Gutch (you must remember him, at Christ's; you saw him, slightly, one day with Thomson at our house), to come and lodge with him, at his house in Southampton Buildings, Chancery Lane. This was a very comfortable offer to me, the rooms being at a reasonable rent, and including the use of an old servant, besides being infinitely preferable to ordinary lodgings *in our case*, as you must perceive. As Gutch knew all our story and the perpetual liability to a recurrence in my sister's disorder, probably to the end of her life, I certainly think the offer very generous and very friendly. I have got three rooms (including servant) under £34 a year. Here I soon found myself at home; and here, in six weeks after, Mary was well enough to join me. So we are once more settled. I am afraid we are not placed out of the reach of future interruptions. But I am determined to take what snatches of pleasure we can between the acts of our distressful drama. . . . I have passed two days at Oxford, on a visit which I have long put off, to Gutch's family. The sight of the Bodleian Library, and, above all, a fine bust of Bishop Taylor, at All Souls', were particularly gratifying to me. Unluckily, it was not a family where I could take Mary with me, and I am afraid there is something of dishonesty in any pleasures I take without *her*. She never goes anywhere. I do not know what I can add to this letter. I hope you are better by this time; and I desire to be affectionately remembered to Sara and Hartley.

I expected before this to have had tidings of another little philosopher. Lloyd's wife is on the point of favouring the world.

Have you seen the new edition of Burns? his posthumous works and letters? I have only been able to procure the first volume, which contains his life—very confusedly and badly written, and interspersed with dull pathological and *medical* discussions. It is written by a Dr. Currie. Do you know the well-meaning doctor! Alas, *ne sutor ultra crepidam!*

I hope to hear again from you very soon. Godwin is gone to Ireland on a visit to Grattan. Before he went I passed much time with him, and he has showed me particular attentions: N.B. A thing I much like. Your books are all safe : only I have not thought it necessary to fetch away your last batch, which I understand are at Johnson's, the bookseller, who has got quite as much room, and will take as much care of them as myself ; and you can send for them immediately from him.

I wish you would advert to a letter I sent you at Grassmere about *Christabel*, and comply with my request contained therein.

Love to all friends round Skiddaw.   C. LAMB.

Letter LXIII.]   *August* 26, 1800.

How do you like this little epigram? It is not my writing, nor had I any finger in it. If you concur with me in thinking it very elegant and very original, I shall

be tempted to name the author to you.   I will just hint
that it is almost or quite a first attempt.

HELEN.

HIGH-BORN Helen, round your dwelling
  These twenty years I've paced in vain :
Haughty beauty, thy lover's duty
  Hath been to glory in his pain.

High-born Helen, proudly telling
  Stories of thy cold disdain ;
I starve, I die, now you comply,
  And I no longer can complain.

These twenty years I've lived on tears,
  Dwelling for ever on a frown ;
On sighs I've fed, your scorn my bread ;
  I perish now you kind are grown.

Can I, who loved my beloved
  But for the scorn " was in her eye,"
Can I be moved for my beloved,
  When she " returns me sigh for sigh ?"

In stately pride, by my bed-side,
  High-born Helen's portrait's hung ;
Deaf to my praise, my mournful lays
  Are nightly to the portrait sung.

To that I weep, nor ever sleep,
  Complaining all night long to her,
Helen, grown old, no longer cold,
  Said, " You to all men I prefer."

By the by, I have a sort of recollection that some-
body, I think *you,* promised me a sight of Wordsworth's
Tragedy.   I should be very glad of it just now ; for I
have got Manning with me, and should like to read it
with him.   But this, I confess, is a refinement.   Under
any circumstances, alone, in Cold-Bath prison, or in the
desert island, just when Prospero and his crew had set
off, with Caliban in a cage, to Milan, it would be a treat
to me to read that play.   Manning has read it, so has

Lloyd, and all Lloyd's family; but I could not get him to betray his trust by giving *me* a sight of it. Lloyd is sadly deficient in some of those virtuous vices. I have just lit upon a most beautiful fiction of Hell punishments by the author of *Hurlothrumbo*, a mad farce. The inventor imagines that in Hell there is a great caldron of hot water, in which a man can scarce hold his finger, and an immense sieve over it, into which the probationary souls are put—

> "And all the little souls
> Pop thro' the riddle holes!"

George Dyer is the only literary character I am happily acquainted with. The oftener I see him, the more deeply I admire him. He is goodness itself. If I could but calculate the precise date of his death, I would write a novel on purpose to make George the hero. I could hit him off to a hair.

George brought a Dr. Anderson to see me. The doctor is a very pleasant old man, a great genius for agriculture, one that ties his breeches-knees with pack-thread, and boasts of having had disappointments from ministers. The doctor happened to mention an epic poem by one Wilkie, called the *Epigoniad*, in which he assured us there is not one tolerable line from beginning to end, but that all the characters, incidents, etc., are verbally copied from *Homer*. George, who had been sitting quite inattentive to the Doctor's criticism, no sooner heard the sound of *Homer* strike his pericranicks, than up he gets, and declares he must see that poem immediately: where was it to be had? An epic poem of 8000 lines, and *he* not hear of it! There must be some good things in it, and it was necessary he should see it, for he had touched pretty deeply upon that subject in his criticisms on the Epic. George has touched pretty deeply upon the Lyric, I find; he has also prepared a dissertation on the Drama and the comparison of the English and German theatres. As I rather doubted his competency to do the latter, knowing that his peculiar *turn* lies in the lyric species of composition, I questioned George what English plays he had read. I found that he *had* read Shakspeare (whom he calls an original, but irregular, genius); but it was a good while ago; and he has dipped into Rowe and Otway, I suppose having found their names in *Johnson's Lives* at full length; and upon this slender ground he has undertaken the task. He never seemed even to have heard of Fletcher, Ford, Marlowe, Massinger, and the worthies of Dodsley's collection; but he is to read all these, to prepare him for bringing out his "Parallel" in the Winter. I find he is also determined to vindicate poetry from the shackles which Aristotle and some others have imposed upon it, which is very good-natured of him, and very necessary just now. Now I am *touching* so *deeply* upon poetry, can I forget that I have just received from Cottle a magnificent copy of his Guinea *Alfred*. Four-and-twenty books to read in the dog-days! I got as far as the Mad Monk the first day, and fainted. Mr. Cottle's genius strongly points him to the *Pastoral*, but his inclinations divert him perpetually from his calling. He imitates Southey, as Rowe did Shakspeare, with his "Good morrow to ye; good master Lieutenant." Instead of *a* man, *a* woman, *a* daughter, he constantly writes, one a man, one a woman, one his daughter. Instead of *the* king, *the* hero, he constantly writes, he the king, he the hero; two flowers of rhetoric, palpably from the "Joan." But Mr. Cottle soars a higher pitch: and when he *is* original, it is in a most original way indeed. His terrific scenes are indefatigable. Serpents, asps, spiders, ghosts, dead bodies, staircases made of nothing, with adders' tongues for bannisters. What a brain he must have! He puts as many plums in his pudding as my grandmother used to do;—and then his emerging from Hell's horrors into light, and treading on pure flats of this earth—for twenty-three books together!   C. L.

To THOMAS MANNING.

LETTER LXIV.] *October* 5, 1800.

C. L.'s moral sense presents her compliments to Doctor Manning, is very thankful for his medical advice, but is happy to add that her disorder has died of itself.

Dr. Manning, Coleridge has left us, to go into the North, on a visit to Wordsworth. With him have flown all my splendid prospects of engagement with the *Morning Post*, all my visionary guineas, the deceitful wages of unborn scandal. In truth, I wonder you took it up so seriously. All my intention was but to make a little sport with such public and fair game as Mr. Pitt, Mr. Wilberforce, Mrs. Fitzherbert, the Devil, etc.— gentry dipped in Styx all over, whom no paper-javelin-lings can touch. To have made free with these cattle where was the harm? 'twould have been but giving a polish to lamp-black, not nigrifying a negro primarily. After all, I cannot but regret my involuntary virtue. Damn virtue that's thrust upon us; it behaves itself with such constraint, till conscience opens the window and lets out the goose. I had struck off two imitations of Burton, quite abstracted from any modern allusions, which it was my intent only to lug in from time to time to make 'em popular.

Stuart has got these, with an introductory letter; but, not hearing from him, I have ceased from my labours, but I write to him to-day to get a final answer. I am afraid they won't do for a paper. Burton is a scarce gentleman, not much known, else I had done 'em pretty well.

I have also hit off a few lines in the name of Burton, being a "Conceit of Diabolic Possession." Burton was a man often assailed by deepest melancholy, and at other times much given to laughing and jesting, as is the way with melancholy men. I will send them to you: they were almost extempore, and no great things; but you will indulge them. Robert Lloyd is come to town. Priscilla meditates going to see *Pizarro* at Drury Lane to-night (from her uncle's), under cover of coming to dine with me . . . *heu tempora! heu mores!*—I have barely time to finish, as I expect her and Robin every minute. —Yours as usual. C. L.

To SAMUEL TAYLOR COLERIDGE.

LETTER LXV.]   *October* 9, 1800.

I suppose you have heard of the death of Amos Cottle. I paid a solemn visit of condolence to his brother, accompanied by George Dyer, of burlesque memory. I went, trembling to see poor Cottle so immediately upon the event. He was in black; and his younger brother was also in black. Everything wore an aspect suitable to the respect due to the freshly dead. For some time after our entrance, nobody spake till George modestly put in a question, whether *Alfred* was likely to sell. This was Lethe to Cottle, and his poor face, wet with tears, and his kind eye brightened up in a moment. Now I felt it was my cue to speak. I had to thank him for a present of a magnificent copy, and had promised to send him my remarks,—the least thing I could do; so I ventured to suggest, that I perceived a considerable improvement he had made in his first book since the state in which he first read it to me. Joseph, who till now had sat with his knees cowering in by the fireplace, wheeled about, and with great difficulty of body shifted the same round to the corner of a table where I was sitting, and first stationing one thigh over the other, which is his sedentary mood, and placidly fixing his benevolent face right against mine, waited my observations. At that moment it came strongly into my mind, that I had got Uncle Toby before me, he looked so kind and so good. I could not say an unkind thing of *Alfred*. So I set my memory to work to recollect what was the name of Alfred's Queen, and with some adroitness recalled the well-known sound to Cottle's ears of Alswitha. At that moment I could perceive that Cottle had forgot his brother was so lately become a blessed spirit. In the language of mathematicians the author was as 9, the brother as 1. I felt my cue, and strong pity working at the root, I went to work, and beslabber'd *Alfred* with most unqualified praise, or only qualifying my praise by the occasional politic interposition of an exception taken against trivial faults, slips, and human imperfections, which, by removing the appearance of insincerity, did but in truth heighten the relish. Perhaps I might have spared that refinement, for Joseph was in a humour to hope and believe *all things*. What I said was beautifully supported, corroborated, and confirmed by the stupidity of his brother on my left hand, and by George on my right, who has an utter incapacity of comprehending that there can be anything bad in poetry. All poems are *good* poems to George ; all men are *fine geniuses*. So what with my actual memory, of which I made the most, and Cottle's own helping me out, for I *really* had forgotten a good deal of *Alfred*, I made shift to discuss the most essential parts entirely to the satisfaction of its author, who repeatedly declared that he loved nothing better than *candid* criticism. Was I a candid grayhound now for all this ? or did I do right ? I believe I did. The effect was luscious to my conscience. For all the rest of the evening Amos was no more heard of, till George revived the subject by inquiring whether some account should not be drawn up by the friends of the deceased to be inserted in Phillips's Monthly Obituary; adding, that Amos was estimable both for his head and heart, and would have made a fine poet if he had lived. To the expediency of this measure Cottle fully assented, but could not help adding that he always thought that the qualities of his brother's heart exceeded those of his head. I believe his brother, when living, had formed precisely the same idea of him; and I apprehend the world will assent to both judgments. I rather guess that the Brothers were poetical rivals. I judged so when I saw them together. Poor Cottle, I must leave him after his short dream, to muse again upon his poor brother, for whom I am sure in secret he will yet shed many a tear. Now send me in return some Greta news.   C. L.

To WORDSWORTH.

LETTER LXVI.]   *October* 13, 1800.

Dear Wordsworth—I have not forgot your commissions. But the truth is (and why should I not confess it?) I am not plethorically abounding in cash at this present. Merit, God knows, is very little rewarded; but it does not become me to speak of myself. My motto is "contented with little, yet wishing for more." Now, the books you wish for would require some pounds, which, I am sorry to say, I have not by me; so I will say at once, if you will give me a draft upon your town banker for any sum you propose to lay out, I will dispose of it to the very best of my skill in choice old books, such as my own soul loveth. In fact, I have been waiting for the liquidation of a debt to enable myself to set about your commission handsomely; for it is a scurvy thing to cry, "Give me the money first," and I am the first of the family of the Lambs that have done it for many centuries; but the debt remains as it was, and my old friend that I accommodated has generously forgot it! The books which you want, I calculate at about £8. Ben Jonson is a guinea book. Beaumont and Fletcher, in folio, the right folio, not now to be met with; the octavos are about £3. As to any other dramatists, I do not know where to find them, except what are in Dodsley's Old Plays, which are about £3 also. Massinger I never saw but at one shop, and it is now gone; but one of the editions of Dodsley contains

about a fourth (the best) of his plays. Congreve, and
the rest of King Charles's moralists, are cheap and acces-
sible.   The works on Ireland I will inquire after; but I
fear Spenser's is not to be had apart from his poems; I
never saw it.   But you may depend upon my sparing no
pains to furnish you as complete a library of old poets and
dramatists as will be prudent to buy; for, I suppose you
do not include the £20 edition of *Hamlet*, single play,
which Kemble has.   Marlowe's plays and poems are
totally vanished; only one edition of Dodsley retains one,
and the other two of his plays: but John Ford is the
man after Shakspeare.   Let me know your will and
pleasure soon, for I have observed, next to the pleasure
of buying a bargain for one's self, is the pleasure of per-
suading a friend to buy it.   It tickles one with the image
of an imprudency, without the penalty usually annexed.

C. LAMB.

To THOMAS MANNING.

LETTER LXVII.]   *October* 16, 1800.

Dear Manning—Had you written one week before you
did, I certainly should have obeyed your injunction; you
should have seen me before my letter.   I will explain to
you my situation.   There are six of us in one department.
Two of us (within these four days) are confined with
severe fevers; and two more, who belong to the Tower
Militia, expect to have marching orders on Friday.   Now
six are absolutely necessary.   I have already asked and
obtained two young hands to supply the loss of the
feverites.   And, with the other prospect before me, you
may believe I cannot decently ask leave of absence for
myself.   All I can promise (and I do promise, with the
sincerity of St. Peter, and the contrition of sinner Peter
if I fail) that I will come *the very first spare week*, and
go nowhere till I have been at Cambridge.   No matter

if you are in a state of pupilage when I come; for I can employ myself in Cambridge very pleasantly in the mornings. Are there not libraries, halls, colleges, books, pictures, statues? I wish you had made London in your way. There is an exhibition quite uncommon in Europe, which could not have escaped *your genius*,—a live rattle-snake, ten feet in length, and the thickness of a big leg. I went to see it last night by candlelight. We were ushered into a room very little bigger than ours at Pentonville. A man and woman and four boys live in this room, joint tenants with nine snakes, most of them such as no remedy has been discovered for their bite. We walked into the middle, which is formed by a half-moon of wired boxes, all mansions of *snakes*—whip-snakes, thunder-snakes, pig-nose-snakes, American vipers, and *this monster*. He lies curled up in folds. Immediately a stranger entered (for he is used to the family, and sees them play at cards,) he set up a rattle like a watchman's in London, or near as loud, and reared up a head, from the midst of these folds, like a toad, and shook his head, and showed every sign a snake can show of irritation. I had the foolish curiosity to strike the wires with my finger, and the devil flew at me with his toad-mouth wide open; the inside of his mouth is quite white. I had got my finger away, nor could he well have bit me with his big mouth, which would have been certain death in five minutes. But it frightened me so much, that I did not recover my voice for a minute's space. I forgot, in my fear, that he was secured. You would have forgot too, for 'tis incredible how such a monster can be confined in small gauzy-looking wires. I dreamed of snakes in the night. I wish to heaven you could see it. He absolutely swelled with passion to the bigness of a large thigh. I could not retreat without infringing on another box; and just behind, a little devil not an inch from my back had got his nose out, with some difficulty and pain, quite through the bars! He was soon taught better manners. All the snakes were curious, and objects of terror: but this monster, like Aaron's serpent, swallowed up the impression of the rest. He opened his cursed mouth, when he made at me, as wide as his head was broad. I hallooed out quite loud, and felt pains all over my body with the fright.

I have had the felicity of hearing George Dyer read out one book of the *Farmer's Boy*. I thought it rather childish. No doubt, there is originality in it (which, in your self-taught geniuses, is a most rare quality, they generally getting hold of some bad models, in a scarcity of books, and forming their taste on them), but no *selection*. *All* is described.

Mind, I have only heard read one book.—Yours sincerely, Philo-Snake, C. L.

LETTER LXVIII.] *November* 3, 1800.

Ecquid meditatur Archimedes? What is Euclid doing? What hath happened to learned Trismegist? Doth he take it in ill part, that his humble friend did not comply with his courteous invitation? Let it suffice, I could not come. Are impossibilities nothing?—be they abstractions of the intellect?—or not (rather) most sharp and mortifying realities? nuts in the Will's mouth too hard for her to crack? brick and stone walls in her way, which she can by no means eat through? sore lets, *impedimenta viarum* no thoroughfares? *racemi nimium alte pendentes?* Is the phrase classic? I allude to the grapes in Æsop, which cost the fox a strain, and gained the world an aphorism. Observe the superscription of this letter. In adapting the size of the letters, which constitute *your* name and Mr. *Crisp's* name respectively, I had an eye to your different stations in life. 'Tis truly curious, and must be soothing to an *aristocrat*. I wonder it has never been hit on before my time. I have made an acquisition latterly of a *pleasant hand*, one Rickman, to whom I was introduced by George Dyer, not the most flattering auspices under which one man can be introduced to another. George brings all sorts of people together, setting up a sort of agrarian law, or common property, in matter of society ; but for once he has done me a great pleasure, while he was only pursuing a principle, as *ignes fatui may* light you home. This Rickman lives in our Buildings, immediately opposite our house ; the finest fellow to drop in a' nights, about nine or ten o'clock— cold bread and cheese time—just in the *wishing* time of the night, when you *wish* for somebody to come in, without a distinct idea of a probable anybody. Just in the nick, neither too early to be tedious, nor too late to sit a reasonable time. He is a most pleasant hand ; a fine rattling fellow, has gone through life laughing at solemn apes ;—himself hugely literate, oppressively full of information in all stuff of conversation, from matter of fact to Xenophon and Plato—can talk Greek with Porson, politics with Thelwall, conjecture with George Dyer, nonsense with me, and anything with anybody ; a great farmer, somewhat concerned in an agricultural magazine ; reads no poetry but Shakspeare ; very intimate with Southey, but never reads his poetry ; relishes George Dyer ; thoroughly penetrates into the ridiculous wherever found ; understands the *first time* (a great desideratum in common minds)—you need never twice speak to him ; does not want explanations, translations, limitations, as Professor Godwin does when you make an assertion ; *up* to anything ; *down* to everything ; whatever *sapit hominem.* A perfect *man.* All this farrago, which must perplex you to read, and has put me to a little trouble to *select,* only proves how impossible it is to describe a *pleasant hand.* You must see Rickman to know him, for he is a species in one ; a new class ; an exotic ; any slip of which I am proud to put in my garden-pot ; the clearest headed fellow ; fullest of matter, with least verbosity. If there be any alloy in my fortune to have met with such a man, it is that he commonly divides his time between town and country, having some foolish family ties at Christchurch, by which means he can only gladden our London hemisphere with returns of light.   He is now going for six weeks.

At last I have written to Kemble, to know the event of my play, which was presented last Christmas.   As I suspected, came an answer back that the copy was lost, and could not be found—no hint that anybody had to this day ever looked into it—with a courteous (reasonable!) request of another copy (if I had one by me), and a promise of a definite answer in a week.   I could not resist so facile and moderate a demand; so scribbled out another, omitting sundry things, such as the witch story, about half of the forest scene (which is too leisurely for story), and transposing that soliloquy about England getting drunk, which, like its reciter, stupidly stood alone, nothing prevenient or antevenient; and cleared away a good deal besides ; and sent this copy, written *all out* (with alterations, etc., *requiring judgment*) in one day and a half!   I sent it last night, and am in weekly expectation of the tolling bell and death-warrant.

This is all my London news.   Send me some from the *banks of Cam*, as the poets delight to speak, especially George Dyer, who has no other name nor idea nor definition of Cambridge.   Its being a market town, sending members to Parliament, never entered into his definition. It was and is simply the banks of the Cam, or the fair Cam, as Oxford is the banks of the Isis, or the fair Isis. Yours in all humility, most illustrious Trismegist,

C. LAMB.

(Read on ; there's more at the bottom.)

You ask me about the *Farmer's Boy*.   Don't you think the fellow who wrote it (who is a shoemaker) has a poor mind ?   Don't you find he is always silly about *poor Giles*, and those abject kind of phrases, which mark a man that looks up to wealth ?   None of Burns's poet dignity.   What do you think ?   I have just opened him; but he makes me sick.

Dyer knows the shoemaker, a damn'd stupid hound in company ; but George promises to introduce him indiscriminately to all friends.

LETTER LXIX.]   *November* 28, 1800.

Dear Manning—I have received a very kind invitation from Lloyd and Sophia, to go and spend a month with them at the Lakes. Now it fortunately happens (which is so seldom the case) that I have spare cash by me, enough to answer the expenses of so long a journey ; and I am determined to get away from the office by some means. The purpose of this letter is to request of you (my dear friend), that you will not take it unkind if I decline my proposed visit to Cambridge *for the present.* Perhaps I shall be able to take Cambridge *in my way,* going or coming. I need not describe to you the expectations which such an one as myself, pent up all my life in a dirty city, have formed of a tour to the Lakes. Consider Grasmere ! Ambleside ! Wordsworth ! Coleridge ! I hope you will. Hills, woods, lakes, and mountains, to the devil. I will eat snipes with thee, Thomas Manning. Only confess, confess, a *bite.*

P.S.—I think you named the 16th ; but was it not modest of Lloyd to send such an invitation ! It shows his knowledge of *money* and *time.* I should be loth to think he meant

> " Ironic satire sidelong sklented
>   On my poor pursie."—BURNS.

For my part, with reference to my friends northward, I must confess that I am not romance-bit about *Nature.* The earth, and sea, and sky (when all is said), is but as a house to dwell in. If the inmates be courteous, and good liquors flow like the conduits at an old coronation, if they can talk sensibly, and feel properly, I have no need to stand staring upon the gilded looking-glass (that strained my friend's purse-strings in the purchase) nor his five-shilling print, over the mantelpiece, of old Nabbs the carrier (which only betrays his false taste). Just as important to me (in a sense) is all the furniture of my world; eye-pampering, but satisfies no heart. Streets, streets, streets, markets, theatres, churches, Covent Gardens, shops sparkling with pretty faces of industrious milliners, neat sempstresses, ladies cheapening, gentlemen behind counters lying, authors in the street with spectacles, George Dyers (you may know them by their gait), lamps lit at night, pastrycooks' and silversmiths' shops, beautiful Quakers of Pentonville, noise of coaches, drowsy cry of mechanic watchmen at night, with bucks reeling home drunk; if you happen to wake at midnight, cries of " Fire !" and " Stop thief !"; inns of court, with their learned air, and halls, and butteries, just like Cambridge colleges; old book-stalls, " Jeremy Taylors," " Burtons on Melancholy," and " Religio Medicis," on every stall. These are thy pleasures, O London ! with thy many sins. O City, abounding in w . . ., for these may Keswick and her giant brood go hang !   C. L.

To WILLIAM GODWIN.

Thursday Morning,
LETTER LXX.]   December 4, 1800.

Dear Sir—I send this speedily after the heels of Cooper (O ! the dainty expression) to say that Mary is obliged to stay at home on Sunday to receive a female friend, from whom I am equally glad to escape. So that we shall be by ourselves. I write, because it may make *some* difference in your marketing, etc.   C. L.

I am sorry to put you to the expense of twopence postage. But I calculate thus : if Mary comes she will—

            eat Beef 2 plates,   .   4d.
  Batter Pudding 1 do. .   .   2d.
  Beer, a pint, .   .   .   2d.
        Wine, 3 glasses,   .   11d. I drink no wine !
        Chesnuts, after dinner, .   2d.
  Tea and supper at moderate
        calculation,   .   .   .   9d.
                                    ____
                                    2s. 6d.
      From which deduct   2d. postage.
                                    ____
                                    2s. 4d.

You are a clear gainer by her not coming.

Wednesday Morning,
December 11, 1800.

LETTER LXXI.]

Dear Sir—I expected a good deal of pleasure from your company to-morrow, but I am sorry I must beg of you to excuse me. I have been confined ever since I saw you with one of the severest colds I ever experienced, occasioned by being in the night air on Sunday and on the following day very foolishly. I am neither in health nor spirits to meet company. I hope and trust I shall get out on Saturday night. You will add to your many favours by transmitting to me as early as possible as many tickets as conveniently you can spare,—Yours truly,   C. L.

I have been plotting how to abridge the Epilogue. But I cannot see that any lines can be spared, retaining the connection, except these two, which are better out.

> " Why should I instance, etc.,
>   The sick man's purpose, etc.,"

and then the following line must run thus,

> " The truth by an example best is shown."

Excuse this *important* postscript.

To THOMAS MANNING.

I have received your letter *this moment*, not having been at the office. I have just time to scribble down the epilogue. To your epistle I will just reply, that I will certainly come to Cambridge before January is out; I'll come *when I can*. You shall have an amended copy of my play early next week. Mary thanks you; but her handwriting is too feminine to be exposed to a Cambridge gentleman, though I endeavour to persuade her that you understand algebra, and must understand her hand. The play is the man's you wot of; but for Heaven's sake do not mention it : it is to come out in a feigned name, as one Tobin's. I will omit the introductory lines which connect it with the play, and give you the concluding tale, which is the mass and bulk of the epilogue. The name is *Jack Incident*. It is all about promise-breaking : you will see it all, if you read the *papers*.

> " Jack, of dramatic genius justly vain,
>   Purchased a renter's share at Drury Lane ;
>   A prudent man in every other matter,
>   Known at his club-room for an honest hatter ;
>   Humane and courteous, led a civil life,
>   And has been seldom known to beat his wife ;
>   But Jack is now grown quite another man,
>   Frequents the green-room, knows the plot and plau
>   Of each new piece,
>   And has been seen to talk with Sheridan !
>   In at the play-house just at six he pops,
>   And never quits it till the curtain drops,
>   Is never absent on the *author's night*,
>   Knows actresses and actors too——by sight ;
>   So humble, that with Suet he'll confer,
>   Or take a pipe with plain Jack Bannister ;
>   Nay, with an author has been known so free,
>   He once suggested a catastrophe—
>   In short, John dabbled till his head was turn'd ;
>   His wife remonstrated, his neighbours mourn'd,

> His customers were dropping off apace,
> And Jack's affairs began to wear a piteous face.
>   One night his wife began a curtain lecture ;
> 'My dearest Johnny, husband, spouse, protector,
> Take pity on your helpless babes and me,
> Save us from ruin, you from bankruptcy—
> Look to your business, leave these cursed plays,
> And try again your old industrious ways.'
>   Jack who was always scared at the Gazette,
> And had some bits of scull uninjured yet,
> Promised amendment, vow'd his wife spake reason,
> 'He would not see another play that season—'
>   Three stubborn fortnights Jack his promise kept,
> Was late and early in his shop, eat, slept,
> And walk'd and talk'd, like ordinary men ;
> No *wit*, but John the hatter once again—
> Visits his club : when lo ! one *fatal night*
> His wife with horror view'd the well-known sight—
> John's *hat, wig, snuff-box*—well she knew his tricks—
> And Jack decamping at the hour of six,
> Just at the counter's edge a playbill lay,
> Announcing that ' Pizarro ' was the play—
> ' O Johnny, Johnny, this is your old doing.'
> Quoth Jack, ' Why what the devil storm's a-brewing ?
> About a harmless play why all this fright ?
> I'll go and see it if it's but for spite—
> Zounds, woman ! Nelson's to be there to-night.' "

N.B.—This was intended for Jack Bannister to speak; but the sage managers have chosen Miss *Heard*, except Miss Tidswell, the worst actress ever seen or *heard*. Now I remember I have promised the loan of my play. I will lend it *instantly*, and you shall get it ('pon honour!) by this day week.

I must go and dress for the boxes ! First night ! Finding I have time, I transcribe the rest. Observe, you must read the last first ; it begins thus :—(The names I took from a little outline G. gave me. I have not read the play.)

> " Ladies, ye've seen how Guzman's consort died,
>   Poor victim of a Spaniard brother's pride,
>   When Spanish honour through the world was blown,
>   And Spanish beauty for the best was known.
>   In that romantic, unenlighten'd time,

A *breach of promise* was a sort of crime—
Which of you handsome English ladies here,
But deems the penance bloody and severe ?
A whimsical old Saragossa fashion,
That a dead father's dying inclination,
Should *live* to thwart a living daughter's passion :
Unjustly on the sex *we* men exclaim,
Rail at *your* vices,—and commit the same ;—
Man is a promise-breaker from the womb,
And goes a promise-breaker to the tomb—
What need we instance here the lover's vow,
The sick man's purpose, or the great man's bow ?
The truth by few examples best is shown—
Instead of many which are better known,
Take poor Jack Incident, that's dead and gone.
Jack," etc. etc. etc.

Now you have it all—how do you like it? I am
going to hear it recited ! ! !   C. L.

To WILLIAM GODWIN.

Letter LXXIII.]   *Late o' Sunday, December* 14, 1800.

Dear Sir—I have performed my office in a slovenly
way, but judge for me. I sat down at six o'clock, and
never left reading (and I read out to Mary) your play till
10. In this sitting I noted down lines as they occurred,
exactly as you will read my rough paper. Do not be
frightened at the bulk of my remarks, for they are almost
all upon single lines, which, put together, do not amount
to a hundred, and many of them merely verbal. I had
but one object in view, abridgment for compression sake.
I have used a dogmatical language (which is truly ludi-
crous when the trivial nature of my remarks is considered);
and, remember, my office was to hunt out faults. You
may fairly abridge one half of them, as a fair deduction
for the infirmities of Error and a single reading, which
leaves only fifty objections, most of them merely against
words, on no short play. Remember, you constituted me

Executioner, and a hangman has been seldom seen to be ashamed of his profession before Master Sheriff. We'll talk of the Beauties (of which I am more than ever sure) when we meet.—Yours truly,   C. L.

I will barely add, as you are on the very point of printing, that in my opinion neither prologue nor epilogue should accompany the play. It can only serve to remind your readers of its fate. *Both* suppose an audience, and, that jest being gone, must convert into burlesque. Nor would I (but therein custom and decorum must be a law) print the actors' names. Some things must be kept out of sight.

I have done, and I have but a few square inches of paper to fill up. I am emboldened by a little jorum of punch (vastly good) to say that next to *one man*, I am the most hurt at our ill success. The breast of Hecuba, where she did suckle Hector, looked not to be more lovely than Marshal's forehead when it spit forth sweat, at Critic-swords contending. I remember two honest lines by Marvel (whose poems by the way I am just going to possess).

> " Where every Mower's wholesome heat
> Smells like an Alexander's sweat."

To THOMAS MANNING.

LETTER LXXIV.]   *December* 16, 1800.

We are damn'd!—Not the facetious epilogue itself could save us; for, as the editor of the *Morning Post* (quick-sighted gentleman!) hath this morning truly observed (I beg pardon if I falsify his *words;* their profound *sense* I am sure I retain;) both prologue and epilogue were worthy of accompanying such a piece; and indeed (mark the profundity, Mr. Manning!) were received with proper indignation by such of the audience only as thought either worth attending to. Professor, thy glories wax dim! Again, the incomparable author of the *True Briton* declareth in *his* paper (bearing same date) that the epilogue was an indifferent attempt at humour and character, and failed in both. I forbear to mention the other papers, because I have not read them. O Professor, how different thy feelings now (*quantum mutatus ab illo professore, qui in agris philosophiæ tantas victorias acquisivisti*),— how different thy proud feelings but one little week ago —thy anticipations of thy nine nights—those visionary claps, which have soothed thy soul by day and thy dreams by night! Calling in accidentally on the Professor while he was out, I was ushered into the study; and my nose quickly (most sagacious always) pointed me to four tokens lying loose upon thy table, Professor, which indicated thy violent and satanical pride of heart. *Imprimis*, there caught mine eye a list of six persons, thy friends, whom thou didst meditate inviting to a sumptuous dinner on the Thursday, anticipating the profits of thy Saturday's play to answer charges: I was in the honoured file! Next (a stronger evidence of thy violent and almost satanical pride) lay a list of all the morning papers (from the *Morning Chronicle* downwards to the *Porcupine*), with the places of their respective offices, where thou wast meditating to insert, and didst insert, an elaborate sketch of the story of thy play; stones in thy enemy's hand to bruise thee with, and severely wast thou bruised, O Professor! nor do I know what oil to pour into thy wounds. Next (which convinced me to a dead conviction of thy pride, violent and almost satanical pride!) lay a list of books which thy un-tragedy-favoured pocket could never answer; Dodsley's Old Plays, Malone's Shakspeare (still harping upon thy play, thy philosophy abandoned meanwhile to Christians and superstitious minds); nay, I believe (if I can believe my memory) that the ambitious Encyclopædia itself was part of thy meditated acquisitions; but many a playbook was there. All these visions are *damned*; and thou, Professor, must read Shakspeare in future out of a common edition ; and, hark ye ! pray read him to a little better purpose.　Last and strongest against thee (in colours manifest as the hand upon Belshazzar's wall) lay a volume of poems by C. Lloyd and C. Lamb. Thy heart misgave thee, that thy assistant might possibly not have talent enough to furnish thee an epilogue! Manning, all these things came over my mind ; all the gratulations that would have thickened upon him, and even some have glanced aside upon his humble friend ; the vanity, and the fame, and the profits (the Professor is £500 ideal money out of pocket by this failure, besides £200 he would have got for the copyright, and the Professor is never much beforehand with the world ; what he gets is all by the sweat of his brow and dint of brain, for the Professor, though a sure man, is also a slow) ; and now to muse upon thy altered physiognomy, thy pale and squalid appearance (a kind of *blue sickness* about the eyelids), and thy crest fallen, and thy proud demand of £200 from thy bookseller changed to an uncertainty of his taking it at all, or giving the full £50.　The Professor has won my heart by this *his* mournful catastrophe.　You remember Marshall, who dined with him at my house ; I met him in the lobby immediately after the damnation of the Professor's play, and he looked to me like an angel ; his face was lengthened, and all over perspiration.　I never saw such a care-fraught visage ; I could have hugged him, I loved him so intensely.　"From every pore of him a perfume fell."　I have seen that man in many situations, and, from my soul, I think that a more god-like honest soul exists not in this world.　The Professor's poor nerves trembling with the recent shock, he hurried him away to my house to supper, and there we comforted him as well as we could.　He came to consult me about a change of catastrophe ; but alas ! the piece was condemned long before that crisis.　I at first humoured him with a specious proposition, but have since joined his true friends in advising him to give it up.　He did it with a pang, and is to print it as *his.*　　　　　　　　　　　　　　　　L.

LETTER LXXV.]   *December* 27, 1800.

At length George Dyer's phrenitis has come to a crisis ;
he is raging and furiously mad.   I waited upon the
heathen, Thursday was a se'nnight.   The first symptom
which struck my eye, and gave me incontrovertible proof
of the fatal truth, was a pair of nankeen pantaloons four
times too big for him, which the said Heathen did perti-
naciously affirm to be new.

They were absolutely ingrained with the accumulated
dirt of ages ; but he affirmed them to be clean.   He was
going to visit a lady that was nice about those things,
and that's the reason he wore nankeen that day.   And
then he danced, and capered, and fidgeted, and pulled up
his pantaloons, and hugged his intolerable flannel vestment
closer about his poetic loins.   Anon he gave it loose to
the zephyrs which plentifully insinuate their tiny bodies
through every crevice, door, window, or wainscot, expressly
formed for the exclusion of such impertinents.   Then he
caught at a proof sheet, and catched up a laundress's bill
instead—made a dart at Bloomfield's Poems, and threw
them in agony aside.   I could not bring him to one
direct reply ; he could not maintain his jumping mind in
a right line for the tithe of a moment by Clifford's Inn
clock.   He must go to the printer's immediately : (the
most unlucky accident !) he had struck off five hundred
impressions of his Poems, which were ready for delivery
to subscribers, and the Preface must all be expunged.
There were eighty pages of Preface, and not till that
morning had he discovered that in the very first page of
said Preface he had set out with a principle of Criticism
fundamentally wrong, which vitiated all his following
reasoning.   The Preface must be expunged, although it
cost him £30, the lowest calculation, taking in paper and
printing !   In vain have his real friends remonstrated
against this Midsummer madness.   George is as obstinate
as a Primitive Christian, and wards and parries off all

our thrusts with one unanswerable fence :—" Sir, 'tis of great consequence that the *world* is not *misled !*"

As for the other Professor, he has actually begun to dive into Tavernier and Chardin's *Persian* Travels for a story, to form a new drama for the sweet tooth of this fastidious age.   Hath not Bethlehem College a fair action for non-residence against such professors ?   Are poets so *few* in *this age*, that He must write poetry ?   *Is morals* a subject so exhausted, that he must quit that line ?   Is the metaphysic well (without a bottom) drained dry ?

If I can guess at the wicked pride of the Professor's heart, I would take a shrewd wager that he disdains ever again to dip his pen in *Prose.*   Adieu, ye splendid theories !   Farewell, dreams of political justice !   Law-suits, where I was council for Archbishop Fenelon *versus* my own mother, in the famous fire cause !

Vanish from my mind, professors, one and all !   I have metal more attractive on foot.

Man of many snipes,—I will sup with thee (Deo volente, et diabolo nolente,) on Monday night, the 5th of January, in the new year, and crush a cup to the infant century.

A word or two of my progress : Embark at six o'clock in the morning, with a fresh gale, on a Cambridge one-decker ; very cold till eight at night ; land at St. Mary's lighthouse, muffins and coffee upon table (or any other curious production of Turkey, or both Indies), snipes exactly at nine, punch to commence at ten, with *argu-ment ;* difference of opinion is expected to take place about eleven ; perfect unanimity, with some haziness and dimness, before twelve.   *N.B.*—My single affection is not so singly wedded to snipes ; but the curious and epicurean eye would also take a pleasure in beholding a delicate and well-chosen assortment of teals, ortolans, the unctuous and palate-soothing flesh of geese, wild and tame, night-ingales' brains, the sensorium of a young sucking pig, or any other Christmas dish, which I leave to the judgment of you and the cook of Gonville.   C. LAMB.

To SAMUEL TAYLOR COLERIDGE.

LETTER LXXVI.]   [No date—end of 1800.]

I send you, in this parcel, my play, which I beg you to present in my name, with my respect and love, to Wordsworth, and his sister. You blame us for giving your direction to Miss Wesley. The woman has been ten times after us about it, and we gave it her at last, under the idea that no further harm would ensue ; but she would *once* write to you, and you would bite your lips and forget to answer it, and so it would end. You read us a dismal homily upon " Realities." We know, quite as well as you do, what are shadows and what are realities. You, for instance, when you are over your fourth or fifth jorum, chirping about old school occurrences, are the best of realities. Shadows are cold, thin things, that have no warmth or grasp in them. Miss Wesley and her friend, and a tribe of authoresses that come after you here daily, and, in defect of you, hive and cluster upon us, are the shadows. You encouraged that mopsey, Miss Wesley, to dance after you, in the hope of having her nonsense put into a nonsensical Anthology. We have pretty well shaken her off by that simple expedient of referring her to you ; but there are more burs in the wind. I came home t' other day from business, hungry as a hunter, to dinner, with nothing, I am sure, of the author but *hunger* about me ; and whom found I closeted with Mary but a friend of this Miss Wesley, one Miss Benjay or Benje ; I don't know how she spells her name. I just came in time enough, I believe, luckily to prevent them from exchanging vows of eternal friendship. It seems she is one of your authoresses, that you first foster, and then upbraid us with. But I forgive you. " The rogue has given me potions to make me love him." Well ; go she would not, nor step a step over our threshold, till we

had promised to come and drink tea with her next night.
I had never seen her before, and could not tell who the
devil it was that was so familiar. We went, however,
not to be impolite. Her lodgings are up two pair of
stairs in East Street. Tea and coffee, and macaroons—a
kind of cake—much love. We sat down. Presently
Miss Benjay broke the silence, by declaring herself quite
of a different opinion from *D'Israeli*, who supposes the
differences of human intellect to be the mere effect of
organisation. She begged to know my opinion. I
attempted to carry it off with a pun upon organ, but
that went off very flat. She immediately conceived a
very low opinion of my metaphysics ; and, turning round
to Mary, put some question to her in French,—possibly
having heard that neither Mary nor I understood French.
The explanation that took place occasioned some embar-
rassment and much wondering. She then fell into an
insulting conversation about the comparative genius and
merits of all modern languages, and concluded with
asserting that the Saxon was esteemed the purest dialect
in Germany. From thence she passed into the subject of
poetry ; where I, who had hitherto sat mute, and a hearer
only, humbly hoped I might now put in a word to some
advantage, seeing that it was my own trade in a manner.
But I was stopped by a round assertion, that no good
poetry had appeared since Dr. Johnson's time. It seems
the Doctor has suppressed many hopeful geniuses that
way, by the severity of his critical strictures in his *Lives
of the Poets*. I here ventured to question the fact, and
was beginning to appeal to *names*, but I was assured "it
was certainly the case." Then we discussed Miss More's
book on education, which I had never read. It seems
Dr. Gregory, another of Miss Benjay's friends, has found
fault with one of Miss More's metaphors. Miss More has
been at some pains to vindicate herself,—in the opinion
of Miss Benjay not without success. It seems the Doctor
is invariably against the use of broken or mixed metaphor,
which he reprobates, against the authority of Shakspeare

himself. We next discussed the question, whether Pope was a poet? I find Dr. Gregory is of opinion he was not, though Miss Seward does not at all concur with him in this. We then sat upon the comparative merits of the ten translations of *Pizarro*, and Miss Benjay or Benje advised Mary to take two of them home (she thought it might afford her some pleasure to compare them *verbatim*); which we declined. It being now nine o'clock, wine and macaroons were again served round, and we parted, with a promise to go again next week, and meet the Miss Porters, who, it seems, have heard much of Mr. Coleridge, and wish to meet *us*, because we are *his* friends. I have been preparing for the occasion. I crowd cotton in my ears. I read all the reviews and magazines of the past month, against the dreadful meeting, and I hope by these means to cut a tolerable second-rate figure.

Pray let us have no more complaints about shadows. We are in a fair way, *through you*, to surfeit sick upon them.

Our loves and respects to your host and hostess. Our dearest love to Coleridge.

Take no thought about your proof sheets; they shall be done as if Woodfall himself did them. Pray send us word of Mrs. Coleridge and little David Hartley, your little reality.

Farewell, dear Substance. Take no umbrage at anything I have written. C. LAMB, *Umbra.*

Land of Shadows,
Shadow Month the 16th or 17th, 1800.

Coleridge, I find loose among your papers a copy of *Christabel.* It wants about thirty lines; you will very much oblige me by sending me the beginning as far as that line,—

"And the spring comes slowly up this way;"

and the intermediate lines between—

> "The lady leaps up suddenly,
>   The lovely Lady Christabel;"

and the lines,—

> "She folded her arms beneath her cloak,
>   And stole to the other side of the oak."

The trouble to you *will be small*, and the benefit to us *very great*.   A pretty antithesis!   A figure in speech I much applaud.

Godwin has called upon us.   He spent one evening here: was very friendly: kept us up till midnight, drank punch, and talked about you.   He seems above all men, mortified at your going away.   Suppose you were to write to that good-natured heathen: "Or is he a *shadow?*"

If I do not *write*, impute it to the long postage, of which you have so much cause to complain.   I have scribbled over a *queer letter*, as I find by perusal, but it means no mischief.

I am, and will be, yours ever, in sober sadness,

C. L.

Write your *German* as plain as sunshine, for that must correct itself.   You know I am *homo unius linguæ :* in English—illiterate, a dunce, a ninny.

To WILLIAM WORDSWORTH.

LETTER LXXVII.]   *January* 1801.

Thanks for your letter and present.   I had already borrowed your second volume.   What most pleases me is, "The Song of Lucy."   *Simon's sickly daughter*, in "The Sexton," made me *cry*.   Next to these are the description of these continuous echoes in the story of "Joanna's Laugh," where the mountains and all the scenery absolutely seem alive; and that fine Shakspearian character of the "happy man," in the "Brothers,"

> ———"that creeps about the fields,
> Following his fancies by the hour, to bring
> Tears down his cheek, or solitary smiles
> Into his face, until the setting sun
> Write Fool upon his forehead!"

I will mention one more—the delicate and curious feeling in the wish for the " Cumberland Beggar," that he may have about him the melody of birds, although he hear them not. Here the mind knowingly passes a fiction upon herself, first substituting her own feeling for the Beggar's, and in the same breath detecting the fallacy, will not part with the wish. The " Poet's Epitaph " is disfigured, to my taste, by the common satire upon parsons and lawyers in the beginning, and the coarse epithet of " pin-point," in the sixth stanza. All the rest is eminently good, and your own. I will just add that it appears to me a fault in the " Beggar," that the instructions conveyed in it are too direct, and like a lecture : they don't slide into the mind of the reader while he is imagining no such matter. An intelligent reader finds a sort of insult in being told, " I will teach you how to think upon this subject." This fault, if I am right, is in a ten-thousandth worse degree to be found in Sterne, and in many novelists and modern poets, who continually put a sign-post up to show where you are to feel. They set out with assuming their readers to be stupid; very different from *Robinson Crusoe*, the *Vicar of Wakefield*, *Roderick Random*, and other beautiful, bare narratives. There is implied an unwritten compact between author and reader ; " I will tell you a story, and I suppose you will understand it." Modern novels, *St. Leons* and the like, are full of such flowers as these—" Let not my reader suppose," " Imagine, if you can, modest !" etc. I will here have done with praise and blame. I have written so much, only that you may not think I have passed over your book without observation. . . . I am sorry that Coleridge has christened his *Ancient Marinere*, a *Poet's Reverie ;* it is as bad as Bottom the Weaver's declaration that he is not a lion, but only the scenical representation of a lion.   What new idea is gained by this title but one subversive of all credit—which the tale should force upon us—of its truth !

For me, I was never so affected with any human tale. After first reading it, I was totally possessed with it for many days.   I dislike all the miraculous part of it; but the feelings of the man under the operation of such scenery, dragged me along like Tom Pipe's magic whistle.   I totally differ from your idea that the *Marinere* should have had a character and profession.   This is a beauty in *Gulliver's Travels*, where the mind is kept in a placid state of little wonderments; but the *Ancient Marinere* undergoes such trials as overwhelm and bury all individuality or memory of what he was—like the state of a man in a bad dream, one terrible peculiarity of which is, that all consciousness of personality is gone.   Your other observation is, I think as well, a little unfounded : the "Marinere," from being conversant in supernatural events, *has* acquired a supernatural and strange cast of *phrase*, eye, appearance, etc., which frighten the "wedding guest."   You will excuse my remarks, because I am hurt and vexed that you should think it necessary, with a prose apology, to open the eyes of dead men that cannot see.

To sum up a general opinion of the second volume, I do not feel any one poem in it so forcibly as the *Ancient Marinere*, and the "Mad Mother," and the "Lines at Tintern Abbey" in the first.

Letter LXXVIII.]   *January* 30, 1801.

I ought before this to have replied to your very kind invitation into Cumberland.   With you and your sister I could gang anywhere; but I am afraid whether I shall ever be able to afford so desperate a journey.   Separate from the pleasure of your company, I don't much care if I never see a mountain in my life.   I have passed all my days in London, until I have formed as many and intense local attachments as any of you mountaineers can have done with dead Nature. The lighted shops of the Strand and Fleet Street; the innumerable trades, tradesmen, and customers, coaches, waggons, playhouses; all the bustle and wickedness round about Covent Garden; the very women of the Town; the watchmen, drunken scenes, rattles; life awake, if you awake, at all hours of the night; the impossibility of being dull in Fleet Street; the crowds, the very dirt and mud, the sun shining upon houses and pavements, the print-shops, the old bookstalls, parsons cheapening books, coffee-houses, steams of soups from kitchens, the pantomimes—London itself a pantomime and a masquerade—all these things work themselves into my mind, and feed me, without a power of satiating me. The wonder of these sights impels me into night-walks about her crowded streets, and I often shed tears in the motley Strand from fulness of joy at so much life. All these emotions must be strange to you; so are your rural emotions to me. But consider, what must I have been doing all my life, not to have lent great portions of my heart with usury to such scenes?

My attachments are all local, purely local. I have no passion (or have had none since I was in love, and then it was the spurious engendering of poetry and books) for groves and valleys. The rooms where I was born, the furniture which has been before my eyes all my life, a book-case which has followed me about like a faithful dog, (only exceeding him in knowledge), wherever I have moved, old chairs, old tables, streets, squares, where I have sunned myself, my old school,—these are my mistresses. Have I not enough, without your mountains? I do not envy you. I should pity you, did I not know that the mind will make friends of anything. Your sun, and moon, and skies, and hills, and lakes, affect me no more, or scarcely come to me in more venerable characters, than as a gilded room with tapestry and tapers, where I might live with handsome visible objects. I consider the clouds above me but as a roof beautifully painted, but unable to satisfy the mind : and at last, like the pictures of the apartment of a connoisseur, unable to afford him any longer a pleasure. So fading upon me, from disuse, have been the beauties of Nature, as they have been confinedly called ; so ever fresh, and green, and warm are all the inventions of men, and assemblies of men in this great city. I should certainly have laughed with .dear Joanna.

Give my kindest love, and my sister's, to D. and yourself; and a kiss from me to little Barbara Lewthwaite. Thank you for liking my play.   C. L.

To THOMAS MANNING.

LETTER LXXIX.]   [*February* or *March*] 1801.

You masters of logic ought to know (logic is nothing more than a knowledge of *words*, as the Greek etymon implies) that all words are no more to be. taken in a literal sense at all times than a promise given to a tailor. When I exprest an apprehension that you were mortally offended, I meant no more than by the application of a certain formula of efficacious sounds, which had *done* in similar cases before, to rouse a sense of decency in you, and a remembrance of what was due to me ! You masters of logic should advert to this phenomenon in human speech, before you arraign the usage of us dramatic geniuses. Imagination is a good blood mare, and goes well : but the misfortune is, she has too many paths before her. 'Tis true I might have imagined to myself, that you had trundled your frail carcass to Norfolk. I might also, and did imagine, that you had not, but that you were lazy, or inventing new properties in a triangle, and for that purpose moulding and squeezing Landlord Crisp's three-cornered beaver into fantastic experimental forms ; or, that Archimedes was meditating to repulse the French, in case of a Cambridge invasion, by a geometric hurling of folios on their red caps; or, peradventure, that you were in extremities, in great wants, and just set out for Trinity Bogs when my letters came. In short, my genius (which is a short word, now-a-days, for what-a-great-man-am-I)! was absolutely stifled and overlaid with its own riches. Truth is one and poor, like the cruse of Elijah's widow. Imagination is the bold face that multiplies its oil; and thou, the old cracked pipkin, that could not believe it could be put to such purposes. Dull pipkin, to have Elijah for thy cook! Imbecile recipient of so fat a miracle! I send you George Dyer's Poems, the richest production of the lyrical muse *this century* can justly boast: for Wordsworth's L. B. were published, or at least written, before Christmas.

Please to advert to pages 291 to 296 for the most astonishing account of where Shakspeare's muse has been all this while. I thought she had been dead, and buried in Stratford Church, with the young man *that kept her company,*—

> " But it seems, like the Devil,
>   Buried in Cole Harbour,
> Some say she's risen again,
>   'Gone prentice to a barber."

N.B.—I don't charge anything for the additional manuscript notes, which are the joint productions of myself and a learned translator of Schiller, John Stoddart, Esq.

N.B. the 2d.—I should not have blotted your book, but I had sent my own out to be bound, as I was in duty bound. A liberal criticism upon the several pieces, lyrical, heroical, amatory, and satirical, would be acceptable. So, you don't think there's a Word's—worth of good poetry in the great L. B.! I daren't put the dreaded syllables at their just length, for my back tingles from the northern castigation. I send you the three letters, which I beg you to return along with those former letters (which I hope you are not going to print, by your detention). But don't be in a hurry to send them. When you come to town will do. Apropos of coming to town : Last Sunday was a fortnight, as I was *coming to town* from the Professor's, inspired with new rum, I tumbled down and broke my nose. I drink nothing stronger than malt liquors.

I am going to change my lodgings, having received a hint that it would be agreeable, at our Lady's next feast. I have partly fixed upon most delectable rooms, which look out (when you stand a tip-toe) over the Thames and Surrey Hills; at the upper end of King's Bench Walks, in the Temple. There I shall have all the privacy of a house without the encumbrance, and shall be able to lock my friends out as often as I desire to hold free converse with my immortal mind ; for my present lodgings resemble a minister's levee, I have so increased my acquaintance (as they call 'em) since I have resided in town. Like the country mouse, that had tasted a little of urbane manners, I long to be nibbling my own cheese by my dear self, without mouse-traps and time-traps. By my new plan, I shall be as airy, up four pair of stairs, as in the country ; and in a garden, in the midst of enchanting (more than Mahometan paradise) London, whose dirtiest drab-frequented alley, and her lowest bowing tradesman, I would not exchange for Skiddaw, Helvellyn, James, Walter, and the parson into the bargain. O her lamps of a night ! her rich goldsmiths, print-shops, toy-shops, mercers, hardwaremen, pastry-cooks, St. Paul's Churchyard, the Strand, Exeter Change, Charing Cross, with the man *upon* a black horse ! These are thy gods, O London ! A'nt you mightily moped on the banks of the Cam ? Had you not better come and set up here ? You can't think what a difference. All the streets and pavements are pure gold, I warrant you. At least, I know an alchemy that turns her mud into that metal,—a mind that loves to be at home in crowds.

'Tis half-past twelve o'clock, and all sober people

ought to be a-bed.   Between you and me the L. Ballads are but drowsy performances.

C. LAMB (as you may guess).

LETTER LXXX.] *April* 1801.

I was not aware that you owed me anything beside that guinea; but I daresay you are right.   I live at No. 16 Mitre Court Buildings, a pistol-shot off Baron Maseres'. You must introduce me to the Baron.   I think we should suit one another mainly.   He lives on the ground floor, for convenience of the gout; I prefer the attic story, for the air.   He keeps three footmen and two maids; I have neither maid nor laundress, not caring to be troubled with them.   His forte, I understand, is the higher mathematics; my turn, I confess, is more to poetry and the belles lettres.   The very antithesis of our characters would make up a harmony.   You must bring the Baron and me together.   *N.B.*—When you come to see me, mount up to the top of the stairs—I hope you are not asthmatical—and come in flannel, for 'tis pure airy up there.   And bring your glass, and I will show you the Surrey Hills. My bed faces the river, so as by perking up upon my haunches, and supporting my carcass with my elbows, without much wrying my neck, I can see the white sails glide by the bottom of the King's Bench Walks as I lie in my bed.   An excellent tiptoe prospect in the best room :—casement windows, with small panes, to look more like a cottage.   Mind, I have got no bed for you, that's flat; sold it to pay expenses of moving,—the very bed on which Manning lay; the friendly, the mathematical Manning !   How forcibly does it remind me of the interesting Otway !   "The very bed which on thy marriage night gave thee into the arms of Belvidera, by the coarse hands of ruffians—" (upholsterers' men), etc.   My tears will not give me leave to go on.   But a bed I will get you, Manning, on condition you will be my day-guest.

I have been ill more than mouth, with a bad cold

which comes upon me (like a murderer's conscience) about
midnight, and vexes me for many hours. I have success-
sively been drugged with Spanish licorice, opium, ipecacu-
anha, paregoric, and tincture of foxglove (tinctura purpuræ
digitalis of the ancients). I am afraid I must leave off
drinking.

To WILLIAM GODWIN.

LETTER LXXXI.]   *June* 29, 1801.

Dear Sir—Dr. Christy's Brother and Sister are come
to town and have shown me great civilities. I in return
wish to requite them, having, *by God's grace*, principles
of generosity *implanted* (as the moralists say) in my
nature, which have been duly cultivated and watered by
good and religious friends, and a pious education. They
have picked up in the northern parts of the island an
astonishing admiration of the great author of the New
Philosophy in England, and I have ventured to promise
their taste an evening's gratification by seeing Mr. Godwin
face to *face ! ! ! !* Will you do them, and me *in* them,
the pleasure of drinking tea and supping with me at the
old number 16 on Friday or Saturday next? An early
nomination of the day will very much oblige yours
sincerely,   CH. LAMB.

To MR. WALTER WILSON.

LETTER LXXXII.]   *August* 14, 1801.

Dear Wilson—I am extremely sorry that any serious
differences should subsist between us, on account of some
foolish behaviour of mine at Richmond ; you knew me
well enough before, that a very little liquor will cause a
considerable alteration in me.

I beg you to impute my conduct solely to that, and not to any deliberate intention of offending you, from whom I have received so many friendly attentions. I know that you think a very important difference in opinion with respect to some more serious subjects between us makes me a dangerous companion; but do not rashly infer, from some slight and light expressions which I may have made use of in a moment of levity, in your presence, without sufficient regard to your feelings—do not conclude that I am an inveterate enemy to all religion. I have had a time of seriousness, and I have known the import-ance and reality of a religious belief. Latterly, I acknow-ledge, much of my seriousness has gone off, whether from new company, or some other new associations; but I still retain at bottom a conviction of the truth, and a certainty of the usefulness of religion. I will not pretend to more gravity or feeling than I at present possess; my intention is not to persuade you that any great alteration is probable in me; sudden converts are superficial and transitory; I only want you to believe that I have *stamina* of serious-ness within me, and that I desire nothing more than a return of that friendly intercourse which used to subsist between us, but which my folly has suspended.

Believe me, very affectionately yours,   C. LAMB.

To THOMAS MANNING.

LETTER LXXXIII.]   [*August*] 1801.

Dear Manning—I have forborne writing so long (and so have you for the matter of that), until I am almost ashamed either to write or to forbear any longer. But as your silence may proceed from some worse cause than neglect—from illness, or some mishap which may have befallen you, I begin to be anxious. You may have been burnt out, or you may have married, or you may have broken a limb, or turned country parson : any of these would be excuse sufficient for not coming to my supper. I am not so unforgiving as the nobleman in Saint Mark. For me, nothing new has happened to me, unless that the poor *Albion* died last Saturday of the world's neglect, and with it the fountain of my puns is choked up for ever.

All the Lloyds wonder that you do not write to them. They apply to me for the cause. Relieve me from this weight of ignorance, and enable me to give a truly oracular response.

I have been confined some days with swelled cheek and rheumatism : they divide and govern me with a viceroy-headache in the middle. I can neither write nor read without great pain. It must be something like obstinacy that I choose this time to write to you in after many months' interruption.

I will close my letter of simple inquiry with an epigram on Mackintosh, the *Vindiciæ Gallicæ* man—who has got a place at last—one of the last I *did* for the Albion :—

> " Though thou'rt like Judas, an apostate black,
> In the resemblance one thing thou dost lack :
> When he had gotten his ill-purchased pelf,
> He went away, and wisely hang'd himself :
> This thou may'st do at last ; yet much I doubt,
> If thou hast any *bowels* to gush out !"

Yours, as ever,   C. LAMB.

LETTER LXXXIV.]   *August* 31, 1801.

I heard that you were going to China, with a commission from the Wedgwoods to collect hints for their pottery, and to teach the Chinese *perspective ;* but I did not know that London lay in your way to Pekin. I am seriously glad of it, for I shall trouble you with a small present for the Emperor of Usbeck Tartary, as you go by his territories : it is a fragment of a " Dissertation on the state of political parties in England at the end of the eighteenth century," which will no doubt be very interesting to his

Imperial Majesty. It was written originally in English for the use of the *two* and *twenty* readers of the *Albion* (this *calculation* includes a printer, four pressmen, and a devil); but becoming of no use when the *Albion* stopped, I got it translated into Usbeck Tartar by my good friend Tibet Kulm, who is to come to London with a *civil* invitation from the Cham to the English nation to go over to the worship of the Lama.

The *Albion* is dead—dead as nail in door—and my revenues have died with it; but I am not as a man without hope. I have got a sort of opening to the *Morning Chronicle*, by means of that common dispenser of benevolence, Mister Dyer. I have not seen Perry, the editor, yet: but I am preparing a specimen. I shall have a difficult job to manage, for you must know that Mr. Perry, in common with the great body of the Whigs, thinks the *Albion* very low. I find I must rise a peg or so, be a little more decent, and less abusive; for, to confess the truth, I had arrived to an abominable pitch; I spared neither age nor sex when my cue was given me. *N'importe* (as they say in French), any climate will suit me. So you are about to bring your old face-making face to London. You could not come in a better time for my purposes; for I have just lost Rickman, a faint idea of whose character I sent you. He has gone to Ireland for a year or two to make his fortune; and I have lost by his going what seems to me I can never recover—*a finished man*. His memory will be to me as the brazen serpent to the Israelites,—I shall look up to it, to keep me upright and honest. But he may yet bring back his honest face to England one day. I wish your affairs with the Emperor of China had not been *so urgent*, that you might have stayed in Great Britain a year or two longer, to have seen him; for, judging from *my own* experience, I almost dare pronounce you never saw his equal. I never saw a man that could be at all a second or substitute for him in any sort.

Imagine that what is here erased was an apology and

explanation, perfectly satisfactory you may be sure for rating this man so highly at the expense of ——, and ——, and ——, and M——, and ——, and ——, and ——. But Mr. Burke has explained this phenomenon of our nature very prettily in his letter to a Member of the National Assembly, or else in Appeal to the old Whigs, I forget which. Do you remember an instance from Homer (who understood these matters tolerably well), of Priam driving away his other sons with expressions of wrath and bitter reproach, when Hector was just dead?

I live where I did, in a *private* manner, because I don't like *state*. Nothing is so disagreeable to me as the clamours and applauses of the mob. For this reason I live in an *obscure* situation in one of the courts of the Temple. C. L.

I send you all of Coleridge's letters to me, which I have preserved: some of them are upon the subject of my play. I also send you Kemble's two letters, and the prompter's courteous epistle, with a curious critique on "Pride's Cure," by a young physician from EDINBRO', who modestly suggests quite another kind of a plot. These are monuments of my disappointment which I like to preserve.

In Coleridge's letters you will find a good deal of amusement, to see genuine talent struggling against a pompous display of it. I also send you the Professor's letter to me (careful Professor! to conceal his *name* even from his correspondent), ere yet the Professor's pride was cured. Oh monstrous and almost satanical pride!

You will carefully keep all (except the Scotch Doctor's, *which burn*) *in statu quo*, till I come to claim mine own. C. LAMB.

To WILLIAM GODWIN.

Letter LXXXV.]   [*Margate ?*] *September* 9, 1801.

Dear Sir—Nothing runs in my head when I think of your story, but that you should make it as like the life of Savage as possible. That is a known and familiar tale, and its effect on the public mind has been very great. Many of the incidents in the true history are readily made dramatical. For instance, Savage used to walk backwards and forwards o' nights to his mother's window, to catch a glimpse of her, as she passed with a candle. With some such situation the play might happily open. I would plunge my Hero, exactly like Savage, into difficulties and embarrassments, the consequences of an unsettled mind : out of which he may be extricated by the unknown interference of his mother. He should be attended from the beginning by a Friend, who should stand in much the same relation towards him as Horatio to Altamont in the play of the "Fair Penitent." A character of this sort seems indispensable. This Friend might gain interviews with the mother, when the son was refused sight of her. Like Horatio with Calista, he might wring her soul. Like Horatio, he might learn the secret *first.* He might be exactly in the same perplexing situation, when he had learned it, whether to tell it or conceal it from the Son (I have still Savage in my head), who might *kill* a man (as he did) in an affray—he should receive a pardon, as Savage did—and the mother might interfere to have him *banished.* This should provoke the friend to demand an interview with her husband, and disclose the whole secret. The husband, refusing to believe anything to her dishonour, should fight with him. The husband repents before he dies. The mother explains and confesses everything in his presence. The son is admitted to an interview with his now acknowledged mother. Instead of embraces, she resolves to abstract herself from all pleasure, even from his sight, in voluntary penance all her days after. This is crude indeed!! but I am totally unable to suggest a better. I am the worst hand in the world at a plot. But I understand enough of passion to predict that your story, with some of Savage's, which has no repugnance, but a natural alliance with it, cannot fail. The mystery of the suspected relationship—the suspicion, generated from slight and forgotten circumstances, coming at last to act as Instinct, and so to be mistaken for Instinct—the son's unceasing pursuit and throwing of himself in his mother's way, something like Falkland's eternal persecution of Williams—the high and intricate passion in the mother, the being obliged to shun and keep at a distance the thing nearest to her heart—to be cruel, where her heart yearns to be kind, without a possibility of explanation. You have the power of life and death and the hearts of your auditors in your hands—still Harris will want a skeleton, and he must have it. I can only put in some sorry hints. The discovery to the son's friend may take place not before the third act—in some such way as this. The mother may cross the street—he may point her out to some gay companion of his as the Beauty of Leghorn—the pattern for wives, etc. etc. His companion, who is an Englishman, laughs at his mistake, and knows her to have been the famous Nancy Dawson, or any one else, who captivated the English king. Some such way seems dramatic, and speaks to the Eye. The audience will enter into the Friend's surprise and into the perplexity of his situation. These Ocular Scenes are so many great landmarks, rememberable headlands and lighthouses in the voyage. Macbeth's witch has a good advice to a tragic writer, what to do with his spectator.

> "*Show* his *eyes*, and grieve his heart."

The most difficult thing seems to be, What to do with the husband? You will not make him jealous of his own son? that is a stale and an unpleasant trick in Douglas, etc. Can't you keep him out of the way till you want him, as the husband of Isabella is conveniently sent off till his cue comes? There will be story enough without him, and he will only puzzle all. Catastrophes are worst of all. Mine is most stupid. I only propose it to fulfil my engagement, not in hopes to convert you.

It is always difficult to get rid of a woman at the end of a tragedy. *Men* may fight and die. A woman must either take poison, *which is a nasty trick*, or go mad, which is not fit to be shown—or retire, which is poor: only retiring is most reputable.

I am sorry I can furnish you no better: but I find it extremely difficult to settle my thoughts upon anything but the scene before me, when I am from home: I am from home so seldom. If any the least hint crosses me, I will write again, and I very much wish to read your plan, if you could abridge and send it. In this little scrawl you must take the will for the deed, for I most sincerely wish success to your play.—Farewell,

C. L.

[*Fragment.*]

I shall be glad to come home and talk these matters over with you. I have read your scheme very attentively. That Arabella has been mistress to King Charles is sufficient to all the purposes of the story. It can only diminish that respect we feel for her to make her turn whore to one of the Lords of his Bedchamber. Her son must not know that she has been a whore: it matters not that she has been whore to a *King:* equally in both cases, it is against decorum and against the delicacy of a son's respect that he should be privy to it. No doubt, many sons might feel a wayward pleasure in the honourable guilt of their mothers; but is it a true feeling? Is it the best sort of feeling? Is it a feeling to be exposed on theatres to mothers and daughters? Your conclusion (or

rather Defoe's) comes far short of the tragic ending, which
is always expected ; and it is not safe to disappoint.   A
tragic auditory wants *blood.*   They care but little about
a man and his wife parting.   Besides, what will you do
with the son, after all his pursuits and adventures ?   Even
quietly leave him to take guinea-and-a-half lodgings with
mamma in Leghorn !   O impotent and pacific measures !
. . . I am certain that you must mix up some strong
ingredients of distress to give a savour to your pottage.
I still think that you may, and must, graft the story of
Savage upon Defoe.   Your hero must *kill* a *man* or *do
something.*   Can't you bring him to the gallows or some
great mischief, out of which she *must* have recourse to an
explanation with her husband to save him.   Think on this.
The husband, for instance, has great friends in Court at
Leghorn.   The son is condemned to death.   She cannot
tease him for a stranger.   She must tell the whole truth.
Or she *may* tease him, as for a stranger, till (like Othello
in Cassio's case) he begins to suspect her for her impor-
tunity.   Or, being pardoned, can she not tease her
husband to get him banished?   Something of this I
suggested before.   *Both* is best.   The murder and the
pardon will make business for the fourth act, and the
banishment and explanation (by means of the *Friend* I
want you to draw) the fifth.   You must not open any of
the truth to Dawley by means of a letter.   A letter is a
feeble messenger on the stage.   Somebody, the son or his
friend, must, as a *coup de main,* be exasperated, and
obliged to tell the husband.   Damn the husband and his
" gentlemanlike qualities."   Keep him out of sight, or he
will trouble all.   Let him be in England on trade, and
come home as Biron does in *Isabella,* in the fourth act,
when he is wanted.   I am for introducing situations, sort
of counterparts to situations which have been tried in
other plays—*like,* but not the *same.*   On this principle I
recommended a friend like Horatio in the "Fair Penitent,"
and on this principle I recommend a situation like Othello,
with relation to Desdemona's intercession for Cassio.

Bye-scenes may likewise receive hints. The son may see his mother at a mask or Feast, as Romeo, Juliet. The festivity of the company contrasts with the strong perturbations of the individuals. Dawley may be told his wife's past unchastity at a mask by some witch-character, as Macbeth upon the heath, in dark sentences. This may stir his brain, and be forgot, but come in aid of stronger proof hereafter. From this what you will perhaps call whimsical way of counterparting, this honest stealing, and original mode of plagiarism, much yet, I think, remains to be sucked. Excuse these abortions. I thought you would want the draught soon again, and I would not send it empty away.—Yours truly,

WILLIAM GODWIN!!!

Somers Town, September 17, 1801.

To THOMAS MANNING.

LETTER LXXXVII.]   *February* 15, 1802.

Apropos, I think you wrong about my play. All the omissions are right. And the supplementary scene, in which Sandford narrates the manner in which his master is affected, is the best in the book. It stands where a hodge-podge of German puerilities used to stand. I insist upon it that you like that scene. Love me, love that scene. I will now transcribe the "Londoner" (No. 1), and wind up all with affection and humble servant at the end.

[Here was transcribed the essay called "The Londoner," which was published some years afterwards in the *Reflector*, and which forms part of Lamb's collected works. He then proceeds] :—

"What is all this about?" said Mrs. Shandy. "A story of a cock and a bull," said Yorick: and so it is; but Manning will take good-naturedly what *God will send him* across the water : only I hope he won't *shut* his *eyes*, and *open* his *mouth*, as the children say, for that is the way to *gape*, and not to *read*. Manning, continue your laudable purpose of making me your register. I will render you back all your remarks; and *I, not you*, shall have received usury by having read them. In the meantime, may the great Spirit have you in his keeping, and preserve our Englishmen from the inoculation of frivolity and sin upon French earth.

Allons—or what is it you say, instead of *good-bye?*

Mary sends her kind remembrance, and covets the remarks equally with me.   C. LAMB.

To Mr. RICKMAN.

LETTER LXXXVIII.]   *April* 10, 1802.

Dear Rickman—The enclosed letter explains itself. It will save me the danger of a corporal interview with the man-eater, who, if very sharp set, may take a fancy to me, if you will give me a short note, declaratory of probabilities. These from him who hopes to see you once or twice more before he goes hence, to be no more seen : for there is no tipple nor tobacco in the grave, whereunto he hasteneth.   C. LAMB.

   16, Mitre Court Buildings,
      Inner Temple.

How clearly the Ghoul writes, and like a gentleman !

To SAMUEL TAYLOR COLERIDGE.

LETTER LXXXIX.]   *September* 8, 1802.

Dear Coleridge—I thought of not writing till we had performed some of our commissions; but we have been hindered from setting about them, which yet shall be done to a tittle. We got home very pleasantly on Sunday. Mary is a good deal fatigued, and finds the difference of going *to* a place, and coming *from* it. I feel that I shall remember your mountains to the last day I live. They haunt me perpetually. I am like a man who has been

falling in love unknown to himself, which he finds out
when he leaves the lady. I do not remember any very
strong impression while they were present; but, being
gone, their mementos are shelved in my brain. We
passed a very pleasant little time with the Clarksons.
The Wordsworths are at Montagu's rooms, near neigh-
bours to us. They dined with us yesterday, and I was
their guide to Bartlemy Fair!

To Mrs. GODWIN.

Letter XC.] [*Early in September* 1802?]

Dear Mrs. G.—Having observed with some concern
that Mr. Godwin is a little fastidious in what he eats for
supper, I herewith beg to present his palate with a piece
of dried salmon. I am assured it is the best that swims
in Trent. If you do not know how to dress it, allow me
to add, that it should be cut in thin slices and boiled in
paper *previously prepared in butter*. Wishing it exquisite,
I remain,—Much as before, yours sincerely,

C. Lamb.

Some add *mashed potatoes*.

To THOMAS MANNING.

Letter XCI.] *London, September* 24, 1802.

My dear Manning—Since the date of my last letter
I have been a traveller. A strong desire seized me of
visiting remote regions. My first impulse was to go and
see Paris. It was a trivial objection to my aspiring mind,
that I did not understand a word of the language, since
I certainly intend some time in my life to see Paris, and
equally certainly intend never to learn the language;
therefore that could be no objection. However, I am
very glad I did not go, because you had left Paris (I see)
before I could have set out. I believe, Stoddart promising
to go with me another year, prevented that plan. My

next scheme (for to my restless, ambitious mind London
was become a bed of thorns) was to visit the far-famed
peak in Derbyshire, where the Devil sits, they say, with-
out breeches. *This* my purer mind rejected as indelicate.
And my final resolve was, a tour to the Lakes. I set
out with Mary to Keswick, without giving Coleridge any
notice, for my time, being precious, did not admit of it.
He received us with all the hospitality in the world, and
gave up his time to show us all the wonders of the country.
He dwells upon a small hill by the side of Keswick, in a
comfortable house, quite enveloped on all sides by a net
of mountains: great floundering bears and monsters they
seemed, all couchant and asleep. We got in in the even-
ing, travelling in a post-chaise from Penrith, in the midst
of a gorgeous sunshine, which transmuted all the mount-
ains into colours, purple, etc. etc. We thought we had
got into fairyland. But that went off (as it never came
again; while we stayed we had no more fine sunsets),
and we entered Coleridge's comfortable study just in the
dusk, when the mountains were all dark with clouds upon
their heads. Such an impression I never received from
objects of sight before, nor do I suppose I can ever again.
Glorious creatures, fine old fellows, Skiddaw, etc. I
never shall forget ye, how ye lay about that night, like
an intrenchment; gone to bed, as it seemed for the night,
but promising that ye were to be seen in the morning.
Coleridge had got a blazing fire in his study; which is a
large antique, ill-shaped room, with an old-fashioned organ,
never played upon, big enough for a church, shelves of
scattered folios, an Æolian harp, and an old sofa, half
bed, etc. And all looking out upon the last fading view
of Skiddaw, and his broad-breasted brethren: what a
night! Here we stayed three full weeks, in which time
I visited Wordsworth's cottage, where we stayed a day
or two with the Clarksons (good people, and most hospit-
able, at whose house we tarried one day and night), and
saw Lloyd. The Wordsworths were gone to Calais.
They have since been in London, and past much time

with us : he is now gone into Yorkshire to be married.
So we have seen Keswick, Grasmere, Ambleside, Ulswater
(where the Clarksons live), and a place at the other end
of Ulswater; I forget the name; to which we travelled
on a very sultry day, over the middle of Helvellyn. We
have clambered up to the top of Skiddaw, and I have
waded up the bed of Lodore. In fine, I have satisfied
myself that there is such a thing as that which tourists
call *romantic*, which I very much suspected before : they
make such a spluttering about it, and toss their splendid
epithets around them, till they give as dim a light as at
four o'clock next morning the lamps do after an illumina-
tion. Mary was excessively tired when she got about
half-way up Skiddaw, but we came to a cold rill (than
which nothing can be imagined more cold, running over
cold stones), and with the reinforcement of a draught of
cold water she surmounted it most manfully. Oh, its
fine black head, and the bleak air atop of it, with a pro-
spect of mountains all about and about, making you giddy;
and then Scotland afar off, and the border countries so
famous in song and ballad! It was a day that will stand
out, like a mountain, I am sure, in my life. But I am
returned (I have now been come home near three weeks;
I was a month out), and you cannot conceive the degrada-
tion I felt at first, from being accustomed to wander free
as air among mountains, and bathe in rivers without
being controlled by any one, to come home and *work*. I
felt very *little*. I had been dreaming I was a very great
man. But that is going off, and I find I shall conform
in time to that state of life to which it has pleased God
to call me. Besides, after all, Fleet Street and the Strand
are better places to live in for good and all than amidst
Skiddaw. Still, I turn back to those great places where
I wandered about, participating in their greatness. After
all, I could not *live* in Skiddaw. I could spend a year,
two, three years among them, but I must have a prospect
of seeing Fleet Street at the end of that time, or I should
mope and pine away, I know. Still, Skiddaw is a fine

creature.   My habits are changing, I think, *i.e.* from
drunk to sober. Whether I shall be happier or not
remains to be proved.   I shall certainly be more happy
in a morning ; but whether I shall not sacrifice the fat,
and the marrow, and the kidneys, *i.e.* the night, glorious
care-drowning night, that heals all our wrongs, pours wine
into our mortifications, changes the scene from indifferent
and flat to bright and brilliant ! O Manning, if I should
have formed a diabolical resolution, by the time you come
to England, of not admitting any spirituous liquors into
my house, will you be my guest on such shameworthy
terms ?   Is life, with such limitations, worth trying ?
The truth is, that my liquors bring a nest of friendly
harpies about my house, who consume me.   This is a
pitiful tale to be read at St. Gothard, but it is just now
nearest my heart.   Fenwick is a ruined man.   He is
hiding himself from his creditors, and has sent his wife
and children into the country.   Fell, my other drunken
companion (that has been : *nam hic cæstus artemque
repono*), is turned editor of a Naval Chronicle.   Godwin
continues a steady friend, though the same facility does
not remain of visiting him often.   That . . . has
detached Marshall from his house ; Marshall, the man
who went to sleep when the "Ancient Mariner" was
reading ; the old, steady, unalterable friend of the Pro-
fessor.   Holcroft is not yet come to town.   I expect to
see him, and will deliver your message.   Things come
crowding in to say, and no room for 'em.   Some things
are too little to be told, *i.e.* to have a preference ; some
are too big and circumstantial.   Thanks for yours, which
was most delicious.   Would I had been with you, be-
nighted, etc.!   I fear my head is turned with wandering.
I shall never be the same acquiescent being.   Farewell.
Write again quickly, for I shall not like to hazard a letter,
not knowing where the fates have carried you.   Farewell,
my dear fellow.   C. LAMB.

To SAMUEL TAYLOR COLERIDGE.

LETTER XCII.] *October* 9, 1802.

CAROLUS AGNUS COLERIDGIO SUO S.

Carissime—Scribis, ut nummos scilicet epistolarios solvam et postremo in Tartara abeam : immo tu potius Tartaricum (ut aiunt) deprehendisti, qui me vernaculâ meâ linguâ pro scribâ conductitio per tot annos satis eleganter usum ad Latinè impure et canino fere ore latrandum per tuasmet epistolas benè compositas et concinnatas percellere studueris. Conabor tamen : Attamen vereor, ut Ædes istas nostri Christi, inter quas tantâ diligentiâ magistri improbâ bonis literulis, quasi per clysterem quendam injectis, infrà supràque olim penitùs imbutus fui, Barnesii et Marklandii doctissimorum virorum nominibus adhuc gaudentes, barbarismis meis peregrinis et aliunde quæsitis valde dehonestavero. Sed pergere quocunque placet. Adeste igitur, quotquot estis, conjugationum declinationumve turmæ, terribilia spectra, et tu imprimis ades, Umbra et Imago maxima obsoletæ (Diis gratiæ) Virgæ, quâ novissime in mentem receptâ, horrescunt subito natales, et parum deest quo minùs braccas meas ultro usque ad crura demittam, et ipse puer pueriliter ejulem.

Ista tua Carmina Chamouniana satis grandia esse mihi constat ; sed hoc mihi nonnihil displicet, quòd in iis illæ montium Grisosonum inter se responsiones totidem reboant anglicè, *God, God,* haud aliter atque temet audivi tuas montes Cumbrianas resonare docentes, *Tod, Tod,* nempe Doctorem infelicem : vocem certe haud Deum Sonantem. Pro cæteris plaudo.

Itidem comparationes istas tuas satis callidas et lepidas certè novi : sed quid hoc ad verum ? cum illi Consulari viro et *mentem irritabilem* istum Julianum : et etiam *astutias frigidulas* quasdam Augusto propriores, nequaquam congruenter uno afflatu comparationis causâ insedisse affirmaveris : necnon nescio quid similitudinis etiam cum Tiberio tertio in loco solicite produxeris. Quid tibi equidem cum uno vel altero Cæsare, cùm universi Duodecim ad comparationes tuas se ultro tulerint? Præterea, vetustati adnutans, comparationes iniquas odi.

Istas Wordsworthianas nuptias (vel potius cujusdam *Edmundii* tui) te retulisse mirificum gaudeo. Valeas, Maria, fortunata nimium, et antiquæ illæ Mariæ Virgini (comparatione plusquam Cæsareanâ) forsitan comparanda, quoniam "beata inter mulieres:" et etiam fortasse Wordsworthium ipsum tuum maritum Angelo Salutatori æquare fas erit, quoniam e Cœlo (ut ille) descendunt et Musæ et ipsi Musicolæ : at Wordsworthium Musarum observantissimum semper novi. Necnon te quoque affinitate hâc novâ, Dorothea, gratulor : et tu certe alterum *donum Dei.*

Istum Ludum, quem tu, Coleridgi, Americanum garris, a Ludo (ut Ludi sunt) maximè abhorrentem prætereo : nempe quid ad Ludum attinet, totius illæ gentis Columbianæ, a nostrâ gente, eadem stirpe ortâ, ludi singuli causa voluntatem perperam alienare? Quæso ego materiam ludi : tu Bella ingeris.

Denique valeas, et quid de Latinitate meâ putes, dicas : facias ut opossum illum nostrum volantem vel (ut tu malis) quendam Piscem errabundum, a me salvum et pulcherrimum esse jubeas. Valeant uxor tua cum Hartleiio nostro. Soror mea salva est et ego : vos et ipsa salvere jubet. Ulterius progrediri non liquet : homo sum æratus.

P.S.—Pene mihi exciderat, apud me esse Librorum a Johanno Miltono Latinè scriptorum volumina duo, quæ (Deo volente) cum cæteris tuis libris ocyùs citiùs per Maria ad te missura curabo ; sed me in hoc tali genere rerum nullo modo *festinantem* novisti : habes confitentem reum. Hoc solum dici restat, prædicta volumina pulchra esse et omnia opera Latina J. M. in se continere. Circa

defensionem istam Pro Pop°. Ang°. acerrimam in præsens
ipse præclaro gaudio moror.

Jussa tua Stuartina faciam ut diligenter colam.

Iterum iterumque valeas :

Et facias memor sis nostri.

LETTER XCIII.]   *October* 11, 1802.

Dear Coleridge—Your offer about the German poems
is exceedingly kind : but I do not think it a wise specula-
tion, because the time it would take you to put them
into prose would be nearly as great as if you versified
them.   Indeed I am sure you could do the one nearly as
soon as the other ; so that instead of a division of labour,
it would be only a multiplication.   But I will think of
your offer in another light.   I daresay I could find many
things, of a light nature, to suit that paper, which you
would not object to pass upon Stuart as your own, and I
should come in for some light profits, and Stuart think
the more highly of your assiduity.   "Bishop Hall's
Characters " I know nothing about, having never seen
them.   I will reconsider your offer, which is very
plausible ; but as to the drudgery of going every day to
an editor with my scraps, like a pedler, for him to pick
out and tumble about my ribbons and posies, and to wait
in his lobby, etc., no money could make up for the
degradation.   You are in too high request with him to
have anything unpleasant of that sort to submit to.

It was quite a slip of my pen, in my Latin letter, when
I told you I had Milton's Latin Works.   I ought to have
said his Prose Works, in two volumes, Birck's edition,
containing all, both Latin and English, a fuller and better
edition than Lloyd's of Toland.   It is completely at your
service, and you must accept it from me ; at the same
time I shall be much obliged to you for your Latin
Milton, which you think you have at Howitt's ; it will
leave me nothing to wish for but the *History of England*,
which I shall soon pick up for a trifle.   But you must

write me word whether the Miltons are worth paying
carriage for. You have a Milton; but it is pleasanter
to eat one's own pease out of one's own garden, than to
buy them by the peck at Covent Garden; and a book
reads the better, which is our own, and has been so long
known to us, that we know the topography of its blots
and dog's-ears, and can trace the dirt in it to having read
it at tea with buttered muffins, or over a pipe, which I
think is the maximum. But, Coleridge, you must accept
these little things, and not think of returning money for
them, for I do not set up for a factor or general agent.
As for the fantastic debt of £15, I'll think you were
dreaming, and not trouble myself seriously to attend to
you. My bad Latin you properly correct; but *natales*
for *nates* was an inadvertency: I knew better. *Progre-
diri*, or *progredi*, I thought indifferent, my authority
being Ainsworth. However, as I have got a fit of Latin,
you will now and then indulge me with an *epistola*. I
pay the postage of this, and propose doing it by turns.
In that case I can now and then write to you without
remorse; not that you would mind the money, but you
have not always ready cash to answer small demands, the
epistolarii nummi.

Your "Epigram on the Sun and Moon in Germany"
is admirable. Take 'em all together, they are as good as
Harrington's. I will muster up all the conceits I can,
and you shall have a packet some day. You and I
together can answer all demands surely: you, mounted
on a terrible charger (like Homer, in the Battle of the
Books), at the head of the cavalry: I will lead the light
horse. I have just heard from Stoddart. Allen and he
intend taking Keswick in their way home. Allen wished
particularly to have it a secret that he is in Scotland,
and wrote to me accordingly very urgently. As luck
was, I had told not above three or four; but Mary had
told Mrs. Green, of Christ's Hospital! For the present,
farewell: never forgetting love to Pipos and his friends.

C. LAMB.

I read daily your political essays. I was particularly pleased with "Once a Jacobin:" though the argument is obvious enough, the style was less swelling than your things sometimes are, and it was plausible *ad populum*. A vessel has just arrived from Jamaica with the news of poor Sam Le Grice's death. He died at Jamaica of the yellow fever. His course was rapid, and he had been very foolish; but I believe there was more of kindness and warmth in him than in almost any other of our schoolfellows. The annual meeting of the Blues is tomorrow, at the London Tavern, where poor Sammy dined with them two years ago, and attracted the notice of all by the singular foppishness of his dress. When men go off the stage so early, it scarce seems a noticeable thing in their epitaphs, whether they had been wise or silly in their lifetime.

I am glad the snuff and Pi-pos's books please. "Goody Two Shoes" is almost out of print. Mrs. Barbauld's stuff has banished all the old classics of the nursery; and the shopman at Newberry's hardly deigned to reach them off an old exploded corner of a shelf, when Mary asked for them. Mrs. Barbauld's and Mrs. Trimmer's nonsense lay in piles about. Knowledge insignificant and vapid as Mrs. Barbauld's books convey, it seems, must come to a child in the *shape of knowledge;* and his empty noddle must be turned with conceit of his own powers when he has learnt that a horse is an animal, and Billy is better than a horse, and such like; instead of that beautiful interest in wild tales, which made the child a man, while all the time he suspected himself to be no bigger than a child. Science has succeeded to poetry no less in the little walks of children than with men. Is there no possibility of averting this sore evil? Think what you would have been now, if, instead of being fed with tales and old wives' fables in childhood, you had been crammed with geography and natural history!

Hang them !—I mean the cursed Barbauld crew, those blights and blasts of all that is human in man and child.

As to the translations, let me do two or three hundred lines, and then do you try the nostrums upon Stuart in any way you please.   If they go down I will bray more. In fact, if I got or could but get £50 a year only, in addition to what I have, I should live in affluence.

Have you anticipated it, or could you not give a parallel of Buonaparte with Cromwell, particularly as to the contrast in their deeds affecting *foreign* States? Cromwell's interference for the Albigenses, Buonaparte's against the Swiss.   Then religion would come in ; and Milton and you could rant about our countrymen of that period.   This is a hasty suggestion, the more hasty because I want my supper.   I have just finished Chapman's Homer.   Did you ever read it? it has the continuous power of interesting you all along, like a rapid original, more than any ; and in the uncommon excellence of the more finished parts goes beyond Fairfax or any of 'em.   The metre is fourteen syllables, and capable of all sweetness and grandeur.   Cowper's blank verse detains you every step with some heavy Miltonism ; Chapman gallops off with you his own free pace.   Take a simile for example.   The council breaks up—

> " Being abroad, the earth was overlaid
> With flockers to them, that came forth ; as when of frequent bees
> Swarms rise out of a hollow rock, repairing the degrees
> *Of their egression endlessly, with ever rising new*
> From forth their sweet nest ; as their store, still as it faded, grew,
> *And never would cease sending forth clusters to the spring,*
> They still crowd out so ; this flock here, that there, belabouring
> The loaded flowers. So," etc. etc.

What *endless egression of phrases* the dog commands !

Take another, Agamemnon wounded, bearing his wound heroically for the sake of the army (look below), to a woman in labour.

> " He, with his lance, sword, mighty stones, pour'd his heroic wreak
> On other squadrons of the foe, whiles yet warm bloom did break

Thro' his cleft veins ; but when the wound was quite exhaust
    and crude,
The eager anguish did approve his princely fortitude.
As when most sharp and bitter pangs distract a labouring dame,
Which the divine Ilithiæ, that rule the painful frame
Of human childbirth, pour on her ; the Ilithiæ that are
The daughters of Saturnia ; with whose extreme repair
The woman strives to take the worst it gives ;
With thought, it *must be, 'tis love's fruit, the end for which she*
    lives ;
The mean to make herself new born, what comforts will redound :
So," etc.

I will tell you more about Chapman and his peculiarities in my next. I am much interested in him.

Yours ever affectionately, and Pi-Pos's.   C. L.

LETTER XCV.]   *November* 4, 1802.

Observe, there comes to you, by the Kendal waggon to-morrow, the illustrious 5th of November, a box, containing the Miltons, the strange American Bible, with White's brief note, to which you will attend; *Baxter's Holy Commonwealth*, for which you stand indebted to me 3s. 6d. ; an odd volume of Montaigne, being of no use to me, I having the whole ; certain books belonging to Wordsworth, as do also the strange thick-hoofed shoes, which are very much admired in London. All these sundries I commend to your most strenuous looking after. If you find the Miltons in certain parts dirtied and soiled with a crumb of right Gloucester, blacked in the candle (my usual supper), or peradventure a stray ash of tobacco wafted into the crevices, look to that passage more especially : depend upon it, it contains good matter. I have got your little Milton, which, as it contains " Salmasius," and I make a rule of never hearing but one side of the question (why should I distract myself?), I shall return to you when I pick up the *Latina opera*. The first Defence is the greatest work among them, because it is uniformly great, and such as is befitting the very mouth of a great nation, speaking for itself. But the second Defence, which is but a succession of splendid episodes, slightly tied together, has one passage, which, if you have not read, I conjure you to lose no time, but read it : it is his consolations in his blindness, which had been made a reproach to him. It begins whimsically, with poetical flourishes about Tiresias and other blind worthies (which still are mainly interesting as displaying his singular mind, and in what degree poetry entered into his daily soul, not by fits and impulses, but engrained and innate), but the concluding page, *i.e.* of *this passage* (not of the *Defensio*), which you will easily find, divested of all brags and flourishes, gives so rational, so true an enumeration of his comforts, so human, that it cannot be read without the deepest interest. Take one touch of the religious part :—"Et sane haud ultima Dei cura cæci —*we blind folks*, I understand it (not *nos* for *ego ;*)— sumus ; qui nos, quominus quicquam aliud præter ipsum cernere valemus, eo clementius atque benignius respicere dignatur. Væ qui illudit nos, væ qui lædit, execratione publica devovendo ; nos ab injuriis hominum non modo incolumes, sed pene sacros, divina lex reddidit, divinus favor : nec tam *oculorum hebetudine* quam *cœlestium alarum umbrâ* has nobis fecisse tenebras videtur, factas illustrare rursus interiore ac longe præstabiliore lumine haud raro solet. Huc refero, quod et amici officiosius nunc etiam quam solebant, colunt, observant, adsunt, quod et nonnulli sunt, quibuscum Pyladeas atque Thescas alternare voces verorum amicorum liceat.

    " Vade gubernaculum mei pedis.
       Da manum ministro amico
       Da collo manum tuam, ductor autem viæ ero tibi ego."

All this, and much more, is highly pleasing to know. But you may easily find it ; and I don't know why I put down so many words about it but for the pleasure of writing to you, and the want of another topic.

    Yours ever,   C. LAMB.

    To-morrow I expect with anxiety S. T. C.'s letter to Mr. Fox.

TO THOMAS MANNING.

LETTER XCVI.]   *November* 1802.

My dear Manning—I must positively write, or I shall miss you at Toulouse. I sit here like a decayed minute hand; (I lie: *that* does not *sit;*) and being myself the exponent of no time, take no heed how the clocks about me are going. You possibly by this time may have explored all Italy, and toppled, unawares, into Etna, while you went too near those rotten-jawed, gap-toothed, old worn-out chaps of hell,—while I am meditating a quiescent letter to the honest post-master of Toulouse. But in case you should not have been *felo de se*, this is to tell you, that your letter was quite to my palate: in particular your just remarks upon Industry, cursed Industry (though indeed you left me to explore the reason), were highly relishing. I have often wished I had lived in the golden age, when shepherds lay stretched upon flowers, and roused themselves at their leisure,—the genius there is in a man's natural idle face, that has not learned his multiplication table! before doubt, and propositions, and corollaries, got into the world!

Now, as Joseph Cottle, a Bard of Nature, sings, going up Malvern Hills,

> " How steep ! how painful the ascent !
> It needs the evidence of *close deduction*
> To know that ever I shall gain the top."

You must know that Joe is lame, so that he had some reason for so singing. These two lines, I assure you, are taken *totidem literis* from a very *popular* poem. Joe is also an Epic Poet as well as a Descriptive, and has written a tragedy, though both his drama and epopoica are strictly *descriptive*, and chiefly of the *Beauties of Nature*, for Joe thinks *man* with all his passions and frailties not a proper subject of the *Drama*. Joe's tragedy hath the following surpassing speech in it. Some king is told that his enemy has engaged twelve archers to come over in a boat from an enemy's country and way-lay him; he thereupon pathetically exclaims—

" *Twelve*, dost thou say? Curse on those dozen villains!"

Cottle read two or three acts out to us, very gravely on both sides till he came to this heroic touch,—and then he asked what we laughed at? I had no more muscles that day. A poet that chooses to read out his own verses has but a limited power over you. There is a bound where his authority ceases.

LETTER XCVII.]   *February* 19, 1803.

My dear Manning—The general scope of your letter afforded no indications of insanity, but some particular points raised a scruple. For God's sake don't think any more of " Independent Tartary." What are you to do among such Ethiopians? Is there no *lineal descendant* of Prester John? Is the chair empty? Is the sword unswayed? Depend upon it they'll never make you their king, as long as any branch of that great stock is remaining. I tremble for your Christianity. They will certainly circumcise you. Read Sir John Mandeville's travels to cure you, or come over to England. There is a Tartarman now exhibiting at Exeter Change. Come and talk with him, and hear what he says first. Indeed he is no very favourable specimen of his countrymen! But perhaps the best thing you can do is to *try* to get the idea out of your head. For this purpose repeat to yourself every night, after you have said your prayers, the words Independent Tartary, Independent Tartary, two or three times, and associate with them the *idea* of *oblivion* ('tis Hartley's method with obstinate memories), or say, Independent, Independent, have I not already got an *independence?* That was a clever way of the old puritans, pun-divinity. My dear friend, think what a sad pity it would be to bury such *parts* in heathen countries, among nasty, unconversable, horse - belching, Tartar - people !

Some say, they are Cannibals ; and then, conceive a Tartar-fellow *eating* my friend, and adding the *cool malignity* of mustard and vinegar ! I am afraid 'tis the reading of Chaucer has misled you ; his foolish stories about Cambuscan, and the ring, and the horse of brass. Believe me, there are no such things, 'tis all the poet's *invention ;* but if there were such darling things as old Chaucer sings, I would *up* behind you on the horse of brass, and frisk off for Prester John's country. But these are all tales ; a horse of brass never flew, and a king's daughter never talked with birds ! The Tartars, really, are a cold, insipid, smouchy set. You'll be sadly moped (if you are not eaten) among them. Pray *try* and cure yourself. Take hellebore (the counsel is Horace's, 'twas none of my thought *originally*). Shave yourself oftener. Eat no saffron, for saffron-eaters contract a terrible Tartar-like yellow. Pray, to avoid the fiend. Eat nothing that gives the heart-burn. *Shave the upper lip.* Go about like an European. Read no books of voyages (they are nothing but lies), only now and then a romance, to keep the fancy *under.* Above all, don't go to any sights of *wild beasts.* *That has been your ruin.* Accustom yourself to write familiar letters, on common subjects, to your friends in England, such as are of a moderate understanding. And think about common things more. There's your friend Holcroft, now, has written a Play. You used to be fond of the drama. Nobody went to see it. Notwithstanding this, with an audacity perfectly original, he faces the town down in a preface that they *did* like it very much. I have heard a waspish punster say, "Sir, why did you not laugh at my jest?" But for a man boldly to face one out with "Sir, I maintain it, you *did* laugh at my jest," is a little too much. I have seen H. but once. He spoke of you to me in honourable terms. H. seems to me to be drearily dull. G———— is dull, then he has a dash of affectation, which smacks of the coxcomb, and your coxcombs are always agreeable. I supped last night with Rickman, and met a merry *natural* captain, who pleases himself vastly with once having made a pun at Otaheite in the O. language. 'Tis the same man who said Shakspeare he liked, because he was *so much of the gentleman.* Rickman is a man "absolute in all numbers." I think I may one day bring you acquainted, if you do not go to Tartary first; for you'll never come back. Have a care, my dear friend, of Anthropophagi! their stomachs are always craving. 'Tis terrible to be weighed out at fivepence a-pound; to sit at table (the reverse of fishes in Holland) not as a guest, but as a meat.

God bless you: do come to England. Air and exercise may do great things. Talk with some minister. Why not your father?

God dispose all for the best. I have discharged my duty.

Your sincere friend, C. LAMB.

LETTER XCVIII.] *February* 1803.

Not a sentence, not a syllable of Trismegistus shall be lost through my neglect. I am his word-banker, his storekeeper of puns and syllogisms. You cannot conceive (and if Trismegistus cannot, no man can) the strange joy which I felt at the receipt of a letter from Paris. It seemed to give me a learned importance, which placed me above all who had not Parisian correspondents. Believe that I shall carefully husband every scrap, which will save you the trouble of memory, when you come back. You cannot write things so trifling, let them only be about Paris, which I shall not treasure. In particular, I must have parallels of actors and actresses. I must be told if any building in Paris is at all comparable to St. Paul's, which, contrary to the usual mode of that part of our nature called admiration, I have looked up to with un-fading wonder, every morning at ten o'clock, ever since it has lain in my way to business. At noon I casually glance upon it, being hungry; and hunger has not much taste for the fine arts. Is any night-walk comparable to a walk from St. Paul's to Charing Cross, for lighting and paving, crowds going and coming without respite, the rattle of coaches, and the cheerfulness of shops? Have you seen a man guillotined yet? Is it as good as hanging? Are the women *all* painted, and the men *all* monkeys? or are there not a *few* that look like *rational* of *both sexes?* Are you and the first consul *thick?* All this expense of ink I may fairly put you to, as your letters will not be solely for my proper pleasure; but are to serve as memoranda and notices, helps for short memory, a kind of Rumfordising recollection, for yourself on your return. Your letter was just what a letter should be, crammed, and very funny. Every part of it pleased me till you came to Paris; then your philosophical indolence, or indifference, stung me. You cannot stir from your rooms till you know the language! What the devil!—are men nothing but word-trumpets? Are men all tongue and ear? Have these creatures, that you and I profess to know *something about*, no faces, gestures, gabble, no folly, no absurdity, no induction of French education upon the abstract idea of men and women, no similitude nor dissimilitude to English! Why, thou cursed Smellfungus! your account of your landing and reception, and Bullen, (I forget how you spell it, it was spelt my way in Harry the Eighth's time), was exactly in that minute style which strong impressions INSPIRE (writing to a Frenchman, I write as a Frenchman would). It appears to me as if I should die with joy at the first landing in a foreign country. It is the nearest pleasure which a grown man can substitute for that unknown one, which he can never know, the pleasure of the first entrance into life from the womb. I dare say, in a short time, my habits would come back like a "stronger man" armed, and drive out that new pleasure; and I should soon sicken for known objects. Nothing has transpired here that seems to me of sufficient importance to send dry-shod over the water: but I suppose you will want to be told some news. The best and

the worst to me is, that I have given up two guineas a
week at the *Post*, and regained my health and spirits,
which were upon the wane. I grew sick, and Stuart
unsatisfied. *Ludisti satis, tempus abire est ;* I must cut
closer, that's all. Mister Fell, or as you, with your usual
facetiousness and drollery, call him, Mr. F + ll, has
stopped short in the middle of his play. Some *friend*
has told him that it has not the least merit in it. Oh
that I had the rectifying of the Litany ! I would put in
a *libera nos (Scriptores videlicet) ab amicis !* That's all
the news. *Apropos :* is it pedantry, writing to a French-
man, to express myself sometimes by a French word, when
an English one would not do as well ? Methinks my
thoughts fall naturally into it.

In all this time I have done but one thing, which I
reckon tolerable, and that I will transcribe, because it
may give you pleasure, being a picture of *my* humours.
You will find it in my last page. It absurdly is a first
Number of a series, thus strangled in embryo.

More news ! The Professor's Rib has come out to be
a disagreeable woman, so much so as to drive me and
some more old cronies from his house. He must not
wonder if people are shy of coming to see him because of
the " snakes."   C. L.

LETTER XCIX.]   *March* 1803.

Dear Manning—I send you some verses I have made
on the death of a young Quaker you may have heard me
speak of as being in love with for some years while I
lived at Pentonville, though I had never spoken to her in
my life. She died about a month since. If you have
interest with the Abbé de Lisle, you may get 'em trans-
lated ; he has done as much for the Georgics.

To SAMUEL TAYLOR COLERIDGE.

LETTER C. *March* 20, 1803.

> Mary sends love from home.

Dear Coleridge—I do confess that I have not sent your books as I ought to have done; but you know how the human free will is tethered, and that we perform promises to ourselves no better than to our friends. A watch is come for you. Do you want it soon, or shall I wait till some one travels your way? You, like me, I suppose, reckon the lapse of time from the waste thereof, as boys let a cock run to waste; too idle to stop it, and rather amused with seeing it dribble. Your poems have begun printing; Longman sent to me to arrange them, the old and the new together. It seems you have left it to him; so I classed them, as nearly as I could, according to dates. First, after the Dedication (which must march first), and which I have transplanted from before the Preface (which stood like a dead wall of prose between), to be the first poem; then comes "The Pixies," and the things most juvenile; then on "To Chatterton," etc.,—on, lastly, to the "Ode on the Departing Year," and "Musings,"—which finish. Longman wanted the Ode first, but the arrangement I have made is precisely that marked out in the Dedication, following the order of time. I told Longman I was sure that you would omit a good portion of the first edition. I instanced several sonnets, etc.; but that was not his plan, and, as you have done nothing in it, all I could do was to arrange 'em on the supposition that all were to be retained. A few I positively rejected; such as that of "The Thimble," and that of "Flicker and Flicker's Wife," and that *not* in the manner of Spenser, which you yourself had stigmatised—and the "Man of Ross,"—I doubt whether I should this last. It is not too late to save it. The first proof is only just come. I have been forced to call that Cupid's Elixir, "Kisses." It stands in your first volume,

as an Effusion, so that, instead of prefixing "The Kiss"
to that of "One Kiss, dear Maid," etc., I have ventured
to entitle it "To Sara." I am aware of the nicety of
changing even so mere a trifle as a title to so short a
piece, and subverting old associations; but two called
"Kisses" would have been absolutely ludicrous, and
"Effusion" is no name, and these poems come close
together. I promise you not to alter one word in any
poem whatever, but to take your last text, where two
are. Can you send any wishes about the book? Long-
man, I think, should have settled with you; but it seems
you have left it to him. Write as soon as you possibly
can; for, without making myself responsible, I feel my-
self, in some sort, accessory to the selection, which I am
to proof-correct; but I decidedly said to Biggs that I was
sure you would omit more. Those I have positively
rubbed off, I can swear to *individually* (except the "Man
of Ross," which is too familiar in Pope), but no others—
you have your cue. For my part, I would rather all the
Juvenilia were kept—*memoriæ causâ*.

Robert Lloyd has written me a masterly letter, con-
taining a character of his father. See how different from
Charles he views the old man! (*Literatim*): "My father
smokes, repeats Homer in Greek, and Virgil, and is learn-
ing, when from business, with all the vigour of a young
man, Italian. He is, really, a wonderful man. He
mixes public and private business, the intricacies of dis-
ordering life, with his religion and devotion. No one
more rationally enjoys the romantic scenes of Nature,
and the chit-chat and little vagaries of his children; and,
though surrounded with an ocean of affairs, the very
neatness of his most obscure cupboard in the house
passes not unnoticed. I never knew any one view with
such clearness, nor so well satisfied with things as they
are, and make such allowance for things which must
appear perfect Syriac to him." By the last he means the
Lloydisms of the younger branches. His portrait of
Charles (exact as far as he has had opportunities of

noting him) is most exquisite:—"Charles is become steady as a church, and as straightforward as a Roman road. It would distract him to mention anything that was not as plain as sense ; he seems to have run the whole scenery of life, and now rests as the formal precision of non-existence." Here is genius, I think, and 'tis seldom a young man, a Lloyd, looks at a father (so differing) with such good-nature while he is alive. Write—

I am in post-haste, C. LAMB.

Love, etc., to Sara, P., and H.

LETTER CI.] *April* 13, 1803.

My dear Coleridge—Things have gone on better with me since you left me. I expect to have my old house-keeper home again in a week or two. She has mended most rapidly. My health too has been better since you took away that Montero cap. I have left off cayenned eggs and such bolsters to discomfort. There was death in that cap. I mischievously wished that by some inauspicious jolt the whole contents might be shaken, and the coach set on fire ; for you said they had that property. How the old gentleman, who joined you at Grantham, would have clapp'd his hands to his knees, and not knowing but it was an immediate visitation of God that burnt him, how pious it would have made him !—him, I mean, that brought the Influenza with him, and only took places for one—an old sinner ; he must have known what he had got with him ! However, I wish the cap no harm for the sake of the *head it fits,* and could be content to see it disfigure my healthy sideboard again.

What do you think of smoking ? I want your sober, *average, noon opinion* of it. I generally am eating my dinner about the time I should determine it.

Morning is a girl, and can't smoke—she's no evidence one way or the other ; and Night is so evidently *bought over,* that he can't be a very upright judge. May be the truth is, that *one* pipe is wholesome, *two* pipes toothsome, *three* pipes noisome, *four* pipes fulsome, *five* pipes quarrelsome, and that's the *sum* on't. But that is deciding rather upon rhyme than reason. . . . After all, our instincts *may* be best. Wine, I am sure—good mellow, generous Port—can hurt nobody, unless those who take it to excess, which they may easily avoid if they observe the rules of temperance.

Bless you, old sophist, who next to human nature taught me all the corruption I was capable of knowing! And bless your Montero cap, and your trail (which shall come after you whenever you appoint), and your wife and children—Pipos especially.

When shall we two smoke again? Last night I had been in a sad quandary of spirits, in what they call the evening; but a pipe, and some generous Port, and *King Lear* (being alone), had their effects as solacers. I went to bed pot-valiant. By the way, may not the Ogles of Somersetshire be remotely descended from King Lear?

C. L.

To THOMAS MANNING.

LETTER CII.]   *April* 23, 1803.

My dear Manning—Although something of the latest, and after two months' waiting, your letter was highly gratifying. Some parts want a little explication; for example, " the god-like face of the first consul." *What god* does he most resemble, Mars, Bacchus, or Apollo? or the god Serapis, who, flying (as Egyptian chronicles deliver) from the fury of the dog Anubis (the hieroglyph of an English mastiff), lighted upon Monomotapa (or the land of apes), by some thought to be Old France, and there set up a tyranny, etc. Our London prints of him represent him gloomy and sulky, like an angry Jupiter. I hear that he is very small, even less than me. I envy you your access to this great man, much more than your séances and conversaziones, which I have a shrewd suspicion must be something dull. What you assert concerning the actors of Paris, that they exceed our comedians, bad as ours are, is *impossible*. In one sense it may be true, that their fine gentlemen, in what is called genteel comedy, may possibly be more brisk and *dégagé* than Mr. Caulfield, or Mr. Whitfield; but have any of them the power to move *laughter in excess?* or can a Frenchman *laugh?* Can they batter at your judicious ribs till they *shake*, nothing loth to be so shaken? This is John Bull's criterion, and it shall be mine. You are Frenchified. Both your tastes and morals are corrupt and perverted. By and by you will come to assert that Buonaparte is as great a general as the old Duke of Cumberland, and deny that one Englishman can beat three Frenchmen. Read *Henry the Fifth* to restore your orthodoxy.

All things continue at a stay-still in London. I cannot repay your new novelties with my stale reminiscences. Like the prodigal, I have spent my patrimony, and feed upon the superannuated chaff and dry husks of repentance; yet sometimes I remember with pleasure the hounds and horses, which I kept in the days of my prodigality. I find nothing new, nor anything that has so much of the gloss and dazzle of novelty as may rebound in narrative, and cast a reflective glimmer across the channel. Something I will say about people that you and I know. Fenwick is still in debt, and the Professor has not done making love to his new spouse. I think he never looks into an almanack, or he would have found by the calendar that the honeymoon was extinct a moon ago. Southey is Secretary to the Chancellor of the Irish Exchequer; £400 a year. Stoddart is turned Doctor of Civil Law, and dwells in Doctors' Commons. I fear *his* commons are short, as they say. Did I send you an epitaph I scribbled upon a poor girl who died at nineteen?—a good girl, and a pretty girl, and a clever girl, but strangely neglected by all her friends and kin.

> " Under this cold marble stone
>   Sleep the sad remains of one
>   Who, when alive, by few or none
>   Was loved, as loved she might have been,
>   If she prosperous days had seen,
>   Or had thriving been, I ween.
>   Only this cold funeral stone
>   Tells she was beloved by one,
>   Who on the marble graves his moan."

Brief, and pretty, and tender, is it not? I send you this, being the only piece of poetry I have *done* since the Muses all went with T. M. to Paris. I have neither stuff in my brain, nor paper in my drawer, to write you a longer letter. Liquor and company and wicked tobacco, a'nights, have quite dispericraniated me, as one may say; but you, who spiritualise upon Champagne, may continue to write long letters, and stuff 'em with amusement to the end. Too long they cannot be, any more than a codicil to a will, which leaves me sundry parks and manors not specified in the deed. But don't be *two months* before you write again. These from merry old England, on the day of her valiant patron St. George.

C. LAMB.

To SAMUEL TAYLOR COLERIDGE.

LETTER CIII.]   *May* 27, 1803.

My dear Coleridge—The date of my last was one day prior to the receipt of your letter, full of foul omens. I explain this lest you should have thought mine too light a reply to such sad matter. I seriously hope by this time you have given up all thoughts of journeying to the green Islands of the Bless'd—(voyages in time of war are very precarious)—or at least, that you will take them in your way to the Azores. Pray be careful of this letter till it has done its duty, for it is to inform you that I have booked off your watch (laid in cotton like an untimely fruit), and with it Condillac, and all other books of yours which were left here. These will set out on Monday next, the 29th May, by Kendal waggon, from White Horse, Cripplegate. You will make seasonable inquiries, for a watch mayn't come your way again in a hurry. I have been repeatedly after Tobin, and now hear that he is in the country, not to return till the middle of June. I will take care and see him with the earliest. But cannot you write pathetically to him, enforcing a speeding mission of your books for literary purposes? He is too good a retainer to Literature to let her interests suffer through his default. And why, in the name of Beelzebub, are your books to travel from Barnard's Inn to the Temple, and thence circuitously to Cripplegate, when their business is to take a short cut down Holborn Hill, up Snow ditto, on to Wood Street, etc.? The former mode seems a sad superstitious sub-division of labour. Well! the "Man of Ross" is to stand; Longman begs for it; the printer stands with a wet sheet in one hand, and a useless Pica in the other, in tears, pleading for it; I relent. Besides, it was a *Salutation* poem, and has the mark of the beast "Tobacco" upon it. Thus much I have done; I have swept off the lines about *widows* and *orphans* in second edition, which (if you remember) you most awkwardly and illogically caused to be inserted between two *Ifs*, to the great breach and disunion of said *Ifs*, which now meet again (as in first edition), like two clever lawyers arguing a case. Another reason for subtracting the pathos was, that the "Man of Ross" is too familiar to need telling what he did, especially in worse lines than Pope told it, and it now stands simply as "Reflections at an Inn about a known Character," and sucking an old story into an accommodation with present feelings. Here is no breaking spears with Pope, but a new, independent, and really a very pretty poem. In fact 'tis as I used to admire it in the first volume, and I have even dared to restore

> "If neath this roof thy *wine cheer'd* moments pass,"

for

> "Beneath this roof if thy cheer'd moments pass."

"Cheer'd" is a sad general word, "*wine-cheer'd*" I'm sure you'd give me, if I had a speaking-trumpet to sound to you 300 miles. But I am your *factotum;* and that (save in this instance, which is a single case, and I can't get at you) shall be next to a *fac-nihil*—at most a *fac-simile*. I have ordered "Imitation of Spenser" to be restored on Wordsworth's authority; and now, all that you will miss will be "Flicker and Flicker's Wife," "The Thimble," "Breathe *dear harmonist,*" and *I believe,* "The Child that was fed with Manna." Another volume will clear off all your Anthologic Morning-Postian Epistolary Miscellanies; but pray don't put "Christabel" therein; don't let that sweet maid come forth attended with Lady Holland's mob at her heels. Let there be a separate volume of Tales, Choice Tales, "Ancient Mariners," etc. A word of your health will be richly acceptable.   C. LAMB.

To Mr. RICKMAN.

LETTER CIV.]   *Saturday Morning, July* 16, 1803.

Dear Rickman—I enclose you a wonder, a letter from the shades. A dead body wants to return, and be inrolled *inter vivos.* 'Tis a gentle ghost, and in this Galvanic age it may have a chance.

Mary and I are setting out for the Isle of Wight. We make but a short stay, and shall pass the time betwixt that place and Portsmouth, where Fenwick is. I sadly wanted to explore the Peak this Summer; but Mary is against steering without card or compass, and we should be at large in Darbyshire.

We shall be at home this night and to-morrow, if you can come and take a farewell pipe.

I regularly transmitted your Notices to the *Morning Post,* but they have not been duly honoured. The fault lay not in me.—Yours truly,   C. LAMB.

To WILLIAM GODWIN.

LETTER CV.]*November* 8, 1803.

My dear Sir—I have been sitting down for three or four days successively to the review, which I so much wished to do well, and to your satisfaction. But I can produce nothing but absolute flatness and nonsense. My health and spirits are so bad, and my nerves so irritable, that I am sure, if I persist, I shall tease myself into a fever. You do not know how sore and weak a brain I have, or you would allow for many things in me which you set down for whims. I solemnly assure you that I never more wished to prove to you the value which I have for you than at this moment; but although so seemingly trifling a service I cannot get through with it: I pray you to impute it to this one sole cause, ill health. I hope I am above subterfuge, and that you will do me this justice to think so.

You will give me great satisfaction by sealing my pardon and oblivion in a line or two, before I come to see you, or I shall be ashamed to come.—Your, with great truth,   C. LAMB.

LETTER CVI.]*November* 10, 1803.

Dear Godwin—You never made a more unlucky and perverse mistake than to suppose that the reason of my not writing that cursed thing was to be found in your book. I assure you most sincerely that I have been greatly delighted with " Chaucer." I may be wrong, but I think there is one considerable error runs through it, which is a conjecturing spirit, a fondness for filling out the picture by supposing what Chaucer did and how he felt, where the materials are scanty. So far from meaning to withhold from you (out of mistaken tenderness) this opinion of mine, I plainly told Mrs. Godwin that I did find a *fault*, which I should reserve naming until I should see you and talk it over. This she may very well remember, and also that I declined naming this fault until she drew it from me by asking me if there was not too much fancy in the work. I then confessed generally what I felt, but refused to go into particulars until I had seen you. I am never very fond of saying things before third persons, because in the relation (such is human nature) something is sure to be dropped. If Mrs. Godwin has been the cause of your misconstruction, I am very angry, tell her; yet it is not an anger unto death. I remember also telling Mrs. G. (which she may have *dropt*) that I was by turns considerably more delighted than I expected. But I wished to reserve all this until I saw you. I even had conceived an expression to meet you with, which was thanking you for some of the most exquisite pieces of criticism I had ever read in my life. In particular, I should have brought forward that on " Troilus and Cressida " and Shakspeare which, it is little to say, delighted me, and instructed me (if not absolutely *instructed* me, yet put into *full-grown sense* many conceptions which had arisen in me before in my most discriminating moods). All these things I was preparing to say, and bottling them up till I came, thinking to please my friend and host the author, when lo ! this deadly blight intervened.

I certainly ought to make great allowances for your misunderstanding me. You, by long habits of composition and a greater command gained over your own powers, cannot conceive of the desultory and uncertain way in which I (an author by fits) sometimes cannot put the thoughts of a common letter into sane prose. Any work which I take upon myself as an engagement will act upon me to torment, *e.g.* when I have undertaken, as three or four times I have, a schoolboy copy of verses for Merchant Taylors' boys, at a guinea a copy, I have fretted over them in perfect inability to do them, and have made my sister wretched with my wretchedness for a week together. The same, till by habit I have acquired a mechanical command, I have felt in making paragraphs. As to reviewing, in particular, my head is so whimsical a head, that I cannot, after reading another man's book, let it have been never so pleasing, give any account of it in any methodical way. I cannot follow his train. Something like this you must have perceived of me in conversation. Ten thousand times I have confessed to you, talking of my talents, my utter inability to remember in any comprehensive way what I read. I can vehemently applaud, or perversely stickle, at *parts ;* but I cannot grasp at a whole. This infirmity (which is nothing to brag of) may be seen in my two little compositions, the tale and my play, in both which no reader, however partial, can find any story. I wrote such stuff about Chaucer, and got into such digressions, quite irreducible into $1\frac{1}{3}$ column of a paper, that I was perfectly ashamed to show it you. However, it is become a serious matter that I should convince you I neither slunk from the task through a wilful deserting neglect, or through any (most imaginary on your part) distaste of " Chaucer ;" and I will try my hand again, I hope with better luck. My health is bad and my time taken up ; but all I can spare between this and Sunday shall be employed for you, since you desire it : and if I bring you a crude, wretched paper on Sunday, you must burn it, and forgive me ; if it proves anything better than I predict, may it be a peace-offering of sweet incense between us. C. LAMB.

To ROBERT SOUTHEY.

LETTER CVII.] *November 7, 1804.*

Dear Southey—You were the last person from whom we heard of Dyer, and if you know where to forward to him the news I now send I shall be obliged to you to lose no time. Dyer's sister-in-law, who lives in St. Dunstan's Court, wrote to him about three weeks ago to the Hope Inn, Cambridge, to inform him that Squire Houlbert, or some such name, of Denmark Hill, has died, and left her husband a thousand pounds, and two or three hundred to Dyer. Her letter got no answer, and she does not know where to direct to him; so she came to me, who am equally in the dark. Her story is, that Dyer's immediately coming to town now, and signing some papers, will save him a considerable sum of money; how, I don't understand; but it is very right he should hear of this. She has left me barely time for the post; so I conclude with love to all at Keswick.

Dyer's brother, who by his wife's account has got £1000 left him, is father of the little dirty girl, Dyer's niece and factotum.—In haste,

Yours truly,   C. LAMB.

If you send George this, cut off the last paragraph.

D.'s laundress had a letter a few days since; but George never dates.

To THOMAS MANNING.

16, *Mitre Court Buildings,*
Saturday, February 24, 1805.

LETTER CVIII.]

Dear Manning—I have been very unwell since I saw you: a sad depression of spirits, a most unaccountable nervousness; from which I have been partially relieved by an odd accident. You knew Dick Hopkins, the swearing scullion of Caius? This fellow, by industry and agility, has thrust himself into the important situations (no sinecures, believe me) of cook to Trinity Hall and Caius College: and the generous creature has contrived, with the greatest delicacy imaginable, to send me a present of Cambridge brawn. What makes it the more extraordinary is, that the man never saw me in his life that I know of. I suppose he has *heard* of me. I did not immediately recognise the donor; but one of Richard's cards, which had accidentally fallen into the straw, detected him in a moment. Dick, you know, was always remarkable for flourishing. His card imports, that "orders (to wit, for brawn) from any part of England, Scotland, or Ireland, will be duly executed," etc. At first, I thought of declining the present; but Richard knew my blind side when he pitched upon brawn. 'Tis of all my hobbies the supreme in the eating way. He might have sent sops from the pan, skimmings, crumpets, chips, hog's lard, the tender brown judiciously scalped from a fillet of veal (dexterously replaced by a salamander), the tops of asparagus, fugitive livers, runaway gizzards of fowls, the eyes of martyred pigs, tender effusions of laxative woodcocks, the red spawn of lobsters, leverets' ears, and such pretty filchings common to cooks; but these had been ordinary presents, the everyday courtesies of dish-washers to their sweethearts. Brawn was a noble thought. It is not every common gullet-fancier that can properly esteem it. It is like a picture of one of the choice old Italian masters. Its gusto is of that hidden sort. As Wordsworth sings of a modest poet,—"you must love him, ere to you he will seem worthy of your love;" so brawn, you must taste it ere to you it will seem to have any taste at all. But 'tis nuts to the adept: those that will send out their tongue and feelers to find it out. It will be wooed, and not unsought be won. Now, ham-essence, lobsters, turtle, such popular minions, absolutely *court you*, lay themselves out to strike you at first smack, like one of David's pictures (they call him *Darveed*) compared with the plain russet-coated wealth of a Titian or a Correggio, as I illustrated above. Such are the obvious glaring heathen virtues of a corporation dinner, compared with the reserved collegiate worth of brawn. Do me the favour to leave off the business which you may be at present upon, and go immediately to the kitchens of Trinity and Caius, and make my most respectful compliments to Mr. Richard Hopkins, and assure him that his brawn is most excellent; and that I am moreover obliged to him for his innuendo about salt

water and bran, which I shall not fail to improve. I
leave it to you whether you shall choose to pay him the
civility of asking him to dinner while you stay in Cam-
bridge, or in whatever other way you may best like to
show your gratitude to *my friend.* Richard Hopkins,
considered in many points of view, is a very extraordinary
character. Adieu. I hope to see you to supper in
London soon, where we will taste Richard's brawn, and
drink his health in a cheerful but moderate cup. We
have not many such men in any rank of life as Mr. R.
Hopkins. Crisp, the barber, of St. Mary's, was just such
another. I wonder *he* never sent me any little token,
some chestnuts, or a puff, or two pound of hair : just to
remember him by. Gifts are like nails. *Præsens ut
absens ;* that is, your *present* makes amends for your
absence.

    Yours,   C. LAMB.

To Miss WORDSWORTH.

LETTER CIX.]   *June* 14, 1805.

My dear Miss Wordsworth—Your long kind letter
has not been thrown away (for it has given me great
pleasure to find you are all resuming your old occupations,
and are better) ; but poor Mary, to whom it is addressed,
cannot yet relish it. She has been attacked by one of
her severe illnesses, and is at present *from home.* Last
Monday week was the day she left me, and I hope I may
calculate upon having her again in a month or little more.
I am rather afraid late hours have in this case contributed
to her indisposition. But when she discovers symptoms
of approaching illness, it is not easy to say what is best
to do. Being by ourselves is bad, and going out is bad.
I get so irritable and wretched with fear, that I con-
stantly hasten on the disorder. You cannot conceive the
misery of such a foresight. I am sure that, for the week
before she left me, I was little better than light-headed.

I now am calm, but sadly taken down and flat. I have every reason to suppose that this illness, like all her former ones, will be but temporary; but I cannot always feel so. Meantime she is dead to me, and I miss a prop. All my strength is gone, and I am like a fool, bereft of her co-operation. I dare not think, lest I should think wrong; so used am I to look up to her in the least and the biggest perplexity. To say all that I know of her would be more than I think anybody could believe, or even understand; and when I hope to have her well again with me, it would be sinning against her feelings to go about to praise her; for I can conceal nothing that I do from her. She is older and wiser and better than I, and all my wretched imperfections I cover to myself by resolutely thinking on her goodness. She would share life and death, heaven and hell, with me. She lives but for me; and I know I have been wasting and teasing her life for five years past incessantly with my cursed drinking and ways of going on. But even in this upbraiding of myself I am offending against her, for I know that she has cleaved to me for better, for worse; and if the balance has been against her hitherto, it was a noble trade. I am stupid, and lose myself in what I write. I write rather what answers to my feelings (which are sometimes sharp enough) than express my present ones, for I am only flat and stupid. I am sure you will excuse my writing any more, I am so very poorly.

I cannot resist transcribing three or four lines which poor Mary made upon a picture (a Holy Family) which we saw at an auction only one week before she left home. She was then beginning to show signs of ill boding. They are sweet lines and upon a sweet picture; but I send them only as the last memorial of her.

" VIRGIN AND CHILD, L. DA VINCI.

" Maternal Lady, with thy virgin grace,
Heaven-born, thy Jesus seemeth sure,
And thou a virgin pure.
Lady most perfect, when thy angel face

Men look upon, they wish to be
A Catholic, Madonna fair, to worship thee.'

You had her lines about the "Lady Blanch." You have not had some which she wrote upon a copy of a girl from Titian, which I had hung up where that print of Blanch and the Abbess (as she beautifully interpreted two female figures from L. da Vinci) had hung in our room. 'Tis light and pretty :—

> " Who art thou, fair one, who usurp'st the place
> Of Blanch, the lady of the matchless grace ?
> Come, fair and pretty, tell to me
> Who in thy lifetime thou mightst be ?
> Thou pretty art and fair,
> But with the Lady Blanch thou never must compare.
> No need for Blanch her history to tell,
> Whoever saw her face, they there did read it well ;
> But when I look on thee, I only know
> There lived a pretty maid some hundred years ago."

This is a little unfair, to tell so much about ourselves, and to advert so little to your letter, so full of comfortable tidings of you all. But my own cares press pretty close upon me, and you can make allowance. That you may go on gathering strength and peace is my next wish to Mary's recovery.

I had almost forgot your repeated invitation. Supposing that Mary will be well and able, there is another *ability* which you may guess at, which I cannot promise myself. In prudence we ought not to come. This illness will make it still more prudential to wait. It is not a balance of this way of spending our money against another way, but an absolute question of whether we shall stop now, or go on wasting away the little we have got beforehand, which my wise conduct has already encroach'd upon one half. My best love, however, to you all ; and to that most friendly creature, Mrs. Clarkson, and better health to her, when you see or write to her.

CHARLES LAMB.

To WILLIAM WORDSWORTH.

LETTER CX.] *June* 26, 1805.

Mary is just stuck fast in " All's Well that Ends Well." She complains of having to set forth so many female characters in boys' clothes. She begins to think Shakspeare must have wanted—imagination ! I, to encourage her (for she often faints in the prosecution of her great work), flatter her with telling her how well such a play and such a play is done. But she is stuck fast, and I have been obliged to promise to assist her. To do this it will be necessary to leave off tobacco. But I had some thoughts of doing that before, for I sometimes think it does not agree with me. Wm. Hazlitt is in town. I took him to see a very pretty girl, professedly, where there were two young girls (the very head and sum of the girlery was two young girls) ; they neither laughed, nor sneered, nor giggled, nor whispered —but they were young girls—and he sat and frowned blacker and blacker, indignant that there should be such a thing as youth and beauty, till he tore me away before supper, in perfect misery, and owned he could not bear young girls ; they drove him mad. So I took him home to my old nurse, where he recovered perfect tranquillity. Independent of this, and as I am not a young girl myself, he is a great acquisition to us. He is, rather imprudently I think, printing a political pamphlet on his own account, and will have to pay for the paper, etc. The first duty of an author, I take it, is never to pay anything. But *non cuivis contigit adire Corinthum.* The managers, I thank my stars, have settled that question for me.

Yours truly, C. LAMB.

To THOMAS MANNING.

LETTER CXI.]   [*July* 27, 1805.]

Dear Archimedes—Things have gone on badly with thy ungeometrical friend ; but they are on the turn. My old housekeeper has shown signs of convalescence, and will shortly resume the power of the keys, so I shan't be cheated of my tea and liquors. Wind in the West, which promotes tranquillity. Have leisure now to anticipate seeing thee again. Have been taking leave of tobacco in a rhyming address. Had thought *that vein* had long since closed up. Find I can rhyme and reason too. Think of studying mathematics, to restrain the fire of my genius, which G. D. recommends. Have frequent bleedings at the nose, which shows plethoric. Maybe shall try the sea myself, that great scene of wonders. Got incredibly sober and regular ; shave oftener, and hum a tune, to signify cheerfulness and gallantry.

Suddenly disposed to sleep, having taken a quart of pease with bacon and stout. Will not refuse Nature, who has done such things for me !

Nurse ! don't call me unless Mr. Manning comes.— What ! the gentleman in spectacles ?—Yes.

 Dormit.   C. L.

Saturday,
 Hot Noon.

To WILLIAM WORDSWORTH.

LETTER CXII.]   *September* 28, 1805.

My dear Wordsworth (or Dorothy rather, for to you appertains the biggest part of this answer by right)— I will not again deserve reproach by so long a silence. I have kept deluding myself with the idea that Mary would write to you, but she is so lazy (or, which I believe is the true state of the case, so diffident), that it must revert to me as usual. Though she writes a pretty good style, and has some notion of the force of words, she is not always so certain of the true orthography of them; and that, and a poor handwriting (in this age of female calligraphy), often deters her, where no other reason does.

We have neither of us been very well for some weeks past. I am very nervous, and she most so at those times when I am; so that a merry friend, adverting to the noble consolation we were able to afford each other, denominated us, not unaptly, Gum-boil and Tooth-Ache, for they used to say that a gum-boil is a great relief to a tooth-ache.

We have been two tiny excursions this Summer, for three or four days each, to a place near Harrow, and to Egham, where Cooper's Hill is: and that is the total history of our rustications this year. Alas! how poor a round to Skiddaw and Helvellyn, and Borrowdale, and the magnificent sesquipedalia of the year 1802! Poor old Molly! to have lost her pride, that "last infirmity of noble minds," and her cow. Fate need not have set her wits to such an old Molly. I am heartily sorry for her. Remember us lovingly to her; and in particular remember us to Mrs. Clarkson in the most kind manner.

I hope, by "southwards," you mean that she will be at or near London, for she is a great favourite of both of us, and we feel for her health as much as possible for any one to do. She is one of the friendliest, comfortablest women we know, and made our little stay at your cottage one of the pleasantest times we ever past. We were quite strangers to her. Mr. C. is with you too; our kindest separate remembrances to him. As to our special affairs, I am looking about me. I have done nothing since the beginning of last year, when I lost my newspaper job: and having had a long idleness, I must do something, or we shall get very poor. Sometimes I think of a farce, but hitherto all schemes have gone off; an idle brag or two of an evening, vapouring out of a pipe, and going off in the morning; but now I have bid farewell to my "sweet enemy," Tobacco, I shall perhaps set nobly to work.   Hang work!

I wish that all the year were holiday; I am sure that indolence—indefeasible indolence—is the true state of man, and business the invention of the old Teazer, whose interference doomed Adam to an apron and set him a hoeing.   Pen and ink, and clerks and desks, were the refinements of this old torturer some thousand years after, under pretence of "Commerce allying distant shores, promoting and diffusing knowledge, good," etc. etc.

I wish you may think this a handsome farewell to my "Friendly Traitress."   Tobacco has been my evening comfort and my morning curse for these five years; and you know how difficult it is from refraining to pick one's lips even, when it has become a habit.   This poem is the only one which I have finished since so long as when I wrote "Hester Savory."   I have had it in my head to do it these two years, but tobacco stood in its own light when it gave me headaches that prevented my singing its praises.   Now you have got it, you have got all my store, for I have absolutely not another line.   No more has Mary.   We have nobody about us that cares for poetry; and who will rear grapes when he shall be the sole eater?   Perhaps if you encourage us to show you what we may write, we may do something now and then before we absolutely forget the quantity of an English line for want of practice.   The "Tobacco," being a little in the way of Wither (whom Southey so much likes), perhaps you will somehow convey it to him with my kind remembrances.   Then, everybody will have seen it that I wish to see it, I having sent it to Malta.

I remain, dear W. and D., yours truly,

C. LAMB.

To WILLIAM HAZLITT.

[LETTER CXIII.]   *November* 10, 1805.

Dear Hazlitt—I was very glad to hear from you, and that your journey was so *picturesque.* We miss you, as we foretold we should. One or two things have happened, which are beneath the dignity of epistolary communication, but which, seated about our fireside at night (the winter hands of pork have begun), gesture and emphasis might have talked into some importance. Something about Rickman's wife; for instance, how tall she is, and that she visits pranked up like a Queen of the May, with green streamers: a good-natured woman though, which is as much as you can expect from a friend's wife, whom you got acquainted with a bachelor. Some things too about Monkey, which can't so well be written: how it set up for a fine lady, and thought it had got lovers, and was obliged to be convinced of its age from the parish register, where it was proved to be only twelve; and an edict issued, that it should not give itself airs yet these four years; and how it got leave to be called Miss, by grace; these, and such like hows, were in my head to tell you; but who can write? Also how Manning is come to town in spectacles, and studies physic; is melancholy, and seems to have something in his head, which he don't impart. Then, how I am going to leave off smoking. O la! your Leonardos of Oxford made my mouth water. I was hurried through the gallery, and they escaped me. What do I say? I was a Goth then, and should not have noticed them. I had not settled my notions of beauty: I have now for ever!—the small head, the long eye,—that sort of peering curve,—the wicked Italian mischief; the stick-at-nothing, Herodias's daughter kind of grace. You understand me? But you disappoint me in passing over in absolute silence the Bleuheim Leonardo. Didn't you see it? Excuse a lover's curiosity. I have seen no pictures of note since, except Mr. Dawe's gallery. It is curious to see how differently two great men treat the same subject, yet both excellent in their way. For instance, Milton and Mr. Dawe. Mr. D. has chosen to illustrate the story of Samson exactly in the point of view in which Milton has been most happy : the interview between the Jewish hero, blind and captive, and Delilah Milton has imagined his locks grown again, strong as horse-hair or porcupine's bristles ; doubtless shaggy and black, as being hairs "which, of a nation armed, contained the strength." I don't remember he *says* black ; but could Milton imagine them to be yellow ? Do you ? Mr. Dawe, with striking originality of conception, has crowned him with a thin yellow wig, in colour precisely like Dyson's ; in curl and quantity, resembling Mrs. Professor's ; his limbs rather stout,—about such a man as my brother or Rickman,— but no Atlas nor Hercules, nor yet so long as Dubois, the clown of Sadler's Wells. This was judicious, taking the spirit of the story rather than the fact ; for doubtless God could communicate national salvation to the trust of flax and tow as well as hemp and cordage, and could draw down a temple with a golden tress as soon as with all the cables of the British navy.

Wasn't you sorry for Lord Nelson ? I have followed him in fancy ever since I saw him walking in Pall Mall (I was prejudiced against him before), looking just as a hero should look ; and I have been very much cut about it indeed. He was the only pretence of a great man we had. Nobody is left of any name at all. His secretary died by his side. I imagined him a Mr. Scott, to be the man you met at Hume's ; but I learnt from Mrs. Hume that it is not the same. I met Mrs. H. one day, and agreed to go on the Sunday to tea, but the rain prevented us, and the distance. I have been to apologise, and we are to dine there the first fine Sunday. Strange perverseness ! I never went while you stayed here ; and now I *go to find you !* What other news is there, Mary ? What puns have I made in the last fortnight ? You never remember them. You have no relish for the comic. "Oh! tell Hazlitt not to forget to send the *American Farmer*. I daresay it is not so good as he fancies; but a book's a book." I have not heard from Wordsworth or from Malta since. Charles Kemble, it seems, enters into possession to-morrow. We sup at 109 Russell Street, this evening. I wish your brother would not drink. 'Tis a blemish in the greatest characters. You send me a modern quotation poetical. How do you like this in an old play? Vittoria Coromboua, a spunky Italian lady, a Leonardo one, nicknamed the White Devil, being on her trial for murder, etc.—and questioned about seducing a duke from his wife and the state, makes answer :—

> "Condemn you me for that the Duke did love me ?
> So may you blame some fair and crystal river,
> For that some melancholic distracted man
> Hath drown'd himself in it."

N.B.—I shall expect a line from you, if but a bare line, whenever you write to Russell Street, and a letter often when you do not. I pay no postage; but I will have consideration for you until Parliament time and franks. Luck to Ned Search, and the new art of colouring. Monkey sends her love; and Mary especially.

Yours truly,   C. LAMB.

To THOMAS MANNING.

LETTER CXIV.]   [*November* 15, 1805.]

Dear Manning—Certainly you could not have called at all hours from two till ten, for we have been only out of an evening Monday and Tuesday in this week. But if you think you have, your thought shall go for the deed. We did pray for you on Wednesday night. Oysters unusually luscious; pearls of extraordinary magnitude found in them. I have made bracelets of them; given them in clusters to ladies. Last night we went out in despite, because you were not come at your hour.

This night we shall be at home ; so shall we certainly, both, on Sunday, Monday, Tuesday, and Wednesday. Take your choice, mind I don't say of one : but choose which evening you will not come, and come the other four.   Doors open at five o'clock.   Shells forced about nine.   Every gentleman smokes or not as he pleases.

.C. L.

To WILLIAM HAZLITT.

LETTER CXV.]   *January* 15, 1806.

Dear Hazlitt—Godwin went to Johnson's yesterday about your business.   Johnson would not come down, or give any answer, but has promised to open the manuscript, and to give you an answer in one month.   Godwin will punctually go again (Wednesday is Johnson's open day) yesterday four weeks next : *i.e.* in one lunar month from this time ; till when, Johnson positively declines giving any answer.   I wish you joy on ending your Search. Mrs. H. was naming something about a " Life of Fawcett," to be by you undertaken : the great Fawcett, as she explained to Manning, when he asked, " *What Fawcett ?*"   He innocently thought *Fawcett the Player*.   But Fawcett the divine is known to many people, albeit unknown to the Chinese inquirer.   I should think, if you liked it, and Johnson declined it, that Phillips is the man. He is perpetually bringing out biographies,—Richardson, Wilks, Foot, Lee Lewis,—without number : little trim things in two easy volumes, price 12s. the two, made up of letters to and from, scraps, posthumous trifles, anecdotes, and about forty pages of hard biography.   You might dish up a Fawcettiad in three months, and ask £60 or £80 for it.   I should dare say that Phillips would catch at it.   I wrote to you the other day in a great hurry.   Did you get it ?   This is merely a letter of business at Godwin's request.   Lord Nelson is quiet at last. His ghost only keeps a slight fluttering in odes and elegies in newspapers, and impromptus, which could not be got ready before the funeral.

As for news, Fenwick is coming to town on Monday (if no kind angel intervene) to surrender himself to prison. He hopes to get the rules of the Fleet. On the same, or nearly the same day, Fell, my other quondam co-friend and drinker, will go to Newgate, and his wife and four children, I suppose, to the parish. Plenty of reflection and motives of gratitude to the wise Disposer of all things in *us*, whose prudent conduct has hitherto ensured us a warm fire and snug roof over our heads. *Nullum numen abest si sit Prudentia.* Alas! Prudentia is in the last quarter of her tutelary shining over me. A little time and I ——; but maybe I may, at last, hit upon some mode of collecting some of the vast superfluities of this money-voiding town. Much is to be got, and I do not want much. All I ask is time and leisure; and I am cruelly off for them. When you have the inclination, I shall be very glad to have a letter from you. Your brother and Mrs. H., I am afraid, think hardly of us for not coming oftener to see them; but we are distracted beyond what they can conceive with visitors and visitings. I never have an hour for my head to work quietly its own workings; which you know is as necessary to the human system as sleep. Sleep, too, I can't get for these winds of a night: and without sleep and rest what should ensue? Lunacy. But I trust it won't.

Yours, dear H., C. LAMB.

To Mr. RICKMAN.

LETTER CXVI.] *January* 25, 1806.

Dear Rickman—You do not happen to have any place at your disposal which would suit a decayed Literatus? I do not much expect that you have, or that you will go much out of the way to serve the object, when you hear it is Fell. But the case is, by a *mistaking* of his *turn,* as they call it, he is reduced, I am afraid, to extremities, and would be extremely glad of a place in an office. Now it does sometimes happen, that just as a man wants a place, a place wants him; and though this is a lottery to which none but G. Burnett would choose to trust his all, there is no harm just to call in at Despair's office for a friend, and see if *his* number is come up (Burnett's further case I enclose by way of episode). Now, if you should happen, or anybody you know, to want a *hand*, here is a young man of solid but not brilliant genius, who would turn his hand to the making out of dockets, penning a manifesto, or scoring a tally, not the worse (I hope) for knowing Latin and Greek, and having in youth conversed with the philosophers. But from these follies I believe he is thoroughly awakened, and would bind himself by a terrible oath never to imagine himself an extraordinary genius again.

Yours, etc.,   C. LAMB.

TO WILLIAM HAZLITT.

LETTER CXVII.]   *February* 19, 1806.

Dear H.—Godwin has just been here in his way from Johnson's. Johnson has had a fire in his house; this happened about five weeks ago; it was in the daytime, so it did not burn the house down, but it did so much damage that the house must come down, to be repaired. His nephew that we met on Hampstead Hill put it out. Well, this fire has put him so back, that he craves one more month before he gives you an answer. I will certainly goad Godwin (if necessary) to go again this very day four weeks; but I am confident he will want no goading. Three or four most capital auctions of pictures are advertised: in May, *Wellbore Ellis Agar's*, the first private collection in England, so Holcroft says; in March, Sir George Young's in Stratford Place (where Cosway lives), and a Mr. Hulse's at Blackheath, both very capital collections, and have been announced for some months. Also the Marquis of Lansdowne's pictures in March; and though inferior to mention, lastly, the Truethsessian Gallery. Don't your mouth water to be here? T'other night Loftus called, whom we have not seen since you went before. We meditate a stroll next Wednesday, fast-day. He happened to light upon Mr. Holcroft, wife, and daughter, their first visit at our house. Your brother called last night. We keep up our intimacy. He is going to begin a large Madonna and child from Mrs. H. and baby. I fear he goes astray after *ignes fatui*. He is a clever man. By the by, I saw a miniature of his as far excelling any in his show cupboard (that of your sister not excepted) as that show cupboard excels the show things you see in windows— an old woman (damn her name!), but most superlative; he has it to clean—I'll ask him the name—but the best miniature I ever saw. But for oil pictures!—what has he to do with Madonnas? If the Virgin Mary were alive and visitable, he would not hazard himself in a Covent Garden pit-door crowd to see her. It isn't his style of beauty, is it? But he will go on painting things he ought not to paint, and not painting things he ought to paint. Manning is not gone to China, but talks of going this Spring. God forbid! Coleridge not heard of. I am going to leave off smoke. In the meantime I am so smoky with last night's ten pipes, that I must leave off. Mary begs her kind remembrances. Pray write to us. This is no letter; but I supposed you grew anxious about Johnson.

N.B.—Have taken a room at three shillings a week, to be in between five and eight at night, to avoid my *nocturnal*, alias *knock-eternal*, visitors. The first-fruits of my retirement has been a farce, which goes to manager to-morrow. *Wish my ticket luck.* God bless you; and do write.—Yours, *famosissimus,* C. LAMB.

To Mr. RICKMAN.

Letter CXVIII.]   *March* 1806.

Dear Rickman—I send you some papers about a salt-water soap, for which the inventor is desirous of getting a parliamentary reward, like Dr. Jenner. Whether such a project be feasible, I mainly doubt, taking for granted the equal utility. I should suppose the usual way of paying such projectors is by patent and contracts. The patent, you see, he has got. A contract he is about with the Navy Board. Meantime, the projector is hungry. Will you answer me two questions, and return them with the papers as soon as you can? Imprimis, is there any chance of success in application to Parliament for a reward? Did you ever hear of the invention? You see its benefits and saving to the nation (always the first motive with a true projector) are feelingly set forth : the last paragraph but one of the estimate, in enumerating the shifts poor seamen are put to, even approaches to the pathetic. But, agreeing to all he says, is there the remotest chance of Parliament giving the projector anything? And *when* should application be made, now, or after a report (if he can get it) from the Navy Board? Secondly, let the infeasibility be as great as you will, you will oblige me by telling me the way of introducing such an application in Parliament, without buying over a majority of members, which is totally out of projector's power. I vouch nothing for the soap myself; for I always wash in *fresh water*, and find it answer tolerably well for all purposes of cleanliness; nor do I know the projector; but a relation of mine has put me on writing to you, for whose parliamentary knowledge he has great veneration.

P. S.—The Capt. and Mrs. Burney and Phillips take their chance at cribbage here on Wednesday. Will you and Mrs. R. join the party? Mary desires her compliments to Mrs. R., and joins in the invitation.

Yours truly,   C. Lamb.

To WILLIAM HAZLITT.

Letter CXIX.]   *March* 15, 1806.

Dear H.—I am a little surprised at no letter from you. This day week, to wit, Saturday, the 8th of March, 1806, I booked off by the Wem coach, Bull and Mouth Inn, directed to *you*, at the Rev. Mr. Hazlitt's, Wem, Shropshire, a parcel containing, besides a book, etc., a rare print, which I take to be a Titian ; begging the said W. H. to acknowledge the receipt thereof ; which he not having done, I conclude the said parcel to be lying at the inn, and may be lost ; for which reason, lest you may be a Wales-hunting at this instant, I have authorised any of your family, whosoever first gets this, to open it, that so precious a parcel may not moulder away for want of looking after.

What do you in Shropshire when so many fine pictures are a-going a-going every day in London ? Monday I visit the Marquis of Lansdowne's, in Berkeley Square. Catalogue 2s. 6d. Leonardos in plenty. Some other day this week I go to see Sir Wm. Young's, in Stratford Place. Hulse's, of Blackheath, are also to be sold this month ; and in May, the first private collection in Europe, Welbore Ellis Agar's. And there are you, perverting Nature in lying landscapes, filched from old rusty Titians, such as I can scrape up here to send you, with an additament from Shropshire Nature thrown in to make the whole look unnatural. I am afraid of your mouth watering when I tell you that Manning and I got into Angerstein's on Wednesday. *Mon Dieu !* Such Claudes ! Four Claudes bought for more than £10,000 ; (those who talk of Wilson being equal to Claude are either mainly ignorant or stupid ;) one of these was perfectly miraculous. What colours short of *bonâ fide* sunbeams it could be painted in, I am not earthly colourman enough to say ; but I did not think it had been in the possibility of things.   Then, a music piece by Titian, a thousand-pound picture, five figures standing behind a piano, the sixth playing—none of the heads, as M. observed, indicating great men, or affecting it, but so sweetly disposed —all leaning separate ways, but so easy—like a flock of some divine shepherd; the colouring, like the economy of the picture, so sweet and harmonious—as good as Shakspeare's *Twelfth Night*,—*almost*, that is.   It will give you a love of order, and cure you of restless, fidgety passions for a week after—more musical than the music which it would, but cannot, yet in a manner *does*, show.   I have no room for the rest.   Let me say, Angerstein sits in a room—his study (only that and the library are shown), when he writes a common letter, as I am doing, surrounded with twenty pictures worth £60,000.   What a luxury!   Apicius and Heliogabalus, hide your diminished heads!

Yours, my dear painter,   C. LAMB.

Mr. Wm. Hazlitt,
    Wem, Shropshire.
In his absence, to be opened immediately.

To THOMAS MANNING.

LETTER CXX.]   *May* 10, 1806.

My dear Manning—I didn't know what your going was till I shook a last fist with you, and then 'twas just like having shaken hands with a wretch on the fatal scaffold, for when you are down the ladder you can never stretch out to him again.   Mary says you are dead, and there's nothing to do but to leave it to time to do for us in the end what it always does for those who mourn for people in such a case.   But she'll see by your letter you are not quite dead.   A little kicking and agony, and then ———.   Martin Burney *took me out* a walking that evening, and we talked of Manning; and then I came home and smoked for you; and at twelve o'clock came home Mary and Monkey Louisa from the play, and there was more talk and more smoking, and they all seemed first-rate characters, because they knew a certain person. But what's the use of talking about 'em? By the time you'll have made your escape from the Kalmuks, you'll have stayed so long I shall never be able to bring to your mind who Mary was, who will have died about a year before, nor who the Holcrofts were! Me perhaps you will mistake for Phillips, or confound me with Mr. Dawe, because you saw us together. Mary (whom you seem to remember yet) is not quite easy that she had not a formal parting from you. I wish it had so happened. But you must bring her a token, a shawl or something, and remember a sprightly little mandarin for our mantel-piece, as a companion to the child I am going to purchase at the museum. She says you saw her writings about the other day, and she wishes you should know what they are. She is doing for Godwin's bookseller twenty of Shakspeare's plays, to be made into children's tales. Six are already done by her; to wit, the *Tempest*, the *Winter's Tale*, *Midsummer Night's Dream*, *Much Ado about Nothing*, the *Two Gentlemen of Verona*, and *Cymbeline*. The *Merchant of Venice* is in forwardness. I have done *Othello* and *Macbeth*, and mean to do all the tragedies. I think it will be popular among the little people, besides money. It is to bring in sixty guineas. Mary has done them capitally, I think you'd think. These are the humble amusements we propose, while you are gone to plant the cross of Christ among barbarous pagan anthropophagi. Quam homo homini præstat! but then, perhaps, you'll get murdered, and we shall die in our beds with a fair literary reputation. Be sure, if you see any of those people whose heads do grow beneath their shoulders, that you make a draught of them. It will be very curious. Oh Manning, I am serious to sinking almost, when I think that all those evenings which you have made so pleasant, are gone perhaps for ever. Four years, you talk of, may be ten, and you may

come back and find such alterations! Some circum
stances may grow up to you or to me, that may be a bar
to the return of any such intimacy. I daresay all this is
hum! and that all will come back; but indeed we die
many deaths before we die, and I am almost sick when
I think that such a hold as I had of you is gone. I have
friends, but some of 'em are changed. Marriage, or some
circumstance, rises up to make them not the same. But
I felt sure of you. And that last token you gave me of
expressing a wish to have my name joined with yours,
you know not how it affected me: like a legacy.

God bless you in every way you can form a wish.
May He give you health, and safety, and the accomplish-
ment of all your objects, and return you again to us, to
gladden some fireside or other (I suppose we shall be
moved from the Temple). I will nurse the remembrance
of your steadiness and quiet, which used to infuse some-
thing like itself into our nervous minds. Mary called
you our ventilator. Farewell, and take her best wishes
and mine.

Good-bye. C. L.

To WILLIAM WORDSWORTH.

LETTER CXXI.]   *June* 1806.

Dear Wordsworth—We are pleased, you may be sure,
with the good news of Mrs. W——. Hope all is well
over by this time. "A fine boy. Have you any more?
—one more and a girl—poor copies of me!" vide *Mr.
H.*, a farce which the proprietors have done me the
honour ——; but I will set down Mr. Wroughton's own
words. *N. B.*—The ensuing letter was sent in answer to
one which I wrote, begging to know if my piece had any
chance, as I might make alterations, etc. I writing on
Monday, there comes this letter on the Wednesday.
Attend!

[Copy of a Letter from Mr. R. Wroughton.]

" Sir—Your piece of *Mr. H.*, I am desired to say, is accepted at Drury Lane Theatre, by the proprietors, and, if agreeable to you, will be brought forwards when the proper opportunity serves. The piece shall be sent to you, for your alterations, in the course of a few days, as the same is not in my hands, but with the proprietors.

" I am, sir, your obedient servant,

" RICHARD WROUGHTON.

[Dated]
" 66, Gower Street,
"Wednesday, June 11, 1806."

On the following Sunday Mr. Tobin comes. The scent of a manager's letter brought him. He would have gone further any day on such a business. I read the letter to him. He deems it authentic and peremptory. Our conversation naturally fell upon pieces, different sorts of pieces; what is the best way of offering a piece, how far the caprice of managers is an obstacle in the way of a piece, how to judge of the merits of a piece, how long a piece may remain in the hands of the managers before it is acted; and my piece, and your piece, and my poor brother's piece—my poor brother was all his life endeavouring to get a piece accepted. I am not sure that, when my poor brother bequeathed the care of his pieces to Mr. Tobin, he did not therein convey a legacy which in some measure mollified the otherwise first stupefactions of grief. It cannot be expected that the present Earl Nelson passes all his time in watering the laurels of the admiral with Right-Reverend Tears. Certainly he steals a fine day now and then to plot how to lay out the grounds and mansion at Burnham most suitable to the late Earl's taste, if he had lived, and how to spend the hundred thousand pounds which Parliament has given him in erecting some little neat monument to his memory.

I wrote that in mere wantonness of triumph. Have

nothing more to say about it. The managers, I thank my stars, have decided its merits for ever. They are the best judges of pieces, and it would be insensible in me to affect a false modesty after the very flattering letter which I have received.

ADMIT

TO

BOXES.

MR. H.

Ninth Night.

CHARLES LAMB.

I think this will be as good a pattern for orders as I can think on. A little thin flowery border, round, neat, not gaudy, and the Drury Lane Apollo, with the harp at the top. Or shall I have no Apollo?—simply nothing? Or perhaps the comic muse?

The same form, only I think without the Apollo, will serve for the pit and galleries. I think it will be best to write my name at full length; but then if I give away a a great many, that will be tedious. Perhaps *Ch. Lamb* will do.

BOXES, now I think on it, I'll have in capitals. The rest, in a neat Italian hand. Or better, perhaps Boxes, in old English characters, like "Madoc" or "Thalaba?"

A-propos of Spenser (you will find him mentioned a page or two before, near enough for an *a-propos*), I was discoursing on poetry (as one's apt to deceive one's self, and when a person is willing to *talk* of what one likes, to believe that he also likes the same, as lovers do) with a young gentleman of my office, who is deep read in Anacreon Moore, Lord Strangford, and the principal modern poets, and I happened to mention Epithalamiums, and that I could show him a very fine one of Spenser's. At the mention of this, my gentleman, who is a very fine gentleman, and is brother to the Miss Evans whom

Coleridge so narrowly escaped marrying, pricked up his ears and expressed great pleasure, and begged that I would give him leave to copy it: he did not care how long it was (for I objected the length), he should be very happy to see *anything by him.* Then pausing, and looking sad, he ejaculated "POOR SPENCER!" I begged to know the reason of his ejaculation, thinking that time had by this time softened down any calamities which the bard might have endured. "Why, poor fellow," said he, "he has lost his wife!" "Lost his wife!" said I, "whom are you talking of?" "Why, Spencer," said he; "I've read the *Monody* he wrote on the occasion, and *a very pretty thing it is.*" This led to an explanation (it could be delayed no longer) that the sound *Spenser,* which, when poetry is talked of, generally excites an image of an old bard in a ruff, and sometimes with it dim notions of Sir P. Sydney, and perhaps Lord Burleigh, had raised in my gentleman a quite contrary image of the Honourable William Spencer, who has translated some things from the German very prettily, which are published with Lady Di. Beauclerk's designs. Nothing like defining of terms when we talk. What blunders might I have fallen into of quite inapplicable criticism, but for this timely explanation!

N.B.—At the beginning of *Edm.* Spenser (to prevent mistakes), I have copied from my own copy, and primarily from a book of Chalmers's on Shakspeare, a sonnet of Spenser's never printed among his poems. It is curious, as being manly, and rather Miltonic, and as a sonnet of Spenser's with nothing in it about love or knighthood. I have no room for remembrances; but I hope our doing your commission will prove we do not quite forget you.

C. L.

To THOMAS MANNING.

LETTER CXXII.]   *December* 5, 1806.

Manning, your letter dated Hottentots, August (the what-was-it?) came to hand. I can scarce hope that mine will have the same luck. China! Canton! Bless us—how it strains the imagination and makes it ache! I write under another uncertainty, whether it can go to-morrow by a ship which I have just learned is going off direct to your part of the world, or whether the despatches may not be sealed up and this have to wait, for if it is detained here, it will grow staler in a fortnight than in a five months' voyage coming to you. It will be a point of conscience to send you none but bran-new news (the latest edition), which, like oranges, will but grow the better for a sea voyage. Oh that you should be so many hemispheres off!—if I speak incorrectly you can correct me—why the simplest death or marriage that takes place here must be important to you as news in the old Bastile. There's your friend Tuthill has got away from France; you remember France? and Tuthill?—ten to one but he writes by this post, if he don't get my note in time, apprising him of the vessel's sailing. Know then that he has found means to obtain leave from Buonaparte (without making use of any *incredible romantic pretences* as some have done, who never meant to fulfil them) to come home, and I have seen him here and at Holcroft's. Arn't you glad about Tuthill? Now then be sorry for Holcroft, whose new play, called the *Vindictive Man*, was damned about a fortnight since. It died in part of its own weakness, and in part for being choked up with bad actors. The two principal parts were destined to Mrs. Jordan and Mr. Bannister, but Mrs. J. has not come to terms with the managers; they have had some squabble; and Bannister shot some of his fingers off by the going off of a gun. So Miss Duncan had her part, and Mr. de Camp took his. His part, the principal comic hope of the play, was most unluckily *Goldfinch*, taken out of the *Road to Ruin*, not only the same character, but the identical *Goldfinch*—the same as *Falstaff* is in two plays of Shakspeare's. As the devil of ill-luck would have it, half the audience did not know that Holcroft had written it, but were displeased at his stealing from the *Road to Ruin*; and those who might have borne a gentlemanly coxcomb with his "That's your sort," "Go it"—such as Lewis is —did not relish the intolerable vulgarity and inanity of the idea stript of his manner. De Camp was hooted, more than hist, hooted and bellowed off the stage before the second act was finished; so that the remainder of his part was forced to be, with some violence to the play, omitted. In addition to this, a whore was another principal character—a most unfortunate choice in this moral day. The audience were as scandalised as if you were to introduce such a personage to their private tea-tables. Besides, her action in the play was gross— wheedling an old man into marriage. But the mortal blunder of the play was that which, oddly enough, Holcroft took pride in, and exultingly told me of the night before it came out, that there were no less than eleven principal characters in it, and I believe he meant of the men only, for the play-bill expressed as much, not reckoning one woman, and one whore; and true it was, for Mr. Powell, Mr. Raymond, Mr. Bartlett, Mr. H. Siddons, Mr. Barrymore, etc. etc., to the number of eleven, had all parts equally prominent, and there was as much of them in quantity and rank as of the hero and heroine— and most of them gentlemen who seldom appear but as the hero's friend in a farce, for a minute or two; and here they all had their ten-minute speeches, and one of them gave the audience a serious account of how he was now a lawyer but had been a poet, and then a long enumeration of the inconveniences of authorship, rascally booksellers, reviewers, etc.; which first set the audience a-gaping; but I have said enough. You will be so sorry,

that you will not think the best of me for my detail;
but news is news at Canton.   Poor Holcroft I fear will
feel the disappointment very seriously in a pecuniary
light.   From what I can learn he has saved nothing.
You and I were hoping one day that he had, but I fear
he has nothing but his pictures and books, and a no very
flourishing business, and to be obliged to part with his
long-necked Guido that hangs opposite as you enter, and
the game-piece that hangs in the back drawing-room, and
all those Vandykes, etc. !   God should temper the wind
to the shorn connoisseur.   I hope I need not say to you,
that I feel for the weather-beaten author, and for all his
household.   I assure you his fate has soured a good deal
the pleasure I should have otherwise taken in my own
little farce being accepted, and I hope about to be acted :
it is in rehearsal actually, and I expect it to come out
next week.   It is kept a sort of secret, and the rehearsals
have gone on privately, lest by many folks knowing it,
the story should come out, which would infallibly damn
it.   You remember I had sent it before you went.
Wroughton read it, and was much pleased with it.   I
speedily got an answer.   I took it to make alterations,
and lazily kept it some months, then took courage and
furbished it up in a day or two and took it.   In less
than a fortnight I heard the principal part was given to
Elliston, who liked it and only wanted a prologue, which
I have since done and sent, and I had a note the day
before yesterday from the manager, Wroughton (bless his
fat face ! he is not a bad actor in some things), to say
that I should be summoned to the rehearsal after the
next, which next was to be yesterday.   I had no idea it
was so forward.   I have had no trouble, attended no
reading or rehearsal, made no interest.   What a contrast
to the usual parade of authors !   But it is peculiar to
modesty to do all things without noise or pomp.   I have
some suspicion it will appear in public on Wednesday
next, for Wroughton says in his note, it is so forward
that if wanted it may come out next week, and a new

melodrame is announced for every day till then; and "a
new farce is in rehearsal," is put up in the bills. Now
you'd like to know the subject. The title is *Mr. H.*, no
more. How simple, how taking! A great H. sprawling
over the play-bill and attracting eyes at every corner.
The story is a coxcomb appearing at Bath, vastly rich—
all the ladies dying for him—all bursting to know who
he is; but he goes by no other name than Mr. H.—a
curiosity like that of the dames of Strasburg about the
man with the great nose. But I won't tell you any more
about it. Yes, I will; but I can't give you an idea how
I have done it. I'll just tell you that after much
vehement admiration, when his true name comes out,
"Hogsflesh," all the women shun him, avoid him, and
not one can be found to change their name for him.
That's the idea. How flat it is here—but how whimsical
in the farce! And only think how hard upon me it is
that the ship is despatched to-morrow, and my triumph
cannot be ascertained till the Wednesday after; but all
China will ring of it by and by. *N.B.* (But this is a
secret). The Professor has got a tragedy coming out,
with the young Roscius in it, in January next, as we say
—January last it will be with you—and though it is a
profound secret now, as all his affairs are, it cannot be
much of one by the time you read this. However, don't
let it go any further. I understand there are dramatic
exhibitions in China. One would not like to be fore-
stalled. Do you find in all this stuff I have written any-
thing like those feelings which one should send my old
adventuring friend, that is gone to wander among Tartars
and may never come again? I don't; but your going
away, and all about you, is a threadbare topic. I have
worn it out with thinking: it has come to me when I
have been dull with anything, till my sadness has seemed
more to have come from it than to have introduced it.
I want you, you don't know how much; but if I had you
here in my European garret, we should but talk over
such stuff as I have written—so. Those *Tales from*

Shakspeare are near coming out, and Mary has begun a new work. Mr. Dawe is turned author; he has been in such a way lately—Dawe, the painter, I mean—he sits and stands about at Holcroft's and says nothing; then sighs and leans his head on his hand. I took him to be in love; but it seems he was only meditating a work,—"The Life of Morland." The young man is not used to composition. Rickman and Captain Burney are well; they assemble at my house pretty regularly of a Wednesday—a new institution. Like other great men I have a public day, cribbage and pipes, with Phillips and noisy Martin.

Good God! what a bit only I've got left! How shall I squeeze all I know into this morsel! Coleridge is come home, and is going to turn lecturer on Taste at the Royal Institution. I shall get £200 from the theatre if *Mr. H.* has a good run, and I hope £100 for the copyright. Nothing if it fails; and there never was a more ticklish thing. The whole depends on the manner in which the name is brought out, which I value myself on, as a *chef-d'œuvre*. How the paper grows less and less! In less than two minutes I shall cease to talk to you, and you may rave to the great wall of China. *N.B.* Is there such a wall? Is it as big as old London Wall, by Bedlam? Have you met with a friend of mine, named Ball, at Canton! If you are acquainted, remember me kindly to him. May be you'll think I have not said enough of Tuthill and the Holcrofts. Tuthill is a noble fellow, as far as I can judge. The H.'s bear their disappointment pretty well, but indeed they are sadly mortified. Mrs. H. is cast down. It was well, if it were but on this account, that T. is come home. *N.B.* If my little thing don't succeed I shall easily survive, having, as it were, compared to H.'s venture, but a sixteenth in the lottery. Mary and I are to sit next the orchestra in the pit, next the tweedledees. She remembers you. You are more to us than five hundred farces, clappings, etc.

Come back one day.   C. LAMB.

To Miss STODDART.

LETTER CXXIII.]   *December* 11 [1806].

Don't mind this being a queer letter.   I am in haste, and taken up by visitors, condolers, etc.

God bless you.

Dear Sarah—Mary is a little cut at the ill success of *Mr. H.*, which came out last night and *failed.*   I know you'll be sorry, but never mind.   We are determined not to be cast down.   I am going to leave off tobacco, and then we must thrive.   A smoking man must write smoky farces.

Mary is pretty well, but I persuaded her to let me write.   We did not apprise you of the coming out of *Mr. H.* for fear of ill luck.   You were much better out of the house.   If it had taken, your partaking of our good luck would have been one of our greatest joys.   As it is, we shall expect you at the time you mentioned.   But whenever you come you shall be most welcome.

God bless you, dear Sarah,

Yours most truly,   C. L.

Mary is by no means unwell, but I made her let me write.

To WILLIAM WORDSWORTH.

LETTER CXXIV.]   *December* 11, 1806.

Mary's love to all of you—I wouldn't let her write.

Dear Wordsworth—*Mr. H.* came out last night, and failed.   I had many fears ; the subject was not substantial enough.   John Bull must have solider fare than a *letter.* We are pretty stout about it ; have had plenty of condoling friends ; but, after all, we had rather it should have succeeded.   You will see the prologue in most of the morning papers.   It was received with such shouts as I never witnessed to a prologue. It was attempted to be encored. How hard!—a thing I did merely as a task, because it was wanted, and set no great store by; and *Mr. H.!!* The number of friends we had in the house —my brother and I being in public offices, etc.—was astonishing, but they yielded at length to a few hisses.

A hundred hisses! (Damn the word, I write it like kisses—how different!)—a hundred hisses outweigh a thousand claps. The former come more directly from the heart. Well, 'tis withdrawn, and there is an end.

Better luck to us.　　　　　　　　　　C. LAMB.

[Turn over.]

P.S.—Pray, when any of you write to the Clarksons, give our kind loves, and say we shall not be able to come and see them at Christmas, as I shall have but a day or two, and tell them we bear our mortification pretty well.

To WILLIAM GODWIN.

LETTER CXXV].　　　　　　　　　　　　1806.

I repent. Can that God whom thy votaries say that thou hast demolished expect more? I did indite a splenetic letter, but did the black Hypocondria never gripe *thy* heart, till thou hast taken a friend for an enemy? The foul fiend Flibbertigibbet leads me over four-inched bridges, to course my own shadow for a traitor. There are certain positions of the moon, under which I counsel thee not to take anything written from this domicile as serious.

I rank thee with Alves, Latinè, Helvetius, or any of his accursed crew? Thou art my friend, and henceforth my philosopher. Thou shalt teach Distinction to the junior branches of my household and Deception to the gray-haired Janitress at my door.

What! Are these atonements? Can Arcadias be brought upon knees, creeping and crouching?

Come, as Macbeth's drunken porter says, knock, knock, knock, knock, knock, knock, knock—seven times a day shalt thou batter at my peace, and if I shut aught against thee, save the Temple of Janus, may Briareus, with his hundred hands, in each a brass knocker, lead me such a life. C. LAMB.

To WILLIAM WORDSWORTH.

LETTER CXXVI.] *Thursday, January* 29, 1807.

Dear Wordsworth—We have book'd off from Swan and Two Necks, Lad Lane, this day (per Coach) the Tales from Shakspeare. You will forgive the plates, when I tell you they were left to the direction of Godwin, who left the choice of subjects to the bad baby, who from mischief (I suppose) has chosen one from damn'd beastly vulgarity (vide *Merch. Venice*) where no atom of authority was in the tale to justify it; to another has given a name which exists not in the tale, Nic Bottom, and which she thought would be funny, though in this I suspect *his* hand, for I guess her reading does not reach far enough to know Bottom's Christian name; and one of Hamlet and grave-digging, a scene which is not hinted at in the story, and you might as well have put King Canute the Great reproving his courtiers. The rest are giants and giantesses. Suffice it, to save our taste and damn our folly, that we left it all to a friend, W. G., who in the first place cheated me into putting a name to them, which I did not mean, but do not repent, and then wrote a puff about their *simplicity*, etc., to go with the advertisement as in my name! Enough of this egregious dupery. I will try to abstract the load of teasing circumstances from the stories and tell you that I am answerable for *Lear*, *Macbeth*, *Timon*, *Romeo*, *Hamlet*, *Othello*, for occasionally a tailpiece or correction of grammar, for none of the cuts and all of the spelling. The rest is my Sister's.——We think Pericles of hers the best, and Othello of mine; but

I hope all have some good. *As you like It*, we like least. So much, only begging you to tear out the cuts and give them to Johnny, as "Mrs. Godwin's fancy"!!—

C. L.

Our love to all.

I had almost forgot, My part of the Preface begins in the middle of a sentence, in last but one page, after a colon, thus—

:—which if they be happily so done, etc.

the former part hath a more feminine turn and does hold me up something as an instructor to young ladies: but upon my modesty's honour I wrote it not.

Godwin told my Sister that the Baby chose the subjects: a fact in taste.

To Rev. W. HAZLITT.

LETTER CXXVII.]   *Temple, February* 18, 1808.

Sir—I am truly concerned that any mistake of mine should have caused you uneasiness, but I hope we have got a clue to William's absence, which may clear up all apprehensions. The people where he lodges in town have received direction from him to forward some linen to a place called Winterslow, in the county of Wilts (not far from Salisbury), where the lady lives, whose cottage, pictured upon a card, if you opened my letter you have doubtless seen; and though we have had no explanation of the mystery since, we shrewdly suspect that at the time of writing that letter which has given you all this trouble, a certain son of yours (who is both painter and author) was at her elbow, and did assist in framing that very cartoon which was sent to amuse and mislead us in town, as to the real place of his destination. And some words at the back of the said cartoon, which we had not marked so narrowly before, by the similarity of the hand-writing to William's, do very much confirm the suspicion.

If our theory be right, they have had the pleasure of their jest, and I am afraid you have paid for it in anxiety. But I hope your uneasiness will now be removed, and you will pardon a suspense occasioned by LOVE, who does so many worse mischiefs every day.

The letter to the people where William lodges says, moreover, that he shall be in town in a fortnight.

My sister joins in respects to you and Mrs. Hazlitt, and in our kindest remembrances and wishes for the restoration of Peggy's health.

I am, Sir, your humble servant,   CH. LAMB.

Rev. W. Hazlitt, Wem, Shropshire.

To THOMAS MANNING.

LETTER CXXVIII.]   *February* 26, 1808.

Dear Missionary—Your letters from the farthest ends of the world have arrived safe. Mary is very thankful for your remembrance of her ; and with the less suspicion of mercenariness, as the silk, the *symbolum materiale* of your friendship, has not yet appeared. I think Horace says somewhere, *nox longa*. I would not impute negligence or unhandsome delays to a person whom you have honoured with your confidence, but I have not heard of the silk, or of Mr. Knox, save by your letter. Maybe he expects the first advances ! or it may be that he has not succeeded in getting the article on shore, for it is among the *res prohibitæ et non nisi smuggle-ationis viâ fruendæ.* But so it is, in the friendships between *wicked men* the very expressions of their goodwill cannot but be sinful. I suppose you know my farce was damned. The noise still rings in my ears. Were you ever in the pillory ?—being damned is something like that. A treaty of marriage is on foot between William Hazlitt and Miss Stoddart. Something about settlements only retards it. She has somewhere about £80 a year, to be £120 when her mother dies. He has no settlement except what he can claim from the Parish. *Pauper est tamen, sed amat.* The thing is therefore in abeyance. But there is love a-both sides. Little Fenwick (you don't see the connection of ideas here; how the devil should you?) is in the rules of the Fleet. Cruel creditors! operation of iniquitous laws. Is Magna Charta then a mockery? Why, in general (here I suppose you to ask a question) my spirits are pretty good; but I have my depressions, black as a smith's beard, Vulcanic, Stygian. At such times I have recourse to a pipe, which is like not being at home to a dun: he comes again with tenfold bitterness the next day.—(Mind, I am not in debt; I only borrow a similitude from others; it shows imagination.) I have done two books since the failure of my farce; they will both be out this Summer. The one is a juvenile book—the *Adventures of Ulysses,* intended to be an introduction to the reading of *Telemachus!* It is done out of the *Odyssey,* not from the Greek (I would not mislead you), nor yet from Pope's *Odyssey,* but from an older translation of one Chapman. The *Shakspeare Tales* suggested the doing of it. Godwin is in both those cases my bookseller. The other is done for Longman, and is *Specimens of English Dramatic Poets contemporary with Shakspeare.* Specimens are becoming fashionable. We have "Specimens of Ancient English Poets," "Specimens of Modern English Poets," "Specimens of Ancient English Prose Writers," without end. They used to be called "Beauties." You have seen "Beauties of Shakspeare :" so have many people that never saw any beauties in Shakspeare. Longman is to print it, and be at all the expense and risk, and I am to share the profits after all deductions; *i.e.* a year or two hence I must pocket what they please to tell me is due to me. But the book is such as I am glad there should be. It is done out of old plays at the Museum, and out of Dodsley's collection, etc. It is to have notes. So I go creeping on since I was lamed with that cursed fall from off the top of Drury Lane Theatre into the pit, something more than a year ago. However, I have been free of the house ever since, and the house was pretty free with me upon that occasion. Damn 'em, how they hissed ! It was not a hiss neither, but a sort of a frantic yell, like a congregation of mad geese, with roaring sometimes, like bears, mows and mops like apes, sometimes snakes, that hiss'd me into madness. 'Twas like St. Anthony's temptations. Mercy on us, that God should give his favourite children, men, mouths to speak with, to discourse rationally, to promise smoothly, to flatter agreeably, to encourage warmly, to counsel wisely, to sing with, to drink with, and to kiss with, and that they should turn them into mouths of adders, bears, wolves, hyenas, and whistle like tempests, and emit breath through them like distillations of aspic poison, to asperse and vilify the innocent labours of their fellow-creatures who are desirous to please them ! Heaven be pleased to make the breath stink and teeth rot out of them all therefore : make them a reproach, and all that pass by them to loll out their tongue at them ! Blind mouths ! as Milton somewhere calls them. Do you like Braham's singing? The little Jew has bewitched me. I follow him like as the boys followed Tom the Piper. He cures me of melancholy as David cured Saul : but I don't throw stones at him as Saul did at David in payment. I was insensible to music till he gave me a new sense. Oh that you could go to the new opera of *Kais* to-night ! 'Tis all about Eastern manners ; it would just suit you. It describes the wild Arabs, wandering Egyptians, lying dervises, and all that sort of people, to a hair. You needn't ha' gone so far to see what you see, if you saw it as I do every night at Drury Lane Theatre. Braham's singing, when it is impassioned, is finer than Mrs. Siddons's or Mr. Kemble's acting ! and when it is not impassioned, it is as good as hearing a person of fine sense talking. The brave little Jew ! Old Sergeant Hill is dead. Mrs. Rickman is in the family way. It is thought that Hazlitt will have children if he marries Miss Stoddart. I made a pun the other day, and palmed it upon Holcroft,

who grinned like a Cheshire cat. (Why do cats grin in
Cheshire?—Because it was once a county palatine, and
the cats cannot help laughing whenever they think of it,
though I see no great joke in it.) I said that Holcroft,
on being asked who were the best dramatic writers of
the day, replied, "HOOK AND I." Mr. Hook is author
of several pieces, *Tekeli*, etc. You know what *hooks and
eyes* are, don't you? They are what little boys do up
their breeches with. Your letter had many things in it
hard to be understood: the puns were ready and Swift-
like; but don't you begin to be melancholy in the midst
of Eastern customs? "The mind does not easily conform
to foreign usages, even in trifles: it requires something
that it has been familiar with." That begins one of Dr.
Hawkesworth's papers in the *Adventurer*, and is, I think,
as sensible a remark as ever fell from the Doctor's mouth.
White is at Christ's Hospital, a wit of the first magni-
tude, but would rather be thought a gentleman, like
Congreve. You know Congreve's repulse which he gave
to Voltaire, when he came to visit him as a *literary man*,
that he wished to be considered only in the light of a
private gentleman. I think the impertinent Frenchman
was properly answered. I should just serve any member
of the French Institute in the same manner, that wished
to be introduced to me. Buonaparte has voted 5000
livres to Davy, the great young English Chemist! but it
has not arrived. Coleridge has delivered two lectures at
the Royal Institution; two more intended, but he did
not come. It is thought he has gone sick upon them.
He isn't well, that's certain. Wordsworth is coming to
see him. He sits up in a two pair of stairs room at the
Courier Office, and receives visitors. . . .

Does any one read at Canton? Lord Moira is
President of the Westminster Library. I suppose you
might have interest with Sir Joseph Banks to get to be
president of any similar institution that should be set up
at Canton. I think public reading-rooms the best mode
of educating young men. Solitary reading is apt to give

the headache. Besides, who knows that you *do* read ? There are ten thousand institutions similar to the Royal Institution which have sprung up from it. There is the London Institution, the Southwark Institution, the Russell Square Rooms Institution, etc.—*College quasi Conlege*, a place where people read together. Wordsworth, the great poet, is coming to town ; he is to have apartments in the Mansion House. He says he does not see much difficulty in writing like Shakspeare, if he had a mind to try it. It is clear that nothing is wanting but the mind. Even Coleridge was a little checked at this hardihood of assertion. Dyer came to me the other evening at 11 o'clock, when there was a large room full of company, which I usually get together on a Wednesday evening (all great men have public days), to propose to me to have my face done by a Miss Beetham (or Betham), a miniature painter, some relation to Mrs. Beetham the Profilist or Pattern Mangle woman opposite St. Dunstan's, to put before my book of Extracts. I declined it.

Well, my dear Manning, talking cannot be infinite I have said all I have to say ; the rest is but remembrances of you, which we shall bear in our heads while we have heads. Here is a packet of trifles nothing worth ; but it is a trifling part of the world where I live : emptiness abounds. But in fulness of affection, we remain yours, C. L.

To WILLIAM GODWIN.

LETTER CXXIX.] *March* 11, 1808.

Dear Godwin—The giant's vomit was perfectly nauseous, and I am glad you pointed it out. I have removed the objection. To the other passages I can find no other objection but what you may bring to numberless passages besides, such as of Scylla snatching up the six men, etc., —that is to say, they are lively images of *shocking* things. If you want a book, which is not occasionally to *shock*, you should not have thought of a tale which was so full of anthropophagi and wonders. I cannot alter these things without enervating the Book, and I will not alter them if the penalty should be that you and all the London booksellers should refuse it. But speaking as author to author, I must say that I think *the terrible* in those two passages seems to me so much to preponderate over the nauseous, as to make them rather fine than disgusting. Who is to read them, I don't know : who is it that reads "Tales of Terror" and "Mysteries of Udolpho"? Such things sell. I only say that I will not consent to alter such passages, which I know to be some of the best in the book. As an author, I say to you an author : touch not my work. As to a bookseller I say, Take the work such as it is, or refuse it. You are as free to refuse it as when we first talked of it. As to a friend I say, Don't plague yourself and me with nonsensical objections. I assure you I will not alter one more word.

.

To Mrs. HAZLITT.

Letter CXXX.]   *Saturday, December* 10, 1808.

There came this morning a printed Prospectus from "S. T. Coleridge, Grasmere," of a Weekly Paper, to be called *The Friend;* a flaming Prospectus. I have no time to give the heads of it. To commence the first Saturday in January. There came also notice of a turkey from Mr. Clarkson, which I am more sanguine in expecting the accomplishment of than I am of Coleridge's prophecy.   C. Lamb.

Mrs. Hazlitt, Winterslow,
    near Sarum, Wilts.

CHAPTER III.

1809–1816.

LETTERS TO MANNING, COLERIDGE, WORDSWORTH,

AND OTHERS.

To THOMAS MANNING.

Southampton Buildings,
LETTER CXXXI.]   *March* 28, 1809.

DEAR MANNING—I sent you a long letter by the ships which sailed the beginning of last month, accompanied with books, etc. Since I last wrote Holcroft is dead. He died on Thursday last. So there is one of your friends whom you will never see again! Perhaps the next fleet may bring you a letter from Martin Burney, to say that he writes by desire of Miss Lamb, who is not well enough to write herself, to inform you that her brother died on Thursday last, 14th June, etc. But I hope *not*. I should be sorry to give occasion to open a correspondence between Martin and you. This letter must be short, for I have driven it off to the very moment of doing up the packets; and besides, that which I refer to above is a very long one; and if you have received my books, you will have enough to do to read them. While I think on it, let me tell you, we are moved. Don't come any more to Mitre Court Buildings. We are at 34, Southampton Buildings, Chancery Lane, and shall be here till about the end of May; then we remove to

No. 4, Inner Temple Lane, where I mean to live and die ;
for I have such horror of moving, that I would not take
a benefice from the King if I was not indulged with non-
residence.   What a dislocation of comfort is comprised
in that word "moving!"   Such a heap of little nasty
things, after you think all is got into the cart : old
dredging-boxes, worn-out brushes, gallipots, vials, things
that it is impossible the most necessitous person can ever
want, but which the women, who preside on these occa-
sions, will not leave behind if it was to save your soul.
They'd keep the cart ten minutes to stow in dirty pipes
and broken matches, to show their economy.   Then you
can find nothing you want for many days after you get
into your new lodgings.   You must comb your hair with
your fingers, wash your hands without soap, go about in
dirty gaiters.   Were I Diogenes, I would not move out
of a kilderkin into a hogshead, though the first had had
nothing but small beer in it, and the second recked claret.
Our place of final destination—I don't mean the grave,
but No. 4, Inner Temple Lane—looks out upon a gloomy
churchyard-like court, called Hare Court, with three trees
and a pump in it.   Do you know it?   I was born near
it, and used to drink at that pump when I was a
Rechabite of six years old.   If you see newspapers you
will read about Mrs. Clarke.   The sensation in London
about this nonsensical business is marvellous.   I remember
nothing in my life like it : thousands of ballads, carica-
tures, lives of Mrs. Clarke, in every blind alley.   Yet in
the midst of this stir, a sublime abstracted dancing-
master, who attends a family we know at Kensington,
being asked a question about the progress of the examina-
tions in the House, inquired who Mrs. Clarke was?   He
had heard nothing of it.   He had evaded this omni-
presence by utter insignificancy !   The Duke should
make that man his confidential valet.   I proposed locking
him up, barring him the use of his fiddle and red pumps,
until he had minutely perused and committed to memory
the whole body of the examinations, which employed the

House of Commons a fortnight, to teach him to be more attentive to what concerns the public. I think I told you of Godwin's little book, and of Coleridge's prospectus, in my last; if I did not, remind me of it, and I will send you them, or an account of them, next fleet. I have no conveniency of doing it by this. Mrs. —— grows every day in disfavour with me. I will be buried with this inscription over me:—"Here lies C. L., the woman-hater:" I mean that hated one woman: for the rest, God bless them! How do you like the Mandarinesses? Are you on some little footing with any of them? This is Wednesday. On Wednesdays is my levee. The Captain, Martin, Phillips (not the Sheriff), Rickman, and some more, are constant attendants, besides stray visitors. We play at whist, eat cold meat and hot potatoes, and any gentleman that chooses smokes. Why do you never drop in? You'll come some day, won't you?

C. LAMB, etc.

To SAMUEL TAYLOR COLERIDGE.

LETTER CXXXII.]   *June* 7, 1809.

Dear Coleridge—I congratulate you on the appearance of the *Friend.* Your first Number promises well, and I have no doubt the succeeding Numbers will fulfil the promise. I had a kind letter from you some time since, which I have left unanswered. I am also obliged to you, I believe, for a review in the Annual, am I not? The *Monthly Review* sneers at me, and asks "if *Comus* is not *good enough* for Mr. Lamb?" because I have said no good serious dramas have been written since the death of Charles the First, except *Samson Agonistes.* So because they do not know, or won't remember, that *Comus* was written long before, I am to be set down as an under-valuer of Milton! O Coleridge, do kill those reviews, or they will kill us; kill all we like. Be a friend to all else, but their foe. I have been turned out of my chambers in the Temple by a landlord who wanted them for himself, but I have got other at No. 4, Inner Temple Lane, far more commodious and roomy. I have two rooms on the third floor and five rooms above, with an inner staircase to myself, and all new painted, etc., and all for £30 a year! I came into them on Saturday week; and on Monday following Mary was taken ill with the fatigue of moving; and affected, I believe, by the novelty of the home she could not sleep, and I am left alone with a maid quite a stranger to me, and she has a month or two's sad distraction to go through. What sad large pieces it cuts out of life!—out of *her* life, who is getting rather old; and we may not have many years to live together. I am weaker, and bear it worse than I ever did. But I hope we shall be comfortable by and by. The rooms are delicious, and the best look backwards into Hare Court, where there is a pump always going. Just now it is dry. Hare Court trees come in at the window, so that 'tis like living in a garden. I try to persuade myself it is much pleasanter than Mitre Court; but, alas! the household gods are slow to come in a new mansion. They are in their infancy to me; I do not feel them yet; no hearth has blazed to them yet. How I hate and dread new places!

I was very glad to see Wordsworth's book advertised: I am to have it to-morrow lent me, and if Wordsworth don't send me an order for one upon Longman, I will buy it. It is greatly extolled and liked by all who have seen it. Let me hear from some of you, for I am desolate. I shall have to send you, in a week or two, two volumes of Juvenile Poetry, done by Mary and me within the last six months, and that tale in prose which Wordsworth so much liked, which was published at Christmas, with nine others, by us, and has reached a second edition. There's for you. We have almost worked ourselves out of child's work, and I don't know what to do. Sometimes I think of a drama, but I have no head for play-making; I can do the dialogue, and that's all. I am quite aground for

a plan ; but I must do something for money. Not that
I have immediate wants, but I have prospective ones.
O money, money, how blindly thou hast been worshipped,
and how stupidly abused ! Thou art health and liberty
and strength ; and he that has thee may rattle his pockets
at the Devil.

Nevertheless, do not understand by this that I have
not quite enough for my occasions for a year or two to
come. While I think on it, Coleridge, I fetch'd away
my books which you had at the *Courier* Office, and found
all but a third volume of the old plays, containing the
White Devil, Green's *Tu Quoque*, and the *Honest Whore*,
perhaps the most valuable volume of them all—*that* I
could not find. Pray, if you can, remember what you
did with it, or where you took it out with you a walking
perhaps ; send me word, for, to use the old plea, it spoils
a set. I found two other volumes (you had three), the
Arcadia, and *Daniel*, enriched with manuscript notes.
I wish every book I have were so noted. They have
thoroughly converted me to relish *Daniel*, or to say I
relish him, for after all, I believe I did relish him. You
well call him sober-minded. Your notes are excellent.
Perhaps you've forgot them. I have read a review in
the *Quarterly*, by Southey, on the Missionaries, which is
most masterly. I only grudge its being there. It is
quite beautiful. Do remember my Dodsley ; and, pray,
do write, or let some of you write. Clarkson tells me
you are in a smoky house. Have you cured it ? It is
hard to cure anything of smoking. Our little poems are
but humble, but they have no name. You must read
them, remembering they were task work ; and perhaps
you will admire the number of subjects, all of children,
picked out by an old Bachelor and an old Maid. Many
parents would not have found so many. Have you read
Cœlebs ? It has reached eight editions in so many weeks,
yet literally it is one of the very poorest sort of common
novels, with the draw-back of dull religion in it. Had
the religion been high and flavoured, it would have been

something.   I borrowed this *Cœlebs in Search of a Wife*, of a very careful, neat lady, and returned it with this stuff written in the beginning :—

> " If ever I marry a wife
> I'll marry a landlord's daughter,
> For then I may sit in the bar,
> And drink cold brandy and water."

I don't expect you can find time from your *Friend* to write to me much; but write something, for there has been a long silence.   You know Holcroft is dead.   Godwin is well.   He has written a very pretty, absurd book about sepulchres.   He was affronted because I told him it was better than Hervey, but not so good as Sir T. Browne.   This letter is all about books; but my head aches, and I hardly know what I write, but I could not let the *Friend* pass without a congratulatory epistle.   I won't criticise till it comes to a volume.   Tell me how I shall send my packet to you?—by what conveyance?—by Longman, Short-man, or how?   Give my kindest remembrances to Wordsworth.   Tell him he must give me a book.   My kind love to Mrs. W. and to Dorothy separately and conjointly.   I wish you could all come and see me in my new rooms.   God bless you all.

C. L.

LETTER CXXXIII.]   *Monday, October* 30, 1809.

Dear Coleridge—I have but this moment received your letter, dated the 9th instant, having just come off a journey from Wiltshire, where I have been with Mary on a visit to Hazlitt.   The journey has been of infinite service to her.   We have had nothing but sunshiny days, and daily walks from eight to twenty miles a day; have seen Wilton, Salisbury, Stonehenge, etc.   Her illness lasted but six weeks; it left her weak, but the country has made us whole.   We came back to our Hogarth Room.   I have made several acquisitions since you saw them,—and found Nos. 8, 9, 10 of the *Friend*.   The account of Luther in the Warteburg is as fine as anything I ever read. God forbid that a man who has such things to say should be silenced for want of £100. This Custom-and-Duty Age would have made the Preacher on the Mount take out a licence, and St. Paul's Epistles would not have been missible without a stamp. O that you may find means to go on! But alas! where is Sir G. Beaumont?—Sotheby? What is become of the rich Auditors in Albemarle Street? Your letter has saddened me.

I am so tired with my journey, being up all night, that I have neither things nor words in my power. I believe I expressed my admiration of the pamphlet. Its power over me was like that which Milton's pamphlets must have had on his contemporaries, who were tuned to them. What a piece of prose! Do you hear if it is read at all? I am out of the world of readers. I hate all that do read, for they read nothing but reviews and new books. I gather myself up unto the old things.

I have put up shelves. You never saw a book-case in more true harmony with the contents than what I've nailed up in a room, which, though new, has more aptitudes for growing old than you shall often see—as one sometimes gets a friend in the middle of life, who becomes an old friend in a short time. My rooms are luxurious; one is for prints and one for books; a Summer and a Winter parlour. When shall I ever see you in them?

C. L.

To THOMAS MANNING.

LETTER CXXXIV.] *January* 2, 1810.

Dear Manning—When I last wrote to you I was in lodgings. I am now in chambers, No. 4, Inner Temple Lane, where I should be happy to see you any evening. Bring any of your friends, the Mandarins, with you. I have two sitting-rooms: I call them so *par excellence*, for

you may stand, or loll, or lean, or try any posture in
them, but they are best for sitting; not squatting down
Japanese fashion, but the more decorous use of the ———
which European usage has consecrated. I have two of
these rooms on the third floor, and five sleeping, cooking,
etc., rooms, on the fourth floor. In my best room is a
choice collection of the works of Hogarth, an English
painter of some humour. In my next best are shelves
containing a small but well-chosen library. My best
room commands a court, in which there are trees and a
pump, the water of which is excellent cold, with brandy,
and not very insipid without. Here I hope to set up my
rest, and not quit till Mr. Powell, the undertaker, gives
me notice that I may have possession of my last lodging.
He lets lodgings for single gentlemen. I sent you a
parcel of books by my last, to give you some idea of the
state of European literature. There comes with this two
volumes, done up as letters, of minor poetry, a sequel to
"Mrs. Leicester;" the best you may suppose mine; the
next best are my coadjutor's. You may amuse yourself
in guessing them out; but I must tell you mine are but
one-third in quantity of the whole. So much for a very
delicate subject. It is hard to speak of one's self, etc.
Holcroft had finished his life when I wrote to you, and
Hazlitt has since finished his life; I do not mean his own
life, but he has finished a life of Holcroft, which is going
to press. Tuthill is Dr. Tuthill. I continue Mr. Lamb.
I have published a little book for children on titles of
honour; and to give them some idea of the difference of
rank and gradual rising, I have made a little scale, sup-
posing myself to receive the following various accessions
of dignity from the king, who is the fountain of honour—
As at first, 1, Mr. C. Lamb; 2, C. Lamb, Esq.; 3, Sir
C. Lamb, Bart.; 4, Baron Lamb, of Stamford; 5,
Viscount Lamb; 6, Earl Lamb; 7, Marquis Lamb; 8,
Duke Lamb. It would look like quibbling to carry it on
further, and especially as it is not necessary for children
to go beyond the ordinary titles of sub-regal dignity in

our own country ; otherwise I have sometimes in my
dreams imagined myself still advancing, as 9th, King
Lamb ; 10th, Emperor Lamb ; 11th, Pope Innocent ;
higher than which is nothing upon earth. Puns I have
not made many (nor punch much) since the date of my
last ; one I cannot help relating. A constable in Salis-
bury Cathedral was telling me that eight people dined at
the top of the spire of the cathedral ; upon which I
remarked, that they must be very sharp set. But in
general I cultivate the reasoning part of my mind more
than the imaginative. I am stuffed out so with eating
turkey for dinner, and another turkey for supper yester-
day (Turkey in Europe and Turkey in Asia), that I can't
jog on. It is New Year here ; that is, it was New Year
half a year back, when I was writing this. Nothing
puzzles me more than time and space ; and yet nothing
puzzles me less, for I never think about them. The
Persian ambassador is the principal thing talked of now.
I sent some people to see him worship the sun on Prim-
rose Hill, at half-past six in the morning, 28th November ;
but he did not come, which makes me think the old fire-
worshippers are a sect almost extinct in Persia. The
Persian ambassador's name is Shaw Ali Mirza. The
common people call him Shaw Nonsense. While I think
of it, I have put three letters, besides my own three, into
the India post for you, from your brother, sister, and
some gentleman whose name I forget. Will they, have
they, did they come safe ? The distance you are at, cuts
up tenses by the root. I think you said you did not
know Kate * * * * * * * * *. I express her by nine
stars, though she is but one. You must have seen her
at her father's. Try and remember her. Coleridge is
bringing out a paper in weekly Numbers, called the
Friend, which I would send if I could ; but the difficulty
I had in getting the packets of books out to you before,
deters me ; and you'll want something new to read when
you come home. It is chiefly intended to puff off Words-
worth's poetry ; but there are some noble things in it by

the by.   Except Kate, I have had no vision of excellence this year, and she passed by like the Queen on her coronation day ; you don't know whether you saw her or not. Kate is fifteen : I go about moping, and sing the old pathetic ballad I used to like in my youth—

> " She's sweet fifteen,
> I'm *one year more.*"

Mrs. Bland sang it in boy's clothes the first time I heard it.   I sometimes think the lower notes in my voice are like Mrs. Bland's.   That glorious singer, Braham, one of my lights, is fled.   He was for a season.   He was a rare composition of the Jew, the gentleman, and the angel ; yet all these elements mixed up so kindly in him, that you could not tell which preponderated ; but he is gone, and one Phillips is engaged instead.   Kate is vanished, but Miss B—— is always to be met with !

> " Queens drop away, while blue-legg'd Maukin thrives ;
> And courtly Mildred dies while country Madge survives."

That is not my poetry, but Quarles's ; but haven't you observed that the rarest things are the least obvious ? Don't show anybody the names in this letter.   I write confidentially, and wish this letter to be considered as *private.*   Hazlitt has written a *grammar* for Godwin. Godwin sells it bound up with a treatise of his own on language ; but the *gray mare is the better horse.*   I don't allude to Mrs. [Godwin], but to the word *grammar,* which comes near to *gray mare,* if you observe, in sound. That figure is called paronomasia in Greek.   I am sometimes happy in it.   An old woman begged of me for charity.   " Ah ! sir," said she, " I have seen better days." " So have I, good woman," I replied ; but I meant, literally, days not so rainy and overcast as that on which she begged : she meant more prosperous days.   Mr. Dawe is made associate of the Royal Academy.   By what law of association I can't guess, Mrs. Holcroft, Miss Holcroft, Mr. and Mrs. Godwin, Mr. and Mrs. Hazlitt, Mrs. Martin and Louisa, Mrs. Lum, Capt. Burney, Mrs.

Burney, Martin Burney, Mr. Rickman, Mrs. Rickman, Dr. Stoddart, William Dollin, Mr. Thompson, Mr. and Mrs. Norris, Mr. Fenwick, Mrs. Fenwick, Miss Fenwick, a man that saw you at our house one day, and a lady that heard me speak of you; Mrs. Buffam that heard Hazlitt mention you, Dr. Tuthill, Mrs. Tuthill, Colonel Harwood, Mrs. Harwood, Mr. Collier, Mrs. Collier, Mr. Sutton, Nurse, Mr. Fell, Mrs. Fell, Mr. Marshall, are very well, and occasionally inquire after you.

I remain yours ever,   CH. LAMB.

To JOHN MATHEW GUTCH.

LETTER CXXXV.]   [*April* 9, 1810.]

Dear Gutch—I did not see your brother, who brought me Wither; but he understood, he said, you were daily expecting to come to town: this has prevented my writing. The books have pleased me excessively: I should think you could not have made a better selection. I never saw *Philarete* before—judge of my pleasure. I could not forbear scribbling certain critiques in pencil on the blank leaves. Shall I send them, or may I expect to see you in town? Some of them are remarks on the character of Wither and of his writings. Do you mean to have anything of that kind? What I have said on *Philarete* is poor, but I think some of the rest not so bad: perhaps I have exceeded my commission in scrawling over the copies; but my delight therein must excuse me, and pencil-marks will rub out. Where is the Life? Write, for I am quite in the dark.

Yours, with many thanks,   C. LAMB.

Perhaps I could digest the few critiques prefixed to the Satires, Shepherds Hunting, etc., into a short abstract of Wither's character and works, at the end of his Life. But, may be, you don't want anything, and have said all you wish in the Life.

To BASIL MONTAGU.

Winterslow, near Sarum,
July 12, 1810.

LETTER CXXXVI.]

Dear Montagu—I have turned and twisted the MSS. in my head, and can make nothing of them. I knew when I took them that I could not, but I do not like to do an act of ungracious necessity at once; so I am ever committing myself by half engagements, and total failures. I cannot make anybody understand why I can't do such things; it is a defect in my occiput. I cannot put other people's thoughts together; I forget every paragraph as fast as I read it; and my head has received such a shock by an all-night journey on the top of the coach, that I shall have enough to do to nurse it into its natural pace before I go home. I must devote myself to imbecility; I must be gloriously useless while I stay here. How is Mrs. M. ? will she pardon my inefficiency ? The city of Salisbury is full of weeping and wailing. The bank has stopped payment; and everybody in the town kept money at it, or has got some of its notes. Some have lost all they had in the world. It is the next thing to seeing a city with the plague within its walls. The Wilton people are all undone; all the manufacturers there kept cash at the Salisbury bank; and I do suppose it to be the unhappiest county in England this, where I am making holiday. We propose setting out for Oxford Tuesday fortnight, and coming thereby home. But no more night travelling. My head is sore (understand it of the inside) with that deduction from my natural rest which I suffered coming down. Neither Mary nor I can spare a morsel of our rest : it is incumbent on us to be misers of it. Travelling is not good for us, we travel so seldom. If the sun be hell, it is not for the fire, but for the sempiternal motion of that miserable body of light. How much more dignified leisure hath a mussel glued to his unpassable rocky limit two inch square ! He hears

the tide roll over him, backwards and forwards twice
a day (as the Salisbury long coach goes and returns in
eight-and-forty hours), but knows better than to take an
outside night place a top on't.   He is the owl of the sea
—Minerva's fish—the fish of wisdom.

Our kindest remembrances to Mrs. M.

Yours truly,   C. LAMB.

To WILLIAM HAZLITT.

LETTER CXXXVII.]   *Thursday* [*August* 9, 1810].

Dear H.—Epistemon is not well.   Our pleasant excur-
sion has ended sadly for one of us.   You will guess I
mean my sister.   She got home very well (I was very
ill on the journey) and continued so till Monday night,
when her complaint came on, and she is now absent from
home.

I am glad to hear you are all well.   I think I shall
be mad if I take any more journeys, with two experiences
against it.   I found all well here.   Kind remembrances
to Sarah,—have just got her letter.

H. Robinson has been to Blenheim.   He says you will
be sorry to hear that we should not have asked for the
Titian Gallery there.   One of his friends knew of it, and
asked to see it.   It is never shown but to those who
inquire for it.

The pictures are all Titians, Jupiter and Ledas, Mars
and Venuses, etc., all naked pictures, which may be a
reason they don't show them to females.   But he says
they are very fine ; and perhaps they are shown separately
to put another fee into the shower's pocket.   Well, I
shall never see it.

I have lost all wish for sights.   God bless you.   I
shall be glad to see you in London.

Yours truly,   C. LAMB.

Mr. Hazlitt, Winterslow,
    near Salisbury.

To Miss WORDSWORTH.

LETTER CXXXVIII.]   [*August* 1810.]

Mary has left a little space for me to fill up with non-
sense, as the geographers used to cram monsters in the
voids of the maps, and call it Terra Incognita. She has
told you how she has taken to water like a hungry otter.
I too limp after her in lame imitation, but it goes against
me a little at first. I have been acquaintance with it now
for full four days, and it seems a moon. I am full of
cramps and rheumatisms, and cold internally, so that fire
won't warm me; yet I bear all for virtue's sake. Must
I then leave you, gin, rum, brandy, aqua-vitæ, pleasant
jolly fellows? Damn temperance and he that first invented
it!—some Anti-Noahite. Coleridge has powdered his
head, and looks like Bacchus, Bacchus ever sleek and
young. He is going to turn sober, but his clock has not
struck yet; meantime he pours down goblet after goblet,
the second to see where the first is gone, the third to see
no harm happens to the second, a fourth to say there is
another coming, and a fifth to say he is not sure he is
the last.

To WILLIAM WORDSWORTH.

LETTER CXXXIX.]   *Friday, October* 19, 1810. *E. I. Ho.*

Dear W.—Mary has been very ill, which you have
heard, I suppose, from the Montagus. She is very weak
and low-spirited now. I was much pleased with your
continuation of the Essay on Epitaphs. It is the only
sensible thing which has been written on that subject,
and it goes to the bottom. In particular I was pleased
with your translation of that turgid epitaph into the plain
feeling under it. It is perfectly a test. But what is
the reason we have no good epitaphs after all?

A very striking instance of your position might be
found in the churchyard of Ditton-upon-Thames, if you

know such a place.   Ditton-upon-Thames has been blessed
by the residence of a poet, who for love or money—I do
not well know which—has dignified every gravestone, for
the last few years, with bran-new verses, all different, and
all ingenious, with the author's name at the bottom of
each.   This sweet Swan of Thames has so artfully diver-
sified his strains and his rhymes, that the same thought
never occurs twice ; more justly, perhaps, as no thought
ever occurs at all, there was a physical impossibility that
the same thought should recur.   It is long since I saw
and read these inscriptions, but I remember the impres-
sion was of a smug usher at his desk in the intervals of
instruction, levelling his pen.   Of death, as it consists of
dust and worms, and mourners and uncertainty, he had
never thought ; but the word " death " he had often seen
separate and conjunct with other words, till he had
learned to speak of all its attributes as glibly as Unitarian
Belsham will discuss you the attributes of the word "God"
in a pulpit ; and will talk of infinity with a tongue that
dangles from a skull that never reached in thought and
thorough imagination two inches, or further than from
his hand to his mouth, or from the vestry to the sounding-
board of the pulpit.

But the epitaphs were trim, and sprag, and patent,
and pleased the survivors of Thames-Ditton above the old
mumpsimus of " Afflictions Sore." . . . To do justice
though, it must be owned that even the excellent feeling
which dictated this dirge when new must have suffered
something in passing through so many thousand applica-
tions, many of them no doubt quite misplaced, as I have
seen in Islington churchyard (I think) an Epitaph to an
infant who died " *Ætatis* four months," with this season-
able inscription appended, " Honour thy father and thy
mother ; that thy days may be long in the land," etc.
Sincerely wishing your children long life to honour, etc.

  I remain,   C. LAMB.

To Miss WORDSWORTH.

LETTER CXL.]   *November* 23, 1810.

We are in a pickle. Mary, from her affectation of physiognomy, has hired a stupid big country wench, who looked honest, as she thought, and has been doing her work some days, but without eating—eats no butter, nor meat, but prefers cheese with her tea for breakfast; and now it comes out that she was ill when she came, with lifting her mother about (who is now with God) when she was dying, and with riding up from Norfolk, four days and nights in the waggon. She got advice yesterday, and took something which has made her bring up a quart of blood, and she now lies in her bed, a dead weight upon our humanity, incapable of getting up, refusing to go into an hospital, having nobody in town but a poor asthmatic uncle whose son lately married a drab who fills his house, and there is nowhere she can go, and she seems to have made up her mind to take her flight to heaven from our bed. Oh for the little wheel-barrow which trundled the hunchback from door to door to try the various charities of different professions of mankind! Here's her uncle just crawled up. He is far liker Death than she. Oh the Parish, the Parish, the hospital, the infirmary, the charnel-house!—these are places meet for such guests, not our quiet mansion, where nothing but affluent plenty and literary ease should abound.—Howard's House, Howard's House, or where the Paralytic descended through the skylight (what a God's gift!) to get at our Saviour. In this perplexity such topics as Spanish papers and Monkhouses sink into comparative insignificance. What shall we do? If she died, it were something: gladly would I pay the coffin-maker, and the bell-man and searchers.   C. L.

To Miss Wordsworth, Grasmere,
     near Kendal, Westmoreland.

To WILLIAM HAZLITT.

LETTER CXLI.]   *Wednesday, November 28, 1810.*

Dear Hazlitt—I sent you on Saturday a Cobbett, containing your reply to the *Edinburgh Review*, which I thought you would be glad to receive as an example of attention on the part of Mr. Cobbett to insert it so speedily. Did you get it? We have received your pig, and return you thanks; it will be dressed in due form, with appropriate sauce, this day. Mary has been very ill indeed since you saw her; that is, as ill as she can be to remain at home. But she is a good deal better now, owing to a very careful regimen. She drinks nothing but water, and never goes out; she does not even go to the Captain's. Her indisposition has been ever since that night you left town; the night Miss W[ordsworth] came. Her coming, and that d——d Mrs. Godwin coming and staying so late that night, so overset her that she lay broad awake all that night, and it was by a miracle that she escaped a very bad illness, which I thoroughly expected. I have made up my mind that she shall never have any one in the house again with her, and that no one shall sleep with her, not even for a night; for it is a very serious thing to be always living with a kind of fever upon her; and therefore I am sure you will take it in good part if I say that if Mrs. Hazlitt comes to town at any time, however glad we shall be to see her in the daytime, I cannot ask her to spend a night under our roof. Some decision we must come to, for the harassing fever that we have both been in, owing to Miss Wordsworth's coming, is not to be borne; and I would rather be dead than so alive. However, at present, owing to a regimen and medicines which Tuthill has given her, who very kindly volunteer'd the care of her, she is a great deal quieter, though too much harassed by company, who cannot or will not see how late hours and society teaze her.

Poor Phillips had the cup dash'd out of his lips as it were. He had every prospect of the situation, when about ten days since one of the council of the R—— Society started for the place himself, being a rich merchant who lately failed, and he will certainly be elected on Friday next. P. is very sore and miserable about it.

Coleridge is in town, or at least at Hammersmith. He is writing or going to write in the *Courier* against Cobbett, and in favour of paper money.

No news. Remember me kindly to Sarah. I write from the office.

Yours ever,   C. LAMB.

I just open'd it to say the pig, upon proof, hath turned out as good as I predicted. My fauces yet retain the sweet porcine odour. I find you have received the Cobbett. I think your paper complete.

Mrs. Reynolds, who is a sage woman, approves of the pig.

Mr. Hazlitt, Winterslow,
    near Salisbury, Wilts.

To HENRY CRABB ROBINSON.

LETTER CXLII.]   [1810.]

Dear R.—My brother, whom you have met at my rooms (a plump, good-looking man of seven-and-forty) has written a book about humanity, which I transmit to you herewith. Wilson, the publisher, has put it into his head that you can get it reviewed for him. I dare say it is not in the scope of your review; but if you could put it in any likely train, he would rejoice. For alas! our boasted humanity partakes of vanity. As it is, he teazes me to death with choosing to suppose that I could get it into all the reviews at a moment's notice. *I!!* who have been set up as a mark for them to throw at, and would willingly consign them all to Megæra's snaky locks.

But here's the book, and don't show it to Mrs. Collier, for I remember she makes excellent *eel* soup, and the leading points of the book are directed against that very process.

Yours truly,   C. LAMB.

To WILLIAM HAZLITT.

LETTER CXLIII.]   *October* 2, 1811.

Dear Hazlitt—I cannot help accompanying my sister's congratulations to Sarah with some of my own to you on this happy occasion of a man child being born.

Delighted fancy already sees him some future rich alderman or opulent merchant, painting perhaps a little in his leisure hours, for amusement, like the late H. Bunbury, Esq.

Pray, are the Winterslow estates entailed? I am afraid lest the young dog when he grows up should cut down the woods, and leave no groves for widows to take their lonesome solace in. The Wem estate of course can only devolve on him in case of your brother's leaving no male issue.

Well, my blessing and heaven's be upon him, and make him like his father, with something a better temper, and a smoother head of hair; and then all the men and women must love him.

Martin and the card-boys join in congratulations. Love to Sarah. Sorry we are not within candle-shot.

                                                              C. LAMB.

If the widow be assistant on this notable occasion, give our due respects and kind remembrances to her.

Mr. Hazlitt, Winterslow,
      near Sarum, Wilts.

To WILLIAM GODWIN.

" Bis dat qui dat cito.'

LETTER CXLIV.]   [1811.]

I hate the pedantry of expressing that in another
language which we have sufficient terms for in our own.
So in plain English I very much wish you to give your
vote to-morrow at Clerkenwell, instead of Saturday.   It
would clear up the brows of my favourite candidate, and
stagger the hands of the opposite party.   It commences
at nine.   How easy, as you come from Kensington (à
propos, how is your excellent family?) to turn down
Bloomsbury, through Leather Lane (avoiding Lay Stall
St. for the disagreeableness of the name)!   Why, it
brings you in four minutes and a half to the spot re-
nowned on northern milestones, "where Hicks' Hall
formerly stood."   There will be good cheer ready for
every independent freeholder; where you see a green flag
hang out, go boldly in, call for ham, or beef, or what you
please, and a mug of Meux's best.   How much more
gentleman-like to come in the front of the battle, openly
avowing one's sentiments, than to lag in on the last day,
when the adversary is dejected, spiritless, laid low!
Have the first cut at them.   By Saturday you'll cut into
the mutton.   I'd go cheerfully myself, but I am no
freeholder (Fuimus Troes, fuit Ilium), but I sold it for
£50.   If they'd accept a copy-holder, we clerks are
naturally *copy*-holders.

By the way, get Mrs. Hume, or that agreeable Amelia
or Caroline, to stick a bit of green in your hat.   Nothing
daunts the adversary more than to wear the colours of
your party.   Stick it in cockade-like.   It has a martial
and by no means disagreeable effect.

Go, my dear freeholder, and if any chance calls you
out of this transitory scene earlier than expected, the
coroner shall sit lightly on your corpse.   He shall not
too anxiously inquire into the circumstances of blood

found upon your razor. That might happen to any gentleman in shaving. Nor into your having been heard to express a contempt of life, or for scolding Louisa for what Julia did, and other trifling incoherencies.

Yours sincerely, C. LAMB.

TO SAMUEL TAYLOR COLERIDGE.

LETTER CXLV.]   *August* 13, 1814.

Dear Resuscitate—There comes to you by the vehicle from Lad Lane this day a volume of German; what it is I cannot justly say, the characters of those northern nations having been always singularly harsh and unpleasant to me. It is a contribution of Dr. Southey's towards your wants, and you would have had it sooner but for an odd accident. I wrote for it three days ago, and the Doctor, as he thought, sent it me. A book of like exterior he did send, but being disclosed, how far unlike! It was the *Well-bred Scholar*,—a book with which it seems the Doctor laudably fills up those hours which he can steal from his medical avocations. Chesterfield, Blair, Beattie, portions from the *Life of Savage*, make up a prettyish system of morality and the belles-lettres, which Mr. Mylius, a schoolmaster, has properly brought together, and calls the collection by the denomination above mentioned. The Doctor had no sooner discovered his error than he dispatched man and horse to rectify the mistake, and with a pretty kind of ingenuous modesty in his note, seemeth to deny any knowledge of the *Well-bred Scholar;* false modesty surely, and a blush misplaced: for what more pleasing than the consideration of professional austerity thus relaxing, thus improving! But so, when a child, I remember blushing, being caught on my knees to my Maker, or doing otherwise some pious and praiseworthy action: *now* I rather love such things to be seen. Henry Crabb Robinson is out upon his circuit, and his books are inaccessible without his leave and key. He is attending the Norfolk Circuit,—a short term, but to him, as to many young lawyers, a long vacation, sufficiently dreary. I thought I could do no better than transmit to him, not extracts, but your very letter itself, than which I think I never read anything more moving, more pathetic, or more conducive to the purpose of persuasion. The Crab is a sour Crab if it does not sweeten him. I think it would draw another third volume of Dodsley out of me; but you say you don't want any English books. Perhaps, after all, that's as well; one's romantic credulity is for ever misleading one into misplaced acts of foolery. Crab might have answered by this time: his juices take a long time supplying, but they'll run at last—I know they will—pure golden pippin. A fearful rumour has since reached me that the Crab is on the eve of setting out for France. If he is in England your letter will reach him, and I flatter myself a touch of the persuasive of my own, which accompanies it, will not be thrown away; if it be, he is a sloe, and no true-hearted Crab, and there's an end. For that life of the German conjuror which you speak of, *Colerus de Vitâ Doctoris vix-Intelligibilis*, I perfectly remember the last evening we spent with Mrs. Morgan and Miss Brent, in London Street,— (by that token we had raw rabbits for supper, and Miss B. prevailed upon me to take a glass of brandy and water, which is not my habit),—I perfectly remember reading portions of that life in their parlour, and I think it must be among their packages. It was the very last evening we were at that house. What is gone of that frank-hearted circle, Morgan, and his cos-lettuces? He ate walnuts better than any man I ever knew. Friendships in these parts stagnate.

. . . . . .

I am going to eat turbot, turtle, venison, marrow pudding,—cold punch, claret, Madeira,—at our annual feast, at half-past four this day. They keep bothering me (I'm at office), and my ideas are confused. Let me know if I can be of any service as to books. God forbid

the Architectonican should be sacrificed to a foolish
scruple of some book proprietor, as if books did not
belong with the highest propriety to those that under-
stand 'em best.   C. LAMB.

To WILLIAM WORDSWORTH.

LETTER CXLVI.]   *August* 14, 1814.

Dear Wordsworth—I cannot tell you how pleased I
was at the receipt of the great armful of poetry which
you have sent me; and to get it before the rest of the
world too! I have gone quite through with it, and was
thinking to have accomplished that pleasure a second
time before I wrote to thank you, but M. Burney came
in the night (while we were out) and made holy theft of
it, but we expect restitution in a day or two. It is the
noblest conversational poem I ever read—a day in Heaven.
The part (or rather main body) which has left the sweetest
odour on my memory (a bad term for the remains of an
impression so recent) is the Tales of the Churchyard; the
only girl among seven brethren, born out of due time, and
not duly taken away again,—the deaf man and the blind
man;—the Jacobite and the Hanoverian, whom anti-
pathies reconcile; the Scarron-entry of the rusticating
parson upon his solitude;—these were all new to me
too. My having known the story of Margaret (at the
beginning), a very old acquaintance, even as long back
as when I saw you first at Stowey, did not make her
reappearance less fresh. I don't know what to pick out
of this best of books upon the best subjects for partial
naming. That gorgeous sunset is famous; I think it
must have been the identical one we saw on Salisbury
Plain five years ago, that drew Phillips from the card-
table, where he had sat from rise of that luminary to its
unequalled set; but neither he nor I had gifted eyes to
see those symbols of common things glorified, such as the
prophets saw them in that sunset—the wheel, the potter's

clay, the wash-pot, the wine-press, the almond-tree rod, the baskets of figs, the fourfold visaged head, the throne, and Him that sat thereon.

One feeling I was particularly struck with, as what I recognised so very lately at Harrow Church on entering in it after a hot and secular day's pleasure, the instantaneous coolness and calming, almost transforming properties of a country church just entered; a certain fragrance which it has, either from its holiness, or being kept shut all the week, or the air that is let in being pure country, exactly what you have reduced into words; but I am feeling that which I cannot express. Reading your lines about it fixed me for a time, a monument in Harrow Church. Do you know it? with its fine long spire, white as washed marble, to be seen, by vantage of its high site, as far as Salisbury spire itself almost.

I shall select a day or two, very shortly, when I am coolest in brain, to have a steady second reading, which I feel will lead to many more, for it will be a stock book with me while eyes or spectacles shall be lent me. There is a great deal of noble matter about mountain scenery, yet not so much as to overpower and discountenance a poor Londoner or south-countryman entirely, though Mary seems to have felt it occasionally a little too powerfully, for it was her remark during reading it, that by your system it was doubtful whether a liver in towns had a soul to be saved. She almost trembled for that invisible part of us in her.

Save for a late excursion to Harrow, and a day or two on the banks of the Thames this Summer, rural images were fast fading from my mind, and by the wise provision of the Regent, all that was country-fy'd in the Parks is all but obliterated. The very colour of green is vanished; the whole surface of Hyde Park is dry crumbling sand (*Arabia Arenosa*), not a vestige or hint of grass ever having grown there. Booths and drinking-places go all round it for a mile and half, I am confident —I might say two miles in circuit. The stench of liquors, *bad* tobacco, dirty people and provisions, conquers the air, and we are stifled and suffocated in Hyde Park.

Order after order has been issued by Lord Sidmouth in the name of the Regent (acting in behalf of his Royal father) for the dispersion of the varlets, but in vain. The *vis unita* of all the publicans in London, Westminster, Marylebone, and miles round, is too powerful a force to put down. The Regent has raised a phantom which he cannot lay. There they'll stay probably for ever. The whole beauty of the place is gone—that lake-look of the Serpentine—it has got foolish ships upon it; but something whispers to have confidence in Nature and its revival—

> At the coming of the *milder day*,
> These monuments shall all be overgrown.

Meantime I confess to have smoked one delicious pipe in one of the cleanliest and goodliest of the booths; a tent rather—

> " Oh call it not a booth !"

erected by the public spirit of Watson, who keeps the Adam and Eve at Pancras (the ale-houses have all emigrated, with their train of bottles, mugs, corkscrews, waiters, into Hyde Park—whole ale-houses, with all their ale !), in company with some of the Guards that had been in France, and a fine French girl, habited like a princess of banditti, which one of the dogs had transported from the Garonne to the Serpentine. The unusual scene in Hyde Park, by candle-light, in open air,—good tobacco, bottled stout,—made it look like an interval in a campaign, a repose after battle. I almost fancied scars smarting, and was ready to club a story with my comrades of some of my lying deeds. After all, the fireworks were splendid; the rockets in clusters, in trees and all shapes, spreading about like young stars in the making, floundering about in space (like unbroke horses), till some of Newton's calculations should fix them; but then they went out. Any one who could see 'em, and the still finer showers of gloomy rain-fire that fell sulkily and angrily from 'em, and could go to bed without dreaming of the last day, must be as hardened an atheist as . . .

The conclusion of this epistle getting gloomy, I have chosen this part to desire *our* kindest loves to Mrs. Wordsworth and to Dorothea.   Will none of you ever be in London again?

Again let me thank you for your present, and assure you that fireworks and triumphs have not distracted me from receiving a calm and noble enjoyment from it (which I trust I shall often), and I sincerely congratulate you on its appearance.

With kindest remembrances to you and your household, we remain, yours sincerely,

C. LAMB and Sister.

To SAMUEL TAYLOR COLERIDGE.

LETTER CXLVII.]   *August* 26, 1814.

Let the hungry soul rejoice, there is corn in Egypt. Whatever thou hast been told to the contrary by designing friends, who perhaps inquired carelessly, or did not inquire at all, in hope of saving their money, there is a stock of "Remorse" on hand—enough, as Pople conjectures, for seven years' consumption; judging from experience of the last two years.   Methinks it makes for the benefit of sound literature, that the best books do not always go off best.   Inquire in seven years' time for the *Rokebys* and the *Laras*, and where shall they be found?—fluttering fragmentally in some thread-paper; whereas thy *Wallenstein* and thy *Remorse* are safe on Longman's or Pople's shelves, as in some Bodleian; there they shall remain; no need of a chain to hold them fast —perhaps for ages—tall copies—and people shan't run about hunting for them as in old Ezra's shrievalty they did for a Bible, almost without effect till the great-great-grand-niece (by the mother's side) of Jeremiah or Ezekiel (which was it?) remembered something of a book, with odd reading in it, that used to lie in the green closet in her aunt Judith's bedchamber.

Thy caterer, Price, was at Hamburgh when last Pople heard of him, laying up for thee like some miserly old father for his generous-hearted son to squander.

Mr. Charles Aders, whose books also pant for that free circulation which thy custody is sure to give them, is to be heard of at his kinsmen, Messrs. Jameson and Aders, No. 7, Laurence Pountney Lane, London, according to the information which Crabius with his parting breath left me. Crabius is gone to Paris. I prophesy he and the Parisians will part with mutual contempt. His head has a twist Allemagne, like thine, dear mystic.

I have been reading Madame Stael on Germany : an impudent clever woman. But if *Faust* be no better than in her abstract of it, I counsel thee to let it alone. How canst thou translate the language of cat-monkeys? Fie on such fantasies! But I will not forget to look for *Proclus*. It is a kind of book which, when we meet with it, we shut up faster than we opened it. Yet I have some bastard kind of recollection that somewhere, some time ago, upon some stall or other, I saw it. It was either that or *Plotinus*, or Saint Augustine's *City of God*. So little do some folks value, what to others, *sc.* to you, "well used," had been the "Pledge of Immortality." Bishop Bruno I never touched upon. Stuffing too good for the brains of such a "Hare" as thou describest. May it burst his pericranium, as the gobbets of fat and turpentine (a nasty thought of the seer) did that old dragon in the Apocrypha! May he go mad in trying to understand his author! May he lend the third volume of him before he has quite translated the second, to a friend who shall lose it, and so spoil the publication, and may his friend find it and send it him just as thou or some such less dilatory spirit shall have announced the whole for the press. So I think I have answered all thy questions except about Morgan's cos-lettuce. The first personal peculiarity I ever observed of him (all worthy souls are subject to 'em) was a particular kind of rabbit-like delight in munching salads with oil without vinegar after dinner—a steady contemplative browsing on them —didst never take note of it? Canst think of any other queries in the solution of which I can give thee satisfaction? Do you want any books that I can procure for you? Old Jimmy Boyer is dead at last. Trollope has got his living, worth £1000 a year net. See, thou sluggard, thou heretic-sluggard, what mightest thou not have arrived at! Lay thy animosity against Jimmy in the grave. Do not *entail* it on thy posterity.

CHARLES LAMB.

To WILLIAM WORDSWORTH.

LETTER CXLVIII.]　　　　　　　　　　*August* 29, 1814.

My dear W.—I have scarce time or quiet to explain my present situation, how unquiet and distracted it is, owing to the absence of some of my compeers, and to the deficient state of payments at E. I. H., owing to bad peace speculations in the calico market. (I write this to W. W., Esq., Collector of Stamp Duties for the Conjoint Northern Counties, not to W. W., Poet.) I go back, and have for many days past, to evening work, generally at the rate of nine hours a day. The nature of my work, too, puzzling and hurrying, has so shaken my spirits, that my sleep is nothing but a succession of dreams of business I cannot do, of assistants that give me no assistance, of terrible responsibilities. I reclaimed your book, which Hazlitt has uncivilly kept, only two days ago, and have made shift to read it again with shattered brain. It does not lose—rather some parts have come out with a prominence I did not perceive before—but such was my aching head yesterday (Sunday), that the book was like a mountain landscape to one that should walk on the edge of a precipice ; I perceive beauty dizzily. Now, what I would say is, that I see no prospect of a quiet half-day, or hour even, till this week and the next are past. I then hope to get four weeks' absence, and if *then* is time enough to begin, I will most gladly do what is required, though I feel my inability, for my brain is always desultory, and snatches off hints from things, but can seldom follow 2 "work" methodically. But that shall be no excuse. What I beg you to do is, to let me know from Southey, if that will be time enough for the *Quarterly, i.e.* suppose it done in three weeks from this date (19th Sept.): if not, it is my bounden duty to express my regret, and decline it. Mary thanks you, and feels highly grateful for your "Patent of Nobility," and acknowledges the author of the *Excursion* as the legitimate Fountain of Honour. We both agree that, to our feeling, Ellen is best as she is. To us there would have been something repugnant in her challenging her Penance as a Dowry : the fact is explicable ; but how few are those to whom it would have been rendered explicit ! The unlucky reason of the detention of the *Excursion* was Hazlitt and we having a misunderstanding. He blowed us up about six months ago, since which the union hath snapt ; but M. Burney borrowed it for him, and after reiterated messages I only got it on Friday. His remarks had some vigour in them ; particularly something about an old ruin being *too modern for your Primeval Nature* and about *a lichen.* I forget the passage, but the whole wore a slovenly air of despatch. That objection which M. Burney had imbibed from him about Voltaire I explained to M. B. (or tried) exactly on your principle of its being a characteristic speech. That it was no settled comparative estimate of Voltaire with any of his own tribe of buffoons—no injustice, even if *you* spoke it, for I dared say you never could relish *Candide.* I know I tried to get through it about a twelvemonth since, and couldn't for the dulness. Now I think I have a wider range in buffoonery than you. Too much toleration perhaps.

I finish this after a raw ill-baked dinner fast gobbled up to set me off to office again, after working there till near four. Oh how I wish I were a rich man! even though I were squeezed camel-fashion at getting through that needle's eye that is spoken of in the *Written Word*. Apropos; are you a Christian? or is it the Pedler and the Priest that are?

I find I miscalled that celestial splendour of the mist going off, a *sunset*. That only shows my inaccuracy of head.

Do, pray, indulge me by writing an answer to the point of time mentioned above, or *let Southey*. I am ashamed to go bargaining in this way, but indeed I have no time I can reckon on till the first week in October. God send I may not be disappointed in that! Coleridge swore in a letter to me he would review the *Excursion* in the *Quarterly*. Therefore, though *that* shall not stop me, yet if I can do anything *when* done, I must know of him if he has anything ready, or I shall fill the world with loud exclaims.

I keep writing on, knowing the postage is no more for much writing, else so fagged and dispirited I am with cursed India House work, I scarce know what I do. My left arm reposes on the *Excursion*. I feel what it would be in quiet. It is now a sealed book.   C. LAMB.

LETTER CXLIX.]   1814.

Dear W.—Your experience about tailors seems to be in point blank opposition to Burton, as much as the author of the *Excursion* does, *toto cœlo*, differ in his notion of a country life from the picture which W. H. has exhibited of the same. But, with a little explanation, you and B. may be reconciled. It is evident that he confined his observations to the genuine native London tailor. What freaks tailor-nature may take in the country is not for him to give account of. And certainly some of the freaks recorded do give an idea of the persons in question being beside themselves, rather than in harmony with the common, moderate, self-enjoyment of the rest of mankind. A flying tailor, I venture to say, is no more *in rerum naturâ* than a flying horse or a gryphon. His wheeling his airy flight from the precipice you mention had a parallel in the melancholy Jew who toppled from the monument. Were his limbs ever found? Then, the man who cures diseases by words is evidently an inspired tailor. Burton never affirmed that the art of sewing disqualified the practiser of it from being a fit organ for supernatural revelation. He never enters into such subjects. 'Tis the common, uninspired tailor which he speaks of. Again, the person who makes his smiles to be *heard* is evidently a man under possession—a demoniac tailor. A greater hell than his own must have a hand in this. I am not certain that the cause which you advocate has much reason for triumph. You seem to me to substitute light-headedness for light-heartedness by a trick, or not to know the difference. I confess, a grinning tailor would shock me. Enough of tailors!

The "'scapes" of the great god Pan, who appeared among your mountains some dozen years since, and his narrow chance of being submerged by the swains, afforded me much pleasure. I can conceive the water-nymphs pulling for him. He would have been another Hylas—W. Hylas. In a mad letter which Capel Lofft wrote to *M*[*onthly*] *M*[*agazine*] Philips (now Sir Richard), I remember his noticing a metaphysical article of Pan, signed H., and adding, "I take your correspondent to be the same with Hylas." Hylas had put forth a pastoral just before. How near the unfounded conjecture of the certainly inspired Lofft (unfounded as we thought it) was to being realised! I can conceive him being "good to all that wander in that perilous flood." One J. Scott (I know no more) is editor of the *Champion*. Where is Coleridge?

That Review you speak of, I am only sorry it did not

appear last month. The circumstances of haste and peculiar bad spirits under which it was written would have excused its slightness and inadequacy, the full load of which I shall suffer from its lying by so long, as it will seem to have done, from its postponement. I write with great difficulty, and can scarce command my own resolution to sit at writing an hour together. I am a poor creature, but I am leaving off gin. I hope you will see good-will in the thing. I had a difficulty to perform not to make it all panegyric; I have attempted to personate a mere stranger to you; perhaps with too much strangeness. But you must bear that in mind when you read it, and not think that I am, in mind, distant from you or your poem, but that both are close to me, among the nearest of persons and things. I do but act the stranger in the Review. Then, I was puzzled about extracts, and determined upon not giving one that had been in the *Examiner ;* for extracts repeated give an idea that there is a meagre allowance of good things. By this way, I deprived myself of *Sir Alfred Irthing,* and the reflections that conclude his story, which are the flower of the poem. Hazlitt had given the reflections before me. *Then* it is the first review I ever did, and I did not know how long I might make it. But it must speak for itself, if Gifford and his crew do not put words in its mouth, which I expect. Farewell. Love to all. Mary keeps very bad.   C. LAMB.

Letter CL.]   1814.

Dear Wordsworth—I told you my Review was a very imperfect one. But what you will see in the *Quarterly* is a spurious one, which Mr. Baviad Gifford has palmed upon it for mine. I never felt more vexed in my life than when I read it. I cannot give you an idea of what he has done to it, out of spite at me, because he once suffered me to be called a lunatic in his Review. The *language* he has altered throughout. Whatever inadequateness it had to its subject, it was, in point of composition, the prettiest piece of prose I ever writ: and so my sister (to whom alone I read the MS.) said. That charm, if it had any, is all gone: more than a third of the substance is cut away, and that not all from one place, but *passim*, so as to make utter nonsense. Every warm expression is changed for a nasty cold one.

I have not the cursed alteration by me; I shall never look at it again; but for a specimen, I remember I had said the poet of the *Excursion* "walks through common forests as through some Dodona or enchanted wood, and every casual bird that flits upon the boughs, like that miraculous one in Tasso, but in language more piercing than any articulate sounds, reveals to him far higher love-lays."   It is now (besides half-a-dozen alterations in the same half-dozen lines) "but in language more *intelligent* reveals to him;"—that is one I remember.

But that would have been little, putting his damn'd shoemaker phraseology (for he was a shoemaker) instead of mine, which has been tinctured with better authors than his ignorance can comprehend;—for I reckon myself a dab at *prose;*—verse I leave to my betters: God help them, if they are to be so reviewed by friend and foe as you have been this quarter!   I have read "It won't do." But worse than altering words; he has kept a few members only of the part I had done best, which was to explain all I could of your "Scheme of Harmonies," as I had ventured to call it, between the external universe and what within us answers to it. To do this I had accumulated a good many short passages, rising in length to the end, weaving in the extracts as if they came in as a part of the text naturally, not intruding them as specimens. Of this part a little is left, but so as, without conjuration, no man could tell what I was driving at. A proof of it you may see (though not judge of the whole of the injustice) by these words. I had spoken something about "natural methodism;" and after follows, "and *therefore* the tale of Margaret should have been postponed" (I forget my words, or his words); now the reasons for postponing it are as deducible from what goes before as they are from the 104th Psalm. The passage whence I deduced it has vanished, but clapping a colon before a *therefore* is always reason enough for Mr. Baviad Gifford to allow to a reviewer that is not himself. I assure you my complaints are well founded. I know how sore a word altered makes one; but, indeed, of this review the whole complexion is gone. I regret only that I did not keep a copy. I am sure you would have been pleased with it, because I have been feeding my fancy for some months with the notion of pleasing you. Its imperfection or inadequateness in size and method I knew; but for the *writing part* of it I was fully satisfied; I hoped it would make more than atonement. Ten or twelve distinct passages come to my mind, which are gone; and what is left is, of course, the worse for their having been there; the eyes are pulled out, and the bleeding sockets are left.

I read it at Arch's shop with my face burning with vexation secretly, with just such a feeling as if it had been a review written against myself, making false quotations from me. But I am ashamed to say so much about a short piece. How are *you* served! and the labours of years turned into contempt by scoundrels!

But I could not but protest against your taking that thing as mine. Every *pretty* expression (I know there were many), every warm expression (there was nothing else), is vulgarised and frozen. But if they catch me in their camps again, let them spitchcock me! They had a right to do it, as no name appears to it; and Mr. Shoemaker Gifford, I suppose, never waived a right he had since he commenced author. God confound him and all caitiffs!　　　　　　　　　　　　　　　　　　C. L.

Dear Wordsworth—You have made me very proud with your successive book presents. I have been carefully through the two volumes, to see that nothing was omitted which used to be there. I think I miss nothing but a character in the antithetic manner, which I do not know why you left out,—the moral to the boys building the giant, the omission whereof leaves it, in my mind, less complete,—and one admirable line gone (or something come instead of it), "the stone-chat, and the glancing sand-piper," which was a line quite alive. I demand these at your hand. I am glad that you have not sacrificed a verse to those scoundrels. I would not have had you offer up the poorest rag that lingered upon the stript shoulders of little Alice Fell, to have atoned all their malice; I would not have given 'em a red cloak to save their souls. I am afraid lest that substitution of a shell (a flat falsification of the history) for the household implement, as it stood at first, was a kind of tub thrown out to the beast, or rather thrown out for him. The tub was a good honest tub in its place, and nothing could fairly be said against it. You say you made the alteration for the "friendly reader," but the "malicious" will take it to himself. Damn 'em, if you give 'em an inch, etc. The Preface is noble, and such as you should write. I wish I could set my name to it, *Imprimatur*, —but you have set it there yourself, and I thank you. I would rather be a doorkeeper in your margin, than have their proudest text swelling with my eulogies. The poems in the volumes which are new to me are so much in the old tone that I hardly received them as novelties. Of those of which I had no previous knowledge, the "Four Yew Trees," and the mysterious company which you have assembled there, most struck me— "Death the Skeleton and Time the Shadow." It is a sight not for every youthful poet to dream of; it is one of the last results he must have gone thinking on for years for. "Laodamia" is a very original poem; I mean original with reference to your own manner. You have nothing like it. I should have seen it in a strange 'place, and greatly admired it, but not suspected its derivation.

Let me in this place, for I have writ you several letters naming it, mention that my brother, who is a picture-collector, has picked up an undoubtable picture of Milton. He gave a few shillings for it, and could get no history with it, but that some old lady had had it for a great many years. Its age is ascertainable from the state of the canvas, and you need only see it to be sure that it is the original of the heads in the Tonson editions, with which we are all so well familiar. Since I saw you I have had a treat in the reading way, which comes not every day, the Latin Poems of V. Bourne, which were quite new to me. What a heart that man had! all laid out upon town schemes, a proper counterpoise to *some people's* rural extravaganzas. Why I mention him is, that your "Power of Music" reminded me of his poem of "The Ballad Singer in the Seven Dials." Do you remember his epigram on the old woman who taught Newton the A B C? which, after all, he says, he hesitates not to call Newton's "Principia." I was lately fatiguing myself with going through a volume of fine words by Lord Thurlow; excellent words; and if the heart could live by words alone, it could desire no better regales; but what an aching vacuum of matter! I don't stick at the madness of it, for that is only a consequence of shutting his eyes and thinking he is in the age of the old Elizabeth poets. From thence I turned to Bourne. What a sweet, unpretending, pretty-mannered, *matter-ful* creature! sucking from every flower, making a flower of everything, his diction all Latin, and his thoughts all English. Bless him! Latin wasn't good enough for him. Why wasn't he content with the language which Gay and Prior wrote in?

I am almost sorry that you printed extracts from

those first poems, or that you did not print them at
length. They do not read to me as they do altogether.
Besides, they have diminished the value of the original,
which I possess as a curiosity. I have hitherto kept
them distinct in my mind as referring to a particular
period of your life. All the rest of your poems are so
much of a piece, they might have been written in the
same week; these decidedly speak of an earlier period.
They tell more of what you had been reading. We were
glad to see the poems "by a female friend." The one of
the Wind is masterly, but not new to us. Being only
three, perhaps you might have clapt a D. at the corner,
and let it have past as a printer's mark to the uninitiated,
as a delightful hint to the better instructed. As it is,
expect a formal criticism on the poems of your female
friend, and she must expect it. I should have written
before, but I am cruelly engaged, and like to be. On
Friday I was at office from ten in the morning (two hours
dinner except) to eleven at night; last night till nine.
My business and office business in general have increased
so; I don't mean I am there every night, but I must
expect a great deal of it. I never leave till four, and do
not keep a holiday now once in ten times, where I used
to keep all red-letter days, and some five days besides,
which I used to dub Nature's holidays. I have had my
day. I had formerly little to do. So of the little that
is left of life, I may reckon two-thirds as dead, for time
that a man may call his own is his life; and hard work
and thinking about it taints even the leisure hours,—stains
Sunday with work-day contemplations. This is Sunday:
and the headache I have is part late hours at work the
two preceding nights, and part later hours over a con-
soling pipe afterwards. But I find stupid acquiescence
coming over me. I bend to the yoke, and it is almost
with me and my household as with the man and his
consort—

> " To them each evening had its glittering star,
> And every Sabbath Day its golden sun "—

to such straits am I driven for the life of life, Time!
O that from that superfluity of holiday leisure my youth
wasted, "Age might but take some hours youth wanted
not!" *N.B.*—I have left off spirituous liquors for four
or more months, with a moral certainty of its lasting.
Farewell, dear Wordsworth!

O happy Paris, seat of idleness and pleasure! from
some returned English I hear that not such a thing as a
counting-house is to be seen in her streets,—scarce a
desk. Earthquakes swallow up this mercantile city and
its "gripple merchants," as Drayton hath it—"born to
be the curse of this brave isle!" I invoke this, not on
account of any parsimonious habits the mercantile interest
may have, but, to confess truth, because I am not fit for
an office.

Farewell, in haste, from a head that is too ill to
methodise, a stomach too weak to digest, and all out of
tune. Better harmonies await you! C. LAMB.

LETTER CLII.]

Excuse this maddish letter: I am too tired to write
in formâ.

1815.

Dear Wordsworth—The more I read of your last two
volumes, the more I feel it necessary to make my acknow-
ledgments for them in more than one short letter. The
"Night Piece," to which you refer me, I meant fully to
have noticed; but, the fact is, I come so fluttering and
languid from business, tired with thoughts of it, fright-
ened with the fears of it, that when I get a few minutes
to sit down to scribble (an action of the hand now seldom
natural to me—I mean voluntary pen-work) I lose all
presential memory of what I had intended to say, and
say what I can, talk about Vincent Bourne, or any casual
image, instead of that which I had meditated (by the
way, I must look out V. B. for you). So I meant to
mention "Yarrow Visited," with that stanza, "But thou

that didst appear so fair;" than which I think no lovelier stanza can be found in the wide world of poetry; —yet the poem, on the whole, seems condemned to leave behind it a melancholy of imperfect satisfaction, as if you had wronged the feeling with which, in what preceded it, you had resolved never to visit it, and as if the Muse had determined, in the most delicate manner, to make you, and *scarce make you,* feel it. Else, it is far superior to the other, which has but one exquisite verse in it, the last but one, or the last two: this is all fine, except perhaps that *that* of "studious ease and generous cares" has a little tinge of the *less romantic* about it. "The Farmer of Tilsbury Vale" is a charming counterpart to "Poor Susan," with the addition of that delicacy towards aberrations from the strict path, which is so fine in the "Old Thief and the Boy by his side," which always brings water into my eyes. Perhaps it is the worse for being a repetition; "Susan" stood for the representative of poor *Rus in Urbe.* There was quite enough to stamp the moral of the thing never to be forgotten; "bright volumes of vapour," etc. The last verse of Susan was to be got rid of, at all events. It threw a kind of dubiety upon Susan's moral conduct. Susan is a servant maid. I see her trundling her mop, and contemplating the whirling phenomenon through blurred optics; but to term her "a poor outcast" seems as much as to say that poor Susan was no better than she should be, which I trust was not what you meant to express. Robin Goodfellow supports himself without that *stick* of a moral which you have thrown away; but how I can be brought in *felo de omittendo* for that ending to the Boy-builders is a mystery. I can't say positively now,—I only know that no line oftener or readier occurs than that "Light-hearted boys, I will build up a Giant with you." It comes naturally, with a warm holiday, and the freshness of the blood. It is a perfect summer amulet, that I tie round my legs to quicken their motion when I go out a maying. (*N.B.*) I don't often go out a *maying;—must*

is the tense with me now.   Do you take the pun ?   Young
Romilly is divine ; the reasons of his mother's grief being
remediless.   I never saw parental love carried up so
high, towering above the other loves.   Shakspeare had
done something for the filial, in Cordelia, and, by implica-
tion, for the fatherly too, in Lear's resentment ; he left
it for you to explore the depths of the maternal heart.
I get stupid, and flat, and flattering.   What's the use of
telling you what good things you have written, or—I
hope I may add—that I know them to be good ?
Apropos—when I first opened upon the just mentioned
poem, in a careless tone, I said to Mary, as if putting a
riddle, " *What is good for a bootless bene ?*"   To which,
with infinite presence of mind (as the jest-book has it),
she answered, " a shoeless pea."   It was the first joke
she ever made.   Joke the second I make.   You distin-
guish well, in your old preface, between the verses of
Dr. Johnson, of the " Man in the Strand," and those
from " The Babes in the Wood."   I was thinking, whether
taking your own glorious lines—

> " And from the love which was in her soul
>   For her youthful Romilly,"

which, by the love I bear my own soul, I think have no
parallel in any of the best old ballads, and just altering
them to—

> " And from the great respect she felt
>   For Sir Samuel Romilly,"

would not have explained the boundaries of prose expres-
sion, and poetic feeling, nearly as well.   Excuse my
levity on such an occasion.   I never felt deeply in my
life if that poem did not make me feel, both lately and
when I read it in MS.   No alderman ever longed after a
haunch of buck venison more than I for a spiritual taste
of that " White Doe" you promise.   I am sure it is
superlative, or will be when *drest, i.e.* printed.   All things
read raw to me in MS. ; to compare *magna parvis*, I
cannot endure my own writings in that state.   The only

one which I think would not very much win upon me in print is "Peter Bell." But I am not certain. You ask me about your preface. I like both that and the supplement, without an exception. The account of what you mean by imagination is very valuable to me. It will help me to like some things in poetry better, which is a little humiliating in me to confess. I thought I could not be instructed in that science (I mean the critical), as I once heard old obscene, beastly Peter Pindar, in a dispute on Milton, say he thought that if he had reason to value himself upon one thing more than another, it was in knowing what good verse was. Who looked over your proof sheets and left *ordebo* in that line of Virgil?

My brother's picture of Milton is very finely painted; that is, it might have been done by a hand next to Vandyke's. It is the genuine Milton, and an object of quiet gaze for the half-hour at a time. Yet though I am confident there is no better one of him, the face does not quite answer to Milton. There is a tinge of *petit* (or *petite*, how do you spell it?) querulousness about it; yet, hang it! now I remember better, there is not; it is calm, melancholy, and poetical. *One* of the copies of the poems you sent has precisely the same pleasant blending of a sheet of second volume with a sheet of first. I think it was page 245; but I sent it and had it rectified. It gave me in the first impetus of cutting the leaves, just such a cold squelch as going down a plausible turning and suddenly reading "No thoroughfare!" Robinson's is entire: I wish you would write more criticism about Spenser, etc. I think I could say something about him myself; but, Lord bless me! these "merchants and their spicy drugs," which are so harmonious to sing of, they limetwig up my poor soul and body, till I shall forget I ever thought myself a bit of a genius! I can't even put a few thoughts on paper for a newspaper. I "engross" when I should "pen" a paragraph. Confusion blast all mercantile transactions, all traffic, exchange of commodities, intercourse between nations, all the consequent civilisa-

tion, and wealth, and amity, and link of society, and
getting rid of prejudices, and getting a knowledge of the
face of the globe; and rotting the very firs of the forest,
that look so romantic alive, and die into desks! *Vale.*

Yours, dear W., and all yours,   C. LAMB.

To ROBERT SOUTHEY.

LETTER CLIII.]   *London, May* 6, 1815.

Dear Southey—I have received from Longman a copy
of *Roderick*, with the Author's Compliments, for which
I much thank you. I don't know where I shall put all
the noble presents I have lately received in that way:
the *Excursion*, Wordsworth's two last vols., and now
Roderick, have come pouring in upon me like some
irruption from Helicon. The story of the brave Maccabee
was already, you may be sure, familiar to me in all its
parts. I have, since the receipt of your present, read it
quite through again, and with no diminished pleasure.
I don't know whether I ought to say that it has given
me more pleasure than any of your long poems. *Kehama*
is doubtless more powerful, but I don't feel that firm
footing in it that I do in *Roderick:* my imagination goes
sinking and floundering in the vast spaces of unopened-
before systems and faiths; I am put out of the pale of
my old sympathies; my moral sense is almost outraged;
I can't believe, or with horror am made to believe, such
desperate chances against Omnipotence, such disturbances
of faith to the centre; the more potent the more painful
the spell. Jove, and his brotherhood of gods, tottering
with the giant assailings, I can bear, for the soul's hopes
are not struck at in such contests; but your Oriental
almighties are too much types of the intangible prototype
to be meddled with without shuddering. One never
connects what are called the attributes with Jupiter.—
I mention only what diminishes my delight at the wonder-
workings of *Kehama*, not what impeaches its power,

which I confess with trembling; but *Roderick* is a comfortable poem.   It reminds me of the delight I took in the first reading of the *Joan of Arc*.   It is maturer and better than *that*, though not better to me now than that was then.   It suits me better than *Madoc*.   I am at home in Spain and Christendom.   I have a timid imagination, I am afraid.   I do not willingly admit of strange beliefs, or out-of-the-way creeds or places.   I never read books of travels, at least not farther than Paris or Rome. I can just endure Moors, because of their connection as foes with Christians; but Abyssinians, Ethiops, Esquimaux, Dervises, and all that tribe, I hate.   I believe I fear them in some manner.   A Mahometan turban on the stage, though enveloping some well-known face (Mr. Cook or Mr. Maddox, whom I see another day good Christian and English waiters, innkeepers, etc.), does not give me pleasure unalloyed.   I am a Christian, Englishman, Londoner, *Templar*.   God help me when I come to put off these snug relations, and to get abroad into the world to come!   I shall be like *the crow on the sand*, as Wordsworth has it; but I won't think on it: no need, I hope, yet.

The parts I have been most pleased with, both on first and second readings, perhaps, are Florinda's palliation of Roderick's crime, confessed to him in his disguise—the retreat of the Palayos family first discovered—his being made king—" For acclamation one form must serve *more solemn for the breach* of *old observances*."   Roderick's vow is extremely fine, and his blessing on the vow of Alphonso :

> " Towards the troop he spread his arms,
> As if the expanded soul diffused itself,
> And carried to all spirits *with the act*
> Its affluent inspiration."

It struck me forcibly that the feeling of these last lines might have been suggested to you by the Cartoon of Paul at Athens.   Certain it is that a better motto or guide to that famous attitude can nowhere be found.   I shall adopt it as explanatory of that violent but dignified motion.

I must read again Landor's *Julian.* I have not read it some time. I think he must have failed in Roderick, for I remember nothing of him, nor of any distinct character as a character—only fine-sounding passages. I remember thinking also he had chosen a point of time after the event, as it were, for Roderick survives to no use ; but my memory is weak, and I will not wrong a fine poem by trusting to it.

The notes to your poem I have not read again : but it will be a take-downable book on my shelf, and they will serve sometimes at breakfast, or times too light for the text to be duly appreciated. Though some of 'em— one of the serpent penance—is serious enough, now I think on't. Of Coleridge I hear nothing, nor of the Morgans. I hope to have him like a re-appearing star, standing up before me some time when least expected in London, as has been the case whilere.

I am *doing* nothing (as the phrase is) but reading presents, and walk away what of the day hours I can get from hard occupation. Pray accept once more my hearty thanks, and expression of pleasure for your remembrance of me. My sister desires her kind respects to Mrs. S. and to all at Keswick.

Yours truly,　　　　　　　　　　　　　C. LAMB.

The next present I look for is the *White Doe.*

Have you seen Mat. Betham's *Lay of Marie?* I think it very delicately pretty as to sentiment, etc.

R. Southey, Esq.,
　Keswick, near Penrith,
　　Cumberland.

　　　　　　　　　August 9, 1815.

Dear Southey—Robinson is not on the circuit, as I erroneously stated in a letter to W. W., which travels

with this, but is gone to Brussels, Ostend, Ghent, etc.
But his friends, the Colliers, whom I consulted respecting
your friend's fate, remember to have heard him say that
Father Pardo had effected his escape (the cunning greasy
rogue!), and to the best of their belief is at present in
Paris. To my thinking, it is a small matter whether
there be one fat friar more or less in the world. I have
rather a taste for clerical executions, imbibed from early
recollections of the fate of the excellent Dodd. I hear
Buonaparte has sued his habeas corpus, and the twelve
judges are now sitting upon it at the Rolls.

Your boute-feu (bonfire) must be excellent of its kind.
Poet Settle presided at the last great thing of the kind
in London, when the pope was burnt in form. Do you
provide any verses on this occasion? Your fear for
Hartley's intellectuals is just and rational. Could not
the Chancellor be petitioned to remove him? His lord-
ship took Mr. Betty from under the paternal wing. I
think at least he should go through a course of matter-
of-fact with some sober man after the mysteries. Could
not he spend a week at Poole's before he goes back to
Oxford? Tobin is dead. But there is a man in my
office, a Mr. Hedges, who proses it away from morning
to night, and never gets beyond corporal and material
verities. He'd get these crack-brain metaphysics out of
the young gentleman's head as soon as any one I know.
When I can't sleep o' nights, I imagine a dialogue with
Mr. Hedges, upon any given subject, and go prosing on
in fancy with him, till I either laugh or fall asleep. I
have literally found it answer. I am going to stand
godfather; I don't like the business; I cannot muster
up decorum for these occasions; I shall certainly disgrace
the font. I was at Hazlitt's marriage, and had like to
have been turned out several times during the ceremony.
Anything awful makes me laugh. I misbehaved once at
a funeral. Yet I can read about these ceremonies with
pious and proper feelings. The realities of life only seem
the mockeries. I fear I must get cured along with

Hartley, if not too inveterate. Don't you think Louis the Desirable is in a sort of quandary?

After all, Buonaparte is a fine fellow, as my barber says, and I should not mind standing bareheaded at his table to do him service in his fall. They should have given him Hampton Court or Kensington, with a tether extending forty miles round London. Qu. Would not the people have ejected the Brunswicks some day in his favour? Well, we shall see.   C. LAMB.

To WILLIAM WORDSWORTH.

LETTER CLV.]   *August* 9, 1815.

Dear Wordsworth—We acknowledge with pride the receipt of both your handwritings, and desire to be ever had in kindly remembrance by you both and by Dorothy. Alsager, whom you call Alsinger (and indeed he is rather *singer* than *sager*, no reflection upon his naturals neither), is well, and in harmony with himself and the world. I don't know how he, and those of his constitution, keep their nerves so nicely balanced as they do. Or, have they any? Or, are they made of packthread? He is proof against weather, ingratitude, meat underdone, every weapon of fate. I have just now a jagged end of a tooth pricking against my tongue, which meets it half way, in a wantonness of provocation; and there they go at it, the tongue pricking itself, like the viper against the file, and the tooth galling all the gum inside and out to torture; tongue and tooth, tooth and tongue, hard at it; and I to pay the reckoning, till all my mouth is as hot as brimstone; and I'd venture the roof of my mouth, that at this moment, at which I conjecture my full-happiness'd friend is picking his crackers, not one of the double rows of ivory in his privileged mouth has as much as a flaw in it, but all perform their functions, and, having performed them, expect to be picked (luxurious steeds !), and rubbed down. I don't think he could be robbed, or have the house set on fire, or ever want money. I have heard him express a similar opinion of his own impassibility. I keep acting here Heautontimorumenos.

Mr. Burney has been to Calais, and has come a travelled Monsieur. He speaks nothing but the Gallic Idiom. Field is on circuit. So now I believe I have given account of most that you saw at our Cabin.

Have you seen a curious letter in the *Morning Chronicle*, by C. L. [Capell Lofft,] the genius of absurdity, respecting Buonaparte's suing out his Habeas Corpus? That man is his own moon. He has no need of ascending into that gentle planet for mild influences.

Mary and I felt quite queer after your taking leave (you W. W.) of us in St. Giles's. We wish we had seen more of you, but felt we had scarce been sufficiently acknowledging for the share we had enjoyed of your company. We felt as if we had been not enough *expressive* of our pleasure. But our manners *both* are a little too much on this side of too-much-cordiality. We want presence of mind and presence of heart. What we feel comes too late, like an afterthought impromptu. But perhaps you observed nothing of that which we have been painfully conscious of, and are every day in our inter-course with those we stand affected to through all the degrees of love. Robinson is on the circuit. Our panegyrist I thought had forgotten one of the objects of his youthful admiration, but I was agreeably removed from that scruple by the laundress knocking at my door this morning, almost before I was up, with a present of fruit from my young friend, etc. There is something inex-pressibly pleasant to me in these *presents*, be it fruit, or fowl, or brawn, or *what not*. Books are a legitimate cause of acceptance. If presents be not the soul of friendship, undoubtedly they are the most spiritual part of the body of that intercourse. There is too much narrowness of thinking in this point. The punctilio of acceptance, methinks, is too confined and strait-laced. I could be content to receive money, or clothes, or a joint of meat from a friend. Why should he not send me a dinner as well as a dessert? I would taste him in the beasts of the field, and through all creation. Therefore did the basket of fruit of the juvenile Talfourd not displease me; not that I have any thoughts of bartering or reciprocating these things. To send him anything in return, would be to reflect suspicion of mercenariness upon what I know he meant a freewill offering. Let him overcome me in bounty. In this strife a generous nature loves to be overcome. You wish me some of your leisure. I have a glimmering aspect, a chink-light of liberty before me, which I pray God may prove not fallacious. My remonstrances have stirred up others to remonstrate, and altogether, there is a plan for separating certain parts of business from our department; which, if it take place, will produce me more time, *i.e.* my evenings free. It may be a means of placing me in a more conspicuous situation, which will knock at my nerves another way, but I wait the issue in submission. If I can but begin my own day at four o'clock in the afternoon, I shall think myself to have Eden days of peace and liberty to what I have had. As you say, how a man can fill three volumes up with an essay on the drama is wonderful; I am sure a very few sheets would hold all I had to say on the subject.

Did you ever read "Charron on Wisdom"? or "Patrick's Pilgrim"? If neither, you have two great pleasures to come. I mean some day to attack Caryl on Job, six folios. What any man can write, surely I may read. If I do but get rid of auditing warehousekeepers' accounts and get no worse-harassing task in the place of it, what a lord of liberty I shall be! I shall dance and skip, and make mouths at the invisible event, and pick the thorns out of my pillow, and throw 'em at rich men's night-caps, and talk blank verse, hoity-toity, and sing— "A clerk I was in London gay," "Ban, ban, Ca-Caliban," like the emancipated monster, and go where I like, up this street or down that alley.   Adieu, and pray that it may be my luck.

Good-bye to you all.   C. LAMB.

To Miss HUTCHINSON.

LETTER CLVI.]   *Thursday, October* 19, 1815.

Dear Miss H.—I am forced to be the replier to your letter, for Mary has been ill, and gone from home these five weeks yesterday.   She has left me very lonely and very miserable.   I stroll about, but there is no rest but at one's own fireside, and there is no rest for me there now. I look forward to the worse half being past, and keep up as well as I can.   She has begun to show some favourable symptoms.   The return of her disorder has been frightfully soon this time, with scarce a six months' interval.   I am almost afraid my worry of spirits about the E. I. House was partly the cause of her illness, but one always imputes it to the cause next at hand; more probably it comes from some cause we have no control over or conjecture of.   It cuts sad great slices out of the time, the little time, we shall have to live together.   I don't know but the recurrence of these illnesses might help me to sustain her death better than if we had had no partial separations.   But I won't talk of death.   I will imagine us immortal, or forget that we are otherwise.   By God's blessing, in a few weeks we may be making our meal together, or sitting in the front row of the Pit at Drury Lane, or taking our evening walk past the theatres, to look at the outside of them, at least, if not to be tempted in.   Then we forget we are assailable; we are strong for the time as rocks;—"the wind is tempered to the shorn Lambs."   Poor C. Lloyd, and poor Priscilla!   I feel I hardly feel enough for him; my own calamities press about me, and involve me in a thick integument not to be reached at by other folks' misfortunes. But I feel all I can—all the kindness I can, towards you all—God bless you! I hear nothing from Coleridge.

Yours truly,   C. LAMB.

To THOMAS MANNING.

LETTER CLVII.]   *December* 25, 1815.

Dear old Friend and absentee—This is Christmas Day 1815 with us; what it may be with you I don't know, the 12th of June next year perhaps; and if it should be the consecrated season with you, I don't see how you can keep it. You have no turkeys; you would not desecrate the festival by offering up a withered Chinese bantam, instead of the savoury grand Norfolcian holocaust, that smokes all around my nostrils at this moment from a thousand firesides. Then what puddings have you? Where will you get holly to stick in your churches, or churches to stick your dried tea-leaves (that must be the substitute) in? What memorials you can have of the holy time, I see not. A chopped missionary or two may keep up the thin idea of Lent and the wilderness; but what standing evidence have you of the Nativity? 'Tis our rosy-cheeked, homestalled divines, whose faces shine to the tune of " Unto us a child was born," faces fragrant with the mince-pies of half a century, that alone can authenticate the cheerful mystery. I feel my bowels refreshed with the holy tide; my zeal is great against the unedified heathen. Down with the Pagodas—down with the idols—Ching-chong-fo—and his foolish priest-hood! Come out of Babylon, O my friend! for her time is come; and the child that is native, and the Proselyte of her gates, shall kindle and smoke together! And in sober sense what makes you so long from among us, Manning? You must not expect to see the same England again which you left.

Empires have been overturned, crowns trodden into

dust, the face of the western world quite changed. Your
friends have all got old—those you left blooming; myself
(who am one of the few that remember you), those golden
hairs which you recollect my taking a pride in, turned to
silvery and gray. Mary has been dead and buried many
years : she desired to be buried in the silk gown you sent
her. Rickman, that you remember active and strong,
now walks out supported by a servant maid and a stick.
Martin Burney is a very old man. The other day an
aged woman knocked at my door, and pretended to my
acquaintance. It was long before I had the most distant
cognition of her; but at last, together, we made her out
to be Louisa, the daughter of Mrs. Topham, formerly
Mrs. Morton, who had been Mrs. Reynolds, formerly Mrs.
Kenney, whose first husband was Holcroft, the dramatic
writer of the last century. St. Paul's Church is a heap
of ruins; the Monument isn't half so high as you knew
it, divers parts being successively taken down which the
ravages of time had rendered dangerous; the horse at
Charing Cross is gone, no one knows whither; and all
this has taken place while you have been settling whether
Ho-hing-tong should be spelt with a ——, or a ——.
For aught I see you might almost as well remain where
you are, and not come like a Struldbrug into a world
were few were born when you went away. Scarce here
and there one will be able to make out your face. All
your opinions will be out of date, your jokes obsolete,
your puns rejected with fastidiousness as wit of the last
age. Your way of mathematics has already given way
to a new method, which after all is I believe the old
doctrine of Maclaurin, new-vamped up with what he
borrowed of the negative quantity of fluxions from Euler.

Poor Godwin! I was passing his tomb the other day
in Cripplegate churchyard. There are some verses upon
it written by Miss ——, which if I thought good enough
I would send you. He was one of those who would
have hailed your return, not with boisterous shouts and
clamours, but with the complacent gratulations of a

philosopher anxious to promote knowledge as leading to happiness; but his systems and his theories are ten feet deep in Cripplegate mould. Coleridge is just dead, having lived just long enough to close the eyes of Wordsworth, who paid the debt to Nature but a week or two before. Poor Col., but two days before he died he wrote to a bookseller, proposing an epic poem on the "Wanderings of Cain," in twenty-four books. It is said he has left behind him more than forty thousand treatises in criticism, metaphysics, and divinity, but few of them in a state of completion. They are now destined, perhaps, to wrap up spices. You see what mutations the busy hand of Time has produced, while you have consumed in foolish voluntary exile that time which might have gladdened your friends—benefited your country; but reproaches are useless. Gather up the wretched reliques, my friend, as fast as you can, and come to your old home. I will rub my eyes and try to recognise you. We will shake withered hands together, and talk of old things— of St. Mary's Church and the barber's opposite, where the young students in mathematics used to assemble. Poor Crips, that kept it afterwards, set up a fruiterer's shop in Trumpington Street, and for aught I know resides there still, for I saw the name up in the last journey I took there with my sister just before she died. I suppose you heard that I had left the India House, and gone into the Fishmongers' Almshouses over the bridge. I have a little cabin there, small and homely, but you shall be welcome to it. You like oysters, and to open them yourself; I'll get you some if you come in oyster time. Marshall, Godwin's old friend, is still alive, and talks of the faces you used to make.

Come as soon as you can. C. LAMB.

 December 26, 1815.

Dear Manning—Following your brother's example, I have just ventured one letter to Canton, and am now

hazarding another (not exactly a duplicate) to St. Helena.
The first was full of unprobable romantic fictions, fitting
the remoteness of the mission it goes upon; in the present
I mean to confine myself nearer to truth as you come
nearer home. A correspondence with the uttermost parts
of the earth necessarily involves in it some heat of fancy;
it sets the brain agoing, but I can think on the half-way
house tranquilly. Your friends then are not all dead or
grown forgetful of you through old age, as that lying
letter asserted, anticipating rather what must happen if
you kept tarrying on for ever on the skirts of creation, as
there seemed a danger of your doing; but they are all
tolerably well and in full and perfect comprehension of
what is meant by Manning's coming home again. Mrs.
Kenney never lets her tongue run riot more than in
remembrances of you. Fanny expends herself in phrases
that can only be justified by her romantic nature. Mary
reserves a portion of your silk, not to be buried in (as the
false nuncio asserts), but to make up spick and span into
a bran-new gown to wear when you come. I am the
same as when you knew me, almost to a surfeiting
identity. This very night I am going to *leave off tobacco!*
Surely there must be some other world in which this
unconquerable purpose shall be realised. The soul hath
not her generous aspirings implanted in her in vain. One
that you knew, and I think the only one of those friends
we knew much of in common, has died in earnest. Poor
Priscilla! Her brother Robert is also dead, and several
of the grown-up brothers and sisters, in the compass of a
very few years. Death has not otherwise meddled much
in families that I know. Not but he has his eye upon
us, and is whetting his feathered dart every instant, as
you see him truly pictured in that impressive moral
picture, "The good man at the hour of death." I have
in trust to put in the post four letters from Diss, and one
from Lynn, to St. Helena, which I hope will accompany
this safe, and one from Lynn, and the one before spoken
of from me, to Canton. But we all hope that these

letters may be waste paper. I don't know why I have forborne writing so long ; but it is such a forlorn hope to send a scrap of paper straggling over wide oceans ! And yet I know, when you come home, I shall have you sitting before me at our fireside just as if you had never been away. In such an instant does the return of a person dissipate all the weight of imaginary perplexity from distance of time and space ! I'll promise you good oysters. Corry is dead that kept the shop opposite St. Dunstan's ; but the tougher materials of the shop survive the perishing frame of its keeper. Oysters continue to flourish there under as good auspices. Poor Corry ! but if you will absent yourself twenty years together, you must not expect numerically the same population to congratulate your return which wetted the sea-beach with their tears when you went away. Have you recovered the breathless stone-staring astonishment into which you must have been thrown upon learning at landing that an Emperor of France was living in St. Helena ? What an event in the solitude of the seas ! like finding a fish's bone at the top of Plinlimmon ; but these things are nothing in our western world. Novelties cease to affect. Come and try what your presence can.

God bless you.—Your old friend,   C. LAMB.

To WILLIAM WORDSWORTH.

LETTER CLIX.]   *April* 9, 1816.

Dear Wordsworth—Thanks for the books you have given me and for all the books you mean to give me. I will bind up the Political Sonnets and Ode according to your suggestion. I have not bound the poems yet. I wait till people have done borrowing them. I think I shall get a chain and chain them to my shelves, *more Bodleiano*, and people may come and read them at chain's length. For of those who borrow, some read slow ; some mean to read but don't read; and some neither read nor meant to read, but borrow to leave you an opinion of their sagacity. I must do my money-borrowing friends the justice to say that there is nothing of this caprice or wantonness of alienation in them. When they borrow my money they never fail to make use of it. Coleridge has been here about a fortnight. His health is tolerable at present, though beset with temptations. In the first place, the Covent Garden Manager has declined accepting his Tragedy, though (having read it) I see no reason upon earth why it might not have run a very fair chance, though it certainly wants a prominent part for a Miss O'Neil or a Mr. Kean. However, he is going to-day to write to Lord Byron to get it to Drury. Should you see Mrs. C., who has just written to C. a letter, which I have given him, it will be as well to say nothing about its fate, till some answer is shaped from Drury. He has two volumes printing together at Bristol, both finished as far as the composition goes; the latter containing his fugitive poems, the former his Literary Life. Nature, who conducts every creature, by instinct, to its best end, has skilfully directed C. to take up his abode at a Chemist's Laboratory in Norfolk Street. She might as well have sent a *Helluo Librorum* for cure to the Vatican. God keep him inviolate among the traps and pitfalls! He has done pretty well as yet.

Tell Miss H[utchinson] my sister is every day wishing to be quietly sitting down to answer her very kind letter, but while C. stays she can hardly find a quiet time; God bless him!

Tell Mrs. W. her postscripts are always agreeable. They are so legible too. Your manual-graphy is terrible, dark as Lycophron "Likelihood," for instance, is thus typified . . . . I should not wonder if the constant making out of such paragraphs is the cause of that weakness in Mrs. W.'s eyes, as she is tenderly pleased to express it. Dorothy, I hear, has mounted spectacles; so you have deoculated two of your dearest relations in life.

Well, God bless you, and continue to give you power to write with a finger of power upon our hearts what you fail to impress, in corresponding lucidness, upon our outward eye-sight!

Mary's love to all; she is quite well.

I am called off to do the deposits on Cotton Wool; but why do I relate this to you, who want faculties to comprehend the great mystery of deposits, of interests, of warehouse rent, and contingent fund? Adieu!

C. LAMB.

A longer letter when C. is gone back into the country, relating his success, etc.—*my* judgment of *your* new books, etc. etc.—I am scarce quiet enough while he stays.

Yours again,

C. L.

To WILLIAM WORDSWORTH.

LETTER CLX.]   *Accountant's Office, April* 26, 1816.

Dear W.—I have just finished the pleasing task of correcting the revise of the poems and letter. I hope they will come out faultless. One blunder I saw and shuddered at. The hallucinating rascal had printed *battered* for *battened*, this last not conveying any distinct sense to his gaping soul. The Reader (as they call 'em) had discovered it, and given it the marginal brand, but the substitutory *n* had not yet appeared. I accompanied his notice with a most pathetic address to the printer not to neglect the correction. I know how such a blunder would "batter at your peace." With regard to the works, the Letter I read with unabated satisfaction. Such a thing was wanted—called for. The parallel of Cotton with Burns I heartily approve. Izaak Walton hallows any page in which his reverend name appears. "Duty archly bending to purposes of general benevolence" is exquisite. The poems I endeavoured not to understand, but to read them with my eye alone, and I think I suc-

ceeded. (Some people will do that when they come out,
you'll say.) As if I were to luxuriate to-morrow at some
picture gallery I was never at before, and going by to-day
by chance, found the door open, and had but five minutes
to look about me, peeped in ; just such a *chastised* peep
I took with my mind at the lines my luxuriating eye was
coursing over unrestrained, not to anticipate another day's
fuller satisfaction. Coleridge is printing "Christabel,"
by Lord Byron's recommendation to Murray, with what
he calls a vision, "Kubla Khan," which said vision he
repeats so enchantingly that it irradiates and brings
heaven and elysian bowers into my parlour while he sings
or says it ; but there is an observation, "Never tell thy
dreams," and I am almost afraid that "Kubla Khan" is
an owl that won't bear daylight. I fear lest it should
be discovered by the lantern of typography and clear
reducting to letters no better than nonsense or no sense.
When I was young I used to chant with ecstasy "MILD
ARCADIANS EVER BLOOMING," till somebody told me it
was meant to be nonsense. Even yet I have a lingering
attachment to it, and I think it better than "Windsor
Forest," "Dying Christian's Address," etc. Coleridge
has sent his tragedy to D[rury] L[ane] T[heatre]. It
cannot be acted this season ; and by their manner of
receiving, I hope he will be able to alter it to make them
accept it for next. He is, at present, under the medical
care of a Mr. Gillman (Killman ?) a Highgate apothecary,
where he plays at leaving off laud—m. I think his
essentials not touched : he is very bad ; but then he
wonderfully picks up another day, and his face, when he
repeats his verses, hath its ancient glory ; an archangel a
little damaged. Will Miss H. pardon our not replying
at length to her kind letter ? We are not quiet enough ;
Morgan is with us every day, going betwixt Highgate
and the Temple. Coleridge is absent but four miles, and
the neighbourhood of such a man is as exciting as the
presence of fifty ordinary persons. 'Tis enough to be
within the whiff and wind of his genius for us not to

possess our souls in quiet. If I lived with him or the Author of the *Excursion*, I should, in a very little time, lose my own identity, and be dragged along in the current of other people's thoughts, hampered in a net. How cool I sit in this office, with no possible interruption further than what I may term *material!* There is not as much metaphysics in thirty-six of the people here as there is in the first page of Locke's "Treatise on the Human Understanding," or as much poetry as in any ten lines of the "Pleasures of Hope," or more natural "Beggar's Petition." I never entangle myself in any of their speculations. Interruptions, if I try to write a letter even, I have dreadful. Just now, within four lines, I was called off for ten minutes to consult dusty old books for the settlement of obsolete errors. I hold you a guinea you don't find the chasm where I left off, so excellently the wounded sense closed again and was healed.

N.B.—Nothing said above to the contrary, but that I hold the personal presence of the two mentioned potent spirits at a rate as high as any; but I pay dearer. What amuses others robs me of myself: my mind is positively discharged into their greater currents, but flows with a willing violence. As to your question about work, it is far less oppressive to me than it was, from circumstances. It takes all the golden part of the day away, a solid lump, from ten to four; but it does not kill my peace as before. Some day or other I shall be in a taking again. My head aches, and you have had enough. God bless you!　　　　　　　　　　　　　　　　　　　C. LAMB.

To Miss MATILDA BETHAM.

LETTER CLXI.]　　　　　　　*East India House, June 1, 1816.*

Dear Miss Betham—All this while I have been tormenting myself with the thought of having been ungracious

to you, and you have been all the while accusing yourself.
Let us absolve one another, and be quiet. My head is in
such a state from incapacity for business that I certainly
know it to be my duty not to undertake the veriest trifle
in addition.   I hardly know how I can go on.   I have
tried to get some redress by explaining my health, but
with no great success.   No one can tell how ill I am
because it does not come out to the exterior of my face,
but lies in my skull, deep and invisible.   I wish I was
leprous, and black jaundiced skin over, and that all was
as well within as my cursed looks.   You must not think
me worse than I am.   I am determined not to be over-
set, but to give up business rather, and get 'em to allow
me a trifle for services past.   Oh! that I had been a
shoemaker, or a baker, or a man of large independent
fortune!   Oh! darling laziness! heaven of Epicurus!
Saint's Everlasting Rest! that I could drink vast pota-
tions of thee thro' unmeasured Eternity—Otium *cum*, vel
sine dignitate.   Scandalous, dishonourable—any kind of
repose.   I stand not upon the dignified sort.   Accursed,
damned desks, trade, commerce, business! Inventions
of the old original busy-body, brain-working Satan—
Sabbathless, restless Satan! A curse relieves: do you
ever try it?

A strange letter to write to a lady; but more honeyed
sentences will not distil.   I dare not ask who revises in
my stead.   I have drawn you into a scrape and am
ashamed; but I know no remedy.   My unwellness must
be my apology.   God bless you (tho' He curse the India
House, and fire it *to the ground*), and may no unkind
error creep into "Marie"/ May all its readers like it as
well as I do, and everybody about you like its kind author
no worse!   Why the devil am I never to have a chance
of scribbling my own free thoughts, verse or prose, again?
Why must I write of tea and drugs, and price goods and
the bales of indigo?   Farewell.   C. LAMB.

Mary goes to her place on Sunday—I mean your maid,
foolish Mary; she wants a very little brains only to be

an excellent servant; she is excellently calculated for the country, where nobody has brains.

Have you seen "Christabel" since its publication?

To H. DODWELL.

LETTER CLXII.]   *July* 1816.

My dear fellow—I have been in a lethargy this long while, and forgotten London, Westminster, Marybone, Paddington—they all went clean out of my head, till happening to go to a neighbor's in this good borough of Calne, for want of whist players, we fell upon *Commerce:* the word awoke me to a remembrance of my professional avocations and the long-continued strife which I have been these 24 years endeavoring to compose between those grand Irreconcileables Cash and Commerce; I instantly called for an almanack, which with some difficulty was procured at a fortune-teller's in the vicinity (for the happy holyday people here having nothing to do, keep no account of time), and found that by dint of duty I must attend in Leadenhall on Wednesy. morning next, and shall attend accordingly. Does Master Hannah give macaroons still, and does he fetch the Cobbetts from my Attic? Perhaps it wouldn't be too much trouble for him to drop the inclosed up at my aforesaid Chamber, and any letters, etc., with it; but the inclosed should go without delay. *N.B.*—He isn't to fetch Monday's Cobbett, but it is to wait my reading when I come back. Heigh Ho! Lord have mercy upon me, how many does two and two make? I am afraid I shall make a poor clerk in future, I am spoiled with rambling among haycocks and cows and pigs. Bless me! I had like to have forgot (the air is so temperate and oblivious here) to say I have seen your brother, and hope he is doing well in the finest spot of the world. More of these things when I return. Remember me to the gentlemen,—I forget names. Shall

I find all my letters at my rooms on Tuesday? If you
forgot to send 'em never mind, for I don't much care
for reading and writing now; I shall come back again
by degrees, I suppose, into my former habits. How is
Bruce de Ponthieu, and Porcher and Co.?—the tears
come into my eyes when I think how long I have
neglected ——.

Adieu! ye fields, ye shepherds and—herdesses, and
dairies and cream-pots, and fairies and dances upon the
green.

I come, I come. Don't drag me so hard by the hair of
my head, Genius of British India! I know my hour is
come, Faustus must give up his soul, O Lucifer, O
Mephistopheles! Can you make out what all this letter
is about? I am afraid to look it over.   CH. LAMB.

Calne, Wilts, Friday,
July something, old style, 1816.

No new style here, all the styles are old, and some of
the gates too for that matter.

[Addressed] H. Dodwell, Esq.,
     India House, London.

In his absence may be opened by Mr. Chambers.

NOTES.

CHAPTER I.

1796–1800.

The Letters of this period are chiefly addressed to Coleridge, then at Bristol. They relate the sad fortunes of the Lamb family, arising out of the death of the mother in September 1796. They are also largely critical, and deal with Coleridge's first published poems, and the joint volume in which Lamb and Charles Lloyd made their earliest appearance in print.

Letter I (p. 1).—Southey had just published his *Joan of Arc*, in quarto. He had produced two years before at Bristol, in conjunction with Robert Lovell, *Poems by Bion and Moschus*. Charles Valentine Le Grice, here mentioned, was schoolfellow with Lamb and Coleridge at Christ's Hospital, as also was James White. The latter published his *Original Letters of Sir John Falstaff* in this year. They were dedicated, in a manifestly satirical spirit, to "Master Samuel Irelaunde." The allusions in the letter to Coleridge's "Numbers" are to the weekly issue of his *Watchman*, which first appeared on March 1, 1796, and expired on May 13. *Conciones ad Populum*, or, Addresses to the People, appeared in November 1795.

Letter II (p. 3).—*Poems on Various Subjects*, by S. T. Coleridge, late of Jesus College, Cambridge, was published this year, and it is to this volume, or the proof-sheets of it sent for inspection, that Lamb here refers as "your poems." The volume contained four sonnets signed C. L., and Coleridge's Preface announced that they "were written by Mr. Charles Lamb of the India House." The other sonnets by Lamb here submitted to Coleridge's opinion appeared in the second edition of Coleridge's Poems, in 1797. The story of the preparation of these small volumes of verse may be read, concurrently with these letters, in Joseph Cottle's *Recollections of Coleridge*, vol. i.

Moschus was Robert Lovell, Southey's brother-in-law, several of whose sonnets were printed by Coleridge in his *Watchman.* He died of fever in this year. The "difference" which Lamb alludes to as having arisen between Coleridge and Southey was the split on the Pantisocratic Scheme which was to have been carried out by the young colonists on the banks of the Susquehanna.

Letter III (p. 10).—The simile of the Laplander,

. . . "by Niemi lake,"

is from Coleridge's *Destiny of Nations.* The allusion to the "Monody on Henderson" in this letter needs explanation. John Henderson was a singular genius and precocious scholar, the son of a Bristol schoolmaster, an account of whom will be found in the appendix to the second volume of Cottle's *Recollections of Coleridge.* Cottle was also the author of the "Monody on Henderson" here referred to. It had appeared in a small volume of poems published, without Cottle's name, at Bristol in 1795. Coleridge had evidently forwarded this volume to Lamb for his opinion. The lines criticised by Lamb occur in the following passage :—

> " As o'er thy tomb, my Henderson ! I bend,
> Shall I not praise thee? scholar, Christian, friend !
> The tears which o'er a brother's recent grave
> Fond nature sheds, those copious tears I gave ;
> But now that Time her softening hues has brought
> And mellowed anguish into pensive thought ;
> Since through the varying scenes of life I've passed,
> Comparing still the former with the last,
> I prize thee more ! The *great,* the *learn'd* I see,
> Yet memory turns from *little men* to *thee.*"

The other "Monody" here criticised is that of Coleridge on Chatterton. The first symptoms of the subsequent coolness between Coleridge and Lamb may here be detected. It had its source in a delicate matter—Coleridge's alterations of Lamb's sonnets. The "Epitaph on an Infant" is the famous one—

" Ere sin could blight or sorrow fade ;"

at which Lamb never tired of laughing, up to the day when he applied it, in his "Essay on Roast Pig," to the infant grunter. Dr. Forster is his playful way of writing Dr. Faustus.

Letter IV (p. 21).—*Your part of the "Joan of Arc."* "To the second book Coleridge contributed some four hundred lines, where Platonic philosophy and protests against the Newtonian hypothesis of æther are not very appropriately brought into connection with the shepherd-girl of Domremi. These lines

disappeared from all editions after the first."—(Dowden's
Southey, in the "Men of Letters' Series.")

The verses on Lamb's grandmother are those afterwards
entitled "The Grandame." See *Poems, Plays, and Essays*, vol.
ii. of this series, p. 8.

LETTER V (p. 23).—The *Salutation*. The inn near Christ's
Hospital where Lamb and Coleridge used occasionally to meet
and discuss poetry after Coleridge's departure from school. See
Lamb's Preface to the 1818 edition of his works.

LETTER VI (p. 26).—The Dactyls here parodied were by
Southey, one stanza of them only being Coleridge's. They
appear in Southey's Collected Poems as "The Soldier's Wife,"
and begin—

> " Weary way-wanderer ! languid and sick at heart,
>   Travelling painfully over the rugged road ;
>   Wild-visaged wanderer ! God help thee, wretched one."

It will be remembered as a curious coincidence that the same
lines attracted the notice of the writers in the *Anti-Jacobin*,
where a very humorous parody of them appears, which may be
compared with Lamb's. Another like experiment in Latin
metres by Southey was there transmuted into the more famous
Knife-Grinder.

*Your own lines, introductory to your poem on 'Self,' run
smoothly and pleasurably.* I am inclined to think that the refer-
ence is to a Fragment by Coleridge called "Melancholy," and
to a poem addressed to Lamb, entitled "To a Friend, together
with an Unfinished Poem." I believe that the unfinished poem
was the Fragment just mentioned. Both were written as early
as 1794, and the Fragment first appeared in the *Morning
Chronicle*.

The poem referred to on the "Prince and Princess" was
that bearing the title "On a Late Connubial Rupture in High
Life," now first submitted to Lamb in manuscript.

LETTER VII (p. 28).—White's *Falstaff Letters* have been
already referred to. Dr. Kenrick's *Falstaff's Wedding* was
published in 1760. "Master Dyer" is the first mention in
these letters of George Dyer. See notes in *Essays of Elia*,
to "Oxford in the Vacation." Bürger's *Leonora*, translated by
William Taylor of Norwich, first appeared in this year.

The Statute de Contumeliâ. See Coleridge's "Lines composed
in a Concert Room." In most editions of Coleridge these lines
are dated 1799, but it will be seen that Coleridge submitted
them to Lamb three years before.

LETTERS VIII, IX, X, XI (p. 32-41).—The following letters tell the sad story of the death of Lamb's mother. Whether the Mr. Norris of Christ's Hospital, here mentioned, is the Mr. Randal Norris, afterwards Sub-Treasurer of the Inner Temple, and to the end of his life Lamb's faithful friend, I cannot say. Mr. Randal Norris's daughter tells me that she knows nothing of her father having ever been connected with Christ's Hospital.

Write as religious a letter as possible. Coleridge, we might be sure, obeyed this touching behest. In Gillman's unfinished *Life of Coleridge* there is given a letter by Coleridge addressed "To a friend in great anguish of mind on the sudden death of his mother." It is beyond all doubt the one addressed on this occasion to Lamb, for, as will be seen, it cites Lamb's particular request for "a religious letter." It runs as follows :—

"Your letter, my friend, struck me with a mighty horror. It rushed upon me and stupified my feelings. You bid me write you a religious letter : I am not a man who would attempt to insult the greatness of your anguish by any other consolation. Heaven knows that in the easiest fortunes there is much dissatisfaction and weariness of spirit : much that calls for the exercise of patience and resignation ; but in storms like these, that shake the dwelling and make the heart tremble, there is no middle way between despair and the yielding up of the whole spirit unto the guidance of faith. And surely it is a matter of joy that your faith in Jesus has been preserved : the Comforter that should relieve you is not far from you. But, as you are a Christian, in the name of that Saviour who was filled with bitterness and made drunken with wormwood, I conjure you to have recourse in frequent prayer to 'his God and your God,' the God of mercies and Father of all comfort. Your poor father is, I hope, almost senseless of the calamity : the unconscious instrument of Divine Providence knows it not, and your mother is in Heaven. It is sweet to be roused from a frightful dream by the song of birds, and the gladsome rays of the morning. Ah ! how infinitely more sweet to be awakened from the blackness and amazement of a sudden horror by the glories of God manifest, and the hallelujahs of angels.

"As to what regards yourself, I approve altogether of your abandoning what you justly call vanities. I look upon you as a man called by sorrow and anguish and a strange desolation of hopes into quietness, and a soul set apart and made peculiar to God : we cannot arrive at any portion of heavenly bliss without, in some measure, imitating Christ. And they arrive at the largest inheritance who imitate the most difficult parts of His character, and, bowed down and crushed under foot, cry in fulness of faith, 'Father, thy will be done.'

"I wish above measure to have you for a little while here :

no visitants shall blow on the nakedness of your feelings ; you shall be quiet, and your spirit may be healed. I see no possible objection, unless your father's helplessness prevent you, and unless you are necessary to him. If this be not the case, I charge you write me that you will come.

"I charge you, my dearest friend, not to dare to encourage gloom or despair : you are a temporary sharer in human miseries that you may be an eternal partaker of the Divine Nature. I charge you, if by any means it is possible, come to me" (Gillman's *Life of Coleridge*, vol. i. p. 338). See, afterwards, poor Lamb's comments on the concluding sentences of this letter.

LETTER XII (p. 41).—Lamb begins to find an interest in books once more. William Lisle Bowles's Poem, *Hope*, appeared this year in handsome quarto. *The Pursuits of Literature*, by T. J. Mathias, was also just published in its complete form, but anonymously.

LETTER XIII (p. 43).—Coleridge had removed about Christmas of this year to a cottage at Nether-Stowey near Bristol, in order to be near his friend Thomas Poole. A letter written to Joseph Cottle, shortly after his arrival, tells the same story of deep melancholy as he had also apparently confided to Lamb :—
"On the Saturday, the Sunday and ten days after my arrival at Stowey, I felt a depression too dreadful to be described,

> 'So much I felt my genial spirits droop,
> My hopes all flat : Nature within me seemed
> In all her functions, weary of herself.'

" Wordsworth's conversation aroused me somewhat, but even now I am not the man I have been, and I think never shall. A sort of calm hopelessness diffuses itself over my heart. Indeed every mode of life which has promised me bread and cheese, has been one after another torn away from me, but God remains."

The rest of Lamb's letter refers to the arrangements in progress for the publication of the second edition (1797) of Coleridge's Poems, with others by Lamb and Lloyd. The sonnet ending "So, for the mother's sake," is that entitled "To a Friend who asked how I felt when the Nurse first presented my Infant to me."

LETTER XIV (p. 46).—Coleridge dedicated the volume of 1797 to his brother, George Coleridge of Ottery St. Mary ; but the sonnets contained in the volume were prefaced by one addressed to Bowles, beginning—

> "My heart has thanked thee, Bowles ;"

and to this sonnet Lamb here alludes.   The lines cited by Lamb, beginning—

"When all the vanities of life's brief day,"

are unknown to me.   His own motto, from Massinger, is from *A Very Woman, or The Prince of Tarent.*   He quoted the scene in which it occurs, twelve years later, in his *Dramatic Specimens.*

Letter XV (p. 49).—The forthcoming volume of 1797 is here under discussion.   The numbers "40, 63," etc., refer to the pages in the first edition of Coleridge's Poems, 1796. "40" is "Absence, A Farewell Ode;" "63" a sonnet, "To the Autumnal Moon;" "84" "An Imitation from Ossian."   In spite of Lamb's remonstrances these were omitted from the second edition.   Of the "Epitaph on an Infant,"

"Ere sin could blight or sorrow fade,"

Coleridge was indeed showing himself "tenacious."   It had already appeared in the *Morning Chronicle,* and the *Watchman.* What lines of Lamb's are referred to, as beginning—

"Laugh all that weep,"

I cannot say.   They did not appear in the forthcoming volume. The sonnet on Mrs. Siddons was a joint composition of Lamb and Coleridge.

The lines "*Dear native brook,*" published first in the *Watchman,* are the well-known sonnet "To the River Otter."   No. "48" is the sonnet "To Priestley," beginning—

"'Tho' roused by that dark Vizir Riot rude";

"52" the sonnet "To Kosciusko"; and "53" that "To Fayette." *The last five lines of* 50 are those which conclude the sonnet to Sheridan.   Sara Coleridge had a share in one poem in the edition of 1796,—that on page 129, here referred to, called "The Production of a Young Lady," on the subject of the loss of a silver thimble.

Letter XVI (p. 52).—*The "divine chit-chat of Cowper"* was, as we learn from a sentence in the following letter, a phrase of Coleridge's own.   Coleridge uses it again in a letter to John Thelwall of December 17 :—"But do not let us introduce an Act of Uniformity against poets.   I have room enough in *my* brain to admire, aye, and almost equally, the *head* and fancy of Akenside and the *heart* and fancy of Bowles, the solemn lordliness of Milton, and the divine chit-chat of Cowper, and whatever a man's excellence is, that will be likewise his fault" (S. T. C. to J. Thelwall, Bristol, December 17, 1796.   Mr. Cosens's MSS.)

LETTER XVII (p. 52).—"*The sainted growing woof*," etc. I have not traced this and the following quotation to their source. Coleridge's Lines on Burns, here referred to, were printed in a Bristol paper, and afterwards included in the poem, "To a friend who declared his intention of writing no more poetry."

LETTER XIX (p. 56).—The lines to his sister were afterwards withdrawn by Lamb from the forthcoming volume, but were printed in the *Monthly Magazine* for October 1797, with the simple heading "Sonnet to a Friend." They will be found on page 4 of the second volume of this series. "David Hartley Coleridge" was now in his second year, having been born September 19, 1796. Priestley's "Examination of the Scotch Doctors" was, I presume, his reply to Dr. Jamieson and others who had criticised his *History of the Corruptions of Christianity*.

LETTER XX (p. 57).—Mention has been already made of Coleridge's contribution to Southey's *Joan of Arc* of certain lines in the second book. Coleridge in later years entirely endorsed his friend Lamb's opinion of the lines. On reading them again he says, 'I was really astonished (1) at the school-boy, wretched, allegoric machinery; (2) at the transmogrification of the fanatic virago into a modern novel-pawing proselyte of the Age of Reason—a Tom Paine in petticoats; (3) at the utter want of all rhythm in the verse, the monotony and dead plumb-down of the pauses, and the absence of all bone, muscle, and sinew in the single lines."

The lines were omitted from all editions of Southey's Poem after the first, but were reprinted by Coleridge under the title of "The Destiny of Nations: a Vision," in his *Sibylline Leaves*, in 1817, and will be found in all complete editions of Coleridge's Poems. Lamb, with characteristic certainty of taste, selects for praise the finest lines of the whole composition—

> " For she had lived in this bad world
>   As in a place of tombs,
>   And touch'd not the pollutions of the dead."

Montauban dancing with Roubigné's tenants, is an incident in Mackenzie's *Julia de Roubigné*—the story which probably suggested to Lamb to attempt prose fiction.

The poem of Coleridge's here referred to as the "Dream" is that afterwards entitled "The Raven: a Christmas Tale told by a schoolboy to his little brothers and sisters," first printed in the *Morning Post* of March 10, 1798, and afterwards reprinted in *Sibylline Leaves*.

My poor old aunt. See Lamb's verses "Written on the Day of my Aunt's Funeral" (*Poems, Plays, and Essays,* p. 16).

No after friendship e'er can raise—from John Logan's poem "On the death of a young lady."

John Woolman. Readers of the *Essays of Elia* will remember the reference to the writings of John Woolman, the Quaker, in the essay "A Quaker's Meeting."

The poem in Southey's new volume which Lamb calls the "Miniature," was actually called "On my own miniature Picture," the "Robert" being of course Southey himself. "Spirit of Spenser! was the wanderer wrong?" is the last line of the poem.

Flocci-nauci-what-do-you-call-'em-ists! may be deemed worthy of a note. "Flocci, nauci" is the beginning of a rule in the old Latin grammars, containing a list of words signifying "of no account," *floccus* being a lock of wool, and *naucus* a trifle. Lamb was recalling a sentence in one of Shenstone's Letters :— "I loved him for nothing so much as his flocci-nauci-nihili-pili-fication of money."

Mr. Rogers is indebted for his story. In a note to "An Effusion on an Autumnal Evening," in the first edition of his Poems, Coleridge had asserted that the tale of Florio in Rogers's *Pleasures of Memory* was to be found in the *Lochleven* of Bruce. As the fruit of Lamb's remonstrance in this letter Coleridge introduced a handsome apology to Rogers in the next edition (1797), admitting that, on a re-examination of the two poems, he had not found sufficient resemblance to justify the charge.

LETTER XXI (p. 63).—*Did the wand of Merlin wave?* Lamb refers to his sonnet, beginning "Was it some sweet delight of Fairy?" In the 1796 edition of Coleridge's Poems the passage had run thus :—

"Or did the wizard wand
Of Merlin wave, impregning vacant air,
And kindle up the vision of a smile
In those blue eyes?"

This, it seems, was an alteration of Coleridge's. In accordance with Lamb's instructions in this letter, the passage appeared in the 1797 edition without the "wizard wand of Merlin." See *Poems*, etc., by Ch. Lamb, p. 1. *Mr.* Merlin, the conjuror, of Oxford Street, was a well-known person at the end of the last century.

LETTER XXII (p. 67).—*Those very schoolboy-ish verses.* See the lines "To Sara and her Samuel," *Poems*, etc., of Ch. Lamb. p. 6.

LETTER XXIII (p. 69).—Compare with previous letter of January 5, 1797.

LETTER XXIV (p. 73).—Charles Lloyd, the son of a banker at Birmingham, lived under Coleridge's roof at Bristol, and at Nether-Stowey from the autumn of 1796 to the close of 1797. He was all his life subject to ill-health and persistent melancholia. The "Dedication" to which Lamb refers is the one to his sister, which introduced his portion of the volume of 1797. It ran thus:—"The few following poems, creatures of the Fancy and the Feeling, in life's more *vacant* hours; produced for the most part by Love in Idleness, are, with all a brother's fondness, inscribed to Mary Ann Lamb, the author's best friend and sister."

LETTER XXV (p. 75).—*The above* was Lamb's poem, "A Vision of Repentance," published in an appendix to the volume of 1797. See *Poems*, etc., of Lamb, p. 13.

LETTER XXVI (p. 76).—*Our little book* was the volume of 1797, which now appeared with the following title-page:— "Poems, by S. T. Coleridge. Second edition. To which are now added Poems by Charles Lamb and Charles Lloyd," followed by the Latin motto of Coleridge, from the imaginary Epistles of Groscollias :—"Duplex nobis vinculum, et amicitiae et similium junctarumque Camenarum ; quod utinam neque mors solvat, neque temporis longinquitas."

The Richardson referred to in this and other letters was evidently some one in authority at the India House, who controlled the important matter of Lamb's occasional holidays.

LETTER XXVII (p. 76).—"Gryll will be Gryll, and keep his hoggish mind."—Spenser, *Faëry Queen*.

Of my last poem. "The Vision of Repentance," mentioned in previous letter. *Riding behind in the basket* alludes to its being relegated to an appendix, with certain others by his two companions.

LETTER XXVIII (p. 78).—*Life of John Buncle*, by Amory. See reference to this book, a great favourite of Lamb's, in the Essay on "Imperfect Sympathies."

LETTER XXIX (p. 79).—Written after Lamb's visit to Coleridge at Nether-Stowey. Talfourd placed this letter in the year 1800, and has been followed by all subsequent editors. Yet, strangely enough, the summer in which it was written is placed beyond all question by the letter itself. The visit to Coleridge of which it tells was for many reasons a memorable one. It was on the evening of the arrival of Lamb and his sister that Coleridge met with the accident to his leg which prevented his accompanying them on a walk, and drew from him the well-known lines, entitled "This Lime-Tree Bower my Prison," containing the apostrophe to Lamb, "My gentle-

hearted Charles," under which Lamb so often affected to wince.
An allusion to Coleridge's injured leg, it will be seen, occurs in
this letter; and a further allusion to little Hartley cutting his
teeth, adds a quite independent corroboration of the date.

LETTER XXX (p. 81).—*A little passage of Beaumont and
Fletcher's.* The lines thus altered are from the "Maid's Tragedy,"
and run thus:—

> " And am prouder
> That I was once your love (though now refused),
> Than to have had another true to me."

When time drives flocks from field to fold. Perhaps a random
recollection of a couplet from the song in *Love's Labour's Lost.*

LETTER XXXI (p. 83).—*The odd coincidence of two young men.*
In the joint volume of 1797 Charles Lloyd republished a series
of sonnets on the death of his grandmother, Priscilla Farmer.
It will be remembered that Lamb's lines, "The Grandame,"
appeared in the same volume.

LETTER XXXII (p. 85). -*I had well-nigh quarrelled with
Charles Lloyd.* This sentence seems to throw light upon the
origin of Lamb's beautiful verses, composed in this very month,
"The Old Familiar Faces," and to suggest a different interpre-
tation of them from that usually given. In my Memoir of
Lamb ("Men of Letters' Series"), I had supposed, in company
with many others, that the allusion in the lines—

> " I have a friend, a kinder friend has no man.
> Like an ingrate, I left my friend abruptly—
> Left him, to muse on the old familiar faces."—

was to Coleridge, between whom and Lamb the relations had,
as we have seen, for some time been rather strained. But it
has been pointed out to me by an obliging correspondent that
the reference in the lines just quoted is more probably to this
temporary rupture with Lloyd; and that the "Friend of my
bosom, thou more than a brother," in the last stanza but one, is
addressed to Coleridge. It is pleasant to think that this should
be the true explanation, and I gladly accept my correspondent's
correction.

Coleridge, as the address at the end of the letter shows, was
now at Shrewsbury, on a visit to the Unitarian minister, the Rev.
A. Rowe, whom he then proposed to succeed in that office.

LETTER XXXIII (p. 87).—Lamb had been introduced to
Southey by Coleridge, as long back as 1795; but, according to
Talfourd, "no intimacy ensued until he accompanied Lloyd in
the summer of 1797 to the little village of Burton, near Christ

Church in Hampshire, where Southey was then residing, and where they spent a fortnight as the poet's guests."

Sir R. Phillips was the proprietor of the *Monthly Magazine*.

Coleridge, in company with Wordsworth and his sister, left England for Germany in September 1798. Coleridge was absent a little less than a year. It was perhaps well for the future relations between him and Lamb that this temporary separation took place. Poetic rivalry and poetic criticism freely indulged on both sides had left bitterness behind. The whole pitiable story may be read, if it is worth reading, in the pages of Cottle's *Early Recollections of Coleridge*. Cottle tells us that Coleridge forwarded to him Lamb's letter, containing the sarcastic *Theses* here propounded, adding "these young visionaries" (meaning Lamb and Lloyd) "will do each other no good." The *Theses* were prefaced by the following remarks :—"Learned Sir, my friend, presuming on our long habits of friendship, and emboldened further by your late liberal permission to avail myself of your correspondence in case I want any knowledge (which I intend to do, when I have no Encyclopædia or Ladies' Magazine at hand to refer to in any matter of science), I now submit to your enquiries the above theological propositions, to be by you defended or oppugned (or both) in the schools of Germany, whither I am told you are departing, to the utter dissatisfaction of your native Devonshire, and regret of universal England ; but to my own individual consolation, if, through the channel of your wished return, learned Sir, my friend, may be transmitted to this our island, from those famous theological wits of Leipsic and Gottingen, any rays of illumination, in vain to be derived from the home growth of our English halls and colleges. Finally wishing, learned Sir, that you may see Schiller, and swing in a wood (*vide* Poems) and sit upon a tun, and eat fat hams of Westphalia,—I remain your friend and docile pupil to instruct,   CHAS. LAMB."

LETTER XXXIV (p. 90).—*Rosamund Gray*, by Charles Lamb, was published in this year, 1798.

LETTER XXXV (p. 90).—The Eclogue here criticised was that entitled *The Ruined Cottage*. See note to "Rosamund Gray" in *Poems, Plays*, etc., p. 388.

How does your Calendar prosper? There would seem to have been an idea of calling the *Annual Anthology* a Calendar or Almanack of the Muses. Southey thus opens his preface to the first volume of the work :—"Similar collections to the present have long been known in France and Germany under the title of *Almanacks of the Muses*."

LETTER XXXVI (p. 93).—Southey, who was now taking Coleridge's place as Lamb's chief literary correspondent, had sent two more Eclogues for his opinion—*The Wedding*, and *The last of the Family.*

LETTER XXXVII (p. 95).—The *Lyrical Ballads*, the joint production of Wordsworth and Coleridge, had just made its appearance, published by Joseph Cottle, at Bristol. It contained four poems by Coleridge, one being the "Ancient Mariner." Lamb's pre-eminence as a critic, at this early age of three-and-twenty, appears wonderfully in his remarks upon this poem. "That last poem, which is yet one of the finest written," evidently refers to Wordsworth's "Lines written a few miles above Tintern Abbey," which come last in the little duodecimo volume.

LETTER XXXVIII (p. 96).—The lines entitled "Mystery of God," or "Living without God in the world," originally appeared in the first volume of Cottle's *Annual Anthology*, published this year, edited by Southey. They will be found in *Poems, Plays*, etc., p. 23. The sonnet referred to would seem to be the one to his sister, already given, "Friend of my earliest years." One of the titles proposed for the *Anthology* was "Gleanings." It was in fact a poetical miscellany to which Coleridge, Southey, Lloyd, and others, including the Cottles, contributed. Two volumes only were published. Pratt, the editor of Pratt's *Gleanings through Wales, Holland, and Westphalia* (1795), was a bookseller at Bath, who published novels and poems, as well as various compilations.

Southey continued to send his poems, as he wrote them, for Lamb's criticisms. The "Witch Ballad" was "The Old Woman of Berkeley," written in this year, as was also "Bishop Bruno." Lamb's "Witch" was the poem originally intended as an episode in *John Woodvil*, but afterwards withdrawn and printed separately. See *Poems, Plays*, etc., p. 66. The "Dying Lover" is the young Philip Fairford mentioned in the poem. George Dyer was at this time preparing a volume of poems. The lines criticised by Lamb occur in an ode "addressed to Dr. Robert Anderson" (*Poems*, by George Dyer : Longman and Co., 1801). Dyer did not accept his friend's correction. The line remains—

"Dark is the poet's eye—but shines his name."

The "two noble Englishmen" were of course Wordsworth and Coleridge. Coleridge, as is well known, parted from Wordsworth and his sister while they were still at Hamburgh.

LETTER XXXIX (p. 99).—*John May* was a gentleman whose acquaintance Southey had made during his first visit to Portugal, and who was thenceforth one of Southey's most intimate friends and frequent correspondents.

LETTER XLI (p. 102).—Most of Southey's poems here referred to will be found in vols. ii. and vi. of the ten-volume edition, collected by himself, 1837. "The Parody" is the ballad called "The Surgeon's Warning." "Cousin Margaret" is the poem "To Margaret Hill."

LETTER XLII (p. 104).—See Southey's lines "To a Spider," vol. ii. of the edition just named.

Sam Le Grice. For some amusing particulars concerning him see *Leigh Hunt's Autobiography,* chap. iii. "He was the maddest of all the great boys in my time : clever, full of address, and not hampered by modesty. Remote rumours, not lightly to be heard, fell on our ears respecting pranks of his among the nurses' daughters. He had a fair handsome face, with delicate aquiline nose and twinkling eyes. I remember his astonishing me when I was 'a new boy,' with sending me for a bottle of water, which he proceeded to pour down the back of G., a grave Deputy Grecian. On the master asking him one day why he, of all the boys, had given up no exercise (it was a particular exercise that they were bound to do in the course of a long set of holidays) he said he had had a 'lethargy.'" He must, however, have had a good heart. See the previous letter of Lamb to Coleridge in which he tells of Sam Le Grice giving up every hour of his time to amuse the poor old father, in the sad period following the death of Lamb's mother.

LETTER XLV (p. 109). — Lamb had been visiting his old haunts, near Blakesware in Herts. See note to "Blakesmoor in Hertfordshire ;" *Essays of Elia,* p. 409.

Gebor is Lamb's spelling of "Gebir"—Landor's poem, which was published in this year.

LETTER XLVI (p. 110). — Thomas Manning, whose name appears here for the first time as Lamb's correspondent, was so remarkable a man as to warrant my giving a few particulars of his life, taken from the Memoir prefixed to his "Journey to Lhasa," in 1811-12 (*George Bogle and Thomas Manning's Journey to Thibet and Lhasa,* by C. R. Markham, 1876).—"He was the second son of the Rev. William Manning, Rector of Diss in Norfolk, and was born at his father's first living of Broome, in the same county, on the 8th of November 1772. Owing to ill-health in early life he was obliged to forego the advantages of a public school ; but under his father's roof he was a close student of both classics and mathematics, and became an eager disciple of the philosophy of Plato. On his recovery he went to Caius College, Cambridge, and studied intensely, especially mathematics. While at Cambridge he published a work on Algebra, and a smaller book on Arithmetic. He passed the final examination, and was expected to be at least second wrangler, but his strong repugnance to oaths and tests debarred him from academic honours and preferments, and he left the university without a degree."

He continued to reside at Cambridge, as tutor at Caius, many years after the time when he should have graduated, and was there when Lamb first made his acquaintance, through the introduction of Charles Lloyd, in the autumn of 1799. "After he had lived at Cambridge for some years he began to brood over the mysterious empire of China, and devoted his time to an investigation of the language and arts of the Chinese, and the state of their country. He resolved to enter the Celestial Empire at all hazards, and to prosecute his researches till death stopped him, or until he should return with success. To enable him to undertake this hazardous enterprise he studied the Chinese language under the tuition of Dr. Hagar in France, and afterwards, with the aid of a Chinese, in London. When the English travellers were seized by Napoleon on the breaking out of war in 1803, Manning obtained leave to quit France entirely owing to the respect in which his undertaking was held by the learned men at Paris. His passport was the only one that Napoleon ever signed for an Englishman to go to England after war began."

The rest of Manning's adventures, and the result of his extraordinary expedition to Lhasa in 1811, as well as Manning's own Journal kept during his travels, will be found in Mr. Clement Markham's volume.

Manning was afterwards Chinese Interpreter to Lord Amherst's Embassy in 1817. He then "returned to England, after an absence of nearly twelve years, apparently a disappointed man. He was in Italy from 1827 to 1829, and then went to live in strict retirement at Bexley, whence he removed to a cottage near Dartford, called Orange Grove. He led a very eccentric life. It is said that he never furnished his cottage, but only had a few chairs, one carpet, and a large library of Chinese books. He wore a milky-white beard down to his waist." He died at Bath on the 2d of May 1840, aged sixty-eight.

The Title of the Play.—Lamb had at first intended to call his play, *John Woodvil*, by a different name—*Pride's Cure.*

CHAPTER II.

1800–1809.

LETTER XLVIII (p. 113).—*Mr. Wyndham's unhappy composition.* Coleridge's criticism on Wyndham's note, contributed to the *Morning Post* in January 1800, is reprinted in the *Essays on his own Times* (i. 261).

LETTER XLIX (p. 114).—"War, and Nature, and Mr. Pitt."
Evidently some popular allegorical print of the day.

LETTER L (p. 115).—*Supposed manuscript of Burton.* See
"Curious Fragments, extracted from a common-place book
which belonged to Robert Burton" (*Poems, Plays, and Essays*,
p. 197).
Olivia was Charles Lloyd's sister.

LETTER LI (p. 116).—*Hetty died on Friday night.* Charles
and Mary's one servant.

LETTER LII (p. 117).—*To lodge with a friend in town.*
John Matthew Gutch, a schoolfellow of Lamb's at Christ's
Hospital, afterwards the editor of *Farley's Bristol Journal.*
The rooms were in Southampton Buildings. Lamb lodged
there occasionally for several years to come. See Letter to
Coleridge, later on, p. 134.

LETTER LIII (p. 118).—*My Enemy's B——* is, I am afraid,
a variation upon "My enemy's dog" in a well-known speech
from *King Lear.*
Mary Hayes. Mary Hayes was an intimate friend of Godwin
and his wife, Mary Wollstonecraft. She wrote in the *Monthly
Magazine,* also a novel called *Emma Courtenay.* "An uncom-
mon book. Mary Hayes is an agreeable woman and a God-
winite." (Southey, *Life and Correspondence,* i. 305.)

LETTER LV (p. 120).—*Lamb is quite enough.* There was
evidently a disposition in the early days of Lamb's friendships
to spell his name with a final e. I have seen it thus mis-
spelt in magazines of the time.
By terming me gentle-hearted in print. See Coleridge's lines,
"This Lime-Tree Bower my Prison," first published in the
Annual Anthology.
I have hit off the following. See "A Ballad: Noting the
Difference of Rich and Poor." *Poems, Plays, and Essays,* p. 68.
W.'s tragedy. "The Borderers." The second edition of the
Lyrical Ballads was published this year.

LETTER LVI (p. 123).—*His friend Frend.* The Rev.
William Frend, who was expelled the University of Cambridge
for tenets savouring of Unitarianism.
George Dyer. See note to the Essay, "Oxford in the Vaca-
tion." *Essays of Elia,* p. 379.

LETTER LVII (p. 125).—*Dr. Anderson.* James Anderson
(1739-1808), writer on Agriculture and Politico-Economical
subjects.

LETTER LX (p. 129).—The references to poems in this letter
are to the second volume of the *Annual Anthology,* just pub-

lished. "Blenheim" is, of course, Southey's well-known ballad ; "Lewti" and the "Raven" are by Coleridge.

Your 141st page refers to the poem "'This Lime-Tree Bower my Prison,' a poem addressed to Charles Lamb, of the India House, London," in which Lamb was styled, "my gentle-hearted Charles."

LETTER LXII (p. 134).—*On a visit to Grattan.* Lamb's own slip of the pen for *Curran.* See Mr. Kegan Paul's *Life of Godwin.*

LETTER LXIII (p. 135).—*Helen.* These verses were by Mary Lamb.

Alfred, an epic poem by Joseph Cottle of Bristol, the bookseller and poet.

LETTER LXIV (p. 139).—*A "Conceit of Diabolic Possession."* See the lines afterwards entitled "Hypochondriacus" (*Poems Plays, and Essays*, p. 204).

LETTER LXVIII (p. 145).—*A pleasant hand, one Rickman.* John Rickman (1771-1840), for many years Clerk-Assistant at the Table of the House of Commons, an eminent statistician, and author of the system for taking the population census, besides many other inventions of greater or less utility. He became the intimate friend of Lamb, Southey, and others of that set.

Mr. Crisp was a barber over whose shop Manning lodged, in St. Mary's Passage, Cambridge.

My Play. "John Woodvil."

LETTER LXXI (p. 150).—*How to abridge the Epilogue.* The epilogue Lamb was writing for Godwin's play, *Antonio.* The next two or three letters deal with the production and the failure of the unfortunate drama. See Mr. Kegan Paul's *Life of Godwin.*

LETTER LXXV (p. 157).—*The Preface must be expunged.* In the British Museum is Lamb's copy of Dyer's Poems. It contains the cancelled preface, and on the margin of advertisement, explaining how the book begins at p. lxix. instead of p. i., Lamb has written, "One copy of this cancelled Preface, snatched out of the fire, is prefixed to this volume." The cancelled preface ran to sixty-six pages, not eighty, as Lamb says to Manning. Writing to G. C. Bedford, 22d March 1817, respecting one of his books then printing, Southey says, "Now, pray, be speedy with the cancels. On such an occasion Lamb gave G. Dyer the title of *Cancellarius Magnus.*" (*Letters of R. S.* i. 428.) For this interesting reference I am indebted to my friend Mr. J. Dykes Campbell.

LETTER LXXVI (p. 159).—*Miss Wesley.* Daughter of Samuel and niece of John Wesley. "Eccentric but estimable," says H. Crabb Robinson in Diary, 27th May 1812.

One Miss Benjay. Miss Elizabeth Benger, authoress of various poems and histories. See *Dictionary of National Biography,* iv. 221.

LETTER LXXVII (p. 162).—The "second volume" that Lamb had borrowed was the second volume of the *Lyrical Ballads,* then just published. The "Song of Lucy" is clearly the lovely lyric beginning—

"She dwelt among the untrodden ways."

Lamb's criticism on the second title of the "Ancient Mariner" proved effectual in the end, but the title was retained until the publication of the *Sibylline Leaves* in 1817. The stanzas referred to by Lamb as "The Mad Mother," are those beginning with the words, "Her eyes are wild." Wordsworth in later editions dropped the original title.

This letter to Wordsworth provoked a reply from the poet, referred to in the following singularly interesting letter of Lamb to Manning, which unfortunately came into my hands too late for insertion in the text, but with which I most gladly enrich my notes. The original, from which I have printed it, was lent me by Rev. C. R. Manning, the nephew of Thomas Manning. It was no doubt omitted by Talfourd because Wordsworth was still living when the *Letters* and the *Final Memorials* were published :—

To Thos. Manning,
  Diss, Norfolk.

February 15, 1801.

I had need be cautious henceforward what opinion I give of the *Lyrical Ballads.* All the North of England are in a turmoil. Cumberland and Westmoreland have already declared a state of war. I lately received from Wordsworth a copy of the second volume, accompanied by an acknowledgement of having received from me many months since a copy of a certain Tragedy, with excuses for not having made any acknowledgement sooner, it being owing to an "almost insurmountable aversion from Letter-writing." This letter I answered in due form and time, and enumerated several of the passages which had most affected me, adding, unfortunately, that no single piece had moved me so forcibly as the "Ancient Mariner," "The Mad Mother," or the "Lines at Tintern Abbey." The Post did not sleep a moment. I received almost instantaneously a long letter of four sweating pages from my Reluctant Letter-Writer, the purport of which was, that he was sorry his 2d vol. had not given me more pleasure (Devil a hint did I give that it had *not pleased me*), and "was compelled to wish that my range of sensibility was more extended, being obliged to believe that I should receive large influxes of happiness and happy Thoughts" (I suppose from the L. B.)—With a deal of stuff about a certain Union of Tenderness and Imagination, which in the sense he used Imagination was not the characteristic of Shakspeare, but which Milton possessed in a degree far exceeding other Poets: which Union, as the highest species of Poetry, and chiefly deserving that name, "He was most proud to aspire to"; then illustrating the said Union by two quotations from his own 2d vol. (which I had been so unfortunate as to miss). 1st Specimen —a father addresses his son :—

> " When thou
> First camest into the World, as it befalls
> To new-born Infants, thou didst sleep away
> Two days : and *Blessings from thy father's Tongue*
> *Then fell upon thee.*"

The lines were thus undermarked, and then followed "This Passage, as combining in an extraordinary degree that Union of Imagination and Tenderness which I am speaking of, I consider as one of the Best I ever wrote !"

2d Specimen.—A youth, after years of absence, revisits his native place, and thinks (as most people do) that there has been strange alteration in his absence :—

> " And that the rocks
> And everlasting Hills themselves were changed."

You see both these are good Poetry : but after one has been reading Shakspeare twenty of the best years of one's life, to have a fellow start up, and prate about some unknown quality which Shakspeare possessed in a degree inferior to Milton and *somebody else ! !* This was not to be *all* my castigation. Coleridge, who had not written to me some months before, starts up from his bed of sickness to reprove me for my hardy presumption : four long pages, equally sweaty and more tedious, came from him ; assuring me that, when the works of a man of true genius such as W. undoubtedly was, do not please me at first sight, I should suspect the fault to lie "in me and not in them," etc. etc. etc. etc. etc. What am I to do with such people ? I certainly shall write them a very merry Letter. Writing to *you*, I may say that the 2d vol. has no such pieces as the three I enumerated. It is full of original thinking and an observing mind, but it does not often make you laugh or cry.— It too artfully aims at simplicity of expression. And you sometimes doubt if Simplicity be not a cover for Poverty. The best Piece in it I will send you, being *short*. I have grievously offended my friends in the North by declaring my undue preference; but I need not fear you :—

> " She dwelt among the untrodden ways
>   Beside the Springs of Dove,
> A maid whom there were few (*sic*) to praise
>   And very few to love.
>
> A violet, by a mossy stone,
>   Half hidden from the eye.
> Fair as a star when only one
>   Is shining in the sky.
>
> She lived unknown ; and few could know,
>   When Lucy ceased to be.
> But she is in the grave, and oh !
>   The difference to me."

This is choice and genuine, and so are many, many more. But one does not like to have 'em rammed down one's throat. "Pray, take it—it's very good—let me help you—eat faster."

The coarse epithet of "pin-point." In the first version of the *Poet's Epitaph*, the line to which we are now accustomed—

> "Thy ever-dwindling soul away,"

ran thus :—

> "Thy pin-point of a soul away."

LETTER LXXVIII (p. 164).—*Barbara Lewthwaite.* The little heroine of Wordsworth's poem "The Pet Lamb."

LETTER LXXIX (p. 166).—*George Dyer's Poems :* Longman and Rees, 1801. The passage about Shakspeare from the long poem called "Poetic Sympathies" in this volume, beginning

> "Yet, muse of Shakspeare, whither wouldst thou fly
> With hurried step, and dove-like, trembling eye ?"

is hardly worth quoting further, but may be referred to by the curious.

John Stoddart, Esq. John, afterwards Sir John, Stoddart, was the brother of Mrs. William Hazlitt (the *first* W. H.) He was a writer in the *Times* — quarrelled with Walter, and set up the *New Times*, a short-lived venture, and went to Malta, where he was Chief Justice. While there he invited S. T. Coleridge to visit him, and the invitation was accepted.

My back tingles from the northern castigation. This allusion, hitherto obscure, is now made quite clear by the letter to Manning, given in the preceding note.

I am going to change my lodgings. The Lambs were now about to leave Southampton Buildings (see Letter LXII.) for Mitre Court Buildings, in the Temple, destined to be their home for the next eight years.

LETTER LXXX (p. 169).—Baron Maseres, Cursitor Baron of the Exchequer. See the Elia Essay, "The Old Benchers of the Inner Temple."

LETTER LXXXII (p. 170).—*Walter Wilson*, bookseller, and aftewards writer, best known as the author of the *Memoirs of Defoe*, to which Lamb was later to contribute some interesting critical matter.

LETTER LXXXIII (p. 171).—See Lamb's Essay on "Newspapers Thirty-five Years Ago," and the note upon it in this edition. He there tells us that this epigram gave the unfortunate *Albion* its *coup de grâce*.

LETTER LXXXV (p. 175).—*Your story.* The story of Godwin's later play of *Faulkener* would seem to be indicated here. That play was built upon Defoe's *Roxana*, and Lamb here suggests that the strange history of Richard Savage's parentage might advantageously be borrowed. *Faulkener* was not produced till 1807, and then unsuccessfully. The following letter evidently refers to the plot of the same proposed drama.

LETTER LXXXVII (p. 179).—*My Play*, "John Woodvil." The copy sent to Manning in the handwriting of Mary Lamb, with various omissions marked and corrections added in the handwriting of Charles, is before me, kindly lent by Mr. C. R. Manning of Diss. In the inside cover of the MS. is pasted a sheet of paper, on which Lamb has written as follows :—

Mind this goes for a letter. (Acknowledge it *directly*, if only in ten words.)

Dear Manning—(I shall want to hear this comes safe.) I have scratched out a good deal as you will see. Generally, what I have rejected was either *false* in *feeling*, or a violation of character—mostly of the first sort. I will here just instance in the concluding few lines of the "Dying Lover's Story," which completely contradicted his character of *silent* and *unreproachful*. I hesitated a good deal what copy to send you, and at last resolved to send the worst, because you are familiar with it, and can make it out ; and a stranger would find so much difficulty in doing it, that it would give him more pain than pleasure.

This is compounded precisely of the two persons' hands you requested it should be.—Yours sincerely, C. LAMB.

I will now transcribe the "Londoner." I have printed this letter, with the accompanying note by Talfourd, but in point of fact the "Londoner" was never published in the *Reflector*. See *Poems, Plays, and Essays*, p. 301.

Letter LXXXIX (p. 180).—This letter is written to Coleridge on the return of Charles and Mary from paying him a holiday visit at Keswick. Thomas Clarkson was then residing in a cottage on Ulswater. See following letter to Manning.

Letter XCI (p. 181).—*Fenwick is a ruined man.* See *Elia Essays*, "The Two Races of Men," and "Newspapers Thirty-five Years Ago."

Letter XCII (p. 185).—The first of several letters in this correspondence written in Latin; and in the present instance, as would appear, in reply to a challenge from Coleridge. The letter as hitherto printed is full of certain mistakes for which Lamb is clearly not responsible. These I have ventured to correct, but I have not thought it desirable to amend the Latinity otherwise in passages where it is certainly not immaculate. The grammar and idiom are frequently so lax as to jeopardise the writer's meaning, but with the assistance of my friend Dr. Calvert of Shrewsbury, I hope I have disentangled most of Lamb's somewhat involved allusions. The letter is interesting as bearing reference to several events of interest in the lives of both Coleridge and Wordsworth. It bears date October 9, 1802. A few days earlier, on October 2, Wordsworth had been married to Mary Hutchinson. On the same day (possibly by mere coincidence) Coleridge had printed in the *Morning Post* the first version of his splendid Ode, entitled "Dejection." In this version the person addressed throughout is a certain "Edmund," and not, as in the later revision of the poem, the "Lady," addressed in the often quoted lines—

> " O Lady, we receive but what we give,
> And in *our* Life alone does Nature live."

That "Edmund," the writer's dearest friend and a great poet, could be no other than Wordsworth we might be sure from internal evidence, even if we had not in this letter a curious confirmation. The *Carmina Chamouniana* refer to Coleridge's " Hymn before Sunrise, in the Vale of Chamouni," then recently printed for the first time in the *Morning Post*. Lamb's allusions will be intelligible to those who recall the passage beginning—

> " Who bade the sun
> Clothe you with rainbows? Who with living flowers
> Of loveliest blue, spread garlands at your feet ?
> God ! God ! the torrents, like a shout of nations,
> Utter ! the ice-plain bursts, and answers God !"

Lamb's flippant parallel "Tod, Tod," should be, I am convinced, "Dodd, Dodd"—the crime and punishment of that certainly "unhappy Doctor" being within the memory of many persons then still living.

The comparisons of the First Consul with the Roman Emperors refer to a series of Essays then recently published by Coleridge in the *Morning Post*. They are reprinted in the *Essays on his own Times:* Pickering, 1850 (vol. ii. p. 478-514). The allusion to the *Ludus Americanus* must perhaps remain unsolved. The "Flying Opossum" was little Derwent Coleridge, then just entering his third year. The child's vain attempts to pronounce the name of this creature in his picture-book, to which he never attained nearer than "Pi-pos," had fastened this nick-name upon the little fellow. "Pi-pos" will recur in many of the succeeding letters.

I append a translation, partly paraphrased, of the entire letter :—

My very dear Friend—"Pay the post, and go to ——" you say ; *i.e.* to Tartarus. Nay ! but have *you* not rather caught a Tartar ? Here have I, for all these years, used my vernacular with (for a writing-clerk) passable elegance ; and yet you are bent on goading me on with your neat and masterly letter, to yelp an answer in such dog-Latin as I may. However, I will try, though afraid my outlandish and far-fetched barbarisms will bring disgrace upon Christ's Hospital, the school still so proud of its learned Barnes and Markland, where in days gone by a wrong-headed master perseveringly drenched me with classical lore. But I must go on as best I can. Come then at my call, all ye troops of conjugations or declensions ! horrible spectres ! and come first and foremost thou—mightiest shadow and image of the Rod—now thank Heaven a thing of the past, the thought of which makes me howl as though I were a boy again !

Your lines written at Chamouni I certainly think very noble, but your English rendering of the echo among the Grisons (*God ! God !*) rather jars upon me. I cannot forget that in your own Cumbrian mountains I heard you rouse the echo (Dodd ! Dodd !) of the unfortunate Doctor's name, a sound by no means divine ! As to the rest, I entirely approve.

Your comparisons also I recognise fully as witty and wise. But how about their truth ? I find you asserting in one breath quite inconsistently, merely for comparison's sake, that the First Consul is endowed with the "irritable mind" of Julius Cæsar, as well as with a "constitutional coolness and politic craft" more appropriate to Augustus : and then in the third place you have taken much trouble to extract a resemblance to Tiberius. Why deal with one or two Cæsars when the whole Twelve are only too ready to offer you their services for comparison ? Besides I respect antiquity too much not to detest unfair parallels.

I am wonderfully pleased to have your account of the marriage of Wordsworth, or perhaps I should say of a certain "Edmund" of yours. All blessings rest on thee, Mary! too happy in thy lot. . . . I wish thee also joy in this new alliance, Dorothy —truly so named, that other "gift of God."

The American "Ludus" of which you prattle so much, Coleridge, I pass over, as utterly abhorrent from a "Ludus" (as such things go). For tell me, what "fun" is there in estranging from ourselves, sprung from the same stock (for the sake of one miserable *jeu d'esprit*), the whole of the Columbian nation. I ask you for a subject for something "Sportive," and you offer me "Bloody Wars."

To wind up, good-bye, and let me know what you think of my Latin style; and wish for me all health and beauty to my "Flying Opossum," or as you prefer to call him the "Odd Fish." Best greetings to your wife and my good Hartley. We are well, self and sister, who desires her best wishes. No more at present. My time is not my own.

I had almost forgotten to tell you that I have two volumes of John Milton's Latin Works, which (*D. V.*) I will have sent with the rest of your books sooner or later by Mary. You know, however, that in such matters I am by no means in the habit of hurrying; and I plead guilty. I have only to say further that they are handsome volumes, containing all J. M.'s Latin works. I am just now myself engaged and deeply interested in his very spirited Apology for the People of England.

I will carefully observe you instructions about Stuart. Good-bye, once more; and O remember me.

LETTER XCIII (p. 187).—*Your offer about the German poems.* Coleridge was to translate some of the best German lyrics into literal prose, and Lamb was then to turn them into verse. One experiment of the kind is Lamb's version of Thekla's Song in "Wallenstein." See *Poems, Plays, Essays*, p. 69.

Your "Epigram on the Sun and Moon." An epigram of Coleridge's contributed this month to the *Morning Post :*—"On the curious circumstance that in the German language the sun is feminine and the moon masculine."

Allen. The schoolfellow of Coleridge and Lamb at Christ's Hospital. Robert Allen went to University College, Oxford, in 1792—the year after Coleridge went to Jesus College, Cambridge. Coleridge visited Allen at Oxford in June 1794, and was introduced by him to Southey. Allen was one of the original Pantisocrats. He was very handsome. See anecdote of him in the Elia Essay, "Christ's Hospital five and thirty years ago."

LETTER XCIV (p. 189).—"*Once a Jacobin.*" An essay of

Coleridge's in the *Morning Post* for October 1802. "Once a Jacobin, always a Jacobin." *Essays on his own Times*, ii. p. 542.

Sam Le Grice.   Lamb's schoolfellow at Christ's Hospital. See Elia Essay, "Christ's Hospital five and thirty years ago," and my notes thereon.

LETTER XCV (p. 191).—S. T. C.'s first letter to Mr. Fox was published in the *Morning Post* of Thursday, November 4, 1802. A second followed on November 9.   Both are included in the *Essays on his own Times*, vol. ii.

LETTER XCVI (p. 193).—Joseph Cottle, the bookseller and publisher, was also, like his brother Amos, a poet.   He produced *Malvern Hills* in 1798.

Alfred, an epic poem, in 1801.

LETTER XCVII (p. 194).—*A merry natural captain.* Captain, afterwards Admiral Burney, who sailed with Captain Cook in two of his voyages.

LETTER XCIX (p. 198).—*On the death of a young Quaker.* See the beautiful verses entitled "Hester" (*Poems, Plays*, etc., p. 69).   Miss Emma Savory of Blackheath, a niece of Hester Savory, has kindly supplied me with a few biographical details. "She (Hester) was the eldest sister of my father, A. B. Savory, and lived with him and his sisters, Anna and Martha, at Pentonville.   She married Charles Stoke Dudley, and died, eight months after her marriage, of fever.   I possess a miniature portrait of her which I greatly value.   My mother used to say that her beauty consisted more in expression than in regularity of features."   I may add that I have seen this miniature which, even after reading Lamb's tender and beautiful lyric, is anything but disappointing.   It is a bright-eyed gypsy face such as we know so well from the canvas of Reynolds.   Miss Savory adds, "I do not think our mother was aware of Charles Lamb's attachment to Hester Savory.   Perhaps she did not know it herself."

LETTER C (p. 199).—This letter refers to the third edition (1803) of Coleridge's Poems, which he had placed in Lamb's hands for revision.   The poem called "The Silver Thimble" is that already referred to, in which Sara Coleridge had some small share.   The verses on "Flicker and Flicker's Wife" were entitled simply, "Written after a Walk before Supper."   They open thus—

> "Tho' much averse, dear Jack, to flicker,
> To find a likeness for friend V—ker,
> I've made this Earth and air and sea
> A voyage of Discovery !

> And let me add (to ward off strife),
> For V—ker, and for V—ker's wife."

Lamb's habitual inaccuracy comes out here also. As for the omission of this *jeu d'esprit* in the forthcoming edition, no one will be found to dissent from his judgment.

LETTER CII (p. 202).—This letter is addressed to "Mr. T. Manning, Maison Magnan, No. 342 Boulevard Italien, Paris."

An epitaph scribbled upon a poor girl. Written upon a young lady of the name of Mary Druitt, at Wimborne, Dorsetshire. The late Mr. J. P. Collier gives a slightly different version of the lines in his "Old Man's Diary" (privately printed). Mr. Collier says that the girl died at the age of nineteen, of smallpox, and that the lines were engraved upon the tomb; but I learn from members of the Druitt family still living at Wimborne that this latter statement is not correct.

LETTER CVI (p. 207).—Lamb's animadversions upon Godwin's lengthy *Life of Chaucer* are as usual admirably just. The work consisted of four-fifths ingenious guessing to one-fifth of material having any historic basis.

Schoolboy copy of verses for Merchant Taylors' boys. The boys were allowed to get help from outside in the composition of their weekly epigrams. In later years we find him making some for the present Archdeacon Hessey and his brother, when at that school.

LETTER CXII (p. 216).—*Farewell to my "Friendly Traitress."* The "Farewell to Tobacco." First published in Leigh Hunt's *Reflector* in 1811, and afterwards in Lamb's collected works in 1818. See *Poems, Plays*, etc., p. 70.

LETTER CXIII (p. 219).—*Mr. Dawe.* See the papers by Lamb, written long afterwards, "Recollections of a late Royal Academician." (*Mrs. Leicester's School*, etc., p. 307.)

Lord Nelson, died October 21, 1805.

Luck to Ned Search. *The Light of Nature*, by Edward Search, Esq., was a work by Abraham Tucker, which Hazlitt was at this time engaged in abridging and editing. His abridgment appeared in 1807.

LETTER CXV (p. 222).—*Life of Fawcett.* "Report was rife that a life of the Rev. Joseph Fawcett, Mr. Hazlitt's early friend, might be expected from the same quarter; but such was not the fact" (*Memoir of Hazlitt*, by his Grandson). Fawcett was a dissenting minister at Walthamstow, who published various *Sermons, Poems*, etc.

LETTER CXX (p. 228).—Addressed:—"Mr. Manning, Passenger on Board the *Thames*, East Indiaman, Portsmouth."

A short postscript to this letter was omitted by Talfourd :—
"One thing more, when you get to Canton you will most likely
see a young friend of mine, Inspector of Teas, named Ball. He
is a very good fellow, and I should like to have my name talked
of in China. Give my kind remembrances to the same Ball."

LETTER CXXI (p. 230).—*The good news of Mrs. W.* Words-
worth's son Thomas was born on the 16th of June 1806.

Mr. H.—See *Poems, Plays*, etc., p. 348 and note.

A young gentleman of my office. We shall have occasion here-
after to mention this fellow-clerk of Lamb's. For an account
of Coleridge's early passion for Evans's sister Mary, see Gill-
man's *Life of Coleridge* and Cottle's *Reminiscences*.

LETTER CXXVI (p. 241).—*The Tales from Shakspeare.* The
plates referred to by Lamb were designed (as is believed) by
William Mulready, then a young man of twenty, and engraved
by William Blake. The "bad baby" was a familiar nickname
for Mrs. Godwin. The subject from the *Merchant of Venice*
was lettered, "Gratiano and Nerissa desire to be married";
the illustration to the *Midsummer Night's Dream* bore for title
"Nic Bottom and the Fairies." In spite of Lamb's objection
to this latter, it is by far the best of all the illustrations, both
in design and drawing, and indicates very clearly the hand of
Blake. The "giants and giantesses" of whom Lamb complains
are certainly too frequent in these illustrations.

LETTER CXXVII (p. 242).—The story of William Hazlitt's
disappearance, which caused anxiety to his family, will be
found in the *Memoir of Hazlitt*, by his grandson (chapter xi.)

LETTER CXXVIII (p. 243).—Talfourd omitted a few sentences
from this letter, which may as well be restored. "Godwin
keeps a shop in Skinner Street, Cornhill ; he is termed chil-
dren's bookseller, and sells penny, twopenny, threepenny, and
fourpenny books. Sometimes he gets an order for the dearer
sort of books (mind, all that I tell you in this letter is true)."

Pauper est tamen, sed amat. Lamb wrote "Pauper est Cinna
sed amat." The source of the quotation is unknown to me.

LETTER CXXIX (p. 247).—The passage about the "giant's
vomit" was from the story of Polyphemus in Lamb's version
of the *Odyssey*.

LETTER CXXX (p. 248).—Coleridge's *Friend* made its first
appearance on the first of June 1809, and its last on March
15, 1810.

CHAPTER III.

1809-1816.

LETTER CXXXI (p. 249).—*Mrs. Clarke.* The mistress of the Duke of York, second son of George III., and Commander-in-Chief of the Forces. "It was established beyond the possibility of doubt that the Duke had permitted Mrs. Clarke to interfere in military promotions ; that he had given commissions at her recommendation ; and that she had taken money for the recommendations." In consequence of the public excitement and indignation on the subject, the Duke resigned his office on the 20th of March of this year.

Godwin's little book. Godwin, *On Sepulchres.*

LETTER CXXXII (p. 251).—*Wordsworth's book.* The Convention of Cintra. "Concerning the relations of Great Britain, Spain, and Portugal to each other, and to the common enemy at this crisis, and specifically as affected by the Convention of Cintra," etc. etc., by W. Wordsworth. Longmans. May 20, 1809.

Daniel, enriched with manuscript notes. These are printed in *Notes and Queries,* 1st Series, vi. 117.

Two volumes of Juvenile Poetry. "Poetry for Children, entirely original." By the Author of *Mrs. Leicester's School.* In two volumes. London. Printed for M. J. Godwin at the Juvenile Library, No. 44, Skinner Street. 1809.

Cœlebs. "Cœlebs in Search of a Wife," by Hannah More, published in 1809.

LETTER CXXXIII (p. 254).—*The rich Auditors in Albemarle Street.* The audience at the Lectures by Coleridge, given at the Royal Institution the year before.

My admiration of the pamphlet. Evidently refers to Wordsworth's pamphlet on the Convention of Cintra, mentioned in the preceding letter.

LETTER CXXXIV (p. 255). *Dr. Tuthill,* afterwards Sir George L. Tuthill, M.D., Physician to Bethlehem, Bridewell, and Westminster Hospitals.

Hazlitt has written a grammar. "A new and improved grammar of the English tongue for the use of schools . . . to which is added a new guide to the English tongue, in a letter to Mr. W. F. Mylius, author of the School Dictionary, by Edward Baldwin, Esq. (Godwin)." 1810.

LETTER CXXXV (p. 259).—See Lamb's Essay "On the Poetical Works of George Wither" (*Poems, Plays, and Essays,* p. 295, and the note upon it, p. 397). The annotated volume is now in the possession of Mr. A. C. Swinburne, who has published a full and very interesting account of it.

LETTER CXXXVI (p. 260).—*Winterslow, near Sarum.* The residence of William Hazlitt, on the border of Salisbury Plain. Charles and Mary Lamb spent their summer holiday with Mr. and Mrs. Hazlitt this year. Basil Montagu had written to Lamb suggesting to him to revise a MS. treatise on the subject of Capital Punishment.

LETTER CXXXVII (p. 261).—*H. Robinson.* Henry Crabb Robinson. See his delightful *Diaries* for constant mention of Charles and Mary Lamb.

LETTER CXXXVIII (p. 262).—*Cram monsters in the voids of the maps.* Lamb was thinking of Swift's lines (in the "Ode to Poetry ") about the geographers who—

> "On Afric downs
> Place elephants for want of towns."

LETTER CXXXIX (p. 262).—*Your continuation of the Essay on Epitaphs.* Wordsworth had published the first part of this essay in Coleridge's *Friend*, February 22, 1810. He published it later in separate form with additions. The "turgid epitaph " referred to was one from a churchyard in Westmoreland, of the year 1693, of which Wordsworth thought it worth while to compose a simpler version in prose.

LETTER CXLI (p. 265). — *Your reply to the Edinburgh Review.* " Reformist's reply to the Edinburgh Review," 1810. "A pamphlet," says Hunt in his *Autobiography*, " which I wrote in defence of the *Review's* own reforming principles, which it had lately taken into its head to renounce as impracticable."

LETTER CXLII (p. 266).—John Lamb's book on the subject of *Humanity* has not yet, I believe, been identified by students of Lamb. From the concluding sentence of this letter we must infer that it dealt chiefly with anti-vivisectionist topics

LETTER CXLIII (p. 267).—The letter congratulates William Hazlitt on the birth of his first child, or at least the first which survived.

H. Bunbury, Esq. (1750-1811). The caricaturist, friend of Johnson, Goldsmith, and Garrick.

Martin and the card-boys. Martin Burney and the rest of the little whist-coterie.

LETTER CXLIV (p. 268).—*To give your vote to-morrow.* H. Crabb Robinson, under date, March 16, 1811, writes: "C. Lamb stepped in to announce Dr. Tuthill's defeat as candidate for the post of physician to St. Luke's Hospital." The contest, Mrs. Procter informs me, was very severe, and many friends of the candidates bought governorships at £50 for the sake of votes. Basil Montagu bought one for Lamb.

LETTER CXLV (p. 269).—*The Well-bred Scholar.* I do not find any work of this name assigned to W. F. Mylins, who was a diligent compiler of school-books. He was a master at Christ's Hospital. Dr. Southey was a brother of the poet.

Going to eat turbot. At the annual dinner of old Christ's Hospital boys.

LETTER CXLVI (p. 271).—*The noblest conversational poem.* Wordsworth's *Excursion*, just published.

The whole surface of Hyde Park is dry crumbling sand. Early in August 1814, the three London Parks were thrown open to the public, in celebration of the Peace between England and France. There were fireworks and illuminations; Chinese Pagodas and "Temples of Concord" were erected; and the Parks were, in fact, converted into a vast Fair. It was two years before they recovered their usual verdure.

"*At the coming of the milder day.*" See Wordsworth's Poem, "Hart-Leap Well"—

> ' She leaves these objects to a slow decay,
> That what we are, and have been, may be known ;
> But at the coming of the milder day
> These monuments shall all be overgrown."

LETTER CXLVII (p. 274).—"*Remorse.*" Coleridge's tragedy, which, owing to the good offices of Lord Byron, had been brought out at Drury Lane, January 23, 1813, with a Prologue by Lamb. It ran twenty nights.

Old Jimmy Boyer. Rev. James Boyer, the former Head-Master of Christ's Hospital, while Lamb and Coleridge were at the school.

LETTER CXLVIII (p. 276).—*Time enough for the Quarterly.* Lamb's forthcoming Review of the *Excursion*. See the Review, and notes thereupon, in *Mrs. Leicester's School and other Writings*, etc., pp. 210 and 395.

LETTER CXLIX (p. 278).—*Your experience about tailors.* The allusion is hardly intelligible. The reference to Burton is obviously to Lamb's Paper "On the Melancholy of Tailors," signed "Burton junior," which appeared first in the *Champion*, December 4, 1814.

W. H. is William Hazlitt, who had lately reviewed Wordsworth's *Excursion* in the *Examiner*. This Review was partially reprinted by Hazlitt in the *Round Table*, 1817.

The melancholy Jew. A Jew of the name of Levi had lately flung himself from the monument in Fish Street Hill.

Another Hylas. "An interesting little love-adventure which he (Hazlitt) met with down at the Lakes while he was on his first experimental trip in search of sitters, is so distinctly alluded to in a letter from Lamb to Wordsworth, that I shall just give what Lamb says about it, premising that Patmore had heard in his time of some story of my grandfather being struck by the charms of a village beauty in Wordsworth's neighbourhood, and of having narrowly escaped being ducked by the swains for his ill-appreciated attentions. Wordsworth had evidently described the whole affair in a letter to Lamb" (*Memoirs of William Hazlitt*, by W. C. Hazlitt, i. 105, 106).

LETTER CLI (p. 283).—*Your successive book presents.* In 1815 Wordsworth published a New Edition of his Poems with the following title :—*Poems by William Wordsworth : including Lyrical Ballads, and the Miscellaneous Pieces of the Author. With Additional Poems, a new Preface, and a Supplementary Essay. In two Volumes.* Among the poems that appeared for the first time in this edition were "Yarrow Visited," "The Force of Prayer: or, The Founding of Bolton Abbey," "The Farmer of Tilsbury Vale," "Laodamia," "Yew Trees," "A Night Piece," and others. It was naturally on these that Lamb made his comments. He also refers to the various changes of text made since the appearance of the previous edition in 1807. Some of the former readings were restored in later editions, perhaps in consequence of Lamb's remonstrances. The admirable line—

"The stone-chat and the glancing sand-piper"

(as Lamb truly says, "a line quite alive") is one of these. It occurs in the beautiful poem "Lines left upon a Seat in a Yew-tree," and in the 1815 edition had given place to the far inferior—

"The stone-chat, or the sand-lark, restless Bird
Piping along the margin of the lake."

The "substitution of a shell" to which Lamb alludes was in the poem "The blind Highland Boy," where the vessel in which the poor boy embarked was originally a washing-tub, but which was now exchanged (at the request of friends whose self-respect was wounded) for a turtle-shell.

The Preface is noble. The allusion in the words that follow is to a mention Wordsworth had made of Lamb, in citing a sentence from his Essay on Hogarth. He there speaks of Lamb as one of his "most esteemed friends." The "printed extracts from those first poems" refers to the extracts from an "Evening Walk" and "Descriptive Sketches," early poems first published in 1793.

The poems "by a female friend" were by Dorothy Wordsworth. "Three short pieces (now first published)," we read in the

Preface, "are the work of a Female Friend, and the Reader to whom they may be acceptable is indebted to me for his pleasure."

An undoubtable picture of Milton. This picture, which came into Charles Lamb's possession after his brother's death, was given by him to Emma Isola.

The Latin Poems of V. Bourne. Cowper's friend, and Master at Westminster School. Lamb, as well as Cowper, wrote and printed various translations from Bourne's Latin Poems.

"*To them each evening had its glittering star*"—from the *Excursion*, Book V. "The man and his consort" are the matron and her husband on whose industrious lives these lines are a comment.

LETTER CLII (p. 286).—"*Yarrow Visited.*" The exquisite stanza referred to I would almost hope there is no need to cite, but it is a pleasure to repeat it :—

> " But thou that didst appear so fair
> To fond imagination,
> Dost rival in the light of day
> Her delicate creation."

The poem called by Lamb the "Boy-builders" is that better known as "Rural Architecture." It was first printed in 1800, and had a final stanza, omitted in 1815, ending with the lines—

> " Then, light-hearted boys, to the top of the crag,
> And I'll build up a giant with you."

I don't often go out a "May"ing ;—"must" is the tense with me now. It is interesting to remember that Hood uses this antithesis with exquisite effect in his "Ode to Melancholy" :—

> " Even as the blossoms of the *May*,
> Whose fragrance ends in *must*."

"*What is good for a bootless bene ?*" The first line of the poem on Bolton Abbey :—

> " ' What is good for a bootless bene ?'
> With these dark words begins my tale ;
> And their meaning is, whence can comfort spring
> When Prayer is of no avail ?"

Who looked over your proof-sheets and left "ordebo" in that line of Virgil ? Wordsworth had cited in his preface Virgil's lines from the first Eclogue about the shepherd and the goats :—

> " Non ego vos posthac viridi projectus in antro
> Dumosa pendere procul de rupe *videbo*."

LETTER CLIII (p. 290).—Southey's *Roderick, the Last of the Goths*, was published in quarto, in 1814.

LETTER CLIV (p. 292).—*Hartley's intellectuals.* Hartley Coleridge, now just nineteen years of age, was at Oxford.

Spend a week at Poole's.   Thomas Poole, a gentleman whose name has occurred already as the friend of Coleridge and Lamb. Poole succeeded to his father's business as a tanner at Nether-Stowey.   Coleridge made his acqaintance, through friends in Bristol, as early as 1794 ; and it was to be near Poole that he went to live at Stowey in the winter of 1796-97.   It was thus that Nether-Stowey became, as Mrs. Henry Sandford, Poole's relative, truly says, "a centre of the leading intellectual impulses of the time."   Among other friends of Poole's were Sir Humphrey Davy, the Wedgwood brothers, and John Rickman ; and in a less intimate degree Wordsworth, Southey, and Clarkson.   Poole retired from business about the year 1804, and thenceforth devoted himself to the interests of his native place, and to all questions affecting the welfare of the labouring classes.   He died in 1837.

LETTER CLV (p. 294).—*Alsager.*   Thomas Massa Alsager. For twenty-eight years attached to the *Times* newspaper, in which he wrote the city and money articles.   He further controlled the musical department of the paper.   He did more than perhaps any man of his time to promote the study and performance of classical chamber music, especially Beethoven's Quartettes.   Hence Lamb's allusion to the propriety of varying the spelling of his name.   He died in 1846.

Heautontimorumenos.   "The Self-tormentor," the title of a comedy of Terence.

Capell Lofft (1751-1824).   The Whig lawyer, writer on legal and political subjects, and poet.   He was a native of Bury St. Edmunds, and brought into notice the Suffolk poet, Bloomfield.   He sometimes printed sonnets with his initials C. L., to the disgust of Lamb who bore the same.

The juvenile Talfourd.   This first mention of one who was afterwards to be Lamb's biographer deserves a word of comment. He was at this time a young man of twenty, living in chambers in Inner Temple Lane, and reading with Mr. Joseph Chitty, the Special Pleader.   Talfourd had just before this been introduced to Lamb at the house of Mr. William Evans, of the India House, and editor of the *Pamphleteer.*   I shall have occasion hereafter to mention this latter gentleman in connection with Lamb and Joseph Cottle.

LETTER CLVI (p. 297).—*Miss Hutchinson,* Mrs. Wordsworth's sister.

LETTER CLIX (p. 302).—*The Political Sonnets and Ode.* The ode was evidently Wordsworth's Thanksgiving Ode, composed on the morning of the day appointed for a General Thanksgiving, January 18, 1816.

The Covent Garden Manager has declined accepting his Tragedy. Coleridge's play *Zapolya.* Though Byron's good offices were ineffectual in getting this second tragedy accepted by the managers, Byron introduced Coleridge to John Murray, which was the means (according to Tom Moore) of its publication as *A Christmas Tale* a year later.

At a Chemist's Laboratory in Norfolk Street. I do not know that Coleridge's biographers mention this temporary lodging of Coleridge's. It could have been but for a few days, for on the very day on which this letter was written, application had been made to Mr. Gillman of Highgate, and a week later Coleridge entered that gentleman's house, destined to be his home until his death, eighteen years afterwards.

LETTER CLX (p. 304).—*The revise of the poems and letter.* The letter referred to was Wordsworth's *Letter to a Friend of Burns,* London, 1816. Wordsworth had been consulted by a friend of Burns as to the best mode of vindicating the reputation of the poet which, it was alleged, had been much injured by the publication of Dr. Currie's *Life and Correspondence of Burns.*

Morgan is with us every day. John Morgan, Coleridge's old Bristol friend, and through life one of his kindest and staunchest supporters. He had a house at Calne, in Wiltshire, where Coleridge lived with him for many months at a time. Lamb was in all probability staying with Morgan when he wrote the letter that follows, dated from that town.

LETTER CLXII (p. 308). Henry Dodwell was a fellow-clerk of Lamb's in the India House. This exquisite letter has never before been printed as a whole. I quoted a portion of it in the notes of a previous volume of this edition. The "Cobbetts" are of course the "Political Registers."

END OF VOL. I

Printed by R. & R. CLARK, LIMITED, *Edinburgh.*